BOSS FIGHT

ALSO BY ANNIE BELLET:

BOOKS V THROUGH VII

THE
TWENTY-
SIDED
SORCERESS

VOLUME
2

BOSS FIGHT

BOOKS V THROUGH VII

ANNIE·BELLET

SAGA PRESS

LONDON SYDNEY **NEW YORK** TORONTO NEW DELHI

AN IMPRINT OF SIMON & SCHUSTER, INC.

1230 AVENUE OF THE AMERICAS, NEW YORK, NEW YORK 10020

SAGA PRESS and colophon are registered trademarks of Simon & Schuster, Inc.
For information about special discounts for bulk purchases, please contact Simon & Schuster Special Sales at 1-866-506-1949 or business@simonandschuster.com.
The Simon & Schuster Speakers Bureau can bring authors to your live event. For more information or to book an event, contact the Simon & Schuster Speakers Bureau at 1-866-248-3049 or visit our website at www.simonspeakers.com.
Also available in a Saga Press hardcover edition.
The text for this book was set in ITC Galliard.
Manufactured in the United States of America
First Saga Press paperback edition January 2017
2 4 6 8 10 9 7 5 3 1
Library of Congress Cataloging-in-Publication Data
Names: Bellet, Annie, author.
Title: Boss fight / Annie Bellet.
Description: First Edition. | New York : Saga Press, [2017] |
Series: [The twenty-sided sorceress ; 2]
Identifiers: LCCN 2016034249 | ISBN 9781481491990 (hardback) |
ISBN 9781481491983 (trade paper)
Subjects: BISAC: FICTION / Fantasy / Urban Life. | FICTION / Fantasy / Paranormal. |
FICTION / Fantasy / Contemporary. | GSAFD: Fantasy fiction.
Classification: LCC PS3602.E6475 B67 2017 | DDC 813/.6—dc23
LC record available at https://lccn.loc.gov/2016034249

DEDICATED TO MATT AND GREG,
WITHOUT WHOM I'D NEVER HAVE TAKEN THIS LEAP.

THE TWENTY-SIDED SORCERESS

series in reading order:

Justice Calling
Murder of Crows
Pack of Lies
Hunting Season
Heartache
Thicker Than Blood
Magic to the Bone

CONTENTS

▶ BOOK V: HEARTACHE   1

▶ BOOK VI: THICKER THAN BLOOD   141

▶ BOOK VII: MAGIC TO THE BONE   269

HEARTACHE

THE TWENTY-SIDED SORCERESS: BOOK V

DEDICATED TO

ALL THE AUTHORS THAT EVER MADE ME CRY,
AND TO JOSS WHEDON, THE WORST OFFENDER. I WAS ANGRY,
BUT NOW I THINK I UNDERSTAND WHAT THEY FELT.

NOT THAT I HAVE FORGIVEN THEM.

CHAPTER ONE ▶

The weather people had been forecasting a blizzard, but the sky was a smoky grey and the town utterly peaceful. Peace might have been nice if I didn't feel like the freaking sword of Damocles was playing hide-and-seek over my head. Alek was scarily full of a desire to keep me in his sights, which didn't help my anxiety levels one bit. I think he would have handcuffed himself to my side if I'd let him. My heart was forecasting doom.

Doom hadn't come. Nothing and nobody had come. Nearly a month had gone by since Samir's last missive to me. The dead apprentice of his, Tess, in my head was so damned sure he was coming for me, and yet . . .

Nobody came. The most eventful thing to happen was Brie's bakery being shut down for health code violations. As the building owner, I'd spent all Friday on the phone begging for a reinspection and silently plotting revenge on the witches. Alek had cautioned that I should be sure they were responsible first. Voice of reason and all. It seemed likely someone had reported the magical cockroach invasion. The roaches were gone. Getting a reinspection was a pain in the ass, though. Neither Brie nor I could even remember the first one. The county bureaucrat might well have been a ninja.

I almost wished for ninjas. It would have given me something to fight against. Instead, I spent four hours on hold and then got told to call back on Monday. Awesomesauce.

I wiped a dust cloth over a shelf that didn't have a speck of dust on it, and wondered where Alek was today. He'd stuck next to me for weeks, hardly leaving my side, and then gone away an hour before, after getting a text message. When I'd asked him where the fire was, he had said only that he'd tell me later.

My door chimed and I turned toward the front of the shop, pulling on magic, almost hoping it was Alek so I could play the annoyed girlfriend. Him leaving like that, given everything going on, it made me even more nervous. I knew the chain around his neck was empty, though he tucked it beneath his shirt, but he'd only shaken his head and told me it was complicated when I asked. We'd come a long way down Trust Lane, but not all the way to Unconditional Trust-ville, I guess.

It wasn't Alek but Brie who came through my door. Or, really, the triple goddesses who masqueraded as a single woman named Brie. She was tall and stacked, with bright red curls always braided up or piled on her head. Today, her hair was neatly pinned back, her cheeks rosy from the chill air. She looked around my game store, peering into the corners, then, satisfied it was empty but for me, she gave me a half-wave and slumped into a chair.

"We're leaving," she said. "We've got to go, tonight. I was hoping you'd keep an eye on the building."

"What?" I pushed my hair out of my face as my guts twisted like rope inside me. "Leaving? For how long? You and Ciaran?"

"We've been called to Ireland," Brie said. Her eyes narrowed and she looked into a middle distance, staring toward the new-release rack but seeing something outside my understanding. She lapsed into Irish. "The Fey are gathering. Ciaran must attend, and where he goes, so go I."

"What about Iollan?" I asked, thinking of the big druid. He and Ezee had seemed to reach a new level in their relationship. Like, having a relationship where they actually mentioned each other to their friends and family.

"Not he," Brie said, her eyes snapping to me as she shook off whatever thoughts had darkened her mood. "The druid cannot return to the Isle. But we must."

"So . . . you'll be back when?"

"I wish I could say."

The door chimed again and Ciaran entered in a sweep of crisp, icy air. The leprechaun wore his usual red coat and had a green army bag, like you'd see in old war movies, slung over one stout shoulder. His red-and-silver hair was tousled and damp, as though he'd showered and hadn't bothered to comb it.

"Brie tell you?" he said, also in Irish.

"She did, though I'm a little confused. Why now? Are you in trouble?" *Trouble I could Fireball, perhaps?* I wanted to add, but made my will save. Or my Wisdom check? Either way.

Ciaran and Brie exchanged a look that didn't help my nerves at all. Then he shrugged one shoulder, the other probably weighted down too much by the rucksack to lift.

"We shall see," he said, lips pressing together at the end. "It has been five hundred years since the last gathering."

"Oh, well, maybe they miss your faces." I tried to smile. "Can I help? Are you magicking yourselves there or something?"

"We have a flight leaving from Seattle tonight. Max is driving us. He'll be walking in here through your back door in a moment." Brie rose, straightening her coat.

Max walked in through the back, setting my wards back there buzzing for a second.

Harper's brother grinned at me. "You really going to leave that door unlocked? Is that safe?"

"Anyone coming to kill me won't care about a ten-dollar lock on a door made of cardboard," I pointed out. "How's it feel to have your license, birthday boy?"

Max had turned sixteen the week before, and the first thing he'd done was go get his license. Levi had gifted the kid a car that was ugly as sin and looked pieced together by a bad game of *Katamari* in a junkyard, but it ran despite being held together with bubblegum and love.

"Car's open if you want to put your stuff in," Max said as Brie and Ciaran both moved toward the back door. "I think they are in a hurry," he added to me as they disappeared down the back hall past the game room.

"Do I get to see the picture?" I resisted the urge to fluff Max's brown hair.

"Oh, God, Harper told you?"

"Dude, really? Of course she told me."

"The camera went weird, I swear. I look like a cross-eyed chipmunk."

"Okay, it can't be that bad."

He shook his head and dragged his wallet out of his down jacket pocket.

It wasn't that bad. It was worse. I'm a terrible person, but I totally laughed. There was no way *not* to laugh. I'm only human. Sort of.

Max yanked his license back and crammed it into his wallet, muttering a bunch of words his mother would have washed his mouth out with soap for if she'd heard him.

"Hey, I'm sorry," I said, trying to stifle the giggles. "It's not so bad."

"Harper said the same thing. Then you know what she said?" Max's lips started to twitch and he was having trouble maintaining the surly-teen-boy act.

"What?"

"'It's just, there's something about your eyes,'" he said in a high, squeaky voice that was supposed to be an imitation of his older sister. "'Something . . . shifty.'" He switched back to his normal voice. "Seriously. Then she laughed so hard, Mom had to tell her to go outside."

"Did you tell her there is a special hell for people who make bad puns?"

Max rolled his eyes, then looked around us at the empty store. "Where is she, anyway?"

"Up at the college, in one of the library silent study rooms. She's got MGL qualifiers to practice for and she says the net up there is better than here. Whole section of this block has turned into an annoying net dead zone. We drop offline all the time." I shrugged. The net was another annoyance; plus, I missed Harper being here, cursing a blue storm. I felt weirdly lonely there in my store, just sitting around dusting things that were already clean and sorting cards already sorted.

Like someone rearranging deck chairs on the *Titanic*.

"Be careful on your drive," I said. I had enough intelligence to know not to question Max's car's ability to even make it to Seattle. His feelings were hurt enough for one day. "The roads and all. You going on to the beach early, then?"

"Yeah, the guys got the house a couple days sooner than we thought." He and some friends had gotten a great deal on a beach house in Washington, it being winter and all. His sixteenth birthday was going a hell of a lot better than mine had.

I was glad he'd be away from Wylde for the week. If shit went down soon, one more person I cared about not in the crosshairs was good. Max had already gotten hurt because of me. I wished I could send them all away. But my friends had made their choice.

I could only hope it was the right one.

I made Ciaran and Brie promise to email me with updates, gave Max a quick hug, and stood in the freezing air to wave them away as Max's patchwork car bumped out of the parking lot and out onto the main road. I watched them disappear down the road and shivered from more than the winter chill. With that damned other shoe waiting to drop, every good-bye right now felt weirdly final.

My shop was so quiet and still when I returned that I almost missed Alek standing like a giant Viking shadow by the center support post. His white-blond hair was messy, the way it looked when he'd been running his hands through it, something he only did when upset or angry. His normally pale blue eyes looked colder than the sky and his mouth was pressed into a tight line.

"What's wrong?" I asked, feeling the metaphorical sword shoe thing lowering over my head.

"Carlos," he said.

"It's Sunday," I said, half to myself. The last few weeks, Carlos, Alek's friend and former mentor among the Justices, had been out of touch.

"He wants to meet. Wants me to meet someone."

"Where? When? Who?" I asked. I pressed my hands against his sides, wanting his heat, wanting to push back the tension and darkness lurking in his face and body.

"New Orleans. As soon as possible. I have no idea," he said. Then he shook his head. "No, I have an idea. I do not like it."

"Does he know about . . ." I looked at the chain disappearing under his collar.

"If I am to meet who I think, yes. He knows I am not a Justice anymore."

Alek's words hung between us, almost tangible, like fog in the air. So. There it was. Finally said.

"What happened, Alek?" I whispered. I had an idea. This, like so much else, was probably my fault. I tried to tell myself that was ego talking, but one couldn't deny the timing or the mounds of circumstantial evidence piling up around us.

"The world changes," he said. His eyes shifted down to my face and he bent, kissing me softly on the forehead. "This is not your fault."

He took a deep breath, his chest swelling big enough that his coat brushed my cheek. I wanted to lay my head against him and tell him everything would work out, but we were beyond lying to each other like that. I hoped.

"Anyway," he said after he let out the breath. "I am not going."

"What? Is this important? Will they try to hurt you?" I added the *try* because there was no way anybody was going to hurt him. Not on my watch.

"It is, and no, I do not think they will. Carlos used our safe code. I do not think he would betray me, not like this. But it doesn't matter. I am not leaving you."

"So, I'll come with you."

"You cannot travel where I would go."

"They have some kind of magical barrier around New Orleans now that keeps out sorceresses?" I tried to smile as I said it, ignoring the painful beating of my heart.

"It is Justice business. I am not sure even I can do what I must, but . . ." He sighed again. "I am not going."

Because of me. The tension in his body wasn't just over worry about the situation. He wanted to go. Something had happened to him. One day, he woke up and wasn't the same. The changes were tiny, things only I had noticed, I thought. The necklace being hidden. His overattentiveness that went beyond worry about Samir. Every time he held me, he had a grip that made me feel like that would be the last time. He was there, almost stifling me, but somehow Alek seemed already gone.

If going, if sorting out this Justice business, would give a piece of him back, I couldn't let him stay. I wanted my Alek back, the man who was always sure of things, who saw the shadows in life and faced them down. Not this Alek who clung to me like the world was ending and I just couldn't see the explosion yet.

"You are going," I said.

"Jade," he started, but I shook my head.

"No. I'm serious. You haven't been you. I don't know what happened, because your stubborn ass won't tell me. But if going to see Carlos and whoever this other mysterious whatever is helps you come to terms with whatever the hell happened? I'm for it."

"I don't know how long I'll be gone," he said, shaking his head slowly, his hair brushing against his cheeks and his expression torn between worry and desire. "What if Samir comes?"

"I've been asking myself that question for twenty-six years," I said as I forced my mouth to form a smile. It kind of hurt, but he needed me to be confident. "He hasn't shown up yet. We're about to get a pile of snow dumped on us. If you are going to leave, you should go. Take care of whatever you need to take care of. Then come home to me."

"I will always come home to you," he said, and I swear to the Universe his eyes looked like he might cry.

The fuck was going on? I shivered again, despite the warm shop, despite his warm arms wrapping around me and pulling me close. Swords. Deck chairs. We were totally screwed—I just didn't know exactly how yet.

"Go," I said to him after he had kissed me hard enough that I wanted him to stay.

Alek pressed his cheek to mine and nodded slowly. When he left, I didn't say good-bye. I refused to, because this felt like good-bye enough.

All I knew was that if the Council of Nine did anything to my lover, I was going to have to go make a whole new cadre of enemies. And if Alek didn't return to me soon, Carlos would be first on my damned list.

Sleeping alone that night, I dreamed of fire and ice. Snow and ash drifting down around me, burning my skin where it touched. Just after five in the morning, I gave up on sleep and started a new play-through of *Skyrim*. The mindless task of leveling skills and crafting a few thousand iron daggers helped distract me, but I was still a bit of a zombie by the time I opened the shop.

"Jade?" Harper said. "Are you listening to me?"

I realized I'd been staring at the monitor, not actually clicking the order button. A glance at the tiny clock in the bottom corner of the screen said it was noon. I wondered how long I'd been standing there, staring. My stomach clenched with hunger, but my mouth tasted fuzzy and sour.

"Yeah?" I said, turning to her.

"You okay?" She peered at me with suspicious green eyes, looking very inquisitive in a fox-like way that made me smile.

"Sure," I lied. "Just thinking about if I should order more custom minis. The last batch was pretty popular."

"Uh-huh." Harper gave me a look that told me exactly what she was willing to pay for the bullshit I was trying to sell her. "I said the snow is starting to fall. I'm going to head up to the college to practice some seriously bad-manner builds. If you don't need me," she added, worry creasing her forehead.

Fucking babysitters. I shook my head. "Nah, I'm good. What if it snows as hard as they say, though?"

"Maybe I'll just hook up with a hot student and sleep over." She grinned.

I couldn't remember Harper ever dating anyone in the last five years, not anybody she'd introduced any of us to. I rolled my eyes at her. "Knock yourself out. But really?"

"Ezee gave me a key to his office. I can crash in the lounge on that floor. It's cool. They have popcorn and everything. Any other questions, Mom?"

"Drive safe," I said, making a shooing motion.

She slung her bag over her shoulder but stopped short. "Are you sure you are okay here alone? I can't believe Alek left like that."

"Stop." I folded my arms across my chest. "First him, now you. Just quit, damnit. Nothing has happened in weeks. I almost wish it fucking would so we could stop walking around on eggshells waiting for sword shoes to fall on us. But Samir hasn't come at us directly, not once. I highly doubt he's going to start. Whatever happens, we'll have stupid amounts of warning. He's all about building terror and shit."

A funny warning bell went off in my head and a thought danced through my mind, as elusive as the snow starting to swirl in glittering flakes outside the store windows. I tried to grasp at it, but it melted away as Harper responded.

"Sword shoe?" Her brown eyebrows rose comically.

"Like waiting for the other shoe to drop. But also like the sword of Damocles, hanging by a freaking thread over me."

"You're weird," she said.

"Thanks, Captain Obvious. Now go before it gets too snowy. I'll be fine."

"But what if Samir does show up?" she said, half-turning toward the door.

"I'll challenge him to a wizard's duel. We'll play magical Rock-Paper-Scissors-Lizard-Spock."

"Like, super weird." Harper grinned. "But what if he sends another assassin?"

"I've taken on every bloody one he's sent. We're all here; they ain't. I think I can handle it. I mean, I've been training my ass off. Seriously, it's so flat, I look Caucasian."

"Hey, I resemble that remark. Okay, fine. Just try not to have too much murderous fun without calling me first, deal?" Harper gave me a quick, tight hug and finally left.

I smiled after her but felt the grin melt from my face as the shop grew silent again. I kind of didn't want to be alone, but everyone was gone. Levi at his shop, probably putting on his fiftieth set of snow tires and chains in the last week on some guy's car. Junebug and Rose at the Henhouse. Alek in NOLA. Ezee and Harper up at the college. Max on the coast. Brie and Ciaran on their way to Ireland.

Yep. Not creepy at all, sitting in my shop alone waiting for sword shoes. Nope.

I texted Steve. Steve had Mondays off. I needed something to distract me, and there was a new expansion of *Carcassonne* to test out. Steve had no idea about any of the weird shit. He wouldn't look at me sideways

14

or be always looking over his shoulder, waiting for the next assassin or whatever Samir had planned now.

I called the county clerk again, trying to get another inspection. If I was going to be here alone, waiting for a random customer or for Steve to show, I figured I could make myself useful. Noon was lunch, apparently, and I got voicemail. I wanted to be able to tell Brie her bakery was open again by the time she returned. This whole mess was stupidly frustrating, and then for them to be called away in the middle? Super lame.

That formerly errant thought, which had been like snowflake and smoke before, crystallized.

Brie's shop shut down. Ciaran recalled to Ireland. Alek sent to New Orleans. The Internet in town being spotty, forcing Harper away from the store more.

All these things leaving me here. Alone.

Another deep shiver went through me as I clutched at my twenty-sided die talisman. Mind-Tess woke up, whispering a warning as Wolf, my spirit guardian, materialized, facing the door, growling.

I knew before I felt the wards hum. Before the door opened, bringing with it cold air, swirling snow, and the one man I had hoped never to see again.

CHAPTER TWO

I wasn't using Tess's magic, but time stood still anyway. My heart stopped. Blood froze in my veins. Samir walked two feet into my shop and stood, almost posed, the light glinting in his golden eyes, his long grey wool coat flaring with his sudden halt.

He was still handsome—his face all angles and evenly tanned skin, his hair black and artfully long over his forehead. Standing utterly still, feeling like a rabbit in the shadow of the hawk, I waited for my heart to reboot. I waited to see if I still felt. Still breathed. Mind-Tess fluttered nervously at the edges of my consciousness like a trapped sparrow.

Then time unfroze. Blood rushed to my head and my heart slammed into my ribcage. I pulled my magic around me, reveling as strength and warmth poured through me.

I was no rabbit. Not anymore.

"So," I said, biting off the word with a murderous smile. "We meet again."

"Still funny, Jess. Or I suppose it is Jade now." Samir smiled. Well, his lips shifted and curved upward, but nothing touched his eyes. They might as well have been molten gold in reality for all the emotion in them.

I wanted to blast him off his smug feet but held my rage in check, trembling with the effort of not unleashing hell on him. My wards were humming and I smelled the honey scent of his power. He wouldn't have walked in there without some kind of protection. Hell, he hadn't even looked at Wolf where she crouched growling, her long tail swishing like a cat's. Either he couldn't see her, or . . .

He wasn't worried. The tiny part of my brain that wasn't insane with hatred told me that should worry *me*.

I unclenched my fists and wrapped my left hand around my talisman, fighting for control of my emotions, of my power.

"It's always been Jade," I said. I sent a tendril of power at him, probing the air around him, ready with a shield if he reacted.

Samir kept smiling. My magic slid off an invisible barrier a few inches out from his body. He was shielding. Damn.

What had I expected? It was never going to be as easy as magically punching my way into his ribcage and ripping out his bleeding, shriveled heart.

"Twenty-six years, and you just walk into my store?" I said. I pulled my magic back, thinking furiously about how to get through his shield. Bring the building down on him? Nobody but me was here. I discarded the idea even as it formed. It would probably just piss him off.

"Things around here have gotten too interesting to resist." He shrugged, never taking that molten gaze off me.

"You mean you finally decided to man up and come after me yourself?"

"Man . . . up?" Samir grinned and took a step forward, reaching a hand out as though he wanted to brush my cheek with it.

I swelled with magic, purple sparks crackling in the air around me. Maybe bringing down the building wouldn't be the worst idea. Not compared to if he touched me. My skin wanted to crawl off and burn itself alive at the suggestion of his hands on my body again.

"You truly think I was working up the courage to face you, child?" He laughed, but he didn't advance farther. "I hate to bruise your ego, my dear, but I have other pursuits in life."

"Yeah, fucking right," I said through gritted teeth. "You've hunted me for years. And now that you've found me again, you just. Won't. Leave. Me. Alone." I bit off every word, spitting them out, my whole body trembling with the effort not to smash him down. My rage scared me a little, scared mind-Tess, too, who had gone silent.

The only one not scared was Samir. He was laughing again, his head thrown back, his eyes finally off me.

I took my chance. The floor in there was concrete under the thin industrial carpet. I slammed my magic down into it, sending a wide crack at Samir. His shield might turn my magic, but I wanted to see how he felt about being sunk into concrete that turned instantly to quicksand beneath his feet.

Samir sprang back and a wave of magic radiated off him, smashing into my own shield and sliding me backward as though I'd been physically shoved. My tailbone jammed into the counter behind me and I heard glass crack. I hoped it was glass, anyway, and not my bones. Pain barely registered, hot but distant, like standing just within the circle of warmth from a bonfire.

The walls groaned, but the building stood. I'd sunk a lot of warding magic into it. A crack and a missing couple feet of flooring wouldn't bring it down.

I'd have to do better. I circled to my right, away from the counter. Wolf circled with me, her lips in a silent snarl.

"I've known where you were for four years, Jade," Samir said.

"Bullshit," I said, but his words were like another blow, and I stopped moving, watching him, ready for another spell if one came. "If that's true, why not come after me four years ago?"

"Why rush? You would have run again. Chasing you around was interesting for a few years, but then it became routine. And I do hate routine. Ask Tess." His smile was back but less confident than before. "Ah, yes, you can't. Poor Tess."

In my mind, the ghost of Tess, her soul, or whatever the hell she was now, agreed with him. Boredom was Samir's true enemy. She assured me that she had known nothing about him being aware the whole time of where I was. Small comfort. I hoped he was lying. Alek could have told me, but Alek was away. Which was good. My love would have just gotten himself killed in minutes trying to defend me.

"Here you stayed, surrounded by your childish games. Quiet and boring as a mouse, scratching away at life. Sad, broken, terrified of shadows. Already-broken toys hold no interest for me."

I studied his face, an odd grief tempering my rage. I had loved him once. But it was so clear now, clearer than ever, pushed home by years and by my new experience of actual love, that what I had felt for Samir had been as immature and naïve as I once had been. And the Samir I had loved so blindly had never been real.

I clung to the rage, shoving away all other feelings. This was not epiphany time. This was supposed to be ass-kicking time.

Him monologuing was good, though. It always killed villains in movies. I tried to keep him talking.

"Why not just fuck off and stay away, then?"

"You got interesting. My little mage. Taking her first heart. Thrilling, isn't it? Gaining power, soaking in the knowledge of another, absorbing their spark into your own growing light until you are the sun and moon and stars."

"Have you spent the last few decades smoking crack? I wish you'd said shit like that when I first met you. I probably would have smothered you in your sleep just to shut you up." I circled more to the right. About seven more steps and I would reach the door.

Not that I should take the fight outside, but I had a dim thought of leading him away from town. This was Wylde; there were woods within a quick run from anywhere, including my store. Out in the open, away from humans and buildings, we could get our wizard dueling on.

"Would anything convince you I am not a monster?" His smile faded, his expression turning to stone.

"Hmm. Sending assassins after me. Fucking up my birth family and getting my father killed. Oh, yeah, that part where you fucking burned everyone I ever loved to death. So. That's a big-ass cup of nope." I willed Wolf to make for the door, trying to telepathically send her the plan. Maybe she could help cover my retreat. She'd hurt him before. It was worth a shot.

"Then there is no use pretending. You know what I want."

"Why did you send the postcard? If you thought I'd run," I added as he raised an eyebrow.

"To see if you would. And when you didn't, I knew that you had grown roots again. I knew that you had something to lose again."

His words worked like a Petrification spell.

"So, you have been fucking with us." It wasn't a question. All the pieces I'd put together too slowly were locking into place. "Why not just kill me?"

Samir shook his head and started to answer, but the chime of my door interrupted him. In my peripheral vision, I saw Steve's head appear, followed by his wide shoulders wrapped up in a green parka. Snow was melting on his chubby, cheerful cheeks. He was smiling as he stomped his feet on the doormat, and raised one hand in greeting as he tugged off his ugly Christmas scarf with his other.

"Steve," I screamed at him, "get out!"

Steve's eyes went wide and his mouth opened as though to ask a question. The words were cut off by a gossamer thread as it flew through the air from Samir and wrapped around Steve's exposed throat. Blood sprayed in fine mist and Steve collapsed to his knees, his hands going to his neck.

I slammed a wave of power at Samir, shoving him back, and sprang for Steve. My fingers felt stiff and numb as I tried to get to the magic garrote cutting its way into Steve's neck. The thread felt like fishing line, slippery with blood and gore. Steve convulsed and choked, blood gushing out of his mouth and air starting to hiss from his cut throat.

Blood, blood everywhere.

"Tess," I cried, not caring that I was talking aloud. I reached for mind-Tess, begging her to help me fix this. She was the caged bird again in my head, her ghost screaming at me to stop trying to save a dead man and pay attention to the enemy coming at me.

I reached for her memories, but there was no time to sift, to learn. No time.

Time. I could do things with time. Things I was learning from Tess. *NO.* Mind-Tess still screaming.

I twisted my magic from defensive shielding and poured my will into it, the desire formed by my need, the thought of what I wanted not even registering at a wholly conscious level.

I wanted Steve to be not dying. I wanted time to save him.

Magic roared in my ears, downing out the voice in my head, the sound of Steve choking to death on his own blood only inches from my face. I wrapped a bloody hand around my talisman and threw my power into action.

Time. I needed more time.

The world faded in a purple spiral, my whole body seizing as magic pooled around me, drowning me. I felt like I'd jumped in a wormhole, all sensation fading as I plummeted into a whirlpool of noise and sensation. I squeezed my eyes shut, hoping I still had eyes. There was noise like rushing water or heavy wind or the beating of a million angry wings.

And then it stopped and the world was quiet. I opened my eyes, staggering as my legs threatened to drop me onto my ass.

I was in my store. No Steve. No blood on my hands. Wolf leaned into me, holding me up as I stumbled forward, toward the door. Samir was talking, saying something about not being ready. I realized I'd let go of my power. I wasn't even shielding. My evil ex was too busy with the sound of his voice to notice yet.

21

He stopped talking and narrowed his eyes. I reached for my power again and was answered with only a thin sputtering trickle, like when the water has been shut off but you still get what's left in the pipes.

What the fuck had I done? Where was Steve? The shop walls were pushing in on me, my head pounding as though I'd slammed it into the wall a few dozen times.

Samir shook his head and started to say something else, but the chime of my door interrupted him. In my peripheral vision, I saw Steve's head appear, followed by his wide shoulders wrapped up in a green parka. Snow was melting on his chubby, cheerful cheeks. He was smiling as he stamped his feet on the doormat, and raised one hand in greeting as he tugged off his ugly Christmas scarf with his other.

Déjà fucking vu.

"Steve," I screamed at him, "get out!"

I knew that Samir would throw the killing magic. I watched it almost in slow motion as it swished through the air, a silvery thread of death.

Springing straight into its path, I felt an odd cold pain in my neck as the thread hit me and then passed right through as though made of nothing more than imagination and smoke.

I tried to cast a spell, to throw up a shield, anything, but magic failed me, flowing out of my veins like sand in a sieve. I grabbed for Steve as he fell, as blood misted from his throat.

Once it hit him, the thread became tangible. I jammed my fingers into it and tried to pull it away from his throat. Cold fire burned into my joints, my skin recoiling from the magic.

"No," I said, over and over. "No, don't you die on me again. No. Steve."

Steve tried to say something, but it came out as an aspirated gush of blood. His eyes bulged.

Then he died in my arms, my fingers numb and clinging to the magic that killed him, buried in his throat.

Only hatred kept me conscious. My eyes were wet with unshed tears, my vision fogging as Samir walked toward me. Wolf snarled and tried to spring at him but hit his shield in a spray of black smoke and disappeared, materializing again three feet beyond him, still snarling.

"Why?" I asked, my voice raw and unable to rise above a stage whisper. My throat felt as though it had collapsed on itself, and my hand slipped from the garrote as trembling took over. My body refused to obey me and I crumpled, half-sitting on Steve's still chest. Broken.

"Give me Clyde's heart," Samir said.

"Why did you do this? He's just a guy."

"Clyde's heart, where is it? Perhaps I will spare the next guy, hmm?" Samir's cold smile was back.

I wanted to kick his teeth in, but I wasn't sure I even had feet. I couldn't feel them, anyway.

"I don't have it," I started to say, but decided not to. He wouldn't believe me. "Just end me," I whispered instead. I couldn't defend myself. Whatever I had done, turning back time like that, it had wiped the floor with me.

I'd defeated myself.

"Kill you? Here? Like this? Oh, Jade. You do not understand, do you? This was just a warning. Give me the heart and spare us both this drama." He smiled down at me with a shake of his head.

"Why won't you?" I screamed. My voice gave out mid-cry. "Please," I added, the word forming on my lips but no sound carrying it out into the room.

"Because, my dear," Samir said, "I'm not bored yet."

He left my shop, his shape a shadow as he disappeared into the swirling snow.

I swallowed tears and nausea, adrenaline draining away as quickly as my magic had. I forced myself to look down at Steve.

"I'm so sorry," I mouthed to him.

He didn't answer. He'd never answer.

Working slowly, my stiff hands and the vast amount of blood causing me to lose my grip constantly, I tugged the garrote from his neck. It was inert now, appearing very much like fishing line. Thin and clear. Like my grief, like the tears running down my cheeks and spilling onto my collarbones.

That's how the deputy from the sheriff's office found me. Kneeling over Steve's corpse, garrote in my bloody hands.

They told me I had the right to remain silent, but it didn't matter. I had no voice and nothing at all to say.

CHAPTER THREE ▶

Snow fell in whirling curtains, the chains on the tires rattling like ghosts as the deputies drove me down the road to the county station. I felt the air on my skin as the bigger deputy, a bearded man whose name I wouldn't have been able to remember on a good day, pulled me out of the back, but my legs wouldn't hold me up. All I saw was Steve's dead face and his eyes clouding over.

I threw up on the stairs and there was nothing in my stomach but yellow bile. They hauled me into the station, still dry-heaving. Heat hit me as we stumbled through the double doors.

Maybe Tess was right. Maybe there was a hell and these were the gates. I choked on more bile and tried to speak, but my throat was still ruined, my jaw like nails and broken glass. I needed my phone call. I had to warn Harper. I had to warn them all. I tried to make my eyes focus, to make Steve's face stop swimming in front of me. *Wolf. Tell Harper that Timmy fell down the well again.* I mentally reached for her, but even thinking hurt. I couldn't see her anywhere. I couldn't call out.

No voice. No guardian. I was alone there. Helpless. Just heat now and the scuffed hardwood floor rising to meet my face like a punch I totally deserved.

▲ ▲ ▲

"You left her cuffed?" A woman's voice was arguing with a man's. Sheriff Lee. "I can't believe you just left her unconscious like that. Where's the damn doctor? Did you even think to call a paramedic? She's covered in blood."

"It's not hers; we checked," a defensive male voice responded.

Hands touched me and I tried to unglue my eyelids. Metal clinked on metal as Lee removed my cuffs. I opened my eyes and met her light brown gaze. My shoulders unkinked as I pulled my hands in front of me, blood rushing back into my fingers with the vengeance of a thousand needles.

Blood. On my hands. Steve's blood. It had dried to a sticky brown color, as though I'd been holding onto something rusted. Broken. Steve. Shit.

"Jade?" Lee said softly.

I dragged my gaze away from my hands and sat all the way up. I was in one of the four holding cells in the back of the county courthouse. Such as it was, anyway. The courthouse was tiny, a converted church that had been added on to for the last century. Two courtrooms, one for traffic, one for everything else. Four cells. The sheriff's office and a bullpen for the handful of deputies. Offices upstairs for the presiding judges, all two of them. Anything serious went up to the state facilities—not that most stuff that happened in Wylde was ever written up. Lee and her shifter deputies kept things quiet and swept the weird shit under the proverbial rug.

I worked my jaw, wincing. I didn't know how long I'd been out, but my magic was there when I reached for it. The stream was thin and weak, but at least I could keep hold of it without vomiting or passing out. I reluctantly let it go and tried out my words. I felt the warm weight of my d20 talisman against my chest beneath my shirt. They hadn't taken that, at least.

"I need to call Harper," I said. My voice was mostly back, thick with grief and pain, but audible at least.

"She's awake? Sheriff, you can't be in there," another male voice, different from the earlier one, called out. Heavy footsteps rounded the corner, and a man who was nearly as wide as he was tall, which wasn't much taller than I, charged down the hall toward my cell. He looked about forty with thinning hair he'd tried to comb over and a suit that had probably been wrinkled before it was crammed into a winter coat. He had a badge clipped to his belt but no gun, just the worn spot on his belt where one would clip on.

"She needs to get checked out by a paramedic," Lee said, straightening up. Very quickly and so softly I wasn't sure I even heard her, she added, "I already called her. You have a lawyer?"

"Call her again. Tell Harper that Samir is here. Tell her to turtle." Harper would know what I meant. We'd been thinking, planning what would happen if or when Samir showed.

"Lee," the angry man said. "You want this in your report, too? One would think you have enough troubles right now."

"She's our suspect," said another man, coming up behind the other. He was the Jack Sprat to Angry Man's rotundity. In his thirties, with sandy hair and bland blue eyes, he wore a button-down shirt with no jacket. He too had a badge but no gun.

"I didn't do it," I said. Partially because I was probably expected to, and partially for Lee. She had to know I didn't do this. She had to believe me.

"Jade, these are detectives with the State Police," she started to say, but Angry Man pushed past her and grabbed my arm.

I almost hit him in the face with my palm like Alek had been teaching me to do, but figured I shouldn't add assault to my growing record. So, I shook his hand off, giving him my best *I will fucking murder you* look instead. I'd learned that from Alek, also. He had a very convincing murder face.

"Come with us," he said.

Apparently, I was a good student, because Angry Man backed off and let me stumble out of the cell on my own. They led me out into the bullpen. It was empty but for Jack Sprat, who preceded us. From there I was taken to the interview room, which was about ten degrees colder than the rest of the building.

I knew from cop shows that this was to make me uncomfortable, but the cool air felt good on my feverish skin. All I needed was a drink of water, ten hours in a shower scrubbing myself down with sand, and I'd feel almost normal again.

Oh, and for Samir to be dead and Steve to be alive. That, too.

I folded my arms on the metal table and put my head down, closing my eyes against the glare of the fluorescent lighting. I'd rested a little, but I was far from strong. Miles and acres and light years and parsecs away from being strong enough. My body felt hollow, like a bell that had been rung too many times and now was left with the semblance of vibration and noise.

"Your name is Jade Crow?" Angry Man asked.

"Lawyer," I said. Fuck these guys. I had such worse problems, they didn't even know.

"You are being charged with first-degree murder," Jack Sprat said. "Why don't you tell us your side? Did that man try to hurt you?"

He probably thought he sounded genuine. He sounded like an asshole.

"Steve," I said, baited into raising my head up and talking. "His name is Steve."

"Was Steve," Angry Man said. His thick lips were pressed into a wormy line in his pallid face, and I started to wish I'd hit him.

"Why did you kill Steve?" Jack Sprat asked.

"I didn't," I said. "Lawyer."

"If you aren't guilty, why do you need a lawyer?" Jack was losing his patience.

I stayed silent and looked down at the table. My hands weren't the only thing covered in blood. I stank of it—my jeans, my shirt, everything was spattered and soaked. I resisted looking across into the two-way glass, not wanting to see myself. I probably looked like a Native American version of *Carrie*. Though my mouth tasted like shit and ass, I didn't want water anymore. I'd just throw it up.

"Look, you'd better talk to us. You know they still have the death penalty in Idaho, right?"

"You want to spend the next decade rotting in the Pocatello Women's Correctional Center?" Jack Sprat added.

"I thought you were supposed to be Good Cop," I said, baring my teeth at him.

The younger detective started to say something, but a quick hand motion from his partner stopped him. Angry Man, now looking more comically sly than angry, approached the table and sat down across from me.

"Look, Jade, we're trying to help you. That crime scene, well, it was ugly. But we do just want to understand. Let's get off on a better foot here, all right?"

"Wait, so now you are Good Cop? I'm so confused." I folded my hands, trying to obscure the worst of the blood. I just wanted to stop thinking about blood. About Steve's blood. My stomach twisted and I swallowed hard to keep the acid down.

"I'm Detective Dickson and this is my partner, Detective Baldwin," Angry Man said.

I tried to choke back a laugh and failed, snorting painfully through my nose. "Wait, so you're telling me that you guys are Dick and Balls?"

"You fucking crazy bitch," Balls growled, coming at me.

Dick could move; I'd give him that. He got between his partner and me and ordered the younger man to go get me a soda.

"Dick and Balls. That's funny," he said, his face tight and his eyes mean in a way that said he was lying through his teeth but still trying for the Good Cop role. Definitely wasn't going to get callbacks for that part.

"What? You guys have never heard that one before? Seriously?" It seemed stupidly obvious, and cops liked nicknames. At least TV cops did.

"There's a blizzard outside, Jade. We just want to get home to our families. So, why don't you go over your version of events and you can have a shower and get some sleep?"

"L. A. W. Y. E. R," I said, spelling it out for him. Then I put my head back down and closed my eyes again.

Balls came back with a cup of coffee, which I didn't touch. The acidic, stale smell alone made me more nauseated. I kept my head down and my eyes closed, ignoring their various questions until they finally left the room after Dick cuffed my right hand to a ring in the table.

Samir was out there. He wanted Clyde's heart. So he'd said.

"A diversion," Tess whispered in my head.

I was inclined to agree. Oh, I was sure Samir did want the heart. Somehow, he knew I hadn't eaten it. Maybe because of the bag. It was Samir's creation, after all, so he might know when something was inside it. I'd given the bag to Alek to hide so I wouldn't be tempted by the power in it. I wanted no part of that evil.

Which, I admit, was looking stupid and squeamish of me now. Samir had been toying with me. Wiping my own floor with me, if I was honest. I didn't want to be honest. I wanted to commit some serious murderating for real.

So, why Clyde's heart? Why kill Steve? What was Samir going to do next and how the hell did I get out of this stupid place and find him?

And what the fuck had I done in my shop?

"You went back in time," mind-Tess said. With my eyes closed, I could see her, the beautiful ghost in my head sitting on a rock inside a silver circle. "That shouldn't have worked."

"It sure fucked me up," I muttered, remembering the weakness, the sputtering and utter failure of my powers.

I reached for my magic again and the tap turned on. More of a bathroom-sink kind of tap than the fire hose I was used to, but better than before.

Maybe enough that I could bust myself out of this joint. There was no clock. I could have been unconscious for minutes or for hours.

Samir knew I had something or, more importantly, someone, more than one someone, to lose now. Again. And he had who knew how much of a head start on hurting them.

Fuck the law. I wasn't staying in here. Gripping my d20 in my left hand, I channeled my magic down my right arm and threaded it around the handcuff.

Wolf appeared beside me and whined, pressing her head against my side. My magic stuttered and halted, fading from my control.

"The fuck you doing?" I whispered to her.

Voices from the bullpen drew my attention just as the door slammed open. A petite woman with wheat-blond hair and bright blue eyes sailed into the room, carrying a briefcase and the air of command. She pulled a chair away from the wall, set her briefcase on the table, and then kicked the door shut with her heel.

I relaxed slightly. Maybe I wouldn't have to add running from the law to my résumé just yet. The cavalry had arrived.

CHAPTER FOUR

Kate Perkins, Esquire, was as much a bomb as she was bombshell. She was joint partner in the only law firm in town, Perkins & Smitt. Harper liked to call them Perky and Smitten, which was apt enough since an astronaut could have seen the giant torch Harrison Smitt was carrying for the beautiful blonde. Kate's real name was Katya Gararin and Harper had told me she was a cougar shifter who had come over from the Ukraine with her family, fleeing the Iron Curtain.

I'd met Kate about three years before when she'd needed documents translated. She'd tracked me down after one of the shifters who owned the RV park outside town, Mikhail, had told her I was fluent and did translation work. I was certified to do work for the court in six different languages, though not all of them under my own name. She'd been a breeze to work for, paid on time, and didn't ask questions.

Since then, I'd been doing odd translation jobs for her when she needed, but I was still surprised she had shown up there. She didn't do criminal law that I knew of beyond the occasional DUI or pot-smoking bust.

"Are you hurt?" Kate said, looking me over.

"Not physically," I muttered. "Are you my lawyer?"

"The Macnulty girl called me. I called Sheriff Lee, who said you'd been arrested for murder. Can we do this in Russian?" she added, switching to Russian with an exaggerated look at the two-way mirror.

"Don't trust Dick and Balls to keep client confidentiality sacred?" I glanced at the mirror also and wished I hadn't. I looked worse than a horror movie in the dark glass. A wraith. A nightmare.

"Dick and . . ." She trailed off and laughed. "Dickson and Baldwin. Nice one."

"I didn't do it," I said in Russian, unable to share her mirth. "The man who did is out there, and he'll do this again."

"I know you didn't do it," Kate said, her own face turning serious in a blink. "I saw the crime scene photos and talked to the coroner."

"Assuring yourself of my innocence before you took me as a client?"

"Yes. I was. I like you, and I owe Alek, but I don't need a first-degree murder case." She sat back in her chair and watched me.

After a long moment, she continued. "As soon as those idiots get their evidence in order, they will also realize it's impossible you did this. I'm going to make them clean you up, and then we'll answer some of their questions. Did you say anything to them yet?"

"Other than calling them Dick and Balls?" I said. "Nope. I can't exactly tell them the full truth. I'd just end up in a straitjacket."

"You are lucky I owe Alek," she said, but her mouth twitched in a half-smile.

Kate left and came back with a Styrofoam cup of water and a warm washcloth. She glared at Dick until he undid my cuff, and they let me wipe off my hands. I resisted quoting Shakespeare, since Lady Macbeth had actually been a killer and I didn't really want to draw unnecessary parallels. But I was freakishly glad to have at least some of the blood off my hands.

"My client is willing to answer some questions," Kate said after looking at me to see if I was ready.

There were only three chairs in the room, so Balls was forced to stand awkwardly against the wall as Dick sat across from us, placing a brown folder on the table.

"Will she answer why she killed Steven Jones?"

"If this is your line, we're done," Kate said, starting to rise from her chair.

"She was kneeling over the body, with the murder weapon in her hands. We have a damned deputy as witness, not to mention whoever called nine-one-one." Dick shook his head.

Someone had called nine-one-one? That explained how quickly the deputy had found me. But no one had been around.

"Male or female?" I asked.

"What?" Balls and Dick both squinted at me.

"The caller. Male or female?"

Dick pulled open the file folder and skimmed down what looked like a report sheet. I wondered again how long I'd been out. Long enough for crime scene photos and for Kate to check with the coroner. I looked down at my hands again and then at the bloody rag.

"Um, did I just destroy evidence?"

Dick and Balls exchanged another look, this one more worried.

"Nobody examined you? Did they at least take pictures?"

"I was kind of unconscious," I said.

"She was out cold. Besides, witness. I told you already."

"Did you process her in at all?" Kate gave the detectives a flat look that said she was super unimpressed.

"She's been charged with murder. The DA will make it official in front of the judge tomorrow. If he can get here with all the damned snow." Dick tapped the folder. "It's all here."

"Did you look at the coroner's report?" Kate spoke like she was dealing with children, each word carefully enunciated.

"Yes." Nods from both men.

"How much did Mr. Jones weigh?"

"A couple hundred, I guess."

"Two hundred-thirty-seven pounds. How much does my client weigh?"

"I've always been taught you don't ask a lady her age or her weight," Dick shot back with an angry smile. The meanness was back in his eyes, but beads of sweat popped out on his forehead like dew.

"One-thirty," I said. I saw where she was going with it, and relief snaked through me. I was about to be exonerated through science. The irony was not lost on me.

"So, this girl took down a man who outweighed her by over one hundred pounds, without defensive marks or bruising on either of them, then used a length of what appears to be guitar string to half sever the victim's head, again without leaving a cut or bruise on herself. Not a mark on her hands. Nothing."

I obediently held my hands up, palms out. Tried really hard not to hear her words and think about Steve's throat gaping. About his dead eyes. I failed and had to turn aside, dry-heaving again. I put my head between my knees to fight the dizziness, but it was a mistake. My pants were coated with blood, and all I could smell was sickness and death.

Kate gently patted my back and made me drink some of the water. I tried to tell her it would just end up on her expensive shoes, but she waved that off.

Both detectives were quiet for a good minute, chewing over what Kate had just pointed out. I probably had sexism on my side on this one, since it was pretty obvious from their expressions that they had no trouble doubting a skinny chick like me with my nonexistent nerd muscles had taken out a big grown man like Steve.

"That's for the DA to decide. She's been arrested. Now, if she has an alternate story she wants to tell, we're listening," Dickson said finally.

"It's okay," I said, looking at Kate. "I'll tell them exactly what happened."

Except, of course, for the parts that would bring the men in lab coats. So, I couldn't tell them the whole truth. I skimmed all the magic parts and waved off a question about the giant crack in the floor from Baldwin. But I gave them the gist. Killer psycho ex-lover out to hurt me, who came to my shop and attacked my friend.

"Describe this guy for us?" Dickson actually had a pen out. He glared at Baldwin when the younger detective snorted and shook his head.

"About six foot one. Black hair a little longer than Balls's over there. Gold eyes; they look like contacts but they aren't. Skin a shade or so lighter than mine, less brown, more just tanned-looking. He was wearing a grey wool coat." *And will probably kill you if you get too close or try to detain him*, I added silently. "He's very dangerous," I said instead. I hoped that Samir would at least be trying to fly below the human world's radar. He'd never drawn huge attention to himself that I knew of, at any rate. Maybe a little law pressure would get him to back down, give me space to come up with a new plan.

I was grasping at desperate straws, I knew, but they were all I had.

"So, this guy came in, killed Steven, and then just walked away? Why was the wire in your hands?" Dickson had his Good Cop face back on, though it was even less convincing than before.

I waited a beat for Kate to say I didn't have to answer that, but I guess she was too busy lawyering to watch the amount of crime shows I had. Instead, she looked at me and raised a perfectly waxed eyebrow.

"I was pulling it out. Trying to help him. He died in my fucking arms and I couldn't do anything." I bit down on the inside of my cheek, tasting blood, trying to focus on anger instead of grief. Instead of my failure. "I couldn't do anything," I whispered, looking away from everyone, my eyes focused on a paint chip on the blank beige wall.

"I think that is enough for you to get started, detectives," Kate said firmly. "My client is exhausted and I'm sure she would like to go home."

"She can't go home," Balls said. "She's under arrest."

"Did you not hear a thing I've said?" Kate pursed her lips, her gaze turning to ice.

"That's for the DA to decide, and the judge. Not us. We made the arrest; we can't just let her walk. She's got to appear tomorrow." Dick ran a hand through his thinning hair, completely screwing up his comb-over.

"I can't stay here," I said to Kate. "He's out there. Who knows what he's doing to my friends?"

"It's snowing so hard, you can't see your shoes. Nobody is gonna be killing anybody tonight, if this guy even exists." Balls gave a disgusted snort.

There was more arguing back and forth, but my head started to pound again and I put it down on the table. The metal felt cold and soothing against my skin. It was clear that Kate had planted doubt in the detectives' minds, but they wouldn't budge on letting me go. It seemed like they'd hustled their asses down there for the sure collar, but now that things were messier than a girl covered in blood writing up a tidy confession, they wanted to pass that buck off to someone else.

Me? I just wanted to murder someone for real. Or sleep. I missed Alek. He'd rip right through these walls, stare down these assholes, and get me out. At least, my tired brain had that fantasy. I knew the reality would be different. Besides, part of me was glad he was gone. At least in NOLA, he was safe from Samir.

Unless somehow Samir had tricked him into going there. I sat up, grasping at that thought, worried more than ever.

"I want my phone call," I said.

"Cell tower is out. Landline is screwed, too. Won't do you any good. Sorry," Balls said in a way that made it clear he wasn't sorry at all.

So, that was it, then. I was stuck in jail for the night while my friends were out there in a frakking blizzard, with my psycho ex stalking them. I tried to tell myself they were capable, smart people who knew the danger, but it was cold comfort.

Kate walked me back to the bathroom as the deputy on duty went hunting through the lockers to find me some sweats and a clean shirt. They made her stay in the room with me while I showered, not that I could have fit through the tiny window anyway. What was I going to do? Charge off naked into a blizzard?

I ignored that I had been about to do something very close to that before Kate showed up, and scrubbed my skin raw. Barely able to stay on my feet but glad for warm clothes and no more blood matting my hair, I stumbled back to my cell and sank down on the thin mattress.

"First thing tomorrow, I'm going to get you out of here. Even if I have to put Ray into a snowplow and drive him here, all right?" Kate smiled at me. I assumed Ray was the district attorney. Or maybe the judge. I wasn't exactly on a first-name basis with either.

"No," I said, trying not to sound ungrateful but feeling surly and exhausted—and scared. "It isn't all right. But what choice do I have?"

"Get some sleep. It's late. You'll barely even notice the night going by. I'll be back soon. Trust me, okay? I'm your lawyer." Kate smiled, patted my shoulder gently, and then left.

Dick and Balls must have left too, because nobody disturbed me. I heard the deputy on duty out there listening to soft jazz, but he left me alone. The lights were dim, only the one in the hallway on and its glow didn't quite reach the bed. I pulled the blanket over myself and lay back, my thoughts charging in crazy circles around my brain. Finally, I reached for my magic and wove a simple ward around the cell, anchoring it to the corners. It wouldn't do much except warn me if someone tried to use magic on me or approached, but even that small bit of supernatural protection made me feel very slightly better.

"Tess," I whispered, reaching into my mind for her memories.

She sat on her rock inside a circle of silver, ephemeral and untouched. Another person who was dead and gone. Only her ghost or whatever it was lived on inside me. Who knows? Maybe I was insane.

Samir was there. My nightmare had come into reality. I needed to think shit through, and now I had all night to do it. Sleep would have to wait.

"Time to play Fact. What do we know or think we know?" Somehow, talking to a ghost in my head made things clearer.

"Samir is still toying with you," Tess said. "He could have killed you."

"You could sound a little less pissy about that," I muttered.

"I died so you could have more strength to defeat him."

"Point taken. Tell me about time travel. How did I do that? You told me it wasn't possible." Thinking about what I'd done pulled up memories of Steve's double death, but I focused on Tess, on her heart-shaped face and sad eyes. Grief had to wait.

"It is possible. With enough power, though until you did that, I didn't think anyone had enough power except perhaps Samir. But it should never be done. It could damage you forever, and it changes the world. You are now living in a different future."

"I don't feel different," I said. I took a deep breath and rubbed my fingers over my talisman. "But what? Thirty seconds of time travel backward made me feel like I'd been trampled by a tarrasque. Not looking to repeat that." *Repeat that, get it? Har har.*

Tess wasn't amused. She paced inside my head.

"I brought him here," I said, thinking over everything Samir had said to me. "He knew where I was. I was right about my magic drawing him to me, just wrong about the details. I've been wrong about a lot." It was like Three Feathers all over again. Had I learned nothing?

And now he was there. He didn't want Clyde's heart. Okay, he probably wanted it, but it was, as Tess had said before, a diversion. Something to taunt me about and give me hope that this all could end in anything other than my death and the death of everyone I cared about.

Max and Alek were both away. Vivian, the local vet and another of my friends, was away as well, seeing her mother in Florida. Brie and Ciaran were in Ireland. So, all of them were out of Samir's immediate reach. I hoped.

If Harper had gotten my message, she and the twins, Junebug, and

Rose, would be gathered at the Hen House, behind my wards. Which might not help them much, but they were all shifters. Not easy to kill. I wanted to send them away, too. Tell everyone to scatter and leave myself as the last target standing, but I knew they wouldn't go.

"You might need them," Tess said, her voice gentle but her memories carrying a hard edge that stung my mind.

I pushed away those thoughts. I wasn't going to use them if I didn't have to. There had to be a way to lure Samir out. This was Wylde. In winter. The town was small; everybody knew everybody. There weren't a lot of places to hide. I supposed he could have just waltzed in and killed some poor family, taking their house. Damnit. More grim thoughts. Fear and doubt swirled around like a maelstrom, and my headache increased. I needed to sleep. I would need strength tomorrow, whatever came.

I turned and put my back to the wall. Wolf materialized and lay next to the mattress, resting her head up on the thin pillow. I combed my fingers through her silky fur and closed my eyes, praying no dreams would come.

The dreams that came for me were more like memories. And in my memories, nightmares walked and pain ruled.

In my memory-slash-nightmare, I stand again in the library in the house on the lake that Samir and I have shared for the last year of my life.

He's gone on a trip, the first time he's left me alone. I'm giddy with the trust but I can't help snooping around. It isn't like Bluebeard, the library isn't off-limits, but he's said there are texts and things I'm not ready for, magic that could be dangerous to learn until I'm strong enough.

Wind blows in over Lake Michigan, bringing the promise of winter ice. The house is warm but I shiver anyway. It feels odd to be alone. Isolated out here. The houses nearest ours are empty for the winter, and the phone works only when it wants to. I grow bored of watching The Princess Bride *for the twentieth time. I'm going to wear out the VHS if I'm not careful.*

So, library it is. I love the feel of the room, like knowledge is oozing from every polished mahogany shelf. Heavy brass lamps with Tiffany glass line the walls, and there are overstuffed leather chairs facing a marble fireplace. And books. Some in cases to protect them, so old that the pages aren't paper but vellum. I can almost smell the ink.

There's one line of shelves that draw me, on the wall farthest from the door. The spines of the books are plain leather, no titles or embossment. Some are stacked in a temperature-controlled case, but there is a row, at least twenty books, that are newer and just resting on the shelf. Journals. I've seen Samir writing sometimes at night when he thinks I'm asleep. It's cute how he nibbles on the tip of his pen, sending covert glances my way with half-slit golden eyes. He keeps a diary. I am glad; it makes him less enigmatic, makes him seem more human. More normal.

Curiosity killed the cat, I think, but remember that satisfaction brought it back and reach for one. I almost expect them to be warded, but there's nothing. A thrill goes through me. I know I shouldn't look. I'd be pissed if he read mine. I mean, if I kept one, which I don't.

Sheepish, I glance around. Still alone. No lightning bolt from the sky has come down on me. This diary looks older and I crack it open. The date reads 1927.

The language is a mix of Latin, Coptic, and Avestan. I'm impressed he knows them. Without my weird talent for languages, there is no way I could read this. I doubt anyone could other than Samir. I wonder exactly how old he is. He told me he was born before Jesus once, but he said it in a joking way, and I'd brushed it off. Suddenly, I'm not so sure.

Curiosity and fascination overrule propriety. I ache to know him better, to learn the things he hints at but won't say. I'll beg forgiveness later, if I even tell him. I go over to the chairs and curl up, deciding if I'm in for a penny, I might as well shove all in.

Six hours and ten journals later, I flee the house in the dark, my heart in my throat and horror filling my soul.

Because I know one thing, a pattern I read over and over and cannot ignore.

Samir is a monster. Samir is going to kill me, eat my heart, and take my power.

The dreams shift. Me running. Getting afraid. Calling him. Demanding an explanation. Unable to tell him how I knew, but hearing the smooth lie in his voice as he tries to soothe me.

I ran home. Home to Ji-hoon, Sophie, Todd, and Kayla. I doomed them.

Fire. The building is burning. Odd black crystals are strewn across the floor of the old school. I run down the same hallways I always run down in this nightmare. I've dreamed it before. A part of me will always be trapped on this night, trying to reach my family before Samir kills them.

The stones have magic. I can hear them. They can hear me. There is some kind of device. I hear them talking. They think it will go off when I open the door, taking us all down. Ji-hoon thinks he can reach the door, get it open before I get there. Set off the bomb. I'm screaming at them to wait even as I hear them taking a vote.

"Live, Jess," Sophie screams. "Run and live."

"We love you," Ji-hoon says in Korean.

The world explodes. Ash and tears are all that is left of me as the dream fades, and I'm still screaming, screaming that I can save them, screaming until all that is left are words and ghosts.

CHAPTER FIVE ▶

"Jade."

Sheriff Lee's voice pulled me from my nightmares, and her hand gripping my shoulder yanked me out of the smoke and debris in my head.

My throat felt raw and my eyes and cheeks were wet. I'd been crying in my sleep. Maybe screaming, too.

"You were calling out in Korean," Lee said, staring at me with curious eyes. "Bad dream?"

The vestiges of the dream still clung to me. Ji-hoon's voice. Sophie seconding his decision. The bomb going off and the whole world collapsing around me.

"Something like that," I said, sitting up. "Is that coffee? What time is it?"

"Just past eight," she said, handing me the mug. "I hope you don't mind, but I went by your place and got you some clothes. I've got your phone and wallet also—I figured you might want them once Perkins springs you. They are still plowing out the main road, but court should open at noon."

Four more hours.

"Are the phones working yet?" I asked after taking a sip of the coffee and frying the taste buds off my tongue.

"Land line is still irregular, but they have the cell tower working." She set a duffle bag I recognized as mine next to the bed.

"Can I make a call?" I set my mug on the floor and then opened the bag. She'd brought me a full change of clothes, right down to underwear. I felt a bit weird about that, since I didn't know Lee all that well. Hell, I wasn't even sure what her first name was.

"Not supposed to, but nobody has to know," Lee said with a smile. "Want a donut, too? You can change back here; the camera is only on the hallway."

"What is your first name?" I asked her. "Or should I just keep calling you sheriff?"

"Rachel," she said.

"Are you in trouble because of me?" I thought back to things that Dick and Balls had said the night before.

"No, not you. Stupid paper-pushing bullshit. This county has always run a little differently, on account of the special nature of many of our citizens. Some people who shouldn't have are starting to take notice. It'll blow over. Always does."

"I'm sorry," I said. "I know this situation isn't helping."

"You didn't kill Steve, did you?" She stared at me evenly, her face unreadable.

"What? No."

"Then this is also not your fault. We'll find the man who did. You focus on staying safe, all right?"

She left then, hopefully to go get me a donut and my phone. I gulped down more coffee and did the world's fastest clothing change. It felt good to be pulling on my own socks, to have a body clean of blood and clothes that smelled only of Tide detergent.

I was going to focus on staying safe. Sort of. Mostly I wanted the hell out of here so I could track down Samir and do terrible things to him. Starting and ending with ripping out his fucking heart. I didn't say any of that to Rachel as she returned with an Old Fashioned and my cell.

Hoping that Harper and the crew were at the Henhouse plotting Samir's doom with brilliant ideas, safe in front of a nice fire, I punched in a number and held my breath. My phone had two tiny bars of reception, but Harper picked up on the second ring.

"Jade? Are you out of jail?" Harper's voice was the best salve to my ruined nerves.

"No, not yet. Perky is coming later to get me. I should be out by one or so. Where are you guys? Is everyone okay?"

"I'm at the college with Ezee and Levi. We got snowed in, but I warned Mom and Junebug. Talked to them about half an hour ago. They are at the Henhouse but in the spare room in the barn, just in case."

So much for my hopeful vision of all my friends together around a roaring fire, plotting revenge.

"Is it true?" Harper said then, her voice getting quieter. "Steve?"

"Yeah," I said just as softly, my throat closing up again. "Samir killed him. I tried to stop it, Harper. I did."

"I know you did," she said. "Lee said you were half-dead when they brought you in. She was real worried, but I figured if you weren't dead, you weren't dying, so I called Perky."

"That's because you are the best," I said. "You should have seen the two jerks I got stuck with. It was like a bad rip-off of *The Closer*. Perky shut them down hard."

We were both silent for a moment, me thinking about Steve and what I would do next, Harper thinking about who knew what.

Harper broke the silence first. "Alek is on his way back. He was trying to get a seat on standby when I called him last night."

I felt a twinge of guilt. Maybe I should have tried to call Alek first, but he was supposed to be across the country and safe. Damnit.

"I haven't called him yet. I will." Rachel was giving me the eye from the hallway, where she stood pretending not to overhear us. "Look, I am not supposed to have a phone and I don't want to get the sheriff in trouble. I'll call you again as soon as I'm out. Get everyone together and stay safe. I don't know what Samir will do next, but he'll come after us again. This is going to get worse."

"Of course it is," Harper said. "It's the boss fight."

I could almost hear her attempt at a smile. "We'll get him," I said with more conviction than I felt. "For Steve."

"For Steve," Harper said, her voice grim.

After that, there was nothing more to say.

Alek's phone went straight to voicemail. I tried not to let it worry me. If he was on a plane, it would be off, right? Nope, not worried at all. I wanted him away from danger, but I also knew he was a badass who could handle himself. If yesterday had taught me anything, it was that going up against Samir wasn't going to be as simple as *Throw a lot of magic at him and win*. He wasn't playing fairly.

He'd isolated me. I was sure he'd waited until I was alone in my shop. I had a suspicion he was behind the trouble with the building and Brie's shop. I doubted he had anything to do with Fey business, but the timing was suspicious as well. Maybe he was behind Alek going to New Orleans. It was hard to quell my paranoid thoughts as I sat alone in the jail cell and waited for Kate Perkins to come bail me out.

When she showed up, she wasn't alone, and I knew from the look on her face that something had happened.

Rachel unlocked my cell and motioned for me to come out. Out in the bullpen, Kate Perkins stood talking to two new detectives. I assumed they were detectives, anyway, from how they stood and the clothing they were wearing.

One was a Hispanic male, somewhere in his thirties, with short brown hair and watchful, heavy-lidded brown eyes. He wore a navy-blue suit without a tie, the cut and material of which was understated but had clearly been tailored for him. He kept in shape, from the way he filled it out. I saw no badge, but he was carrying a gun in a shoulder holster under the suit jacket. I'd lived with Alek enough to recognize the shape.

His partner was a stout white woman in her fifties, crow's-feet and worry lines clashing with the laugh lines in her sharp face. Her hair was also cut short and iron grey. She had on a thick sweater and dark jeans, with her badge and gun clipped to her belt. She looked me over with a cool, assessing gaze, and I couldn't tell if she liked what she saw.

I followed Rachel over to them. We were the only ones in the building and it felt strangely subdued. A shiver of foreboding crawled up my spine but I shoved it away. I wasn't handcuffed, and at least Dick and Balls weren't here with their accusing, closed-minded looks. Things could've been worse.

"What happened?" I asked as I stopped next to Kate.

"They are dropping the charges." She had her hip up on one of the cluttered desks and a grim look on her face.

"They?" I said, jerking a thumb at the two new people. The scent of mint tickled my nose in a way that wasn't natural. Magic was present. I focused on the woman but didn't probe at her with my own magic. She had some kind of ward on, centered on a simple silver cross around her neck. Things were getting interesting again quickly.

"I am Senior Detective Hattie Wise," the woman said. "Everyone just calls me Hattie." She nodded to the man and added, "And this is Special Agent Salazar."

"Special agent? You FBI or something?" I looked the man over again.

"Something like that," he said with a bland smile.

"So, where are Dick and Balls?" I asked.

"Jade," Kate admonished with a discreet cough, hiding a grin behind her hand.

"Dick and . . ." Hattie threw back her head and laughed from her belly. "Oh, I'm going to remember that one."

"Hattie is their supervisor with the Staties," Kate said.

"My sympathies," I said.

"We're sorry about the mistake," Hattie said, sobering quickly. "You *are* free to go, but we were hoping you would come with us instead."

"There's been another murder just like your friend's," Salazar added.

Time stopped as my stomach turned into a twisting rope and the room started to spin.

"Who?" I'd just talked to Harper an hour before. She had said everyone was safe. Alek? *No, no, no, not him. Not any of them. Please, merciful Universe, please.*

"Jade. Breathe, Jade," Kate was saying over and over as she gripped my arm. "It was the librarian, Peggy Olsen."

"Peggy? But I hate her," I blurted. At the look on Salazar's and Hattie's faces, I probably should have kept that tidbit to myself. "I mean, she's not someone Samir should go after. He wants to hurt me. Killing people I don't like makes no sense." I couldn't make it line up. Peggy seemed like such a random choice, unless he was just killing everyone I'd come in contact with. I really hated that thought and shoved it away into the throw-up-over-later file.

"You witnessed the first murder. We'd like you to come see the second scene. Maybe you can help us figure out why this man is doing this? Kate said you know him," Hattie said.

"I did. A long time ago. He's stalked me for years. I thought he was here to kill people I care about before coming for me, but . . . Peggy? Makes no sense." I shook my head. More death. I hadn't liked her, but she didn't deserve this. "Are you sure it was him?"

Murders didn't happen there that often, though we'd had our share the last year, some perpetrated by yours truly, but there was a chance that Peggy had hexed the wrong person or something and this was unrelated.

"The coroner is waiting with the body. She was killed early this morning or late last night. He says it was the same kind of wire used yesterday on your friend. I think it would be too big a coincidence, no?" Salazar said.

I took a deep breath and nodded. It was clear that I was now free to go because this murder had been committed while I was locked up in here. I was now doubly glad I hadn't blasted my way out last night, though the illogical part of me wished I could have stopped Samir from hurting another person. He'd gone after Peggy for some reason, and as much as I loathed the idea of seeing another crime scene, of seeing anything that would remind me of Steve's horrific death, I needed information. Samir was still way out ahead of me, and if I was going to pwn this boss fight, as Harper would put it, I needed all the tiny advantages I could muster.

"All right," I said. "Let me grab my stuff and I'll go with you. I want to help if I can."

Rachel brought me my coat, wallet, and shoes as I gathered up the duffle bag and said goodbye to the holding cell for what I prayed was forever. I thanked her again and then whispered, "You might want to get your family out of town for a few days and warn the pack to stay away."

She leaned in and searched my face with troubled eyes. "How bad is this?"

"Bad," I said. "Samir is a sorcerer."

"Fuck," she said. She took a deep breath and tucked her chin down. "Take care of yourself, Jade Crow. Us wolves haven't forgotten what you did for us. Wylde's pack is here if you need us."

I nodded and blinked back a tear. I needed all the help I could get, but I wasn't going to use the shifters as cannon fodder. I'd figure a way out of this, find a way to face Samir again one on one and beat him.

I didn't have any other fucking choice.

Hattie and Salazar were already outside, sitting in a huge black SUV.

The day was overcast but the snow had stopped. Someone had shoveled the stairs, and snow piled in dirty drifts up to my waist. I climbed into the back seat and buckled my seatbelt. The SUV looked like it could handle the roads, at least.

"So," I said as we pulled out of the parking lot and onto the main road, "which one of you is Mulder?"

CHAPTER SIX ▶

Peggy the librarian had lived on the south side of town in a housing suburb called Dogwood Park. The park in question was a single block wide and two blocks long, with a playground now buried under a couple feet of fresh snow. The play structure stuck up from the snow like a lurking beast, red-painted metal glinting like spilled blood where the snow hadn't covered it. Peggy's two-story bungalow backed up to the park. It was easy to spot, because there were two police cars, about twenty neighbors in bathrobes and parkas, and a shitload of yellow crime scene tape.

I was surprised our local news station wasn't on it, but things around Wylde had a habit of not getting reported in a timely manner. People there liked their peace and quiet, for very good reason. This was supposed to be a sanctuary for the supernatural, a place where they had existed more or less peacefully for over a century.

Until I showed up. I mentally stuck another black *X* in the *I suck* column, then tried to shrug it off.

"You coming?" Salazar asked me.

I took another deep breath of cold air and nodded. I didn't want to walk into that house. No more crime scenes. No more death. There was too much of it in my life.

But I had to know why Peggy had been targeted. There were pieces in play I didn't see yet; that much was obvious. Samir wanted to fuck with me, to fuck up my life, kill my friends, and just win the award for ultimate evil ex-boyfriend. I wanted to kill him, because that was the only way any of this would end. To do that, I had to get the bastard to stand still and fight me.

And to do that, I had to find him. Had to figure out what he was doing and why.

Peggy's house smelled like mint, rosemary, and death. I stretched out my magical senses and saw where her wards had been smashed apart. There were broken lines of fine dust—powdered herbs, perhaps—along the windowsills. Motes of it still swirled. She'd tried to protect herself, but I couldn't tell if they were normal, everyday wards or if she'd been afraid of something. Someone.

The front entry divided into three rooms with a narrow staircase leading up. The room at the back looked like a small bathroom. To the right was the kitchen. To the left, the living room.

That was where Peggy had died. A deputy gave us little booties for our feet after we stamped the snow off, and I pulled a pair of latex gloves from the offered carton. I didn't want to touch anything anyway, but this was a crime scene, so it was better to be careful. A tall, gaunt white man stood wearing scrubs, waiting by the body. I assumed he must be the coroner.

Blood misted a nice set of blue-and-white porcelain vases. The carpet was a soft earth tone with a very subtle maple leaf pattern in it. One of the pictures, an oil painting of a black cat and a vase of wild irises, was crooked on the far wall. There was no television, just a coffee table, two linen-colored stuffed chairs, and a Victorian-style brown couch.

My eyes took in these details in stutter step, skipping around the room, looking at everything but the body sprawled on the other side of the coffee table. I forced myself to look, trying to see Peggy and not relive Steve's murder.

She lay on her back, arms wide, legs together and bent to the side, slightly tucked beneath her, as though she'd been kneeling and fallen backward. Her throat was open, the wire still embedded in the wound. Her hair was loose around her head, partially matted with blood. I hadn't realized how long it was, since she had always had it tucked into a tidy bun every time I'd seen her. There was something nobody had mentioned yet, however. I moved closer to the body, trying not to step in blood.

"She's dressed," Hattie commented.

"And her chest has been blown open, maybe by a gun?" Salazar added. He glanced behind him at the coroner. "Nobody mentioned that."

"Didn't want to touch anything till you got here," the coroner said. "And we didn't find a gun."

I felt like I was caught in a cop movie again, listening to the two of them. I turned a manic giggle into a cough.

"You gonna vomit, don't do it on my crime scene," Hattie said, glaring at me. I think she knew I wasn't about to vomit.

I forced away the crazy thoughts, the unreality of the last twenty-four hours, and made myself look at Peggy. Grey edges of rib bone were visible through her mangled blue sweater. Unidentifiable lumps of lung and whatever else we carry around in our chest cavities gleamed wetly in the morning light spilling through the sheer curtains. I didn't need to touch her to know what had happened.

"Her chest wasn't blown open. There was no gun. I think you'll find someone removed her heart." It almost physically hurt to say the words aloud, but life was going from worse to worser and down the handbasket express to worstest.

"Fuck," Hattie said very softly as she reached up and rubbed her own chest in an almost unconscious gesture. Her expression told me she knew exactly what a missing heart meant.

The coroner took the four steps to get to me and bent over the body. He probed the open chest wound and I turned my head. I didn't need to watch that. It was like someone mixing gravel and Jell-O.

"She's right, heart is missing. I'll be damned."

You and me both, dude, I thought, but kept it to myself. I looked at Hattie and flicked my eyes to the others in what I hoped was an obvious way. I couldn't tell her much with everyone standing around. I didn't know who was a normal or not. I had a sneaking suspicion that Salazar wasn't, but he'd done nothing overtly that said Supernatural-R-Us.

"Dan, why don't you go get some fresh air? Take the deputy with you. Too many bodies in here. I'll call you back in when we're ready for the processing, all right?" Hattie said.

Dan, the coroner, raised a salt-and-pepper eyebrow but shrugged and left. We waited until the front door had closed behind them before Hattie nodded to me.

"Start talking," she said.

"What about—" I asked, jerking my head at Salazar. I moved away from Peggy's body as I did, putting my back to the wall with the least amount of blood on it and facing so that I wouldn't have to see her lying there if I was careful about it.

"I'm an eagle," he said, obviously expecting that to make sense to me.

Which, sad to say, it totally did. Shifter it was. Right.

"You?" I asked Hattie. "Witch?"

She snorted. "That's me, though my fellow officers like to use a *B* instead of the *W* most of the time. And you?"

I was surprised no one had told her. It was pretty much an open secret what I was these days, ever since I'd gone toe-to-toe with a corrupt shifter Justice a couple months back.

"So, you don't talk to the Wylde coven much?" I asked, dodging the question for just a moment longer. I didn't know how they were going to react to what I had to tell them. I wasn't sure how much I even should. I needed more information before I spilled my guts.

I really had to stop thinking about spilling guts. Stat. I swallowed bile and focused on my gloved hands for a moment.

"No," Hattie said after exchanging a glance with Salazar. "I'm a solo practitioner. Never much cared for politics. I have to play them enough in my job as it is."

I took another deep breath and regretted it as mint and blood and urine soaked my senses. Samir had killed Peggy for a reason, all right. He was harvesting hearts. He would have taken her power, minimal though it was, and all her knowledge. He'd know everything she knew, have access to all her memories, if my experience with heart-nomming was any guide to go on. I had to talk to her coven, to warn them. I'd only seen them all together once, when I'd gone and laid down the new threefold law about fucking with me and my friends. I'd recognized a few faces then, but names were eluding me. Shit.

"Jade?" Hattie prompted. "What's going on here?"

"And don't feed us a line. This is serious. There's going to be human heat on these killings, and we need to stop them before it gets too big to manage." Salazar moved a couple of steps toward me, his eyes intent on my face.

I made myself look back at Peggy. Samir had done this. He would keep doing this or maybe worse. I had to stop him, and I clearly wasn't going to be able to do it alone. Keeping the truth from Hattie and Salazar would just get them hurt if they went after Samir without knowing. I could almost hear Alek's voice in my head telling me that the truth was a good thing, and suddenly I missed him like hell. He'd know what to do; he'd have stood here with me, solid and warm and smart.

And he'd have told me to trust, to take the leap and give these people whatever information I had. To save lives if I could.

I pushed back my longing for Alek and nodded slowly. "Let me explain," I said with a slight smile. "No, there is too much. Let me sum up."

Not *Princess Bride* fans, these two, because neither gave any sign they recognized the line. So much for trying to smooth things. I sighed.

"Samir, the man who did this? He's a sorcerer. And so am I."

CHAPTER SEVEN

We moved to the kitchen and sat in Peggy's chairs. There was a cold cup of tea with the bag still in it on the kitchen table. I tried not to think about her last moments and instead let the words spill out of me as I gave Hattie and Salazar a rough sketch of what I thought was going on and who the players were.

My story summed up was pretty thin and sad, even to my own ears. There was so much I had to leave out, partially because a lot of it would implicate me in a metric butt-load of crimes, and partially because that stuff might be a distraction. The important thing was that they understood how dangerous Samir was, and that he wasn't going to stop.

"Summers!" I said, breaking off what I had been saying about Samir in mid-sentence as I remembered the name of one of the women in Peggy's coven. "Joyce Summers. She runs a no-kill shelter, Pet Haven. I saw her at the coven meeting. She'll know who the rest are. Do you have Peggy's phone? They'll all be in there, I bet."

"One moment," Hattie said. Both she and Salazar were sitting on the edge of their chairs, not writing anything down, just staring at me with grim faces. "The heart-eating thing, it's real? It really works that way?"

"Yes," I said. "All the horror stories you might have heard about sorcerers? They are probably all about Samir. If he's decided to gain power and knowledge by eating the witches, he's going to keep going until we're down thirteen women." I didn't know why he was doing it. They hadn't been that powerful, but maybe it was more than what their magic could add. Memories and experiences, I knew firsthand, were powerful things in their own right.

"How many hearts have you eaten?" Salazar asked, his tone deceptively light compared to the intense look in his eyes. His gaze was very eagle-like, now that I thought about it, and I felt like a mouse under it.

I was no mouse. "How long have you been beating your wife?" I shot back, folding my arms over my chest.

One corner of his mouth lifted and he inclined his head. "Fair enough," he said in a way that told me this wasn't a conversation either of us wanted to have. "It was a poorly phrased question."

"Look," I said, relenting a little. "Hypothetically and off record and all that, if I did kill anyone ever in my life? It would only be because they were trying to kill me first." Which was mostly true. Ignoring the times it hadn't been true. But partial truth was still like being honest, right? Baby steps.

"I have to call my boss," Salazar said. "If it is as you say, this is going to get much worse."   -

He rose and walked up the stairs, leaving Hattie and I sitting, staring at each other.

"I never thought your kind were quite real. Even living in Wylde all my life. I guess this place attracts all things eventually." She shook her head.

"Thank you for not freaking out and hating me just for being what I am," I said. Which wasn't exactly what I meant, but she seemed to understand.

"You haven't given me cause. I've been on this job too long to judge things by their reputation anymore. And the worst I've seen? It was done by humans to humans. The normals do more damage to themselves than the supernatural ever could."

Supernaturals could be pretty damn bad, but I didn't say that aloud. I thought about Bernard Barnes and the rotting wolves he'd been magically freezing and using as batteries, and shivered, rubbing my hands along my arms. The latex gloves stuck to my sleeves weirdly and reminded me I was at a crime scene. Sitting in a house with a dead woman who used to hate me.

"So, the wire, you said it was magic?" Hattie said after a couple of silent minutes.

"It was when he used it on . . . my friend." I had trouble getting Steve's name out. It felt too real to say it aloud, like invoking his death. "I tried to get in the way, and it went right through me. I think it has to be driven by his power and only works on the target. Made my throat raw as hell, though—I could barely talk for hours."

"Tried to get in the way? So, he threw it, not used it like a garrote?"

"Yeah, it just flew through the air." I touched my neck. "Right through me."

"He could have killed you then?" Hattie had her inscrutable cop face back on.

"I think so," I said. I hadn't mentioned Wolf. No point even trying to explain that part. It didn't matter. I'd been so weak, so distraught. I'd almost wanted to die just so it would end. Not a thought I wanted to dwell on in that moment. Or ever.

"He said he wasn't 'bored enough yet,'" I added. I caught her gaze with mine and leaned forward. "He's evil, detective. Pure selfish evil."

Salazar came down the stairs with an annoyed look on his face. He waved off our questioning glances and pressed his lips together. "Let's get the coroner in to handle the scene. Crime scene folk have arrived, too. Is there any magic around we should be aware of?"

I pulled on my magic, letting my senses stretch out. The broken wards were fainter now. I sensed none of Samir's sickly sweet magic.

"I think it's safe," I said.

Hattie let the deputy and coroner back in. She started questioning the deputy about the scene while Salazar looked around for Peggy's phone. I hung out in the kitchen, feeling useless and tired. I decided to call Harper and went to get my phone from my jacket where it was hung in the hall. I would see if Alek was back yet, and make sure everyone was okay, but as I pulled out my phone, Hattie reappeared with the deputy in tow.

"What was the name of that friend of the victim's?" she asked.

"Joyce Summers; why?" I slid my phone into my jeans pocket. *Please don't say she's dead, please don't say she's dead, please don't say it.*

"Yeah, that's the one," the deputy said, running a hand through his thinning hair.

"She's the next-door neighbor. She's over there right now waiting to give an official statement," Hattie said. "Joyce Summers is the one who found the body."

Joyce Summers wasn't someone I'd said more than four or five words to in all the years I'd been in Wylde, but I'd known who she was because of my dealings with Vivian Lake, the local vet, and because Harper had a serious soft spot for stray animals. Joyce was in her fifties, with brown hair that was too evenly colored to have gotten that brown by natural means, and skin so pale the veins in her cheeks showed through like rivers on a map. Her eyes were puffy as she greeted us with the perfunctory stiffness of someone going into mild shock and showed us where to hang our coats.

From the smell alone, it was easy to tell that Joyce loved and owned a lot of pets, but while it was noticeable, it wasn't that overwhelming. It smelled like a house where animals ruled with decorum, musk and coffee underlying the hint of air freshener and mint. Her house was cluttered with comfortable furniture and cat trees, her carpet littered with cat toys. There were at least four of the critters in view, and I gently stroked a big calico cat who was resting on the back of an overstuffed chair.

Joyce did an almost-comical double take as Hattie sent the deputy out and the four of us sat down.

"What is she doing here?" she demanded, rousing from her grief-stricken torpor. She pointed a trembling finger at me.

"Saving your ass, I hope," I said.

"Ladies," Hattie said. "Jade is helping us with the investigation. Can you walk us through what happened? Do you know who killed your friend?"

Joyce dropped her hand into her lap and sniffed hard. She started to speak but stopped and looked at Salazar, then at Hattie with a question on her face.

"I'm Special Agent Salazar," Salazar said in a patient voice. "I'm an eagle shifter and I know what you are already, so you can speak freely."

"We always check on each other after a storm, because we live alone, you see. My husband and I separated recently. He moved out just last month and I'm not used to being on my own. Peggy and I, well, you know. She is our leader." Joyce stopped and sniffed again. She pulled a wadded-up handkerchief out of a drawer in the sewing table next to her and dabbed at her nose.

"I tried to call, but she didn't pick up. I saw lights on and thought maybe she had her phone off. When she didn't answer the door, I just went in. We don't lock our doors much around here, as the detective can tell you, Agent," Joyce said.

"And that's when you found her?" Salazar prompted.

Joyce nodded and tears started to leak from her eyes. She dabbed at those, too.

"She was . . . I mean. Blood. Everywhere. I . . . I'm sorry. Do I have to talk about this? What is the point? I know who did it." Her expression hardened and she looked at me.

"Wait a minute," I said, holding up my hands in mock surrender. "Don't you even try to pin this on me. I have an airtight alibi." I refrained from saying I'd been locked up in jail all night. Joyce didn't need to know that part.

"Not you," she said. "Though you're the cause, all right. It was that golden-eyed demon, Mr. Cartwright. He did this, sure as the sun rises in the east."

I sat back in the chair, disturbing the cat behind me. She got up and jumped down, giving me a look fit to kill. I rubbed my palms on my thighs.

"You know Samir?" I asked. "Do you know why he did this?"

Joyce pressed her lips together into a thin line. She looked at Hattie, then shifted her gaze to Salazar. When they both were silent, expectant in their expressions and posture, she looked back at me and nodded. I wanted to yank her out of her chair and drag the answers out of her, but I forced myself to be calm. She'd been through a hell of a shock; I could take a moment to be patient.

"You have to understand. We didn't know what was going on. It was just a way to make a little extra money, which the shelter needed. The library too, and Alice's son needed braces, and . . . well. Extra money isn't something folks like us can turn down." She clutched at her dirty handkerchief like it was a security blanket.

"Money?" I said. "From Samir? For what?"

"For you," she said softly. "He was paying us to keep an eye on you."

"When? How long?" I spat the questions out, my brain spinning.

"Oh, gosh. Three years now, at least." Joyce looked down at her hands.

I closed my eyes and wrapped my willpower around my temper. I took a deep breath and tried to think calm thoughts. So, Samir had been telling the truth, it seemed. He had known where I was. What I was doing. I might have noticed one or two people watching me. Even in a small town, seeing someone over and over when you aren't friends would start to stand out. But a whole coven? That was thirteen different women, all probably pillars of the community, thirteen spies to rotate around. I thought of how many had kids or relatives they bought games for. How many times I'd run into people at the grocery store or Brie's or one of the pubs.

"You didn't think that was odd?" Hattie asked. "A man paying you to spy on a woman?"

"Oh, we did, a bit. He said he was her father, and up until last year, none of us had ever met him. But we all thought Jade was a witch, a solo practitioner like yourself, Hattie. He was just asking for updates on what she did, who she talked to. We figured we were going to keep tabs on her anyway; why not take the money? Peggy promised we would warn Jade if anything happened. Until, well, until we realized what you were."

"Then Peggy tried to run me out of town," I said. "They know; I gave them the basic details."

"She knew you'd bring trouble down on us. We can't be involved with sorcerers. Nothing good ever comes of that. And now she's dead. He killed her, didn't he? Took her heart. Oh, my poor Peggy." Joyce started crying again, sniffling and snorting into her kerchief. A tuxedo cat unwound itself from its perch in a cat tree by the front window and went over to her, pressing himself against her legs.

"We stopped reporting to him," she said after choking back a few more sobs. She scratched the cat's ears. "Is that why he did this? I told her it was a bad idea. I told her."

"You have to get the coven out of town," I said to Joyce, glancing at Hattie and Salazar. The agent and the detective were being very quiet for people interviewing a witness. "He's not going to stop. Samir wants your powers, but I think he really wants your memories, your knowledge."

"Stop saying his name," she whispered, looking around as though he might pop out of the shadows.

"He's not Voldemort," I said more sharply than I meant. "He's a man, an evil, awful person, but still just a man. His name isn't going to summon him. Hell, who fucking knows if it is even his real name?"

"You should never have come here," Joyce said.

"It's about five years too late for that, lady. Have you contacted the rest of the coven? I'm serious. Wylde isn't going to be a safe place for witches for a while." I glanced at Hattie again as I said it. Peggy had known about her; that much was obvious, since Joyce knew who she was. And what Peggy had known, Samir now knew. My brain balked at the possibilities.

"I already activated the phone tree, right after I called nine-one-one and asked for Hattie here." Joyce pulled the cat into her lap.

"How much does Samir know?" I asked her. "What did you tell him about me and my friends?"

"Everything," she said in a whisper, not meeting my gaze. "He knows about the Macnulty girl, her family. Those handsome twins. Your store. We told him whatever details he asked. It was all very mundane, harmless knowledge, really."

I stood up and yanked my phone out of my pocket. This was worse than I'd thought. He had Peggy's memories, but he also had years of reports on me and my new life. Years to get to know where I went, what I did, whom I saw.

Where I went.

Harper. The Henhouse. *Shit.*

As if by fucking magic, my phone rang, playing Harper's song.

I flicked it to answer and put it to my ear as dread turned my stomach into self-animating ropes.

"Jade? They're being attacked. Mom said there were men. At the house. Levi's driving us there. Please, Jade. Come." Harper's voice cracked into a shriek.

"On my way," I said. I jammed my phone into my pocket and crossed the living room. "I need a ride," I said to Salazar and Hattie as they followed me.

"What is it?" Salazar asked as I threw open the front door.

"Samir is attacking my friends. I have to get to the Henhouse B&B; do you know it?" I directed the last part at Hattie as I strode toward the SUV parked outside the crime scene next door.

"I do," she said, huffing as she tromped over the un-shoveled snow, her shorter legs sinking her deeper. "But the roads aren't good, and besides, I can't just leave the crime scene."

I stopped, shivering in the cold air. My coat was still hanging inside Joyce's house.

"You saying you won't get me there? You won't help me? Don't you want to catch the killer?"

"Jade," Salazar said in a hushed voice, glancing around. No one was still lingering in the cold now that the body had been removed. We stood alone in a tomb-quiet sea of white. "We can't. We're no match for a sorcerer. I've been ordered to spin the story for the humans and then back down."

So. He was saying it wasn't their fight.

Well, fuck them. They were right. It wasn't their fight.

It was mine.

And I didn't need a damn car. I gathered my magic, power filling my blood, racing along with all the strength of my fear and anger.

I was a motherfucking sorceress and I was going to fly.

CHAPTER EIGHT ▶

I'd never managed to fly before. I could leap and glide, sort of an extended long jump where I just refused to touch the ground for as long as I could suspend my disbelief and trust my magic to hold me aloft. But flying had been out of my grasp.

No more. I shot into the air a good fifty or sixty feet, Superman-style, one fist thrust ridiculously in front of me, the other clinging with total terror to my d20 talisman. Tears streamed from my eyes and froze to my cheeks until I shoved magic out in front of me, pushing a shield out to block the worst of the wind and the cold.

The landscape was black-and-white from up here, houses zipping away beneath me as I hurtled through the air in the general direction of the Henhouse B&B. With the snow covering roads and landmarks, I could only go by the sun and my own sense of direction. The Henhouse had a bright red roof on it, with enough of a slope that I figured some red would show through even with the heavy snowfall.

Horror pictures flickered through my brain. Rose and Junebug strapped to a giant bomb. Samir torturing them. My friends arriving before I did and being cut down by screaming men with giant machine guns. Images of me arriving and finding only silence and everyone dead, bodies laid out, throats open, eyes staring blank and cold at the sun.

I shoved those thoughts away, stuffed them into my power, gathered my anger and my fear, and fed it all into the magic. No one was going to die. Only Samir.

A giant plume of black smoke drew my gaze as I soared over the trees. I corrected my course, heart in my throat. The Henhouse was on fire.

I tried to drop down near the clearing where the buildings were burning, but landing proved harder than it looks in the movies. I didn't so much glide down out of the sky as plummet like a meteor into the snow.

Fresh powder snow? Not as soft as it looks. Shivering, the wind half knocked out of me, I climbed to my feet and ran toward the burning house. The roof had caved in and taken most of the second floor with it. Acrid smoke, tasting of ash and the sickly sweetness of Samir's magic, filled my nose and mouth. I plunged through the door, yelling for Rose. Paper curled with heat and caught on the walls, the curtains burned, and a huge burning beam dropped as I charged into the entry, cutting off the stairs and living room. I sent my magic out like a wave, trying to feel for life, for anything. Only fire.

"Jade!" Harper's voice reached me through the roar of the blaze, and I stumbled free of the house as something else crashed behind me. More beams. The whole place was burning to the ground with a vengeance.

Harper, Ezee, and Levi had just arrived, Levi's four-wheel-drive still steaming in the parking area, his tire chains packed with snow. I stumbled toward them, going for Harper as she tried to rush past me.

"They weren't in the house," I said, remembering. "No one is there."

I hoped I wasn't lying. The house had felt like no one was alive—no one, not even a shifter, could live through that kind of blaze. If Rose or Junebug were in there, they'd have escaped or already be dead.

"The barn," Harper said. Her expression went from relief back to panic, and she turned and bolted for the barn.

The barn wasn't on fire, but it had taken a lot of bullets. The wood was chewed up with hundreds of holes, chunks and splinters sticking out from the doors like spines.

The horses were dead. Something had ripped one of them apart; the other two had died from gunfire. Though my ears rang after the mad flight and the roar of the house fire, the barn felt eerily silent and still.

"Oh, God," Harper whispered, looking into each stall, her movements growing more panicked as she went. "Oh, God." She slammed shut a stall door and kicked over a bucket, a litany of curses pouring from her mouth as she searched.

My legs felt like lead but I climbed up the ladder into the loft. Sleeping bags were still lying on mounded-up hay. A turned-over milk crate had a thermos and a stack of playing cards on it. A broken mug lay on the floor nearby. No sign of Harper's mom or Levi's wife. The upper door was open, a rifle on the floor by it. Hay was everywhere.

Something glinted in the hay by the door, too big to be spent casings and too small to be a gun or knife. A cell phone.

"Is that Mom's?" Harper said. Her voice was soft, flat, as though she'd shouted herself out.

I held up the phone. "Yeah," I said. "They aren't here. There aren't any bodies. No blood. Maybe they escaped?"

"In this snow? Junebug could fly off, but Mom couldn't get away without leaving a trail. Come on." She didn't wait for me as she turned and climbed down the ladder.

"Blood," Levi said as we met up with the twins on the side of the barn. "Junebug's."

"How can you tell?" I asked.

"I know my wife," he said grimly.

"No fox tracks?" Harper said, looking around.

The ground there was a mess from boots tramping it down. I was no tracker, but I could recognize boot tread and that many feet had been there. Samir had brought in help. It figured. He'd used people to abduct my family, too. The bastard seemed to hate getting his hands dirty unless he had to.

More information about him, but useless unless I could find a way to turn it to my advantage. I sighed and followed Ezee and Levi through the snow. My skin was turning from brown to blue in the cold and I pumped more magic through myself to keep from shivering.

"Where is your coat?" Ezee asked.

"I left it in town."

The blood droplets ended in the trees, as did the boot tracks. Someone, or maybe two someones, had come in here and tried to follow Junebug but given up quickly.

"Just drops," Ezee said to Levi, rubbing his twin's shoulder reassuringly. "Takes more than a flesh wound to hurt your girl. She's okay."

"Unless they got her," Levi muttered, shaking Ezee's hand off.

"We need to go back, look for where the tracks go."

Something rustled above us and I readied magic, pooling purple fire in my hand.

Junebug, in owl form, dropped gracefully out of the trees and shifted as she hit the snow, effecting a far better landing than I had. She practically jumped into Levi's arms, tears on her cheeks.

"No point tracking them. They came in snowmobiles," she said, then looked at Harper. "Rosie's gone."

"The house is burning. No one is in the barn," Harper said. "What happened?"

"She made me fly away. I got hit—just a graze," she added quickly as Levi growled. "I didn't want to leave her, but nobody argues with Rose." Junebug turned imploring eyes on Harper. "She said she'd be right behind. But they had her pinned. I tried to fly back, but two of the men came after me. They took her. There were too many, Harper. I'm sorry."

"No," Harper said, her voice still deadly quiet, as cold as the snow surrounding us. "Not your fault. Was she still alive?"

"Yes," Junebug said. "I heard her swearing at them."

"He'll keep her alive," I said with as much confidence as I could muster. "He'll use her as bait for the rest of us. This is what he did to me before. Taking people I love and hurting them to hurt me."

"So, we go get her. And kill him." Harper turned and strode back through the trees.

My cell phone rang. I fumbled it from my jean's pocket. Unknown number. But I knew who it was.

"You fucking bastard," I said as I answered. "Is she alive?"

"Jade, of course she's alive." Samir's slimy, smooth voice was jarring in my ears. I wanted to reach through the phone and rip his heart out from there.

If only I could figure out that spell. Fucker.

"What do you want?" I said, playing the game.

Harper had stopped and turned. Everyone gathered closer, their shifter senses allowing them to hear the phone call just as well as if I'd put him on speaker.

"I want Clyde's heart. It's mine. So nice of you to keep it for me, but I think one life is worth another, no?"

"I give you the heart, you give back Rose? Unharmed?" I ground the words out, looking at Harper.

"Well, she's not entirely unharmed. Put up quite the fight for an old fox. But she's alive. For now. Bring me the heart, and she can stay that way," Samir said.

I didn't need Alek's power of truth detection to know he was a lying son of a bitch. Harper growled, her lips curling back in a snarl that looked at odds with her human face.

"I don't have the heart," I said. "I don't even know where it is."

"But you know who does," Samir said. It was not a question.

"I do," I said, thinking of Alek. I had no idea where Alek was, however. "It will take some time." I needed to buy us time. Buy Rose time. We had to have a plan, and maybe I could get ahead of Samir, use this to lure him into a trap of my own. Something, anything. I hadn't saved Rose from that evil warlock Barnes just to let her die like this.

"Call this number in two hours. I don't hear from you, it's only her dead body you'll find." Samir hung up.

I shivered, nearly dropping the phone. Harper wrapped an arm around me, and we leaned into each other for a long moment. She was warm and solid and I wanted to hug her forever. To keep her safe, to wipe the anger and sadness from her unhappy face.

"He's not going to release her, is he?" Harper said, pulling away so she could look me in the eye.

I swallowed the giant lump in my throat. "No," I said softly. "He'll find a way to screw up the trade, turn it into a trap."

"It's freezing out here," Ezee said. "The barn still stands. Come on. We can talk and form a plan. We will figure this out."

Glad for someone else taking charge, I followed them back to the barn. Junebug started crying again as she saw the horses. Then she punched a wall so hard, the entire barn shuddered and groaned. Levi wrapped an arm around her and spoke in soft tones until she looked like she wasn't about to murder someone, guiding her up the ladder to the loft.

I dragged a sleeping bag around me, glad for the warmth.

"Should we call the fire department? Can they even get out here?" Levi asked.

"No," Harper said. "Let it burn itself out. We can't save the house. The snow will keep it contained."

"At least Max isn't here," I said, trying to find a silver lining.

"Max," Harper said. She reached into her coat and started to pull out her phone but stopped. "No. He's safe where he is. If I tell him anything, the idiot might try to come back and help."

"So, what do we do now?" Ezee asked.

"Is Steve really dead?" Levi asked at the same time.

"And they thought you did it?" Harper added.

Everyone looked at me. I drew the sleeping bag closer, as though it could shield me from their questioning gazes, from their expectation that somehow I could fix all this.

I had to find a way. This was all my fault.

"Yes," I said. "Samir killed Steve. He also killed Peggy Olsen."

That brought on more questions. I gave them the very rough sketch of what had happened and what I knew.

"Witches were spying on you the whole time and they didn't think that was really fucking creepy?" Harper's voice was almost back to normal, a slow-burning anger warming it again.

"Guess not," I muttered. "We have to come up with a new plan, though. Only Alek knows where the heart is. And Samir won't let Rosie go alive anyway. We can't make the trade."

"Yeah, it sounded like *Trap Here* all over it, just from the tone in his evil fucking voice," Harper said. Relief flooded through me. I had been worried she wouldn't understand why we couldn't just obey the ransom demand.

Alek didn't answer his phone. Straight to voicemail. Ezee started to look worried as I jammed my phone back into my pocket.

"Yosemite isn't around, is he?" I asked him.

Ezee shook his head. "He doesn't exactly carry a phone, but he said he had something to do this week. Related to Brie and Ciaran being out of town, I guess."

"What now?" Levi said. He chewed on his lower lip as he looked over at his twin. "It looks like it is just us."

"Junebug, how many were here? Did you see Samir? He's got dark hair, gold eyes, and is tall, but not as tall as Alek or Yosemite." I turned to Junebug.

"Nobody is as tall as Yosemite," Harper said with a snort. There was color in her cheeks, and I hoped that meant she was coming out of shock.

"No," Junebug said. "Nobody like that. There were men, maybe fifteen? Some were shifters. I smelled wolf and bear. The men who came into the woods looking for me were wolves for sure." She ran a hand through her tangled hair and winced.

Why hadn't Samir even been with them? He'd been confident they could handle the shifters? Had he known that only two were here? It bothered me, but I couldn't work out why it should. He was playing a game, and I didn't have the rulebook. I had two hours to figure out what to do, and time was slipping away as we sat there. Looking around the loft again, my gaze rested on the broken mug. It was earthenware, glazed blue with a green handle.

"Harper," I said as an idea took nebulous shape in my brain. "Did Rose make that mug?"

"What? Oh, yeah, that's one of her oldest ones. Why?" Harper looked at the mug and then back at me.

I left the warmth of the sleeping bag and picked up the biggest intact chunk. Closing my eyes, I focused and pushed my magic into the cup. Harper's mother had thrown the clay, worked it with her hands, given this object form and purpose. Part of her would be infused it in, bonded forever to it through intention and the power of creation. Every cup of coffee she'd drunk from it, every moment it had lived on her shelf and been a part of her day-to-day life would have reinforced the bond.

A bond I could track.

The spell snapped into place and I felt a strong pull to the west. Rose. Alive.

"I can track her," I said. I met four grim faces. "I don't know what we'll find, but she's alive and this mug can take us to her. Maybe we can rescue her."

"You've got my axe," Ezee said.

"And my sword," Levi added.

"That would be a lot more comforting if either of you had weapons or knew how to use them," I said, my heart lifting at their unquestioning decision that they were in this with me. I didn't want to get them hurt or killed, but I couldn't face down fifteen shifters on my own, rescue the lady, and fight Samir. I needed help. I'd made the decision to stay in Wylde and stop running.

Now it was time to fight.

"We have teeth and claws," Levi said.

"And a rifle," Junebug added. "With the Idaho State Fair sharpshooting champion to fire it." Her expression was stubborn and stopped any objection Levi might have made. "If I shift, I'll still be injured, so I'm more use in this form. My human isn't bleeding." Her eyes dared Levi to object. He was smarter than that and just nodded and kissed her fiercely on the lips.

"And my magic," I said, feeling the pull of Rose's location. "Once we know where they are keeping Rose, we can form a better plan than *Think positive and get lucky*, all right? So, let's drive out of here before someone shows up and tries to arrest me for arson."

With the kind of week I was having, it was totally possible that could happen.

"Think we can win?" Ezee said to me softly as we left the barn and tromped through the dirty, churned-up snow toward Levi's car.

"We're gamers," Harper answered before I could. "We always win."

I prayed to the universe that she was right and clung to the locating spell with every ounce of hope I had left.

CHAPTER NINE

The spell led us away from town. Levi found ways to keep us heading more or less straight at it, but we had to drive over roads still clogged with snow, lumbering our way toward an unknown destination.

Nobody talked much. We were alone in our thoughts. I sat up front, focusing on the spell, trying to pinpoint where they might be holding Rose.

"I know where we are going," Ezee said suddenly.

"Old church?" Levi asked.

"I think so. What else is out here? Turn around; go back to Red Rock."

"Old church?" I looked at Levi's profile as he jammed on the brakes and executed a three-point turn in the middle of the road.

"There's an old church, sometimes used as a grange, rented to groups, that kind of thing, just out Red Rock Road. You keep pointing in its direction, more or less. Don't know why I didn't see that."

"'Cause I'm prettier and smarter," Ezee said with forced joviality.

"Don't get too close," I said. "They'll probably watch the road."

When we pulled up after following the new road for a mile or so, I couldn't see a church, just a lot of trees lining the roadway. The spell tugged hard, and the road there had been used recently, tire and snow-tread tracks all over it. Levi turned the car around, facing it outward. He looked back at Junebug.

"You are staying here," he said in a tone that brooked no argument. "You keep that rifle ready, because if we come out of there in a hurry, I want you ready to get us out of here."

She made a face but nodded. "I'll set up in the back and cover your asses," she said.

I shivered in the chill air as we climbed out, the weak winter sun doing nothing to warm up the day. At least Rachel had brought me my hiking boots and wool socks, so my feet weren't as miserable as the rest of me. Jeans and a long-sleeve shirt with no coat was shitty winter wear.

Pushing aside my discomfort, I let the anticipation of getting to do something, anything, to strike back at Samir warm me.

"Here," Harper said. "Take my coat. It's not great for this but better than just your shirt." She slipped out of her quilted leather jacket and handed it over.

"But won't you be cold?" I asked, taking it anyway.

"I have fur," she said. "That spell say Mom is in there?"

I refocused on the chunk of mug in my hands. "Yes, definitely close," I said.

Levi, Ezee, and Harper all shifted to their animal forms as we headed into the woods. It was easier going beneath the trees. The thick canopy had stopped a lot of the snow, and as long as I avoided the tree wells, I never sank more than ankle-deep. We reached the edge of the trees without hearing or seeing anyone.

The church had probably been built sometime around the turn of the nineteenth century and not updated much since. It was a squat, grey rectangular building with narrow windows and heavy wooden doors. I saw no movement around the building. Coyote-Ezee, his brown body low to the snowy ground, crept along the edge of the parking lot while the rest of us waited hidden in the tree line. No one fired at him. Snowmobiles, four of them, were pulled up under a carport that was definitely a late add-on to the church. Those were the only vehicles, which bothered me. Coyote-Ezee made his way to them, running low and fast over the ground. He crouched for what felt like eternity next to the door, so still I could barely make him out.

Finally, he slipped away from the church, made a quick circuit of the clearing, and came back around to us. We pulled back quietly into the trees and everyone shifted back to human. I let go of the locating spell and tucked the ceramic fragment into Harper's coat.

"Anything?" Levi asked.

"At least three inside; I could hear them talking. I don't think they are expecting anything. There's definitely a bear in there." Ezee took a deep breath and looked at me.

"Have you guys been inside this place?" I asked.

"Yeah." Levi answered. "It's pretty much a big room up top with a side office space. Then it has a basement, which is where the kitchen is, with a couple bathrooms in back."

"Windows or doors downstairs?" Harper asked.

"Some narrow windows near the ground, but they'll be pretty well snowed under if they aren't boarded up for the winter. There's a storm door in back, leads down to the hall by the bathrooms, if I remember right. No windows in the bathrooms."

I nodded. "Rose isn't going to stay in there easily. I bet they've got her downstairs."

"Makes sense. Locked in a bathroom. That's where I would put someone. Only one door, no windows, mostly underground. She won't be able to get out easily." Harper nodded along with me.

"Is your evil ex-boyfriend here?" Ezee asked.

"I don't know," I said. "This feels weird to me, like we're missing something. Only four snowmobiles? Where are the rest of the people who attacked the Henhouse?"

"It's a trap?" Levi said.

"What time is it?" I asked, even as I pulled out my phone and checked. We had less than an hour until Samir's deadline. "He's had an hour since we talked, bit more, to go elsewhere or send people to try to find me? I don't know."

"Your spell said Mom is here. I'm going in, trap or not." Harper folded her arms over her sweater, glaring at me.

"We're not warriors," I said. "You are shifters, sure, but we aren't exactly equipped for battle. These guys could be mercenaries or something."

"What did we do when that warlock guy tried to kill Mom and Ezee?"

"Fought him," I said. "Well, I saved your asses, anyway." I tried to grin, but my face didn't want to obey.

"And the undead guy who tried to wipe out your people? What happened to him?"

"He's dead," I said, "But I didn't kill him. I just freed the spirit that did it."

"And when the ninja assassin came to take you out?"

"I killed him," I said, my voice softer now.

"And that corrupt Justice who tried to blow up all the wolves?" Harper raised her chin and stared me down. "Or those two sorcerers who showed up to take us all out and summon a super-evil Irish badass with slavering hell-beasties?"

"Okay," I said, seeing her point. "You're right. We should be glad that there are fewer people here, I guess, and that they are just shifters, eh? We'll worry about Samir later. Let's go get Rosie."

The plan we worked out, crouched there in the snow, was stupidly simple. I'd walk toward the front doors and do a lot of showy magic, keep myself shielded against bullets, and create a nice distraction. Levi, Ezee, and Harper would go around and break in the storm doors, searching the lower level for Rose first and then coming up the front to meet me or running away out the back if they found her.

I'd destroy the snowmobiles, or maybe steal one, and meet them back at the car. Or fly away, which was my backup plan, now that I knew I could fly. Of course, if I flew, I'd have to land again, and I wasn't in a super hurry to repeat that experience.

Unless Samir was there. I had no idea how I was going to fight him, but at least out there, I could unleash some real magic and not have to worry about taking the town out with me. If he was there, well, things were going to get very dangerous. For him.

One problem at a time, I told myself. First, I had to go get the attention of people with guns.

I'd marched up on dudes with guns before, so I had a weird feeling of déjà vu. This time, however, I wasn't going to waltz in under a fake flag of truce. This time, I was going in, magic blazing. If I could figure out how.

Pulling my power into a shield was second nature now, so I was pretty sure I could stop bullets from making me into a colander. If I'd had time to stop and think about it, I would have been impressed with how much magic I was able to toss around these days. The training was paying off.

Those kinds of thoughts just led to thinking about my failure to save Steve, so I shoved them away as soon as they surfaced and concentrated on my path toward the main door. There was about twenty yards of open ground to cover.

Unless I didn't go through the door. Rule number one of adventuring? Always look up. The counterpart of that is mistake number one of horror movie survival, which is never looking up.

The roof of the church was sloped but not super steep. There was a bell tower that was boarded up with a metal spike on it that might have been a weathervane sometime in the previous century. Thick snow coated the roof in drifts, and parts had sloughed off with their own weight, but there was enough in piles that I thought I could effect a landing without breaking my legs.

Time to fly again.

"Okay, when I land on the roof, make a break for the back door," I said to my friends.

"Land on the roof? What?" Harper looked at me like I was crazy.

I probably was. I felt a little crazy. Glad to be out of jail and doing something, anything, to strike back at Samir. To act instead of react.

I grinned at her. "Just watch, grasshopper."

I threw myself into the air before I thought about how stupid my plan was, crashing upward through the trees. Branches slapped my face, evergreen needles catching and tangling in my braid. Snow went right down the back of my jacket, bringing out a yelp of surprise that I quickly swallowed. I hurtled a good hundred feet up and pulled downward with my magic to stop myself. I hung in the air, feeling pretty pleased. Jade Crow one, gravity zero.

A coyote, a wolverine, and a fox, all about twice the size of the wild version or more, glided through the forest and got into position below me. From up there, I could see the SUV, though not Junebug.

Shouting rang out from inside and the front door of the church opened. A man in a grey-and-white camouflage coat emerged, looking toward the trees I'd just sailed out of. He was a shitty adventurer but a great horror movie victim. He scanned the treeline but missed the floating woman in the sky. If I'd been closer and more sure of the angle, I would have Magic Missiled his ass.

He went back inside, and I flew toward the church, angling my descent to hit the biggest lump of snow on the roof. This landing went much better, as I used my magic like a jetpack, pulling myself toward the target spot, then pushing away as I came close, so that my descent slowed. Thinking about it like thrusters in a science fiction movie helped a ton. I'd never been a huge fan of Mandalorians from *Star Wars*, but the jetpack thing was suddenly a whole lot more cool-seeming.

If only I'd had badass body armor, too. And a lightsaber.

Instead, I had magic. I hit the roof and let out a whoop as I thumped down. I wrapped my power around me in a shield in case the idiots started shooting through the roof, and kept making lots of noise.

Voices and then bodies appeared. Two men charged out, guns in their hands, pointing and yelling at me. They took shots but I glided forward, using my magic to keep me just over the snow and to hold my balance on the ridge of the church. Their shots went wild, one glancing off my shield but the others missing me by what felt like miles.

Then one of the men shifted, turning into the biggest black bear I hoped ever to see. He let out a roar and jumped, flying upward through the air and gaining the lower edge of the roof. It held his weight. Not good. I threw a wave of force at him, slamming the bear off the roof edge and back to the snow below.

Counterforce is a bitch, apparently. My push knocked me backward, and I lost concentration as I rolled down the other side of the roof. Wrapping magic around me, I rolled through the thick snow and regained my feet as the giant bear rounded the side of the church and flew at me. Snow melted off my face as I rubbed my hands over myself quickly, checking for injury. My jeans and coat were soaked and I knew I'd be a human icicle if I stood still out there long enough. No danger of that. I heard more gunfire and braced for impact, but it was muffled. Coming from the other side of the church, or perhaps inside. I hoped it wasn't from inside.

I had big-ass-bear trouble to worry about. Harper and the twins would have to handle their own problems.

The bear charged, and I threw lightning from my hands. It fizzled and arced away from the shifter. Damn.

Time for fire. This much cold and wet, and the church being mostly stone, I didn't have to worry about burning down the forest or the building. I threw a Fireball right into the bear's face from nearly point-blank range. He roared in pain and rage and sprang aside, plunging his burning body into the snow. Acrid smoke steamed off him as he twisted and came to his feet again, snarling.

Okay. Maybe too much snow for fire.

"My magic will tear you apart," I yelled at the bear. "Whatever Samir is paying you, it isn't worth your life. Run now, and I let you live."

The bear snarled, and a huffing roar barked from his mouth. I think the bastard was laughing at me.

Another ball of fire stopped that. He turned aside so it didn't catch him straight on, instead frying a painful-looking swatch of charred hair and flesh down one of his ginormous sides.

My body hurt, my feet were numb with cold, and I was burning through a lot of magic. Time to end this. Somehow. I was going to have to kill the bear.

He'd signed up for this, but I was still tired of death. No time for second-guessing or mercy. The bear clearly had no intention of showing me any.

I brought another ball of fire into my hands, making it smaller but pouring in as much will and heat as I could. I pictured more than fire; I pictured napalm, Greek fire, the worst grease fires I'd ever seen while working in commercial kitchens. I poured every memory of fire I had into the magic, honing the spell until it was a swirling purple-and-green sphere of death. I took every last second I could, waiting until I felt the breath of the great bear upon me, until he was only one more preternaturally quick step away.

Then I unleashed my ultimate Fireball. It burned right through his side as he tried to twist again. But he was too close. He crashed into me and we fell, the snow beneath me melting away from the focused heat engulfing us both.

All my magic went right into my shields, more on instinct than by design. I closed my eyes and tried not to breathe. The bear convulsed and I shoved hard, managing to roll away from him and escape the conflagration.

A man in fatigues was watching, his gun loose in his hand and pointed at the ground, as I rose slowly to my feet. I raised a hand, gathering magic in my palm.

He dropped his gun and ran.

"Heh, normals," I muttered. At least one person here had some sense. Which was good, because I was exhausted. My body felt like it had been steamrolled by a dire bear. Funny, that.

"Jade!" Ezee's voice brought me back to planet Earth and roused me from my tired fugue.

Turning, I saw him coming around the side of the church. "Okay?" I said, my voice barely above normal, but he was a shifter and heard me just fine.

"Rosie is unconscious. Something's got her bound and we think it's magic. Levi got shot, but he'll live. Come on."

"What about the other guys?"

"Levi and I killed a wolf. Harper took out a human. Nobody else down there." Ezee had blood spatter on his shirt, but from how he was moving, I didn't think it was his.

The sound of a snowmobile caused us both to jerk our heads around, but it was the one smart dude running away. I wondered if Junebug would pick him off or let him go.

I stumbled down through the storm doors to the basement. Levi waited at the bottom of the stairs, an appropriated gun in his hands. His face was paler than it should have been for a full-blood Nez Perce, but his eyes were clear, and he nodded to me as I stepped over the savaged body of a man in grey-and-black fatigues and made my way into the basement. Rose hadn't been locked in a bathroom but was chained by a thin silver wire to a thick wooden chair. Harper paced around her mother, clearly wanting to do something but afraid to fuck with whatever magic was holding her.

The sickly-sweet scent of Samir's power washed over me in a wave and I gagged.

"Don't touch anything," I said, even though they all clearly had the picture. I pulled on more magic, digging deep. I was closer to the edge of my limits than I'd thought. Wolf appeared beside me and whined, pushing on my hip with her nose.

I stepped back and looked down at her. "Can you help?"

"Who are you . . . Oh. Holy shitballs." Harper took a step back as Wolf let herself become visible to the rest of the group.

She circled Rose and then looked back at me with unfathomable night-sky eyes. Then her huge jaws closed on the chain. Silvery smoke puffed into the air as the chain unraveled and curled like a snake, twisting for a moment in the air as though in death throes and then dissipating.

Rose groaned and her eyelids fluttered.

"Mom, Mom," Harper rushed to her side as Wolf backed off and flopped down on the floor.

I looked at my Undying friend and whispered my thanks. Her sides were heaving as though what she had done had taxed her greatly, but watching Harper and Rose embrace was thanks enough for both of us. I went to Wolf and threaded my hand into her thick, warm fur. She felt as solid and comforting as ever.

"We should get out of here," Levi said.

"No telling when the rest will come back or where Jade's evil ex is," Ezee added, going to Rose's side and helping her stand.

She leaned heavily on Harper and Ezee, unable to stand under her own power. Pain lined her face, and her eyes were puffy and red as though she'd been crying. She looked around and violently shook her head.

"Where is Max?"

"Max? He's in Washington, Mom. Remember?" Harper said, her fore-head creasing.

"No, he was here. That golden-eyed monster had him here. He took him upstairs after he talked to Jade. Where is my baby? Where is my boy?" Her voice got louder, stronger, and yet rougher and more broken with each word.

I ran up the steps two at a time. The main floor of the church was empty. The pews had been pushed to the sides, blankets folded on the seats. A couple of shotguns leaned against one wall, but otherwise, the place was abandoned. There was an office and another bathroom, both empty as well of anything useful. No clues about Max, no sign he'd even been here.

No sign of anything but a skeleton crew left to guard Rose. A polished chunk of obsidian resting on one of the folding card tables in the main room caught my eye. I had seen stones like it before. Without even having to summon my magic, I felt Samir's power, his presence. That rock was like the ones he'd used in the school to feed my dead family's voices to me, drawing me into his trap.

I blasted it to pieces without half a thought.

My phone, somehow undestroyed by bad landings and crushing bears, began to play the *X-Files* theme song.

Unknown caller.

With shaking fingers, I pulled it out. The screen was cracked but I was able to flick it to answer.

Samir was on the other end, and before he spoke, I knew deep in the despairing depths of my shrinking heart exactly what he would say.

CHAPTER TEN ▶

Alek called me just after Samir hung up on me. He was at the Henhouse and crazy-worried. I told him to wait in the barn and stay out of sight. We took the snowmobiles and met up with Junebug, transferring the half-conscious Rose to the car. I went with Junebug while the other three drove escort on our stolen snowmobiles.

Samir wanted Clyde's heart. He had arranged to meet us at the old rock quarry. Max's screams had confirmed he was still alive, for the moment.

It was a trap. Another one. But we were tired, injured, and I was running out of juice. Chasing down Samir and playing his games was taking too big a toll on me, but I didn't know how to stop.

Not without getting Max killed, and I wasn't willing to let that happen. I wasn't dead yet, and nothing short of total annihilation was going to stop me from continuing to fight Samir.

We'd saved Rose, at least. One down, one to go.

I had never been so happy to see anyone as I was to see Alek. He looked tired but was in one piece. I practically flew from the car over to him as he emerged from the barn. His big arms wrapped around me, pulling me into his warm embrace, and for a long moment, I let myself cling to him, breathing in his heat and his strength.

"I should never have left you," he murmured into my hair.

"Are you okay?" I asked, ignoring his stupid statement.

"No," Alek said. "But I'm here, and we'll deal with one thing at a time."

I pulled back reluctantly and looked up at him. "What happened?"

"Long story," he said. He looked past me at the others. "For another day."

I wasn't sure we had another day, but he was right. One problem at a time.

Ezee carried Rose into the barn. Someone, I was betting Alek, had dragged the dead horses away.

It turned out that wasn't Alek but Yosemite. The big druid walked in through a stall and nodded at us. We all gave each other the quick explanation of the previous events, from Steve's death through my arrest to the capture of Rose and Max. Yosemite had come and given the horses to the earth. He was done with his druid business and there to help, he said, as long as it meant not leaving the forest.

"I need Clyde's heart," I said, looking at Alek.

"You told me never to give it to you," he said. Though his ice-blue gaze was calm, his lips pressed into a tight line.

"Fuck what I said. Making the trade is the only card we have left. It's a trap, sure thing. But we need to find Samir, save Max, and end this damn thing if we can. If I can." I folded my arms over my chest, willing him to see the necessity.

"You're going to hand the heart over to Samir?" Levi asked.

"Just like that?" Ezee added.

"If it will save Max, I'll do it," Harper said, her voice tight and gravelly. "Fuck the heart. This is my brother's life."

"Samir is going to kill him anyway; Jade said so before about Rosie." Junebug stretched out a hand toward Harper.

"I'm not going to hand him the heart," I said before this could turn into a fight. Everyone was on edge and I couldn't let them turn on each other.

I took a deep breath. I had a shitty plan, but it was better than no plan.

"I'm going to pretend to hand it over. We get to the quarry with the heart, see what is what. Then I'm going to eat Clyde's heart and rain down all hell upon that bastard." Which I should have done already, I knew. I didn't want Clyde's evil inside me. I hadn't wanted his power, his memories. Universe knew what he'd done, but I was willing to bet it made a sick serial killer like Bernard Barnes look like a Bundy in diapers.

"You said it was power you didn't want," Alek said gently in Russian. "You told me to hide it for just this reason. So you wouldn't weaken in your resolve if things got tough."

"I was an idiot," I said to him in the same language. The others were looking between us like kids watching a Ping-Pong match, but I shrugged off their questioning eyes.

"I've been weak," I continued. "Samir killed Steve. Right in my fucking shop. He died in my arms and I couldn't do anything. Do you see what he's done? Destroyed my friends' lives. He's probably torturing the kid while we sit here and argue. I have to stop him, Alek. I have to protect them. Save them.

"No more weakness," I added. "No more squeamishness on my part getting anyone killed. I need more power, and I'm going to take it."

"Jade," Alek said. His eyes were sad and his voice thick with resignation.

I knew I'd won. Go me.

"Take her to the heart," he said to Yosemite.

The big man looked between us and took a deep breath. "All right," he said. He rose and squeezed Ezee's shoulder. "It isn't far."

Alek and Yosemite had hidden the bag with Clyde's heart about a ten-minute walk from the Henhouse. Two huge fir trees towered over a large rock. The stone was cracked in half, as though Paul Bunyan had split it with an axe. I knew from Alek and Yosemite's reactions that this was not how they had left it.

The bag was on the rock. The snow around us was pristine, only the bare grey stone a sign that something wasn't right, that this place had been disturbed.

I walked to the stone and picked up the bag.

It was empty.

"We can't stay here," Levi said.

"Splitting the party hasn't been working out well for us," Ezee added. He stood shoulder to shoulder with his twin. Though they looked different, Ezee with his clean-cut, professorial appearance and Levi with his tattoos, piercings, and Mohawk, their expressions were identically stubborn.

"Rose has to sleep or she won't heal. She's practically in a coma." I couldn't let them come to the quarry with me. Nobody else was allowed to get hurt, damnit. This was my fight.

"I'll take her to my grove," Yosemite said. "Nothing can approach without me knowing. We should be safe there."

"Thank you," Ezee said. He glanced at Junebug and then to Levi, his meaning clear.

Junebug sighed. "Going to try to leave me out of this fight, too, aren't you?" she said to her husband.

Levi crossed to her and slid his arms around her waist. He pressed his lips to her ear and spoke so quietly, I couldn't pick up the words. Her expression grew grim, but she finally nodded.

"I'll help you with Rose," she said to Yosemite.

"You should all go with Rose," I said, knowing that even though it was futile to argue, I had to at least try. My stubborn-ass friends were going to get themselves hurt or killed. "This is a sorcerer fight."

"That he's brought shifters into," Alek said. "That alone would make it my fight. Shifters working for a sorcerer? Against their own?"

"How is the Council even putting up with this? Where are the Justices?" Levi asked. His eyes flicked to the chain around Alek's neck.

Alek bent his head and took a deep, slow breath. Then he pulled the chain out of his collar and yanked it off. The empty links fell to the barn floor.

"There are no more Justices," he said, his voice seeming to echo around the wooden walls.

"What happened in New Orleans?" I asked, breaking the stunned silence that had descended.

"There is no time to explain. I am not even sure what is happening. The world is changing, but we have more immediate trouble."

"Yeah, like saving my brother," Harper said. She clenched her fists at her sides and turned. "No more arguing. We're going with you, Jade, so suck it up and let's move."

I had nothing to say to that. They were going to go get Max with or without me, and I was their only chance of killing Samir. I couldn't fight him and my friends. I had to pick my battles. So, I followed Levi out to his SUV with a heavy heart. The upside was that I was too exhausted and angry to be afraid. Only rage simmered in my veins, rage and power.

The last time I'd been out to the abandoned quarry, I'd killed a man and eaten his heart. Time for an encore.

CHAPTER ELEVEN

Samir waited in the quarry. We drove as far as we could in the snow with the SUV, then Levi and I left the car and rode tandem on one of the stolen snowmobiles. The whole drive, I talked with mind-Tess, both of us picking over as much about Samir as we could remember.

He loved objects, was very good at crafting them. This much was becoming painfully obvious. The stones, the wires, who knew what else? I couldn't rely on him using something like that, but I could at least try to be aware of anything he was holding or had around him. Samir had been careful with Tess as well as with me to never reveal a lot about his power. Just enough, mostly showy things, to get us interested, to prove he was like us. From there, he'd played the lover and teacher, his habits and demeanor insultingly similar, as though Tess and I were interchangeable parts in his life. Toys to him.

At least Tess had known. She had played him as he played her. I'd had no excuse. I'd been starry-eyed, thrilled to finally find someone like me, someone who understood and wasn't afraid of my magic. My shifter family had cast me out. My human family had tried to help me, teaching me to use role-playing games to help focus and control my powers, but even they hadn't really gotten it. They didn't know what it felt like to have magic flowing through your blood in all its hot, elemental glory. To know that if you could just put enough into it, focus your will enough, you could change the whole freaking world and make the stars dance at your fingertips.

Samir had understood, and he had played the perfect boyfriend and mentor. Too perfect.

Tess tried to console me with the knowledge that I must have been suspicious on some level, or I never would have sought out his journals, never would have gone questing for the things he didn't tell me. I was not mollified with that thought. I should have been more suspicious. Done more. Fought him sooner instead of running and running. What had he called me? A mouse. Yeah, I'd been a fucking mouse.

And now more people were getting hurt, were getting killed because of me.

Wolf materialized by my side as I strode over the snow toward the flat plateau at the base of the quarry. The boulders blocking off the entrance carried a thick frosting of snow, and the whole landscape looked glaringly white in the afternoon sun, the snow glittering like a million diamonds. At the edge of my vision, I made out a tall, dark shape standing over another dark shape. Samir and Max.

Alek, the twins, and Harper had reluctantly agreed to take the flank and let me do the approach. We paused at the boulders and I looked over at the huge white tiger to my left. He sniffed at the air, his giant head swinging from side to side as he curled his lip back, tasting as well as smelling.

"Shifters?" I whispered.

Tiger-Alek shook his head. The wind was low but present, coming toward us from down the quarry. Any of the mercenaries helping Samir would have had to be behind us to conceal themselves from his powerful senses. It appeared that Samir was alone with Max.

Somehow, that worried me even more.

Wolf and I walked side by side, my right hand on her back, buried in her warm fur, my left clutching my d20 talisman. I let my magic flow into and around me, formless for the moment, awaiting my will. I wanted to be ready to attack or to shield, and had to hope that between Wolf and all the training I'd been doing, it would be enough. If I could draw Samir away from Max, the others might be able to get him. They'd promised to make his safety a priority, and I knew that Harper at least would keep that promise. The twins too. Alek I was worried about, but he had a stubborn sense of duty, so I had to hope he'd see to their safety and trust me to fight my own battle.

The snow was melted away in a small area around Samir, the brown-and-grey ground barren. Max was prone and bent backward over a flat stone, held by magic that stung my senses even from thirty feet away. I recognized the dark bonds holding him. Samir had definitely eaten Clyde's heart and taken his powers.

My evil ex rested his hand lightly on Max's chest. Max was still breathing, his body twitching in the bonds, his breath escaping in gasps that puffed like smoke in the cold air.

"Let him go," I said, slowing my advance. "You already have the heart." I kept my eyes on Samir but tried to pick out details with my peripheral vision. Nothing moved in the quarry.

"You did a terrible job of hiding it. Leaving it in my own bag. It was far too easy." Samir lifted a shoulder in a half-shrug and pressed down on Max's chest. Max screamed, and I heard fox-Harper snarl behind me.

I waved her back and took another step toward Samir. Something glinted at his throat. A necklace of some kind, with a smoky crystal spinning slowly on a silver chain. That worried me, too, but it gave me ideas. I was going to get rid of that necklace first, if I could separate him from it. Magic was clearly in use there, his sickly-sweet power radiating from his body, centered on the spinning stone.

Tess hadn't known I could see the magic of other sorcerers, so perhaps

Samir didn't either. A small advantage, but I needed every single one I could get.

"Let him go," I repeated. "You want a heart? Come take mine."

Tiger-Alek roared behind me and I twisted and yelled at him to stay back. He crouched ten feet off, snarling more quietly.

"Your heart is already as good as mine," Samir said with an exaggerated sigh. "You are starting to bore me, Jade Crow. I thought you'd put up a better fight than this."

"To be fair," I muttered, "that makes two of us."

Samir laughed. I wondered that I had ever found him attractive. His face was handsome, but he was beautiful the way that a scorpion could be beautiful. When he dropped the pretense of being a feeling, non-evil person, he was as alien to me as an insect. But worse, because a scorpion would sting out of its nature. Samir did it for fun.

"You ever thought about taking up a real hobby?" I asked, moving forward another couple steps. I could make out Max's face now, his brown eyes open, his cheeks hollow and his mouth open. "Underwater basketweaving in the Marianas Trench? Spelunking inside a volcano?"

"I enjoy many hobbies." Samir pressed down on Max's chest and the black bonds binding him constricted. Max screamed, his voice nearly gone, more of an echo of a scream than the real thing, as though his throat was raw and his vocal cords worn away.

"Let. Him. Go." I was nearly to the open ground now. "Why are you so afraid to fight me?"

"Afraid to fight you?" Samir laughed again, but his golden eyes turned sharper and the stone at his neck started to spin more rapidly. "You think this is only about you?"

I stepped onto the open ground, finding my footing in the slick mud, and pulled my magic in around me. I could blast him backward, maybe. If I hit hard enough and caught him by surprise. I just needed to move him away from Max and my friends would have a chance to get to safety.

"You aren't hurting him because of me? Really?"

"Oh, that's definitely a side benefit. You should see your face right now. You're a mess. So desperate, so tired, so sad." Samir smiled, baring his teeth. "It's nearly time to end this. The mortals are getting restless. Their time is ending, too. Like ants in a flood, they don't see it yet. Magic is rising, Jade. You could have ruled with me."

"Okay, now you are talking the crazy talk." One more step, then I'd throw the spell. Rip that necklace off, crush the stone. Whatever it was couldn't be good.

"Soon, I'll take care of you. But you've still got a little fight left. Here? Now? This particular little show isn't about you."

He leapt backward, springing away and into the snow behind Max. The stone stayed, hanging in the air, spinning and spinning like a crystal dreidel.

"It has never been you I'm afraid of," Samir added. He flung his hands out and the crystal exploded.

His retreat left me, Max, and wolf alone inside the circle of bare ground. Circle. *Fuck*.

I threw myself at Max, pulling my magic into a shield as molten power smothered us like a tidal wave. I knew within an instant that my shield wouldn't hold as the air left my lungs and my body remembered the light weight of the dire bear with sudden fondness compared to this crushing pain. Wolf threw herself onto me, her fur expanding into darkness, flowing over both of us like a blanket of night.

The pressure lifted and I could breathe. I clung to Max, to my own power, and rode out the wave as it slammed us down a final time.

The darkness enclosing me grew thin and cold. Light shone through in pinpricks, then in beams, until Wolf's magic turned to golden sunlight. And just like sunlight, it faded, shining with warmth and power for a golden moment, and then gone like the sun dipping behind the horizon.

"Wolf," I screamed. I cast out my hands, reaching for her. I pushed my mind out, too, hunting for the feel of her nearby. I always knew when she was here, a shadow, a presence. She was as much a part of me as my skin.

It was like fishing without a lure. My lines floated in the water, drifting, cut, useless.

Wolf was gone.

Max gasped and groaned beneath me. The rock was pulverized and we lay in a jumbled pile of gravel and mud. I dragged up the vestiges of my magic and climbed to my feet, looking for Samir.

Samir was gone as well. In the distance, I heard a snowmobile start up. Harper sprang into the circle and turned human, grabbing Max, checking him over, babbling words that hardly made sense as she told him to lie still, that he'd be okay.

"He ran," Levi said, stumbling to my side as he shifted from wolverine to human in a blink. "Alek tried to give chase but got thrown aside." He pointed to Alek's body.

I sprinted through the snow, barely conscious, hardly able to breathe.

Alek had shifted to human and he lay on his back, gasping. Alive. Relief flooded through me, taking the adrenaline with it. I collapsed to my knees and wrapped my arms around him.

Wolf was gone. Dead? I didn't know. I shoved aside the crushing fear and clung to my lover. He was alive. Max was alive.

Samir was right. I still had fight left in me. The endgame was coming; I felt it. He'd attracted a lot of notice with his stunts there. While he seemed to not care, he'd always been circumspect, as most of us supernaturals were, about rousing human interest and ire. He couldn't keep doing what he was doing without attracting more notice.

I had a feeling the next time he came for me, it would end things. One way or another.

"Jade," Harper screamed, bringing me back to the present. "Help me; something is wrong with Max!"

I stumbled to my feet, looking down at Alek.

"Wind knocked out," he said. "Go, I'm fine."

Max lay where I'd left him, groaning, his face contorted in agony. I reached for my magic and saw the dark bindings still around him. It was like the unicorn all over again, only this time, I had no help from the very essence of the forest.

I tore into the twisting magic, but it was like trying to rip apart smoke with my bare hands. The bindings dissipated and reformed, coming back like a hydra for every link that I burned.

"No," I muttered. "Don't you die on me, Max. Not today."

"I'm sorry," he said. Blood sprayed in pink foam from his lips. "Love you, Harper."

The bonds dug deeper, binding and smothering. I felt Max's life like a tiny candle, flickering beneath all that darkness. I tried to fan it with my magic, to recreate the power I'd used to save the unicorn.

There wasn't enough strength left in me, or maybe without the unicorn's own power, it would never have worked.

I failed. Max's heart stopped. One moment, he was breathing beneath my hands, alive to my magic. The next, the bonds constricted and the lights went out.

Harper's wail was joined by Ezee and Levi's, preternatural, haunting, and utterly broken. Hot tears rolled down my cheeks, and I opened my mouth and joined my song of grief to theirs.

CHAPTER TWELVE ▶

Harper carried Max's body to the car. She wouldn't let anyone else touch him. I rode behind Alek on a snowmobile, not wanting to face my friend. Not wanting to sit enclosed with grief and the dead body of another person I had failed to save.

Tears froze to my cheeks, and despite Alek's bulk and warmth, I was chilled to the bone and all cried out by the time we reached the smoldering remains of the Henhouse. Yosemite met us there. He looked at our faces and spoke not a single word. Our expressions told the story enough.

It was slow going through the trees to his grove, and the sun started to sink in the sky. We had to abandon the snowmobiles partway into the wood as the terrain grew too rough and the brush too thick. I didn't see the grove until Yosemite parted a thick wall of brambles with the wave of one of his massive hands.

A huge ancient oak, its branches a perfect canopy and still leafy green despite the winter, shrouded a clearing. Beneath the oak, the ground was open and uncovered, no trace of snow. Tiny purple flowers bloomed as though it were summer and the air was warm. Under the tree was a small hut formed of earth and branches.

Beneath my feet I felt a heavy throb, as though the land itself here had a heartbeat. I bent and laid my fingers against the grass, pressing my magic down into the earth. A node, the confluence of magical ley lines that traced the whole of the planet. True wild magic. I'd touched ley lines before, though I'd never tapped one. It was too dangerous. The magic within couldn't be contained for long and violently resisted attempts to channel it. I'd never felt a node this strong, not even the one that Barnes had tried to tap with his ritual the last summer. It didn't surprise me that the druid had his grove here. This place was infused to the molecules with magic.

For the first time in days, I almost felt safe.

The hut was bigger on the inside than it looked. Rose was awake and Harper went to her, collapsing in her mother's lap. I hovered at the door but stayed outside, turning away as soon as I registered that everyone within was whole and sound. I couldn't take more grief, not right now.

Instead, I found a place in the flowers and knelt. I reached for Wolf again, but the void was still there. She was gone.

Alek sat behind me and pulled me back against him. We rocked there in each other's arms for a long time as the sun sank out of sight into the trees. There was nothing to say. I had lost another fight against Samir, had lost my guardian. She was one of the Undying. *Undying, my ass.* Wolf had given herself to save me. Her death was another notch on the stick of my failures.

The best I could hope for was that the kind of magic Samir had thrown at us to kill her had taxed him as much as it would have taxed me. I remembered the crushing wave of power and didn't think I could have done anything so strong. Hopefully, he was exhausted.

Finally, in Alek's arms, warm for the first time that day, I fell into exhausted and fitful sleep.

We buried Max at dawn. Yosemite opened a grave in the earth and we threw flowers picked from the grove in before the earth swallowed Max forever.

No one said any words. Rose and Harper stood holding hands, fat, silent tears slowly dripping down their cheeks. Ezee and Levi and Junebug held hands as well. A united front, brought closer in grief and pain.

It didn't seem right, leaving Max in an unmarked grave. I looked around and settled on the biggest rock I could see.

"Alek," I whispered. "Can you move that?" I pointed at the stone, which was about twice the size of my head.

Alek nodded and lifted it as though it were a bag of groceries. He carried it to Max's grave. I knelt and put one hand on the stone and the other on my talisman. Sleeping in Alek's arms, or perhaps sleeping on top of a huge active node, had revived my magic. I felt almost normal. Too angry to be tired anymore.

I channeled magic, going on will and instinct more than practice. The stone shifted and changed under my power, its mass converting to dark blue crystal. I anchored it in the earth, sending crystal roots out to hold it against earthquake, human intervention, or inclement weather. This stone would stay put short of someone digging it out with a backhoe.

"Thank you," Harper said to me as I finished.

I shook my head and turned, walking back to the grove. She had nothing to be thankful for. All I had done was get her brother killed. A stupid gesture at his grave? Meaningless. My magic was useless if I couldn't protect the people I loved.

I had to convince them to leave, to go into hiding. Samir had said he was getting tired of this game. Well, good. I was tired of it too. If they hid and I offered myself up, perhaps he and I could have a final battle.

One was I fairly sure I'd lose. I needed more power. More of a plan. More knowledge. Instead, all I knew was that Samir liked objects and he liked to get his hands on them.

Oh, and he really wanted to fuck up and kill everyone I ever loved. Totally useless knowledge.

I waited as everyone filed back into the grove.

"We have to run," I said, though by *we* I did mean everyone but myself.

"Fuck that," Harper said. There were nods all around and grim, determined faces. Great.

"I'm going to get you all killed. This is a sorcerer problem. I've failed, okay? Don't you see? This is all my fault." My nails dug into my palms and I blinked back tears. I had to make them understand.

"Your fault?" Harper said, raising a hand to forestall Levi and Ezee, who had both opened their mouths at the same time. "You killed Steve? You kidnapped and killed my brother?"

"Because of me," I said. "If I weren't here, Samir wouldn't have come after them. He only wants to hurt all of you because of me." I paced away from them and turned back. "This is why I should have left a long time ago."

I'd chosen to stay and fight, to stop running. To live. It had felt so good to be a part of something again, to have a lover and friends and a place to belong. I'd forgotten the part where it would all be ripped horribly away from me.

"Fuck. You." Harper stalked toward me, a growl issuing from her human throat. Her green eyes flared gold for a moment and her lips curled back in a snarl.

"Let's play *It's a Wonderful Life*, the Jade Crow version. So what if you'd left? Mom would be dead by now, starved and drained like a fox battery by that Barnes guy. Hell, so would Ezee. Maybe the rest of us. We weren't exactly winning that fight before you showed up."

"I could have left after that," I said weakly. "Everything bad that has happened since has been my fault, because of Samir."

"And let all the wolves die? Let Eva destroy the packs and become the Stalin version of the alpha of alphas? Was that Samir? I don't think so."

"Someone would have stopped her," I muttered.

"You stopped her. You threw yourself on a freaking bomb. You got shot for us. You saved my mom and Ezee. You didn't kill Max, Jade. Your evil fucking ex did. Don't you dare try to take on the blame for that. He has to pay. He has to suffer and die."

"At what cost?" I asked her.

"Any. Fucking. Cost," Harper said. She was toe-to-toe with me, staring into my eyes with a fire I'd never seen in her. "Samir is going to die. And the only way to kill a sorcerer is for another sorcerer to eat their heart. So, stop throwing yourself a fucking pity party for shit you didn't do, and man up. We're in this together and we need you."

I wrapped my arms around her, hugging her fiercely to me.

"I love you, furball," I said. "I'm so sorry."

"I love you, too," she whispered, gripping me hard enough to bruise my ribs. "Now let's stop talking about turning tail and figure out how we destroy that motherfucker."

We spent the morning brainstorming in the grove. By midday, we were all tired of talking in circles, trying to decide how to get Samir to hold still long enough to really fight him. It seemed we would have to wait for him to come to us. Yosemite had the most strength there in the grove, and he would be able to sense anyone approaching, so it seemed like a good spot to make our stand.

We needed supplies. It was dangerous to leave, but neither the druid nor I could conjure food, weapons, ammo, or blankets. The hut had the bare bones of things, some dried food and a couple blankets, but nothing that could last days and support eight people.

Alek and I, and the twins, decided to hike out. The twins would go for weapons. Levi had another rifle stashed at his shop, and Ezee said he'd put a call in to the wolf pack, certain they could help hook him up. Freyda hadn't left town, which worried me. I hoped my message to Sheriff Lee had gotten through.

The day was grey and dim outside the magical grove. Occasional snow spit from the sky, more ice than flakes. We reached the barn and split up, Alek and I taking his truck, Levi and Ezee taking snowmobiles.

"Any sign of trouble, you GTFO," I warned them.

"No shit, Sherlock," Levi said with a half-assed grin.

"Do you smell smoke?" Alek asked, turning his face into the wind.

"I smell the burned building over there," I said, though my nose was too numb to smell much of anything. I kept my eyes off the wrecked heap of the Henhouse. So many happy hours spent inside those walls. It was just a burned-out shell now, hollow and broken.

"No," Ezee said, sniffing also. "I smell smoke. Fresh smoke." He looked around and then pointed. "There."

In the distance, a huge black cloud hung in the air. It looked like storm clouds, but the season was wrong for that kind of storm, and the cloud was too black, too thick. Too low.

"That's Wylde," I said softly, giving voice to what we were all probably thinking. "That's the direction of town."

CHAPTER THIRTEEN ▶

Alek drove his truck at not quite ludicrous speed. I'd made Levi and Ezee stick to the plan. Alek and I would investigate the smoke; they would go get weapons and stuff.

Wylde was burning. Smoke billowed down the main street as we drove past the gas station and courthouse.

My shop was at the heart of the conflagration. Two fire engines were trying to stem the damage, but the water seemed to be making the fire angrier. Every cop car in the county, plus two state patrol vehicles, created a blockade of the main strip. Police in hospital masks and heavy jackets were trying to wave back the mass of onlookers as people desperately jostled for both a view and to stay away from the worst of the radiating heat.

Alek pulled up a block away, and I was out of the truck before it had fully stopped moving. I ran toward the fire, reaching out with my magic, already sensing Samir's power somehow involved. The fire reacted to my own power by flaring up, bright orange flames roaring into the sky. My whole building was a raging inferno, but flames were already jumping farther along, catching the roofs of the buildings next door.

Apparently, Samir was done with subtle. He was trying to burn down the entire town.

"Jade!" Rachel Lee ran toward me, waving her arms.

"What happened?" I yelled over the noise of shouting people, crackling and roaring fire, and the scream of more sirens as another fire engine came up from the other side.

"It won't stop burning," she yelled back. "Went up half an hour ago. Fire chief says he's never seen the like."

"It's magic," I said. It wasn't going to stop. There was something fueling it. I didn't think Samir would stand at the center of such a blaze, if he were even capable of it.

He likes objects. Making things, mind-Tess whispered.

I closed my eyes and pushed my magic back at the building, forming it like a probe. I ignored the renewed pulse of the fire, the answering song of Samir's sickly-sweet power, and tried to feel for a catalyst. There, in my shop. That was the center, a knot of magic holding the fire in its grasp, fueling it.

I was too far away to undo the knot, to destroy whatever was anchoring the spell.

Pulling off my jacket, I looked over at Alek. He shook his head with a warning, an unhappy look on his face.

"Hold this," I said. I stripped out of my shirt next, then my jeans, panties, socks, and shoes.

"Jade," Alek said softly as he took my clothes from me. The wind and noise stole the sound of my name from his lips, but I made out the word.

"What are you doing?" Rachel yelled as I started walking, totally naked, straight at the fire.

"It won't stop without help," I yelled back at her. "Tell them to let me through."

Rachel, to her credit, didn't argue, just started shouting at the firemen to let me through.

Not that they listened. To their eyes, a naked Native American woman wearing only a necklace was walking right at a million-alarm fire. Men in heavy gear tried to grab me.

The time for subtlety was past. I used magic to more or less gently shove them aside. The fire brought sweat to my face, whispering of the heat to come as I neared the building. I pulled my magic around me. I'd survived a damned bomb. I could manage a little fire. Fire and me had always seemed to have an understanding.

I had Haruki's power inside me as well. Fire had been a favorite of his. He knew its ways, knew glyphs to summon it and to quell it. I painted myself with glyphs of pure magic, covering my skin in a second glittering shield as purple fire formed its own marks along my body.

Then I stepped into the blaze. My eyes watered and I didn't want to risk breathing, so my lungs felt tight and empty.

This won't kill me, I told myself. I didn't need to breathe. The fire left my skin alone. It felt as though I'd walked into a dry sauna, oppressive but not unbearable. I walked over the remains of my life there, eyes mostly closed against the thick smoke. I moved by instinct and memory, not sight.

This store had been my home, my sanctuary, for nearly six years. Every miniature I'd painted there, every comic I'd bought and sold, every dragon my friends and I had slain together. All the happiness I'd had in decades was in flames, burning away as though it had never mattered.

But it had. I used those memories to strengthen my shield. Samir was trying to take everything from me, but I still had my family. Their love. The laughter and tears and hopes that we had all shared.

I still had everything that this store represented.

This was still my town, and I wasn't going to roll over and let it burn. I reached the center of the fire and pressed my magic out, feeling for the thing I'd sensed from outside.

The catalyst was not a rock. A snake that looked to be formed of lava and hellfire uncoiled from the center of the blaze, its mouth open in a silent hiss. Or perhaps not so silent, but I couldn't hear anything over the crackle and roar of the flames in my ears.

I dodged as it struck, and my hip slammed into a fallen beam. Part of the upstairs had collapsed down, the subflooring giving way as the fire ate it. Rolling while holding tightly to the glyph shield keeping me safe from the flames, I lashed out with my feet, slamming into a coil of the firesnake.

It felt like I kicked a block of steel. Pain jarred up my legs and I skidded back, ash and smoke swirling up around me, blocking what little vision I had.

The snake struck again, this time catching my left arm. Its molten teeth bit through my shield. Pain so hot it became cold again radiated into my arm, and the smell of cooked meat filled my nostrils. I rammed a bolt of pure force into the snake's head from point-blank range with my right hand, knocking it back and away from me.

My left arm hung useless and numb. I was glad for the numb. That jolt of pain had nearly knocked me out. I renewed my shield as I scrambled back, my smoke-teared eyes hunting for the snake. I missed Wolf more than ever as I tried to regain my feet and get my back up against something more solid than burning wood.

I couldn't fight fire with fire. I had to stop just reacting.

Dragons, I thought. *What if this were a red dragon?*

We'd have boned up on ice spells, ice enchantments, and fire-protection gear. That was what a good adventurer would have done.

Tess had told me my gift, my specialty in sorcery, was elemental magic. It was freaking winter outside this raging inferno. There was snow everywhere and freezing air.

I reached for it, envisioning myself like the center of a black hole, sucking in as much air as I could. The fire flared and grew as I pulled oxygen into it, but I held on, focusing on the cold. Focusing on how it had felt to fly through the air, tears freezing to my cheeks as I raced to try and save Rose and Junebug.

Then I visualized deeper. Glaciers. Swirling blizzards. Dry ice. Cold so strong that blood would freeze in the veins of living things. I set my will on that cold, pushed my magic into ice around me.

The snake struck again, twisting and lashing out as I hit it with the strongest cold area-of-effect spell I could muster. Ice and snow blasted out from my body, the air freezing instantly. Ice formed and encased the snake, catching it in a deadly embrace.

More of the second floor collapsed under the weight of flame and magic. I'd be buried before I killed the damn snake at this rate. Unless I could slow down time.

I reached for Tess's magic then, slowing time around the snake and me. Holding three spells at once made my head spin and my stomach turn to cheese curds. My knees gave out and I fell forward, but I clung to the magic, pouring everything I had into the ice.

The snake's body hardened and grew dark. Embers flared and died in the pits of its eyes.

Then the fire died as though it had never been. I let go of all of my spells and knelt, hands and knees on the floor, gasping in cold, smoky air. The floor was freezing, rimed with frost, and no more flames licked at the building.

Voices roused me from my exhausted slump. Shouting from outside.

I made myself stand and walk toward the street. The entry was mostly crushed, the building half collapsed, but I clambered over fallen beams and charred wall. Firemen stood around, some pointing, many talking at once, as I strode out of the building toward Alek.

"Jade." Rachel rushed at me, grabbing a blanket from a surprised fireman and throwing it around me.

I winced as the cloth hit my injured arm. The numbness was wearing off and it felt like my flesh was still on fire.

Alek reached us a moment later, his glare driving back the two men trying to approach. People were yelling a lot of things, but compared to the roar of the fire, it was almost eerily quiet.

I looked back at my building. The blaze was completely out. Smoke still hung above the building, but nothing seemed to burn or smolder within. Score one for me, I guess.

I wanted to curl up in a ball and sleep for a thousand years, but I pulled the blanket around myself and tried on a smile for Alek's sake.

"I'm okay," I lied. My shop was gone. The picture that Ji-hoon had drawn for me, the last remnant of the people I'd lost, was gone as well. It was the only thing I'd truly prized, the one possession I'd carried through the decades. I'd just performed a crazy amount of magic, further weakening myself. And I'd done it in front of a hundred people, some of whom were definitely normals. Added to my aching arm, it all summed up to very not okay.

"Let's get you to the truck before anyone starts asking what happened," Alek said. He pushed my clothes into Rachel's arms and swept me up like a child.

I was almost used to him carrying me at this point. It was sort of our thing. I perform big magic; Alek sweeps me off my feet when I'm too tired to stay on them. I was supposed to protest, but I was too fucking tired.

Nobody tried to stop us. Awe and disbelief painted the faces around us as Alek strode back to the truck.

Detective Hattie Wise and Agent Salazar waited by the truck, unhappy looks on their faces.

"You are causing a lot of trouble," Hattie said.

"I didn't start the damn fire," I said as Alek growled at her to get out of his way.

"This is getting national media attention," Salazar said. His lips were pressed into a tight line and his forehead creased with worry marks. They both looked like they'd aged a decade since I'd seen them.

"That's your problem," I said. "Remember? You can't stop a sorcerer. So, get out of my way. Unless you want to arrest me for putting out a fire."

Hattie nodded slowly. Salazar looked like he wanted to protest, but she laid a hand on his arm and pulled him back.

Alek set me down on the bench seat. Rachel laid my clothes in my lap. "Get the wolves out," I told her. "Get away from here. This might get worse." I could only hope that Samir would come for us in the woods and stop fucking up my town. My shop was gone. There was nothing left for him there.

"Good luck, Jade," she said, her dark eyes solemn. "And thank you."

I didn't know what she was thanking me for. Maybe putting out the fire. It was hard to tell and I was too tired to care. I clutched the blanket around myself and passed out even as Alek started the engine.

CHAPTER FOURTEEN

The bird hits the glazed windowpane with a sickening thud. Tess runs out the door, ignoring the call of her grandmother to stop, to leave it be.

The bird is dead. Its neck is twisted and Tess cries. Something strange and cold unfurls within her, swirling through her mind. She begs God to let the bird live again, to turn it away from the window.

The world swirls around her. The cabin looks as though it is no thicker than her paper dolls, an image she could push over with the shove of one of her tiny hands.

"NO!" Gran's voice cuts through the chill and the world stops its slow spin.

"Heal him," Tess says, pushing out her lower lip. "I wanted to fix it. To stop the bird from hitting the window."

"You cannot do this, honey-child. Ever. God wills what happens and what does not." Gran takes the bird from Tess's hands. "We'll give him a proper burial."

Later, sitting at the hearth and watching Gran spin in the waning light, Tess gets the courage to ask.

"What was happening? I felt all cold, and the world started to spin and spin."

"It's your gift. Like your mama before you. You have a feel for time, for the way the world and stars and all the heavens move." Gran sighs and stills the drop spindle, setting it in her lap.

Tess stays quiet. Gran never talks about Tess's mama. Not ever.

"She had the sight, which has passed you by, I pray to Jesus. Your mama saw the devil coming and she tried to change the future. Look at me, child. No one can change the future. Only God can stand up to the devil. But my baby tried."

Gran's eyes leave Tess's face and focus on something Tess can't see, a distance she senses but does not understand.

"She gave her life to you," Gran says after a long, long silence that leaves Tess fidgeting and wondering if Gran has fallen asleep with her eyes open. "Like Jesus dying for us, she tried to give her life to you, to die for your sins."

"I'm a good girl," Tess says, distressed. She says her prayers every night. She walks all the way to church twice a week, and she always asks God to forgive her when she has bad thoughts about the mean Camberly boys.

"You are," Gran agrees. "But you must never turn back time. Your mama tried it, the night she died. I can't say for sure if she managed, but I've never known a woman able to survive what she did. A baby, neither."

"How did she die?" Tess whispers. She has an idea, a vague memory that is impossible. A beautiful woman with long brown hair leaning over her, whispering in a language Tess did not understand. Telling her to eat, to remember, to live.

Telling her to fight the devil.

"She gave her life for yours," Gran says. Her grey braids bob as she shakes her head. "That's enough woolgathering. Go wash your hands and say your prayers."

Tess kneels by her bed. She closes her eyes and tries to remember the beautiful woman.

Words tumble from her lips, but they aren't her usual prayers.

"Lucifer has golden eyes. The man comes, Mama. The devil is coming to burn and burn us all. The devil is going to end the world. Lucifer will wake the dragon."

▲ ▲ ▲

ANNIE BELLET

I awoke with strange words and memories on my lips, shaking myself out of Tess's memory, or her dreams. It was hard to tell them apart. Tess stayed silent in my mind, her ghost weeping softly at the edge of my consciousness. She was terrified.

I didn't blame her. I was in the barn, up in the loft. Alek's warm body was pressed against my back. Light filtered in through the bullet holes. It was still daylight.

"Hey," I said, not sure if he was awake.

He was. "You want water or clothes first?" he asked.

"Water," I said. My mouth tasted of ash and blood.

My left arm was still pink and raw but healing. I splashed water over it after taking a deep drink. Minimal pain, just the sting, no worse than a papercut but less annoying. My fingers flexed fine. I'd live.

"What happened in the fire?" Alek said as he handed me my clothing.

"Some kind of magical snake thing. Like a salamander without legs, I guess. Lava snake? Who knows? The important thing is that it tried to eat me and I kicked its ass."

I was filthy, covered in ash and soot. I wondered if the hose still worked but was too tired to climb down and find out. It was probably frozen solid, anyway. All I'd do would be to make myself wet, dirty, and cold. So, I sucked it up and pulled on my clothing. At least it was dry, warm, and less dirty than my skin.

My hair was unraveling from its braid. I did what I could with it, twisting it into a thick knot at the base of my neck. I was halfway tempted to tell Alek to chop it all off, but it could be saved with a hot shower and conditioner. A few hours with a brush and a lot of patience wouldn't have hurt, either. I had none of the above, but I still had my vanity. I loved my hair. It was staying, itchy and annoying though it was at the moment.

"Where are Ezee and Levi?" I asked, looking around. "How long was I out?"

"A couple of hours. They are getting supplies. It'll be dark soon. We're

112

going to stay here for the night and head to the grove at first light."

"Do the others know? If we don't come back, they might come looking for us." I knew that Harper would. She was stubborn that way. Given his relationship with Ezee, there was a good chance Yosemite would go with her. Then we'd be all split up again, ripe for picking off. I didn't like that idea at all.

"Yes. Ezee called Harper. Cell phones are magical, aren't they?" Alek smiled gently at me.

I felt my jeans pocket. My phone was missing. "Don't suppose you know where mine is?" I asked.

"Dead somewhere along the way," Alek said. "That's my guess. It wasn't on you or in the clothes you handed me."

"Damn. Not again." My life was hell on phones. And clothing, for that matter. At least this time, I'd saved my shirt and Harper's jacket.

Alek raised his head, listening, his body tense. He relaxed quickly as the sound of a car crunching on ice and gravel reached my less-sensitive ears.

"Twins?" I asked, though his posture already told me he recognized the vehicle.

I wrapped my hand around my talisman just in case. It had survived the fire just fine, but I kind of figured it would. The d20 was as much a part of me as Wolf.

Shit. *As Wolf had been.* I sucked in a deep breath to quell my grief. For a moment, I'd forgotten.

"Hey," Levi called out.

"Up here," Alek called down to him.

They had backpacks full of granola bars, jerky, and dried fruit. We ate a quick meal, nobody talking much for a while as the sun faded away. I hated winter. It got dark so early and it felt like the sun took its sweet time rising too, like it was too cold to get up and it just hung around considering not making the effort.

"Town didn't burn, I heard," Ezee said after a while. "Thanks to a crazy naked woman."

I gave them the CliffsNotes version.

"Shit, lady." Levi grinned at me, his teeth white in the growing gloom, his face in shadow, only his piercings catching the light and glinting silver.

"I know I can't talk Harper out of her revenge," I said, burrowing into one of the sleeping bags and leaning back against Alek. "But you two should take Rose and Junebug and get the hell out of here. This is my fight."

"Fuck that," they said in unison.

"Samir came here, burned our town, killed our friends, and is trying to destroy the rest of our friends. We aren't abandoning you," Levi said.

"I'd be insulted you are even asking us to, but I know your heart is in the right place. Stupid, but in the right place." Ezee pulled a blanket around his shoulders and moved a mound of hay to help pillow his head.

"I don't know if I can win," I murmured. I barely said the words aloud, but my friends had preternatural hearing, so it didn't matter.

Alek's arms tightened around me and he nuzzled my ear.

"You are the strongest person I've ever met," he said. "And you are not alone."

"Damn straight," Levi said.

"Correct, but never straight," Ezee added. I heard the smile in his voice even as the light faded too much for me to make out his features. It was an old joke with us.

"I feel like we're always behind. I can't pin Samir down. I don't even know what his real game is, what he really wants. He could have killed me by now." At least, I was pretty sure he could have. Maybe Wolf had been more of a deterrent than I thought, but it seemed like Samir was up to more than just toying with me. That, or I truly didn't comprehend the depths of his evil. Little from column A, little from column B?

"It's obvious what game he's playing," Levi said with a snort. "*Human Occupied Landfill*, live-action version."

"What?" I said. I hadn't thought about that obscure game in a long time. I'd had a copy in the game store, but mostly as a novelty item.

"Think about it," Ezee said. "How do you start a live-action game of *HoL*?"

"Set a couch on fire in someone's basement?" I tried to think, remembering something along those lines from the back of the book.

"Exactly." Levi chuckled.

"If we're playing *HoL*," I said. "I guess you all took the 'running blindly into eternal damnation because you think you can win' skill, eh?"

"I think we all took that skill at char gen," Ezee said.

"Except Alek," Levi added. "He took the 'make sharp things go through soft things that scream and bleed' skill."

I managed a laugh at that as Alek nuzzled my cheek with a soft chuckle. Laughing felt good, a little painful but cleansing.

"I like this skill," Alek said.

He was right; I wasn't alone. I was loved and surrounded by those I loved.

That's what terrified me. I had so much to lose. And I didn't want to lose any more.

There had to be a way to protect them all. I closed my eyes, but it was a long time before I slept again. Samir would come at me again. He would finish me himself; I was certain of that. He was hands-on; he'd want to see the life leave my eyes, watch me die as he bit into my heart and stole my soul. Watch the pain in my face as he destroyed everyone I loved, as he broke me before the end.

He would come to me.

I had to be ready. So, I spent most of the night taking a tour of the memories in my head. Thinking about power, about magic, and ley lines, and how to save the people I loved.

When dawn came, I was tired but determined. And I had a terrible, terrible plan.

CHAPTER FIFTEEN

We arrived at the grove to find that Freyda and the Wylde wolf pack had beaten us there sometime in the night. At a glance, the alpha of alphas didn't look like much. She was tall and lean, with pale skin and wheat-colored hair. Freckles dotted her nose, giving her a younger, cuter appearance that almost mocked the worry line in her forehead and the deep knowledge in her blue eyes. She was holding the wolf pack together and had beaten all challengers to her role. Underestimating Freyda was not something that anyone did twice.

"Not what I had in mind when I told the sheriff to tell you to get out of town and get to safety," I said after we exchanged cautious greetings.

"You think we would run? There are strange wolves here, invading my territory without asking for passage. A man who smells of death and old blood leads them. He tried to hire some of my people." She spit into the flowers, then glanced at Yosemite where the big druid lurked near the hut, and inclined her head in apology.

"As though we would fight against the woman who saved us all," she continued.

"Jade thinks everyone should run away and let her fight Samir all alone," Harper said with an exaggerated eye-roll.

I glared at Harper and sighed. I was done fighting with everyone over who could stand with me. Freyda had been around a long time. She wasn't stupid. I hoped she would realize when enough was enough and vanish when the time came.

"You may stay," I said, pretending it was my decision. I could cling to the illusion of choice and control, right? "But the sorcerer is mine. I'm the only one who can kill him. If you want to keep the mercenaries he brought with him off my back, I'd appreciate it. I won't interfere with that."

Freyda looked me over and gave a small shake of her head. I could only imagine how I appeared. Dressed all in black, filthy from the fire, my black hair tangled in a halo around my probably exhausted-looking face. From her expression, she didn't think I could kill a flea, much less Samir, but she had the intelligence or at least the grace to not say so.

We worked out that the wolves would set up in the forest around the grove. They would be the early warning system and try to pick off Samir's men before too many reached us. Working as a pack, we hoped they could drive Samir and his people toward the grove. Yosemite was strongest there, and the thick brambles would limit the effectiveness of guns, hopefully edging the fight into melee range, where the shifters and I could have a better chance of engaging the foe.

It wasn't much of a plan, but when you break eggs, you have to make omelets.

After that, it was a waiting game.

Know something else that druid hovels don't come with? Showers.

I heated water over a propane camp stove and ran a washcloth over my face and neck. The tan cloth turned instantly black, as did the water as soon as I dunked it again.

"Hey," I said to Rose as I gave up on cleanliness. "You feeling okay?"

"I'm healing," she said. Her expression was grim and lined with grief. "As for the rest, well. Max isn't the first baby I've lost. It don't get easier."

I shivered at the hollow pain in her voice. "I'm sorry, Rosie," I said softly.

"Don't start that again," she said, looking at me with fever-bright eyes. "You just promise to keep my Azalea safe. And you kill that devil who took my Max from us."

Devil. Her use of that word echoed Tess's dream memory and ran a different kind of shiver down my spine.

"I promise," I said, meeting her gaze without flinching. "I am going to keep you all safe. Nobody else dies. Not on my watch."

With that said, I left the hut and went to find the druid.

Yosemite was at the edge of the grove, watching me approach as though he'd been waiting for me. Knowing the unfathomable ways of druids, he probably had been.

"Iollan," I said, using his given name instead of his nickname. I continued in old Irish so that Harper, Ezee, and Levi, who were all sacked out on blankets on the other side of the clearing, wouldn't be able to understand us if they overheard.

"That tree teleportation thing you did when we were fighting the Fomorians," I said. "Do you have to use trees? Could you teleport more than one person at a time?" We'd leapt into a tree portal, voluntarily and with haste. I had something else in mind this time.

He was silent a long time, his eyes fixed on my face as though it were a book he could read. Then he sighed and ran a hand through his thick red curls.

"I would say it is not possible, but we are in my grove. Here, many things might be possible."

"Because we are on the biggest node I've ever felt?" I asked, curious if he could feel it, could maybe even tap its power.

"Partially. There is a reason the Eldertree grows here," he said, gesturing at the huge oak. "You want me to take people away from here?"

"Yes," I said simply. "When the fighting reaches us, when Samir shows up, I want you to get everyone out. Everyone," I repeated. "Except me."

Yosemite turned away and ran his fingers along a blackberry cane, tracing lines and thorns. The cane went from winter brown to summer green as I watched, then faded again back to dull, dormant.

"This is a hard thing you ask."

"I cannot watch them die," I said softly, glancing back to where my friends rested. "I need to be able to fight Samir without worrying. This is not their battle anymore. Please, Iollan. Please help me."

"Will they forgive me?" he asked, more to himself than to me. "Will he?"

I had no answer for him. I knew he and Ezee had a troubled relationship. Ezee had described it as a bird loving a fish once, but they'd grown closer over the last month. Turmoil does that, I suppose. Some people it rips apart. Others it binds together, paring us down to our core values and desires, showing us just how damned important the ones we love are, how important that love is all by itself.

I was counting on his love for my friend. Counting on his own desire to keep them from dying, using it to get my way. I would have felt worse about manipulating the druid like this, but I needed to save my friends.

Harper wanted her vengeance, but she couldn't have it. It would only get her killed. I wasn't sure I could defeat Samir, but I'd hatched a plan.

"Do you have a plan?" Yosemite asked, almost as if reading my mind.

I looked up at him. He'd stepped back toward me and I'd forgotten how huge he was. He had a good six inches on Alek, who had a nearly a foot on me. For a moment, Yosemite seemed as old and solid as the oak above us.

"I do," I said. "I need to know they are safe, or I won't be able to do what is necessary."

"Does your plan involve destroying my grove?" A dark glint of humor lurked in his eyes and the corners of his mouth twitched beneath his beard.

Maybe he could read my mind. Damnit.

"Possibly," I said. I didn't really know. It had a good chance of it, though. What I planned wasn't subtle.

"Will you survive?"

"Samir won't," I said with more conviction than I felt. That was all the answer to Yosemite's question I was planning on giving.

"If you do, you'll have your hands full apologizing," he said, the smile gone.

"I'll burn that bridge when I come to it," I muttered. Alek would forgive me. Eventually.

"All right, Jade Crow. I give you my oath. When the fighting starts, I will take them away." He sighed heavily and shook his head. "What about the wolves?"

I repressed my feelings of triumph. This was not something to celebrate, but just knowing that I had Yosemite helping me, that my friends had a chance to escape and live, lifted a weight from my shoulders, unbending my spine.

"Freyda isn't an idiot," I said. "She'll do what she must out there against the other shifters. If it gets too dangerous, she'll pull back the pack." That I was sure of, more or less. She was a survivor, and her skin in this game was thin. She loved Wylde and felt duty-bound as the alpha of alphas, but she wouldn't risk her pack on a suicide mission. She was happy enough to leave Samir and the true war to me.

If only my own damn friends were that pragmatic. Rushing into certain doom because they thought they could win was definitely a feat those loveable bastards all had in common; the twins were right about that.

"How quickly can you get them away?"

He rubbed his beard in a gesture that mimicked Ezee's usual joking one, looking almost professorial himself.

"Not quickly. I will have to use the earth to transport them away. We will not get very far, and I will need them clustered. Especially if they are unwilling."

"Oh, they'll be unwilling," I said.

"Aye." Yosemite gave me a sardonic look. I supposed I was being Captain Obvious again.

"So, you'll have to wait and do it when they are distracted. That'll be more dangerous." I didn't like it, but it was the best plan we had. "How far can you get them?"

"A couple miles. I have a destination in mind. That will be almost equally dangerous. If I lose my grip on anyone, they could be lost and end up who knows where, if the earth spits them back out at all."

Great. So, if this went wrong, my friends could all be lost in time and space. Awesomesauce.

"I know it isn't the best plan. But staying here and watching them die while I'm too distracted to save them is worse. Just . . . do what you can." By which I meant *save them all*, but I decided to stop saying the obvious while I was ahead. He'd agreed to try and given me his oath. That was all I needed.

Yosemite moved away from me and I took the hint, walking back into the grove. I sank down on the warm bed of flowers and lay back. Summoning my magic, I gently probed the node. Raw power sang beneath me, as vast and unknowable as the ocean.

Yep, terrible plan. But it was the only one I had.

I guessed I had taken the same damn feat at char gen. Go me.

Alek found me lying there and sprawled beside me. Everyone else was still curled up, though Levi and Junebug were talking softly. The air had an expectant quality, though the day felt slow and lazy in the artificial warmth of the grove.

"What are you planning?" Alek said to me in Russian. He clearly didn't want anyone understanding our conversation.

"To kill Samir," I said, evading his question as best I could.

"You are too calm," he said. His ice-blue eyes caught my gaze and held it, assessing.

"I could freak out more," I offered. "But I'm tired and I think I should save my energy."

"Wolf is gone?" he asked after a moment of silence stretched between us.

I closed my eyes at the pain those words roused in me and nodded.

"Whatever she did, trying to stop Samir's magic, it killed her."

"She is Undying. They cannot die. By definition." Alek shook his head.

"More by legend," I said. "Before, all my life, I could sense her presence. Even when she wasn't nearby or visible, I knew she was there. Like my shadow. Not always visible, but when conditions are right, it is always following. Now? Nothing. I feel like a ship whose anchor has been cut."

"You are not without harbor," he said, his voice low and soothing.

I crawled into his arms, burying my head into his chest. He'd forgive me when Yosemite took them away; I was sure of it.

But only if I lived. I was equally sure that Alek would never forgive me for dying.

"I'm going to try," I murmured into his chest. "I'm going to win. No one else is going to die because of me."

"I know," he said. "You will do what you must, kitten. No one will die because of you. Steve, Peggy, Max, they weren't your fault."

"Close enough," I muttered. "No one else. No one." Those words were my litany, my new compass point in the storm.

"We cannot take responsibility for the actions of others," Alek said. "Only our own."

"What happened in New Orleans?" I asked him, wanting to change the subject before he coaxed me into spilling my plan and ruining the surprise.

His body stiffened and he rubbed his nose in my hair, his arms tightening around me.

"It is a long story," he said after a moment. "The Justices have been dissolved. Our powers and feather of office stripped from us. The Council has gone silent, for the most part."

"For the most part?" I leaned back and looked up at him.

His blue eyes were shadowed and staring into the middle distance.

"I think one of the Council tried to kill me," he said. "Carlos and . . ." He trailed off and pressed his lips together. "Carlos and I stopped them."

"Is Carlos okay?"

"He'll live," Alek said grimly. "Barely survived, but he made the right choice when the time came. I do not know what will come of this. I do not think I understand the world anymore."

"Was it because of Eva?" I thought about the wolf Justice who had tried to become alpha of alphas, who had tried to destroy the Peace and broken all her vows as Justice.

"I believe she was more of a symptom than the disease," Alek said.

I studied his face. I could only imagine how hurt he must feel about it all, how lost. Over half a year before, when I'd met him, he had been so sure of right and wrong, the perfect judge, jury, and executioner.

"What are you thinking about?"

"How full of vim and vigor you were when we met."

"As opposed to the old man I am now?" he said, smiling a little.

"More like how you waltzed into my shop and accused me of murder. And here we are, waiting for a guy to show up so I can murder the hell out of him." I nipped his chin, wanting him to keep smiling. I wanted to remember him like this, big and strong and curled around me with eyes full of love. I wanted to take his belief in me and forge it into invincible armor.

"Life is strange," he said. "I never thought I would have a mate. I have always been a Justice, since I was barely more than a cub. It was who I am."

"It *is* who you are. Remember what you told me about balance? You have justice in your soul, Aleksei Kirov. You can't help but do what you think is best for everyone around you. It's annoying but kind of endearing, too."

"Only kind of endearing?" He kissed me, pulling me into an embrace so tight that I had to protest lest I lose a rib.

It almost worried me how affectionate he was being. How he clung to me like I was his anchor in a storm. It almost felt like he knew I was going to try and send him away. As though he knew what I was planning. I shoved all that aside. This was potentially our last day together. I couldn't let doubt or fear stop me. I loved this man, every damn inch and frustrating flaw. Every perfect muscle and stubborn devoted molecule of him.

He was right. He was my mate. He was mine, damnit, just as I belonged in a strange way to him. Maybe I'd always known it, since those first uncomfortable moments in my store where I was both attracted to and appalled by him.

He might never forgive me, but I would keep him safe. I was going to protect my own. No more running for me. No more letting people die because I flinched at doing the hard things I needed to do. No more weakness.

"I love you," I murmured to him. Then his lips came down over mine and we forgot we weren't alone for a while. If anyone noticed us curled among the flowers, they were too smart to say a word.

CHAPTER SIXTEEN ▶

It was near dusk, the sun a bloody blur behind flat grey clouds, when the forest fell utterly silent. Winter wasn't a loud season in the woods, but the branches still rustled, a few birds still flitted here and there. The woods had a living, breathing quality to them, a background noise to fill even my duller senses.

Quiet could mean only one thing. Trouble. *Something wicked this way comes*, mind-Tess whispered to me.

Yosemite rose to his feet, and around us, my friends shifted form. Rose emerged from the hut as a fox and paced up to be with her daughter, red and grey next to each other.

I admit it felt somewhat comforting to have a twelve-foot tiger at my side. He was huge and solid and I loved Alek all the more in that moment as eerie silence descended upon our ragtag band of wannabe warriors.

The last stand.

I met Yosemite's eyes as I let my magic flow into me. "What is it?"

"Something is coming, but I can't track it, or perhaps them? It feels like they are all around us." The big druid turned slowly in a circle, his eyes hunting the shadows beyond the grove.

"What about Freyda? Can you sense her?" I wanted to tell him to do it now, to get everyone out right damn now, but I couldn't. Not yet. He couldn't get them far enough that they would be out of the fight, not for certain. I knew my bullheaded friends would turn around and charge right back to try and help me. Even in this terrain, in winter, a few miles wouldn't slow down a giant Siberian tiger, not for long.

"I can't sense the wolves. They are too far out."

The staccato burst of gunfire punctuated his statement and we all stiffened, turning toward the noise.

Owl-Junebug lifted off from her perch on a lower branch of the oak.

"Stop," I called to her, but she ignored me, soaring up into the gloom.

Wolverine-Levi whined low in his throat, clearly no happier about her decision to go take a look than I had been. The thick hair on his back stood up and his huge claws dug into the earth as he watched her fly away.

"Back up," I said to my friends. "Closer to the tree. It can guard our backs."

Alek swung his head toward me, his tiger eyes suspicious. I wondered if he still had the power to detect lies. I wasn't outright lying, as impure as my motives were. The great oak would guard our backs. It would also help group everyone together so that when Samir showed and the fighting started for us, Yosemite could get them out.

Except Junebug, who spiraled above us, scouting. I hoped she had enough sense to stay out of the fight if she was beyond Yosemite's reach. She wasn't much of a fighter in her animal shape, built more for silent speed and grace than brawn.

Something huge moved just beyond the grove, a white shadow in the dark brambles.

Junebug screamed a warning, banking to the south. Another crack of gunfire snapped through the air and she swung sideways and plummeted into the trees below.

A giant white bear smashed into the brambles, bursting through and into the grove as wolverine-Levi screamed challenge and ran in the direction his wife had fallen.

I couldn't let him get far. Things were happening too quickly.

"Iollan," I yelled. "Oath!"

I sent a bolt of pure force into the face of the giant bear, forcing it to slow its charge as it twisted aside. Its teeth were as long as my arm, its mouth opened wide enough to swallow half my torso and not even have to burp. This beast made the bear I'd defeated before look like a child's toy, cuddly and small.

Yosemite was chanting, green light spilling from the ancient oak tree. Tendrils of it started to wrap around my friends, pulling them backward.

Tiger-Alek snarled and broke free of the druid's grasp.

"No," I cried out, sending more magic into the bear. Its hide started to smolder as raw fire burned into it. I wasn't pulling punches. The finale of this wouldn't depend just on my own power, so I wasn't holding reserves. I had to keep my friends clear of this thing long enough for Yosemite to get them out.

Tiger-Alek hesitated as a glowing ball flew into the clearing, landing nearly at my feet. The sickly-sweet smell of Samir's magic flowed over me in a wave.

I grabbed at the glowing stone, trying to fling it away with magic.

Too late. Alek threw himself at me, carrying me beyond the stone.

It burst like a grenade, molten bits of pain lancing through my legs. Tiger-Alek screamed above me, roaring. His blood showered me as molten stone ripped straight through his chest, but he rolled before he crushed my body beneath his.

I struggled to my feet, saying his name over and over. To my right, Ezee and Levi had engaged the bear, using their superior speed to avoid his deadly strikes. The two foxes defended the druid, who was on his side, unmoving. Blood gushed from beneath his hands where they pressed into his throat.

No more green light. No more chanting. I watched as Yosemite's eyes shut, his face a mask of pain.

"Samir," I screamed. It was all falling apart. This wasn't how things were supposed to go.

Beside me, Alek groaned and shifted to his human form. Even in this form, he was covered in blood.

"Alek," I said. "Get back, get back."

He tried to rise but fell, his legs refusing to allow him to stand. I grabbed at his arms, trying to pull him up, to get him to the hut. I had to protect him. His blue eyes widened and he tried to shove me aside, his mouth forming a warning cry.

Force slammed into my back, knocking me over Alek's body. I rolled and regained my feet, twisting to face Samir.

My evil ex strode into the grove like he owned the place. Not a hair on his head was out of order, his coat looking like it had been dry-cleaned that morning, and his smile chilled my blood. Behind him, four wolves crashed out of the woods, springing at Rose and Harper where they guarded Yosemite's fallen body.

"Stop," I said, my voice weak in my ears. "This isn't about them. Fight me. Fight me."

In the corner of my vision, I watched in horror as Ezee failed his saving throw and the bear's jaws snapped on his flank. Wolverine-Levi leapt to the bear's back, clawing huge chunks of flesh, but the bear shook his twin like a wet rat and threw the coyote's much-smaller body into the brambles, where he hit with a sickening smack and lay still.

I threw a fireball into Samir's smirking face. No warning, no gesture, just raw fire fueled by pain, hate, and rage.

The fire cleaved around him, washing off his shields like Moses parting the bloody ocean.

Laughing madly, Samir threw another glowing stone at Harper and her mother. I lashed out with my power and knocked it away, where it exploded in a blast of heat against the ancient oak. Wood chips flew like shrapnel and a wolf screamed in pain as it was caught in the deflected blast. Harper went for the wounded wolf, but its bigger companion hit her from the side, taking advantage of her single-minded focus. She howled in agony as its jaws closed down on her shoulder, ripping into her flesh.

There were too many things to fight. We were losing and my distraction wasn't helping. Inside my mind, Tess was screaming at me to go after Samir. Focus on him. If we could beat him, then we could worry about the others.

The plan. It was all I had.

Samir came at me, gossamer wire spreading with a golden glow between his fingers.

"Fuck, no," I said, pushing more power into a shield around me. I had to close the distance. My legs felt like they'd gone through a meat grinder and my shoes were filling with blood, but I swallowed the agony and charged Samir.

Alek beat me to him, shifting in mid-leap as he went for the sorcerer.

The golden threads tore into Alek's head and chest as he carried them both to the ground. A wave of magic blew Alek aside as though he were a leaf on a vent, and his tiger-body twisted and rolled, leaving Samir kneeling with a snarl on his face.

I reached for the node beneath me as I ran forward. Forcing myself not to look at Alek, not to think about what might be happening to my lover, I opened my body to the raw power of the ley lines.

It felt like I was trying to swallow the ocean. Power filled me, stretching my metaphysical skin until I felt like a magic sausage. A magic pressure cooker ready to explode.

I hit him full force before he'd gained his feet, slamming my body into his, locking us together with my arms as I fought a war with the node, trying to channel all the power toward one purpose. Total and utter annihilation of Samir.

We tumbled to the ground and he tried to fight me off, but I clung with every ounce of strength left in me.

Something inside broke open, like a joint popping into place. Pain faded away. My mind cleared. All at once, the raging ocean of power became a spear in my hand, bent and shaped to my will, ready for use.

I opened my eyes.

We had rolled and turned, so I could see most of the grove beyond Samir's shoulder. Harper was down in a bleeding heap, her mother standing over her, also bleeding from too many cuts and bites to count. Yosemite lay still, his hands no longer stemming the blood flowing from the wound in his throat. Even as time seemed to slow and hang around me, I watched as the bear smashed Levi to the ground, fur and flesh flying.

Then I saw Alek. He was back in human form, blood gushing from a gaping wound in his chest. Deep cuts oozed and smoked in his face. He stretched a hand toward me, trying to rise.

Samir and I were pressed body to body, heart to heart. I heard his heartbeat, felt his magic battering me. I let go of him and space opened between us as we both struggled to our knees. He was still in arm's reach. His heart in arm's reach.

And I hesitated.

This was my future. I had the node at my fingertips, ready to smash through Samir's chest. To drag his heart from his body and end him forever. Mind-Tess screamed inside me to act, to do it.

And then what? Watch Alek die? My friends had fallen. I had failed every single one of them. Again.

What kind of life would I lead? Was this my fate, to watch everyone I loved die over and over? To fail to protect anything at all? I would triumph, perhaps. Be safe, perhaps. But the price. Oh, the price.

It was too high.

My hesitation cost me.

Samir struck, his hand growing glowing claws as he plunged it into my chest, smashing apart the remnants of my shields, and pulled my still-beating heart from my body.

Just as it had when I'd fought and killed Tess, time slowed down even more. The world went silent other than the roaring of my own heartbeat in my ears. I clung to the node magic even as Samir laughed. Clung to the magic and formed a desperate plan that was so idiotic, even Tess stopped yelling inside my mind, shocked to silence.

"Stupid girl," he said, raising my heart to his lips.

I moved my lips, trying to speak, and he hesitated.

"What? Last words? Come on, then." All illusion of sanity and beauty was gone from his features. His handsome face was twisted into a mocking grimace, his eyes blazing molten gold. Lucifer, indeed.

Harper had asked me what I thought would have happened if I hadn't come to Wylde. She'd pointed out that there would be a lot of dead people. Perhaps she'd been right. There were too many dead already. I was the cause, no matter what she'd said. Samir had once again taken everything I loved, had broken me completely.

I didn't want to live anymore. Not in this world, the one where even if I won, I lost. Lost too much. Too many.

It was not better to have loved and lost. The poet got that totally wrong.

It was better to love and win.

I turned the node power from a spear into a portal, reaching deep into Tess's memories, into her mother's memories. A beautiful dark-haired woman giving her life for a baby so that her baby in turn could give her life to a stranger.

My lips moved again, and this time I managed the words.

"Control-Z, motherfucker."

CHAPTER SEVENTEEN

The world went black. Not the black of night or when you squeeze your eyes shut, but a deep and unending darkness that stared into me with Nietzschean horror. An abyss as complete as I could ever have envisioned, glaring into what some might call my soul.

I came apart, the magic unraveling. I felt my body burning away, my essence dispersing into that darkness. There was no pain, no sense of hot or cold. Just . . . nothingness.

Clinging to the thought of a new future, of undoing what I had done, of saving my friends, I fought the unmaking. I held tight to the tiny kernel of hope, of belief that I could change the world, that I was strong enough to affect the entire universe.

Nothingness faded and was replaced by a presence that terrified me more. Something squeezed on whatever remained of me, pressing in on the ember of my life. Every dream I'd had—every wish, every heartache, every memory—compressed into that tiny spark.

I refused to let go. I wasn't ready to die yet. I had too much work left to do, even though my burning brain couldn't quite recall what all I was doing there.

Like a chewed-up cherry pit, the universe spat me back out.

▲ ▲ ▲

"Jade?" Yosemite's voice called to me down a long tunnel, and I opened my eyes with a gasp.

I was on my knees in the grove, clutching my d20 so tightly, it had left a mark in my palm. Wildly, I looked around.

Gunfire burst in the distance and owl-Junebug took flight from the oak.

I hadn't gone back very far, but I was frozen for a moment with utter joy at seeing them alive. I had done it; I had undone the terrible future.

Now to change it, to keep the reality I'd just escaped from happening again. I'd watched Steve die twice; I wasn't going to repeat that mistake. I reached for my magic and nearly passed out. Red dots swam across my vision. It was like reaching for Wolf after she had gone. Nothing responded, not even the tiniest ember of power.

"Fuck," I muttered. Then the future came flooding back to me full force and I struggled to my feet.

A shadow moved in the brambles beyond the grove.

"Iollan," I cried. "Get us out."

I didn't know how I was going to fight Samir when my magic was drained, but escaping and living another day sounded good enough. I would come up with a new plan after we were away. After my friends were safe and whole and alive.

I hadn't fucking time-traveled just to watch them all die again. Not again. Not ever again.

A shot rang out, and Junebug fell in a puff of feathers. I'd forgotten that part, my brain a mush of what was, what had been, and what might be.

Levi tried to run for her and I threw myself in his direction as Yosemite chanted.

The bear crashed through the brambles. I had no magic to stop him this time or slow his charge, and he sprang at Harper and her mother.

Green light wrapped around Levi and jerked him backward. The druid was trying to hold us together, keep us close enough to transport away.

Samir. The exploding stones. That had been next, the glowing rock and the death and pain that had followed.

I twisted and threw my hands out, working on instinct and memory as the stone flew into the grove. I punched it with my fists like spiking a volleyball, knocking it away. Alek hit me from the side and we tumbled over. The stone exploded, but the tree and hut blocked the worst of it this time. Molten pain stung my leg, but Iollan's chant carried on.

He hadn't been hit. I had already altered the future. Maybe we had a chance.

Green light enshrouded us and I clung to the giant tiger as hard as I clung to consciousness. Holding onto Alek was easier. My mind swam and reeled, bile rising in my throat. Ezee and Levi were wrapped in green tendrils, snapping at them with their teeth but unable to break free.

"Don't fight it," I screamed, hoping my friends would understand. "Trust me. We have to go."

I watched a red form streak by us as Alek shifted to human, holding on to me with his arms, no longer fighting the druid's magic. Harper.

"Harper," I yelled.

She dodged around the bear, heading for where Junebug had fallen. She was too far; the green tendrils from the oak couldn't reach her.

"Harper!" The ground started to swallow us, the earth shaking as the sky above began a strange and lazy spiral counter-clockwise.

She slammed into some kind of magical net and was thrown down. I watched her body spin. Samir stepped out of the brambles as the giant white bear backed away from the druid's magic.

I clawed at Alek, trying to free myself. I couldn't leave Harper behind. I felt so weak, my body full of lead and sand, unresponsive. I had no magic. I had no way to help her.

My eyes met her gaze as the white bear closed his jaws on her flank.

I screamed and shoved at Alek again, and then the green light pulled us down, covering us over. We fell through a spinning vortex of green fire, heat and cold licking at my skin.

No magic. I felt it, a void where my power should have been. I couldn't protect them.

Samir would come at us again and again, hunting me, hurting me until there was no hurt left to inflict. Only then would he take my heart.

"I love you," I whispered into Alek's chest. "I love you forever."

Then I let go of him and kicked him as hard as I could, thrusting him away from me.

I heard him call my name, and then the light engulfed me and I sank into oblivion.

CHAPTER EIGHTEEN

Harper felt the bear's teeth crush her hip. She ripped herself from his grasp, snarling and crawling away on broken limbs. Agony was a molten knife in her body, and her spine gave out.

The green light had faded. Everyone was gone. Somewhere in the woods, Junebug was down, injured or dying. Or dead.

Anger smoldered inside her. They were supposed to fight.

Jade had promised they would fight. She had said she had a plan. Running was not the damned plan.

And they'd left her. Her and Junebug. To die.

Harper shifted, her human legs barely working better than her fox ones had. The smell of old blood and death washed over her as she dragged herself backward, waiting for the white bear to end her suffering.

The bear had backed away. Instead, a tall man with dark hair and a grey wool coat walked toward her, a smile on his face that froze her blood.

"Samir," she said.

He lashed out with his hand, and magic pounded into her breastbone. Her heart stuttered as renewed agony smashed through her. Harper grabbed for him, struggling to get up, throwing a wild punch and snapping with her inadequate human teeth.

He rained down blow after blow until her ribs gave out and she couldn't breathe, much less rise. Adrenaline and desperation were a strong antidote to the crushing pain, but her body was numb and refused to obey. Refused to fight.

Et tu, Brute? she thought.

Why had Jade run without fighting? It didn't make sense. Harper's mind played the scene over and over. Junebug tumbling from the sky. Jade, kneeling on the ground, yelling at the druid to get them out of there.

Why had she been kneeling? Harper's mind fixated on that moment. Jade had been standing, radiating magic strongly enough that Harper could taste it, like ozone in the air before a storm.

Then, as though time had skipped a beat, her friend had been kneeling. No magic coming off her. She'd punched that glowing rock out of the air with her fists. Not with power. Jade always used magic, so why hadn't she then?

Harper's mind spun as consciousness warred with survival instinct.

"She left you." Samir's voice intruded. "Turned tail and ran. I admit I didn't expect that."

Harper forced her eyes open. The bastard stood over her, staring down into her face. A crease between his eyebrows gave him a quizzical expression, and Harper almost believed him, believed that he was uncertain. She hadn't expected Jade to run either. Something had happened. Something had gone wrong. She still saw Jade's face, her friend's dark eyes begging for her understanding as the druid's magic took her friends away. She'd seen the terror on that face, the horror at leaving Harper behind.

Maybe she had planned to run. Maybe she hadn't.

Harper pushed away her anger and fought the poison of betrayal. "Trust me," Jade had screamed.

Harper had to trust her. Not that it mattered. The smug, evil asshole above her was a much bigger problem.

She licked her lips, blood stinging tiny cuts around her mouth as her tongue spread the wealth. Working her jaw, Harper tried to think of a really badass thing to say for her last words. Her mind was fogging, her heartbeat so slow, she wasn't even sure it still worked. She was definitely dying, she thought.

So, she went with the first words that came to mind.

"You go to hell," she gasped, snarling up at Samir.

"Ladies first," he replied.

Then his boot came down and Harper had nothing more to say.

THICKER THAN BLOOD

THE TWENTY-SIDED SORCERESS: BOOK VI

DEDICATED TO

ALL THOSE WHO GET KNOCKED DOWN,
BRUSH THEMSELVES OFF, AND GET BACK UP AGAIN.
YOU HAVE A SUPERPOWER THAT SHOULD
NOT BE UNDERESTIMATED.

CHAPTER ONE ▶

The diner was nearly empty when I stumbled in, looking for coffee and a plate full of fat and protein to soothe my starving stomach. I was glad for the lack of people to stare at me, but the emptiness meant the waitress had no one else to pester.

"What's your story, honey?" she asked me as she leaned a hip against my table, holding the coffee pot precariously in one hand. She was plump with wide blue eyes and had probably been pretty before smoke and sun and the disappointment of years working in a diner in the middle of nowhere got to her.

"I used to be a sorceress," I told her. "Until I took an arrow to the knee."

"Sure you did," she said with a small shake of her head, easing away from me like I was rabid. "Holler if you want a refill."

All right, so it was a bad joke. But it was true. Only instead of an arrow, I'd burned myself out by pulling some seriously timey-wimey shit. I'd created a freaking save file in real life. Which was pretty cool. And I'd saved my friends from my psycho ex. I'd saved Alek.

Well, saved most of my friends. My every thought was haunted by that sickening puff of feathers as Junebug was shot out of the sky, and Harper streaking past me, out of reach of Iollan's spell. I still saw

Harper's face every time I closed my eyes. I'd failed her the worst.

I shoved away those thoughts. It was funny, almost, that in saving everyone, in resetting the entire world a few minutes back, and getting the druid to teleport us all to here-and-gone, I'd lost the very power that had made Samir hunt me. Not that I expected for a minute he would stop, even if I was an ex-sorceress. My wounds were healing, so I guess I was only a powerless sorceress and still not human. He'd eat my heart; it would just make less of a meal at the moment.

Because the power *was* gone. *Poof.* No more. I could reach inside me and there was nothing there but a vast empty hole. A dry well. I couldn't have lit a candle or a match with it. Or bent one of the tarnished and chipped spoons on the table in front of me.

No magic. Not a drop. Not even mind-Tess chiding me in my brain anymore. All my ghosts were silent, though their memories still floated around in my head. They were just memories now, however, no more distinct than my own. Even my talisman, the silver d20 necklace, was damaged. Where the one had been on the die was just a pockmark now, a divot. It hung from my neck, a cold reminder that I was totally powerless.

Which really sucked. Because I wanted to find Samir and rip his fucking heart out and swallow it whole.

Literally.

Iollan's spell had spit me out on the edge of the wilderness. I'd stumbled, too stubborn to freeze to death, until I found Highway 95. A trucker couple had picked me up and taken me to Boise. I was surprised they'd bothered, since I looked like death with bruises everywhere and lots of drying blood on my leg. They'd accepted most of the story, and I seeded in enough details about getting away from an abusive boyfriend that they left me alone. I got to pass out somewhere warm; they got to feel like they were doing a good deed. Everybody won.

I had slept fitfully, my dreams turning to nightmares as I watched everyone I loved die over and over, Harper's look of utter betrayal the last thing I saw before I awoke. The couple wanted to help me in Boise, but I told them I had an aunt there, and in the end, they hadn't pressed too much.

I had no aunt there, obviously, but I did have a stash. Nothing says *low point in life* more than breaking into your own storage unit. I had no identification, no money, and I looked like someone who had been through some serious shit. Filthy, bloody, tired as hell. So, I waited for full dark and climbed a fence instead of trying to bluff my way past the gate guy, glad I had opted for a combination lock.

I had a few units like this all over the States, prepped for if or when I had to run away without taking anything with me. Much as it sucked to admit, my paranoia was saving my ass again. The unit had cash, changes of clothes, and a new ID that would let me hide while figuring out my next move. *Just call me Jade fucking Bourne.*

A motel room and a shower later, I'd crashed out again, risking the nightmares for more sleep in the hope that my magic would return. Morning brought nothing but the sound of cars passing on the nearby freeway. So, there I sat, in a diner, alone and powerless, trying to plot my next move.

I was tempted to try to call Alek or the twins. It had been over a day since the fight. I had no idea if they were safe or together. There was a burner phone in my pocket. I gave in, trying Alek's number. I had to know.

It went straight to voicemail. I'd half-expected that, since we'd ditched our stuff before preparing for the final battle, worried that Samir might use human technology to track us somehow. He was using mercenaries, both shifter and human, after all, and he'd used humans to keep track of me, apparently, all these years in Wylde. I tried the twins and Harper's numbers after that, fighting the tears that threatened to spill as each number went straight to voicemail. Out of desperation, I called Brie's number, too, hoping she might have forwarded her bakery phone to a cell or something. I had no way to reach her or Ciaran, my leprechaun neighbor. They were in Ireland still, doing Universe knew what. It wasn't like they could help right now, anyway. That number went to voicemail too, for the bakery. No answer from anyone. No help.

I hadn't felt this alone in over twenty-five years.

It was safer this way. I knew that. Samir wanted me. He'd come after me. I hoped. I remembered his words, his gloating about how he'd known where I was, how this was about more than just me. What if he didn't come after me?

I chewed my way through a plate of waffles and bacon, every bite like swallowing sand. I had to think about this logically.

We'd fought. I'd lost. Well, I'd almost won. I could have killed him, turned that pure bolt of power from the ley lines on him and taken him out.

It only would have cost me everyone I loved to do it. So, I hadn't.

What did that tell me? That I could have won. We weren't as mismatched as it seemed. Well, if I had my magic. Samir wasn't some all-powerful being. I could kill him.

With magic.

That stupid pesky detail kept coming back.

Break it down, I told myself. I needed magic to fight Samir. I needed to know what else he might be up to, and if he had any weaknesses. I'd learned a hard lesson fighting him; now I needed to put what I'd learned to use.

Operating under the idea that I could get my magic back was part one. I'd slept most of the last twenty-four hours, but maybe whatever I'd done would take more time to heal. Which was the bitch of it, because I didn't have time. Samir had clearly chosen now to come after me for a reason, and he wasn't afraid of doing big shit humans might notice. Killing the librarian witch and burning my store with the fire elemental or whatever the fuck that was had shown that as much as anything.

Alek had made it pretty clear the Council of Nine was out of the picture—some kind of infighting going on there—so even Samir threatening shifters wasn't going to cause them to send help. I knew of no other magical source of assistance. Mostly things that went bump in the night hid from the human world, keeping to the edges. Humans outnumber us millions to one, after all, and magic had been fading from the world for a long time. As Brie had once told me, the time of gods had come and gone. Which royally sucked, because I could have really used some divine intervention right about then.

I'd ditched my allies to try to protect them. Going back was option one, I supposed. I thanked the waitress absently as she refilled my coffee. The morning was slipping away; a few diners had come and gone while I sat, lost in thought. I couldn't go back. Not without magic. I was worse than useless to them this way.

"So, go get your mojo back," a gentle male voice said to me.

I spilled coffee all over the table as my hand jerked in surprise. Sitting across from me, where I swear there hadn't been anyone before, was a mid-forties-looking Native man with short black hair and dark eyes that held flickers of red in their depths. Not human.

"Let me get you a washcloth, honey," the waitress said, coming over and helping me contain the coffee spill. She didn't even look at the man or offer him anything, which was my second clue that he wasn't normal.

I decided to say nothing about him either, in case my suspicion was accurate. "Thanks," I said to her again. A family of four came in and saved me from having to say more.

"You done yet?" the man asked.

"Who are you? They can't see you, can they?" I whispered, trying not to look like a crazy lady.

"Of course not. I'm not here." He leaned back and smiled.

"Ash?" I guessed. Half guessed, because my brain provided me an image of a man who looked like him but younger, bending over my mother, Pearl. A memory that wasn't mine.

"Good to see I didn't breed stupid," my biological father said. Well, the whatever-the-fuck vision or hallucination of my father said. "You asked for deus ex machina; here I am."

"Awesome," I said, trying to wrap my brain around this. "How do I get my magic back?"

"Come see me," he said.

I wondered if there had ever been an actually helpful vision anywhere in the history of magical shit happening, or if they were all so damned cryptic.

"Great, where are you?" I asked, keeping my voice low and trying not to get openly annoyed. Though if he was in my head or whatever, he'd know I was frustrated, anyway.

"You don't know, so I can't tell you," he said with a sad shake of his head.

"Super fucking useful," I muttered.

"What's that?" the waitress asked as she passed by me again.

"Nothing," I said quickly. "I'm good." I waited until she walked back to the front again before leaning forward and asking, "So, how do I find you?"

"If only you knew someone who knows things," he said. I could see a little of my own face in his, though I hoped my smart-ass smile didn't look so annoyingly smug.

"I don't know—" I started to say, then stopped. I did know someone who knew things, someone whose job it was to accumulate knowledge. It was a long shot, sure, but looking at my options, any shot was something.

"Good," he said. His body became translucent. "Find me, and I will show you who you are."

"Wait," I said, but he was gone. I went and found the waitress, tipping generously when I paid.

"Hey," I asked her before I left. "There a library nearby? Where I could use a computer?"

"You can catch a bus easy enough to the one at Hillcrest, or go all the way downtown," she said. "They don't open until ten, though, I don't think."

"Thanks," I said. I walked out into the winter sunlight with a plan. First step, find a computer and see if the Archivist had a website or phone number. Second step, question mark, question mark, question mark. Third step, magic.

CHAPTER TWO

Turns out, Noah Grey, Archivist and vampire, did, in fact, have a website. I had no idea what to Google, but I knew where his warehouse-slash-home was, so I ended up looking at a Street View map until it identified the building. There was a nice blue arrow with a pop-up leading to a website.

I guess you really can find anything on the Internet these days.

Leaving the main library, I walked across Capitol and waited until I was in a snowy park near a museum to dial the number off the site. A woman picked up the call.

"Noah Grey, please," I said, unsure if I should use his name or just call him by his apparent title.

"Mr. Grey is not available; may I take a message?" the pleasant voice on the other end replied.

I pressed my lips together and withheld swearing at her. "He'll want to talk to me," I said. I had no idea if that were true, but I could at least try.

"I'm sure he will," she said, her tone still frustratingly smooth. "If you'll leave your name and number, he will return your call at his earliest convenience."

"This is Jade Crow," I said. I rattled off the number of the burner cell, though I was sure they had it already, now that I'd called him on it. "My offer is open for an hour, no more," I added, taking a risk. "He'll want to hear it."

She repeated the number, confirming, and then hung up on me. I paced the edge of the park, not knowing what else to do. Without the Archivist's information, for which I had nothing to trade at the moment, I wasn't sure how I'd even go about finding dear old Dad. A father I hadn't even known I had until this last year.

Worst case, I supposed, would be finding my way back to Three Feathers and asking my mother. She'd banned me from there a second time now, so I could only imagine how *that* reunion would go.

It didn't matter. Nothing mattered now except getting my magic back, finding Samir, and finishing him. This time, without my friends getting killed around me. I'd pack them into boxes and ship them to Australia to keep them safe if I had to. Samir was my problem. I should have faced him on my own.

I should have faced him years before. This was my failure, and I was going to fix it.

My phone rang and I fumbled it on with chilled fingers.

"Hello?" I said.

"Ms. Crow," said a cool voice on the other end. Noah Grey.

"I need your help," I said. I gave him the barest sketch of the events of the previous week, eliding much of it. I finished with "I have to find someone and was hoping you would know where I could look."

"You want to find your father," he said. I had half-expected him to know that somehow. It was just easier to accept that there was a lot I didn't understand about the world and just roll with it.

"Do you know where he is?" I asked.

"Yes," Noah said. "I do. It's complicated. Plus, we have a bargain that must be struck. I do not run a charity. You will come here."

"To Seattle?" I said, buying myself time to think. He knew where Ash was, which was great. I had nothing to trade, which was not so great.

I wondered if the Archivist took IOUs and then decided I really didn't want to owe this guy anything. Seattle was about seven to eight hours' driving from Boise.

"Where are you?" he asked.

I hesitated. The Archivist was, from what Yosemite had told me, an information and magical-items dealer. Forbidden knowledge, hidden things, that stuff was his specialty. His information was for sale, and I could think of one powerful dude with deep pockets who would love to know where I was.

"I am not going to sell you to Samir," Noah said, his voice taking on a weary edge. Apparently, my hesitation had spoken volumes.

"How do I know that?" I said.

"He uses my competition. I have no business dealings with him."

"You have competition?" I asked. That did surprise me. How many people were in this business? Also, Noah hadn't seemed like the encouraging competition kind of guy.

"I have one competitor. Who enjoys the protection of a very powerful sorcerer," he said, and I could almost picture the vampire's angular face looking annoyed at me.

"Boise," I said. Fuck it. I had so few options. I had to trust someone, at least for the moment.

"I'll have a driver there within an hour. Give me an address."

I told him the location of the main library and went back to wait. It was one of the longest hours of my life.

The driver the Archivist sent was a short, compact woman with a friendly smile and no small-talk skills. She made it clear with one-word answers and grunts that she wasn't going to talk to me, not about herself, about Noah, anything. She asked if I wanted music, and when I said no, she went back to driving.

It was a long seven hours.

It was spitting rain in Seattle, the temperature somewhere in the fifties. We pulled up at the warehouse I'd been to before, but this time, I was led through a lower side door into what appeared to be a very normal living room. The two armchairs and the single sofa were comfortable microfiber and modern in their red, grey, and white color scheme. I dropped my bag and waited for my host, trying to contain my nervousness.

Noah didn't keep me waiting long. He glided into the room, just as eerily still and calm as last time. His eyes were flat silver, inhuman, his face angular and almost pretty. We were nearly of a height and stared at each other eye to eye.

"Ms. Crow," he said, indicating I should sit.

"Hi," I said. I picked a chair and sat. I was acutely aware that I was at a bigger disadvantage now than I had been last we met. I had no magic to defend myself, no Wolf, no friends. Just my charming wit and desperation. It was not a great bargaining position.

"We can skip the small talk, if you wish?" he said after a moment when I said nothing else, his lips curving in a self-aware kind of smile.

"I need to know where my father is," I said.

"That is all you want?" he asked.

I started to say yes but closed my mouth on the words. This felt like a situation where you are about to use a Wish in a D&D game and the GM asks if you are sure of the wording. I didn't want to fuck this up. So, I sat there and thought about what I really wanted.

"No," I said slowly, drawing the word out into multiple syllables. "I want to know where he is. I would also like to know where Samir is, what he's doing, and especially if my friends are safe." There, that sounded like a good wish list. I pressed my lips together and wondered if I should have just asked for the moon and stars while I was at it.

"Your friends? Not a very specific request." Noah tipped his head to one side, the motion studied and precise.

"You don't know who my friends are?" I asked. I folded my arms over my chest and glared at him. He knew, I was guessing, but was messing with me. Not cool. I realized getting angry with the one person who could potentially help me right now was stupid, but I didn't care. They say freedom is another word for nothing left to lose for a reason, I guess.

He tipped his head back straight. "I do. I suppose I should not tease. I can do these things for you, perhaps. What will you offer in return?"

"I'll translate whatever you want," I said. I'd thought this over in the car. Last time, he'd wanted my services as a translator, since I spoke and read literally every language ever. "I'll give you a month of services after this whole mess is resolved." It seemed like a lot, and I was going to have fun explaining to Alek why I was going to be living in Seattle translating Universe knew what, but this would be worth it. I hoped.

Plus, it wasn't like I had a game store to run anymore. I swallowed that lump of pain before I thought about it too hard.

"No," Noah said. "I cannot accept future service from someone who is planning to take on Samir."

"Aw, what? You don't think I can win?" I said.

"I believe you have the best chance of anyone who has ever lived," he said with what would have been a shrug on a human but for him was a very measured lift and fall of his shoulders, too planned and precise to look natural.

"But not enough to bet on me coming back," I said. "Fine, what do you want?" Despair, my old friend, crept back into the house of my heart. I had nothing to give.

"A drop of your blood," the vampire said.

Yeah, because that didn't sound dangerous at all. Nope.

"Why?" I asked. Blood was a powerful thing magically, blood freely given even more so. I shuddered to think what this guy would want with mine.

Noah smiled, his eyes mercurial. "I believe there is a quaint human phrase about beggars and choosers."

"Will you use it to harm me or anyone I care about?"

"No," he said, his head shake emphatic. "I will promise that much."

I folded my legs up under me and wrapped my arms around my knees. His offer seemed crazy good. Which worried the shit out of me.

"You'll give me all the information I asked for, in exchange for a single drop of blood?"

"Yes and no, Ms. Crow." He chuckled, a dry, soft sound like wind in leaves at his own rhyme. "I will do better than that. I will also give you the help you need to get what you want."

"To kill Samir?" I asked. I rubbed my talisman, pressing my thumb over the divot.

"As a side effect, yes, I suppose so. I would not mind certain people who enjoy his protection losing it, for example." No doubt about it; Noah Grey's full smile was something sharp and white, and terrifying to behold.

I closed my eyes for a moment and saw Harper's face again, her look of pain and utter betrayal as I left her behind. For her, for Wolf, for Max, for my old family. For everyone I had loved and been unable to protect. I could do a deal with the devil for them. No sweat.

"A drop of blood, then," I said, opening my eyes.

Noah left and came back with a needle in sterile packaging and a petri dish. I almost joked that he should put on a lab coat but decided not to push my luck. Taking the drop of blood was quick and painless. I'd been worried that open blood would make him go all psycho vamp, but apparently, that wasn't a thing. He stayed utterly calm and professional the whole time.

I stuck my bleeding finger into my mouth. The pinprick wound would close in seconds, but it was instinctive.

"What would you like to know first?" he said, taking a seat again.

"You don't have to make calls or send out imps to do your bidding or something?" I raised an eyebrow.

"I have had over eight hours, Ms. Crow. There are things I cannot yet tell you, but any information I have at this moment, I will give."

"One, call me Jade, please. Two, how did you know what else I'd ask for? We only talked about my father."

It was his turn to raise an eyebrow.

"Okay, point taken. Tell me about my friends." I sighed. I supposed my questions weren't all that unpredictable. Who knew what this guy already knew about me, anyway? Probably way more than I was comfortable with.

"That will have to wait for the details," he said, lifting a hand to forestall my protest. "Someone will be here in the morning who can better answer."

"Who?" Alek? I hoped and also didn't hope that he was coming here. I wasn't sure I could face him yet. He'd be so pissed at me for leaving him like that. Justifiably pissed, heh.

"The druid, Iollan. He would not tell me who was with him and our method of communication is imprecise, but he agreed to come talk to you. He must wait for dawn, however."

Yosemite. I felt a small weight lift from me. If he was alive and safe, there was every chance the others were as well. *Except Harper.* Fuck. I couldn't let my fears for her cloud what I had to do. There was nothing I could do, not now. If she was alive, she was alive. If she were dead, she was at least beyond harm. And the furball would want me focused on killing Samir; I knew that much.

One big worry down. If the druid was safe, odds were good that Alek, Rosie, and the twins were as well. Maybe even Junebug and Harper. I had to cling to hope.

"What about Samir?" I asked.

"He is still around Wylde, as far as I can confirm." Noah's eyes narrowed and he looked almost annoyed. "I cannot confirm what he is doing there, but he has pulled in a large force of humans and shifters. I am not fond of guessing, but I believe his plans are larger than just killing you."

I thought about the few words Samir and I had exchanged. He'd told me, as I tried to save Max, something about magic rising, about ruling, that this wasn't just about me. He'd sounded like a crazy person, and I'd been a little distracted by my dying friend, but his words haunted me now.

"They are," I said. "He said something about mortals and ruling, about magic rising up again."

"I am working on discovering what he wants. The area around Wylde is strong with latent magic, as you found out. It is worrying that he is so interested in it. Unfortunately, the Hearteater is not easy to have followed. Spies around him tend to die or disappear." Noah shook his head, the gesture the most natural and unconscious one I'd ever seen him make.

"Hearteater? Samir has, like, a title?" Of course he did. Meh.

"He is known by many names," Noah said.

"Well, that leaves dear old bio-dad," I said. Knowing where Samir was didn't help me right now. I couldn't face him without magic. Whatever he was up to was probably really bad, and I wasn't even going to consider giving myself over to him in hopes of saving my friends. I'd had that thought a few times and looked down that road, seeing only ruin. I trusted this vampire more than I would ever trust Samir.

Noah flashed his white, sharp teeth in a smile. "That is where things get complicated."

"Go on," I said, resting my chin on my bent knees.

"Your father is in prison."

"Prison?"

"Oh, it gets better," Noah said. "He is in a secret prison the government runs to lock away dangerous inhuman elements. They also lock up people and creatures they do not understand."

"So, to talk to him, I have to get him out of jail?" I thought about what Noah was saying. Also what he wasn't saying. It didn't sound like a prison that had visiting hours. "What is my father?"

"You are unlikely to believe me if I tell you. Also, that was not in our bargain."

"Really?" I rolled my eyes at him. I knew I should have been more specific, but I was going to have questions, damnit. "This stems right from our bargain and might be relevant. I have to talk to him, but if he's dangerous, I kind of need to know that, don't you think?"

"He is dangerous, though I doubt so to you," Noah said. "He is also in the prison voluntarily. He is in the do-not-understand category and, I am sure, can leave anytime under his own power. The government could hardly stop him."

From the Archivist's smile, I knew there was so much context I was missing in what he was saying. It frustrated me, but punching my host and source of information seemed less than wise. Fun, but maybe not a good option. For now.

"Okay, wise guy, how do I get him out?"

"You don't," Noah said, that sharp smile back and wider than ever. He rose to his feet. "But I believe your assistants are pulling up as we speak. Shall we go meet them, and then we can discuss how to break into this prison, yes?"

"I have assistants?" I said. This whole conversation had run away from me.

"You do now," Noah said as he glided from the room, leaving the door open for me to trail behind, curious and utterly confused.

HARPER

Harper squeezes her hands into damp fists at her sides, shutting down her senses as best she can. She pretends she doesn't hear the faint scrape of a bare foot on the loft floor, the rustle of loose hay being disturbed. Max smells nervous, something he'll have to work on.

The faintest brush against her side and then . . . Bells tinkle and she spins, catching Max's bony wrist in her hands.

"You lose," she says with a snort. "Maybe you aren't cut out to be a thief."

"Uncle Darragh says we got Tinker blood," Max says. His mouth puckers into a pout and freckles stand out on his cheeks like the dots on the exclamation points of his anger.

Harper almost reminds him that he's no blood of theirs at all, much less Uncle Darragh's kin, but she swallows those words. They'll just hurt him, and anyway, who cares where he came from? He's hers now; Mom said so. Her responsibility.

"Maybe," she says with a quick shrug that sets the bells looped over her belt to chiming again. "But you need a lot more practice if we're to run off with the Travelers and steal our way across the world."

"You make it look so easy," Max says, not ready to abandon his grumpy mood.

"That's 'cause I'm older, faster, and prettier than you," she says, and tweaks his nose, leaping back into the hay as he dives for her.

Max tumbles down on top of her and pain radiates up her sternum. Harper gasps and tries to push him away. He rises, kicking her hard in the ribs.

"Max, stop!"

He kicks her again, his face red and distorted through her tears, hardly looking like Max at all. Again, and again, and again. Harper curls up, trying to dodge the blows. Her body won't do more than that, her limbs leaden. Then Max is on top of her, his nails biting into her throat.

"You let me die," he hisses, his little boy's face melting away into a man's as flames ignite in his eyes. "You were supposed to protect me and you let me die."

"Max." Harper tries to choke out his name. "Max."

Consciousness brought only more pain to Harper. Someone all too alive and real, unlike Max, kicked her ribs one last time before standing back as she gasped and choked awake. She peeled one eye open, the other too

ANNIE BELLET

swollen to obey. Her nose already told her at least two men were in the room, and one of them was her brother's killer. No forgetting his scent. Not ever.

"Samir," she said through cracked and bleeding lips.

The floor under her face was old oak boards, rough and splintered from years of use and hard cleaning. It told her only that she could be in one of a hundred old houses or cabins strewn across the edges of the Frank. The air still smelled like her familiar woods underneath the stink of men. Her arms were numb and chained behind her, but she wiggled her toes and felt them respond. Nothing was too broken. A tight collar squeezed her neck, and she guessed it was chained too. No shifting into a fox for her, not right now. Chains were too tight and fox legs didn't bend the same way. What was painful as a human could seriously damage a fox's joints. She didn't see much immediate chance for escape.

Not that there was much to hope for in general. She was alone, hurt, and abandoned.

But not dead yet. In her position, Harper figured she'd take what she could get.

"Harper, my dear," Samir said. "What will I do with you?"

"Come closer," she said, baring her teeth. Her blurred vision gave her a clear view of his boot. Maybe if he came closer, she could gnaw him to death. Brilliant plan.

His boots moved across the floor toward her. Samir crouched down by Harper's shoulder, and she forced her head to turn as much as it could. Nausea and pain put dancing red dots in her vision, but she wanted to look Max's killer in the eye.

He looked clean and composed, dressed in a thick sweater and dark trousers. A small ruby-colored crystalline vial hung from a heavy gold chain, his only jewelry, looking like a cosplayer's necklace and totally out of place against his mundane clothing. A knife, like something out of a survival catalog, rested loosely in his grip. For a moment, Harper's

162

brain froze, fear washing through her and shoving back the pain. Knife. Death. This was the end of the line.

Then sense kicked in. He'd brought her here, wherever here was, tied her up tightly so she couldn't shift, and was talking to her. Whatever his stupid and totally evil plan was, her death wasn't in the cards yet. He wanted something from her or thought he could use her.

That thought filled her with a different kind of fear. Jade and the others had left her, but Harper wasn't crazy or dumb enough to believe they'd meant to. She'd seen the horror on Jade's face. Some plan had gone wrong.

Harper half-chuckled, half-gagged on her own spit and blood at that thought. Everything had gone wrong.

"Something funny?" Samir said. His eyes narrowed into piss-colored slits. Harper refused to think about him in flattering terms like handsome or golden-eyed. He wasn't getting an inch of her brain space that way. Not a bit.

"You," Harper said. "How you still think you can win."

"I've already won," Samir said. He gave a slight shake of his head and his lips twisted into a smirk. "It was never a contest. I thought you'd have noticed that by now."

"If you've won, why am I still alive?" She spat the words out with as much venom, and actual blood, as she could muster, trying to spatter some on his knees. That would show the bastard. *Yeah.*

"You like games, yes? Think of it like chess. The pieces are still on the board, but checkmate will not occur for a few more turns. There is nothing you or anyone else can do about it, but you are all too stubborn or stupid to see the end, so the game must be played out."

Samir grabbed Harper's bloody tee shirt in one hand and started cutting it off her. She tried to crawl away from his touch, but there was nowhere to go. Her arms and legs were hog-tied, her neck cranked cruelly back as well. She was able to squirm an inch before the strain nearly caused her to black out.

"You going to rape me?" she asked. "How fucking stereotypical."

"Rape you? No. I don't fuck animals." Samir gathered the bloody pieces of her shirt into his hand and wiped them over a gash in her stomach. White-hot pain lanced up her belly, and Harper was almost glad she couldn't see her own body very well.

He rose to his feet, and Harper heard what sounded like her shirt remains being put into a plastic bag.

"That should be enough for a trail," Samir said.

"We will backtrack from where we took that one," the other man said. His voice had an accent that sounded similar to Alek's. "We make it look good, they will follow."

"See it done. Be ready. No mistakes this time. No one escapes. There's no more time to waste," Samir said, dismissing the man.

Harper forced her fogged brain into gear. Samir was going to use her bloody shirt to lead the others to her, from the sounds of it. She could draw some assumptions from that, she figured. Her friends were still alive and not being held somewhere else. They also potentially didn't know that she was alive, and they definitely didn't know where she was, though it seemed she was the cheese in Samir's mousetrap.

Good thing none of my friends are mice, Harper thought. They would come for her. She knew that in the marrow of her own tired bones. They hadn't abandoned her.

"You think they'll fall for such an obvious trap?" she asked, fighting to turn her head and shoulders enough to see Samir again. No dice.

His boots moved away, and the sharp citrus and medical smell of cleaning agents wafted through the air. Then he returned, kindly crouching down again and sitting on his heels so she could see his smug-ugly face. *Smugly face, yeah.* He stared down at her, rubbing her blood off his hands fastidiously with a baby wipe.

"They won't have a choice. Jade will come for you. She always comes for those she loves."

"You say that like it's a bad thing."

"It's going to get her killed." Samir lifted one shoulder in a half shrug.

"Hasn't yet," Harper said.

He pressed his lips into a tight line, and she knew that she'd found at least one crack in his disgustingly competent armor.

"You like games such as chess, yeah?" Harper continued.

"I do," Samir answered.

"Then you should kill me now," Harper said.

"I don't follow."

"Zugzwang," Harper said.

"Zugzwang? That's what I am doing. Forcing Jade to come straight to me." His eyes were slits again and his lips curled back from his teeth. Perhaps he thought he was smiling, but there was too much annoyance and frustration in his expression to fool her.

Harper forced another pained chuckle. "Maybe. But in game theory, it's a forced move that turns a win into a loss. That's what is happening. That's what you are doing. Drawing the one person I know can kill you right to you."

"Jade is no threat to me," he said.

"Yet she's out there, alive and kicking." *Please let her be alive and kicking*, Harper added silently.

Samir sighed again. "Not for long. She'll come for you. Or she won't. Perhaps she will run again. It won't matter soon, anyway."

It won't matter soon? So, it does matter now? Why? Harper's desperate mind raced along a million paths. *Got to keep him talking like a Bond villain*, she decided.

"Soon? I thought you said it doesn't matter at all."

"It doesn't. She doesn't. She's just a loose end I should have tied up years ago." Samir rose to his feet.

"What happens soon?" Harper blurted, desperate to keep him talking. She bit the inside of her cheek and craned her head to keep him in sight.

"I become a god," he said, rubbing his thumb along the ruby vial hanging from his neck.

Harper let her head drop. Then Samir's boots moved away, and she heard a door open and close as he left her alone in the room.

Well. Fuck.

CHAPTER THREE ▶

Noah led me down a hallway and then a set of short stairs and into a part of the warehouse that looked like a loading dock. There were a huge metal door slowly rolling down and a small group of people waiting for us. The space looked too big to fit with the footprint of the warehouse, and not for the first time, I wondered what exactly was going on with this place. The vampire had a lot of secrets to protect; I supposed it only made sense that his place of business, and probably his home, was protected by magical as well as material means.

Around me were corrugated metal walls stretching up about twenty feet to a beamed ceiling in shadow overhead. The floor was concrete, clean and grey. Parked just inside the doors, its engine still ticking as it cooled and rainwater condensed on its windshield and hood, was a giant RV. Beside it, a black motorcycle leaned on a kickstand. Arrayed in front of the vehicles were three people. No, four people. I did a double take and felt my cheeks heat up at how obvious I'd just been.

There were two women sharing a wide wheelchair, their bodies joined at the hips, with four arms but only two visible legs. They looked back at me with nearly identical half-smiles, amusement in their dark brown eyes. They looked to be in their mid-twenties and probably Hispanic in ancestry. One had long black hair twisted up in a bun and held with rainbow hair sticks. The other had short hair cut angularly to chin length and dyed a deep green.

Beside the twins were two other people. One was a tall blonde woman who was glaring at Noah. By *tall* I mean well over six feet. She could have given Alek a runoff for tallest blond in the room. On the other side of the wheelchair, hanging back almost in the shadow of the RV, was a slender man with olive skin and light brown hair cut shaggy around his face. I picked male by default because I couldn't tell, honestly. Something about the face said masculine, the angle of his jaw and the thickness of his brows, but I just wasn't sure.

"Archivist," the blonde giant said.

"This is Jade Crow, your client," Noah said, motioning to me. "I am sure you are hungry after your long drive. We can discuss details at dinner. It should be ready now."

"Introductions first, then dinner." The woman looked me over, a real obvious head-to-toe kind of look, and pressed her lips together. I supposed I didn't look like much right now.

"Very well. Jade Crow, this is Kira Kirovna, who will be helping you get to your father," Noah said.

"Jones," Kira said. "Kira Jones." She glared at the vampire, but she was wasting it on his wall-like exterior.

Kirovna was the female surname form of Kirov. Kira. I actually staggered back a single step.

Ice-blue eyes. Check. White-blond hair, check. Giant height, check. Overwhelming attitude of superiority and confidence? Check, check, check.

"You're Alek's sister," I blurted.

She snarled, full-on lips-back-from-teeth, wild-animal kind of snarling. Next to Kira, the green-haired twin reached out a hand as though to restrain her.

"How do you know my brother?" Her eyes went to icy slits, another facial expression I knew so well. Even if Noah hadn't "slipped" and said her last name, I was pretty sure I'd have figured out quickly who she was.

I hesitated for a moment, staring at her, calculating my answer. Then I mentally said *fuck it* and told the truth. I was too damn tired to play games, and I wasn't going to let the vampire suck me into this weird social situation, whatever this was.

Vampire. Suck. Yeah, I was tired.

"I'm his mate," I said.

She laughed. Not a nice laugh, either, though it was full-bellied and loud. She walked toward me and I held my ground. Without magic to defend myself, watching a tiger—even one in human form—stalk toward me was unnerving. Running away seemed like a stupid idea, though.

"You are telling the truth," she said as she towered over me. "Alek. And a human."

"I'm not a human," I muttered.

Kira leaned toward me almost as if she was going to kiss me and took a deep breath. "No, you certainly aren't," she said, twisting a bit of her hair around one gloved finger. "What are you?"

"We can discuss this over dinner," Noah said. His tone was steel, and even Kira, after glancing at him, didn't argue, instead nodding curtly.

Turning my back on her and following Noah out of that room was nerve-racking. I figured this was going to be the best dinner party ever.

Dinner was laid out in yet another room I hadn't seen. There was a huge table that looked like something out of a medieval war room, its dark wood scarred and shined from years of use. I don't know what kind of food I expected, maybe a seven-course meal with complex French names, but instead, we had fried chicken piled on platters, a huge bowl of mashed potatoes, and a plate of biscuits. There was enough chicken to feed an army.

Or, as it turned out, a small group of hungry shifters and one sort of ex-sorceress.

ANNIE BELLET

The conjoined twins wheeled up next to me at the table. The slender man took the seat across from us. Noah took the head of the table at the end away from the food, leaving the other end seat or a side seat across from the twins to Kira. She took the end of the table and pulled off her leather jacket, draping it over the chair. She was wearing a black tee shirt underneath that said EVIL DEAD on it with a hand reaching up.

"You a fan of horror movies?" I asked her. I was going to be super amused if Alek's sister was a nerd.

She raised an eyebrow and went back to ignoring me in favor of stuffing her face with chicken.

The twins introduced themselves as Cora, the dark-haired one, and Alma, the green-haired one. They both had slight accents that, plus their names, reaffirmed my assumption of Hispanic heritage.

"We're jaguar shifters," Cora added. "If you were curious."

I was. I opened and then closed my mouth on a lot of questions that really were none of my business. Like, how did they shift when they were joined together? Were they two jaguars when shifted?

"I'm Jaq, with a *Q*," the man across from me said. He inclined his head slightly.

In the brighter light of the dining room, I still couldn't quite make up my mind about his gender, but I reached for chicken and decided it didn't matter. I'd ask him later, if we had a chance to talk, what pronoun he preferred. I had a suspicion that it wouldn't be the first time someone was unsure. I figured it was best to just approach things directly.

We ate in near-silence under the watchful and, if I was reading his mostly flat expression correctly, amused eye of the vampire. If the circumstances hadn't been so strange, my own situation so dire, and my brain so exhausted, I might have found it funny. Here I was, eating dinner with a six-foot-six giant blonde tiger and a set of twins. It was like a bizarro-world version of my life.

Only, in this world, I had no guardian, no magic, and still had a psycho

170

ex who wanted to kill me. I felt a deep pang for all I had lost and quickly threw it into a mental black box.

Most of the food vanquished, Noah finally got down to details.

"I have brought Kira and her team here," he said, addressing me, "to help you get to your father. I believe they are uniquely equipped for this."

"He means *insane enough to do jobs for a vampire*," Kira said. She had no trace of Alek's Russian accent. "And, I'm guessing, the only people he could find on short notice."

"Alek said you were a bounty hunter or something?" I said.

Her lip curled. She really hated hearing his name. I wondered what their falling-out had been. Alek hadn't said much, but nothing in his words about her had led me to believe it was something super serious. Of course, when you don't talk to a sibling for a decade, I should have guessed it *was* serious.

"Sometimes." Alma jumped in. "Mostly, we solve problems."

"Jade has a problem," Noah said. "She needs to get into a very secure facility to talk to her father."

"Wait, we're not breaking him out?" I asked.

"No," the Archivist said. His toothy smile was back. "We're breaking you in."

"That's what she said," Cora stage-whispered with a giggle.

Kira shot the twins a suppressing glare. "What prison? Where?"

"It doesn't have a name, but some call it Custer due to the location. It is in South Dakota, Harding County."

"A prison without a name? This sounds peachy as fuck." Kira wiped her fingers on an already-greasy napkin and then folded her arms over her chest.

"It's a secure facility for supernatural beings, run by a shadow organization inside the government. Jade's father is in there. Not," he said, holding up a palm in the universal shut-up-and-wait gesture, "because he did anything. But because he chose to be. He is, my source tells me, asleep, and has been for over forty years."

"He's been . . . asleep?" I looked at Noah, wondering why he hadn't told me this earlier. "For practically my whole life?" The chicken and potatoes I'd eaten turned to lumps in my stomach.

"That is why you must go," Noah said. "I believe he will awaken for you."

"You believe? But you don't know?" I pressed. Visions did a jig in my head of going through whatever mad scheme we'd have to go through to even get into this place and then ending up sitting there as humans in riot suits stormed after me while my father slept on, oblivious.

"Secure government prison for supernatural things?" Kira stood up. "No. That's a bag of nope tied with a nope bow and with a big fat nope cherry on top."

Wow, Alek's sister really was a nerd. I was willing to bet he had no idea. In a non-bizarro world, Kira and I might have been friends. I filed that into the sad thoughts file, which was overflowing lately into a sad thoughts filing cabinet.

I stood too. It did sound insane; I didn't blame her for thinking so at all. But . . . I had no choice. I stepped in front of her, which was one of the more terrifying things I'd ever done in my life.

"If you don't help me," I said, "there's a better than good chance Alek will die." Technically, he already had.

She looked down at me with eyes colder than I'd ever seen Alek's. "I don't care," she said, biting off the words one by one. Then she shoved me aside and stormed out the door.

Jaq rose. "I'll talk to her," he said, walking around the table to follow her out.

I stood there, back against the wall, breathing hard and trying not to start smashing tableware. Eventually, the twins turned their chair, catching my attention, and looked at me.

"You really his mate?" Cora asked.

"Really," I said. I missed him like hell right then, even worse than before. "What happened between them?"

"He killed a friend of ours," Alma said after a moment and a heavy glance exchanged with her twin. Her lips pressed into a pale line.

"As Justice," Cora added. She ran a nervous hand through her green hair, spiking it up in different directions.

I realized she meant Alek's role. Justice. Something else he'd likely lost because of me. I started to say something like *He wouldn't do that* but shut my mouth. Alek would, I knew. He'd have a reason, of course, and I doubted their friend had clean hands if a Justice had been sent after them, but . . . I knew Alek. We'd met with him accusing me of murder, after all. He would always do what he felt was right, no matter the consequences.

Noah reentered the room before I could frame a response or another question, making me realize I'd never even seen him leave.

"Kira has agreed to stay the night and hear out my inside man in the morning," he said. "There is a room for everyone if you want it, though she claims you will all stay in your vehicle." The vampire's nose wrinkled slightly as he said that, as though he could hardly imagine why anyone would choose an RV over a proper bed.

"Yeah, we're good," Cora said. "We can find our way back." She and her twin took the hint and left the room.

I followed Noah again down another hallway that could have been the same or different from any of the others I'd come down. This place was a maze, which I guessed was intentional. He showed me to a small room that had a single bed and an attached bath with shower. My backpack was already there, sitting on a padded bench at the foot of the bed.

"Sleep, Jade," he said, his voice and expression almost gentle. "I will wake you when the druid arrives."

"What if Kira won't help me?" I asked. I didn't want to sleep, though my body certainly did. It was definitely in healing mode, begging me for rest even though I'd spent a lot of time sleeping the last two days. Or maybe three days? I was losing track of time. How long had everyone been out there, running and hiding, without me?

"She will," Noah said. "She is hardly in a position to turn down what I offer her. Leave the tiger to me." He left, closing the door behind him.

That didn't sound ominous at all. Nope. I let it go. I took a long shower, not letting myself cry, and then changed into clean-ish clothing before lying down on the bed. Sleep took forever to find me. It brought only worry and nightmares, and no rest at all.

HARPER

Harper knew she must have passed out for a while. The pain in her abdomen had faded, which hopefully meant the gash she'd felt earlier but couldn't see had closed finally. Her head still throbbed like someone had wrapped it in a towel and beaten her with a sack of oranges, but opening her eyes to the dim light didn't make her want to barf anymore. She knew from smell and sound that she was alone in the room. Somewhere beyond the wall at her back, she heard the cry of a chickadee.

So, there were likely evergreens nearby. Harper filed that information away and twisted her neck as best she could, taking in the room now that she was alone and conscious enough to evaluate.

She was in a windowless wooden box, as far as she could tell, with a bolt screwed into the floor behind her anchoring the collar and chain around her neck. There were tiny wood shavings and lighter wood around the base of the bolt, so it was probably a new addition to the room. Biting her blood-crusted lip, Harper managed to spin a few degrees. A cheap card table stood against the wall near the door. Only one door. Her way out.

She'd read stories of foxes chewing off their limbs to escape snares, but her mouth wouldn't reach her shoulder, so that lame plan was totally out. Harper flexed her wrists, testing the strength of the cuffs. They felt like heavy iron, and the sound that issued from them as she twisted her hands experimentally confirmed it. She lay still, heart pounding in her throat, waiting to see if anyone came to the too-loud sound of clanking chain and metal, but the house seemed eerily quiet.

Twisting her hands had opened the scabs on her wrists, renewing the sharp pains and waking up blood-starved appendages with the death of a thousand needles. Harper twisted some more, her shoulders screaming a protest she ignored, and felt her hands start to slip as her skin pulled and tore. More blood. That was what she needed. Slippery, beautiful blood.

They stretched and strained in the darkness, Harper quoted to herself as a distraction, channeling her inner Bess, *and the hours crawled by like years.* No one was coming for her by moonlight, not if she had anything to say about it. *And everyone figured poetry was a useless life skill.*

Her left hand came free of its cuff with a sickening, moist pop. She was able to turn fully on her side and use the sore hand to free her still-trapped right one, gouging into her own wrist until her thumb dislocated with another moist, grinding pop.

Hands. She had them now. Such as they were. Harper lost a few minutes to lying on the floor, breathing through the pain. She wanted to shift to her fox self and get away from it, but her neck and feet were still trapped. One step at a time.

Un-dislocating a thumb was not as simple as it looked in the movies. She managed to jam it back into position, but her right hand was an aching mess that didn't want to obey her commands. *Fat fucking patootie,* she told it silently. She had work to do. She felt along the collar with her left hand and got lucky. It was a bolt mechanism, with a metal pin tucked through to hold it in place. Clearly, Samir hadn't expected her to be able to get her hands free and unlock herself.

She wanted to fling the stupid collar across the room, but she carefully lowered it to the floor with as little noise as she could. Her feet were still chained to the collar and cuffs, and bolted into the floor. She'd been put into a rough hog-tie, the chains intersecting and locked together at the ankles.

Unfortunately, the manacles on her ankles weren't bolt-and-pin but sported a pair of heavy iron locks keeping the chain affixed to them. Harper allowed herself exactly three deep, aching breaths of freak-out time looking at the stupid locks, then realized her fox ankles would slip right out of them now that her body wasn't contorted into crazy positions.

"Total failfish," she muttered.

She reached into the Veil, letting her human body slide away into warm grey mist and her fox body emerge. She remembered the pain of the bear's teeth ripping into her flank, but enough time must have passed, because while she was sore, her body felt whole and her legs slipped easily out of the manacles. It would have taken at least two days to heal this much in the mists. Harper pushed that thought away. Worrying about her friends wouldn't get her out of this house. One panic attack at a time was enough.

More smells and sounds flooded her senses now that Harper could think without the pain from her human self distracting her. Shifter musk, wolf and bear, lingered in the air. A slightly cooler breeze caught her attention, coming from what she'd thought was a solid wall behind her.

There was a window in the room, she discovered, but it was nailed over with a thick piece of plywood. Harper considered trying to get it loose and escape that way, but her ears picked up slight movement and the vibration of voices coming from beneath her. She'd probably pushed her luck with the chains in terms of noise. A huge piece of wood being pried off a window wouldn't be silent.

Most of the old cabins and farmhouses around the Frank were no more than two stories, so there was that, at least. Harper slunk up to the door and pressed her nose to the crack beneath it. She smelled nothing but drying mud, faint shifter musk, and citrus cleaner fluid. No one seemed to be moving around upstairs, but she waited another full count of sixty. If there was a sentry outside the door, he'd have shifted his weight, she thought. She still heard nothing close by.

Pulling her human form back sucked balls, but she couldn't open the door with her fox paws—not quietly, at any rate. Her right hand throbbed and wouldn't grip the doorknob, so Harper gently turned it with her left. It was unlocked and didn't appear to have any wicked spells on it, either.

Praise Jeebus for hubris, I guess.

Harper eased the door open, wincing as the old hinges squealed. She hovered in the doorway, taking in a narrow view of a hallway. She was at the end of it, two rooms off to the right, one off to the left that smelled like a bathroom, a linoleum floor starting just over the threshold. Beyond the room to the left was a stairway down. She slid out of the room, trying not to touch anything and leave more of a blood trail than she had to, and carefully closed the door behind her.

Slipping back into her fox form, Harper crept down the hall, pausing every few steps to listen, nose in the air, wary of any sign of Samir or the men with him. She pressed her nose to the bottom of the first door on the right, picking up stronger musk smells. Bear shifter, probably the big white bastard who had bitten her ass. No sound, though. She guessed this room was used for sleeping or something and decided not to risk opening the door.

The second room smelled strongly of Samir. His honey-sweet, almost-cold scent irritated her nose and made her growl. She stayed away from that door, guessing that he'd put some kind of ward like Jade used on his own room. That would be a bad way out.

Harper flattened herself to the floor at the top of the stairs and poked her head over. The stairwell was unlit, but enough light filtered in from the hall and the window in the bathroom to let her make out a door at the base, which was closed. Light and shadow flickered under the uneven seam of the door and a soft male laugh filtered up. Definitely people down there.

Harper backed up along the hallway to the bathroom, the one room she hadn't explored yet. It dated the house to the 1970s with its yellow-and-green patterned linoleum and lime green bath and shower combination.

But it had a half-size window over the toilet. A window with a latch. Harper took a deep breath and then pulled on her human form again. She was getting dizzy from going back and forth between injured, aching human and mostly healed fox. It was annoying. All her human form wanted to do was rest in the mist and heal itself. Not today. *Biblethump*.

She eased the bathroom door closed and flipped the lock, hoping if anyone came up there, they would assume it was a compatriot inside and not an escaped prisoner. Gritting her teeth, she climbed up on the toilet and used both hands to force the iced-over window open. Cold air blasted her face, clearing some of the pain fog from her mind. It also reminded her she was about to jump out a second-story window in only ripped jeans and a bra. Classic.

Harper narrowed her eyes against the freezing air and the bright daylight. It was late afternoon, she guessed, the pale winter sun dipping behind the house. So, she was facing west. It wasn't much, but it was something. Immediately below her was snow piled up where it had been dumped off the roof. A few skeletal bushes dotted the snow beyond, and then it was open space for a good two hundred feet until huge pine trees rose up. Harper didn't see any movement or sentries posted here, though the chill air carried voices to her from somewhere very nearby.

Now or never, she told herself. No reason to stay. Dangerous to drop like this, but the alternative was sit there and wait for someone to find her. Terribad choices all around. If she could get to the trees, she stood a chance.

Sure, she thought. *A chance against a sorcerer and a pack of mercenary wolves and shit. 'Cause I'm an expert woodsman.*

These were her woods, at least. She didn't know the Frank completely, nobody could, but these woods felt familiar enough to give her hope. She doubted they were too far outside Wylde. If she could get away, she would deal with the next issue of figuring out where to go. *First steps go first.*

Harper sucked in a painful breath, dragged herself up into the window, and tried to lever out over the side. Her injured hand gave out from under her and she tumbled forward, headfirst, at the snow. She reached for her fox in midair, twisting even as her other body took over. Her landing would have made a cat laugh, but she slammed into the snow mostly feetfirst, the fresh powder just enough over the more-packed snow to cushion her fall. The bush under it wasn't too thrilled, branches crackling beneath the snowpack.

She lay in the snow for a moment to catch her breath and listen. Movement drew her eyes to the treeline. A huge wolf emerged from the trees, and Harper's heart stopped beating for a long moment as he seemed to look directly at her. She was a shifter fox, oversized for her animal and bright freaking red. No snow coat for her. Snow had half-buried her, but she wasn't sure it would be enough. Any minute, he'd start howling. The bloody, crushing jaws of the white bear danced through her memory.

Then the wolf turned and loped to the side, moving along the edge of the woods. He hadn't seen her. She didn't dare cut out into the unbroken snow behind the house, however. Wolves, like many predators, liked to sight-hunt. Movement would catch his eye faster than anything she could do.

Carefully, Harper let herself slip backward in the snowbank until her butt pressed up against the house. She twisted and gained better footing, her ears flicking about to catch any sign she had been noticed. Hugging the house, she slunk through the snow to peer around the corner.

The coast here was clear; the muddy, snowy ground around it was chewed up and filthy from vehicles and boots. Three SUVs were pulled up next to a long driveway. Movement in the trees beyond the cars caught her eye, and Harper picked out the shape of another wolf. His back was to her, his job clearly to watch the woods, not the camp, but she pressed herself down against the snow and shivered.

Too many sentries. She wasn't sure how to get out of there, how to reach the woods. The snow she was in was too white, Harper realized. If she could get to the mud, she would at least blend in there a little better. Keeping an eye on the sentry, she crept across terrifyingly open ground to the nearest vehicle and slunk under it, flattening herself near a tire where the shadows and dirt would hide her. The SUV one over from her hiding spot had a minor gas leak, her nose told her. Not super useful, but it might conceal her smell as she hid there.

She lay there, warm inside her thick fur, ears twitching to gather information from behind her, her eyes focused on the wolf ahead of her. The distance to the trees here was maybe a hundred and fifty feet. All open ground. Probably a field in the summer, but now it was half frozen mud and half pristine, deep snow with only a few trails marring it where the wolves had moved through on patrol. She heard low voices and people moving behind her and sank even flatter to the ground.

After a long moment, Harper made herself twist around and look the other way, though she hated turning her back on the wolf. Ahead of her now was the front of the house. It gave her no information, looking, as she'd suspected, like any one of a couple dozen ramshackle places built edging the Frank during good times and gone to let for hikers and the like in recent years, if they didn't just stand completely boarded and vacant. There was a slouching porch with two chairs on it, one occupied by a big man in a green parka. Cigar smoke wafted toward Harper, and in the slowly dying daylight, she saw the cherry glow in his hand. The white bear, she thought, unconsciously baring her teeth.

There was a gravel drive that had been plowed leading into trees beyond her line of sight, and more vehicles, two big trucks and a domestic sedan, parked across the way. The trucks had big cages in their beds, heavy metal contraptions that reminded Harper of her first and only trip to the circus. She'd hated seeing the big cats crammed into things like that. Max had too; he'd cried and wailed the whole time until the babysitter brought them home and vowed never to do Rosie a favor again.

Thinking about Max brought the void screaming up in her mind, and she pushed the black pit of despair down. No time for that. This is was time for escaping. Then she could find the cavalry, figure out the plan, and come back to enact terrible, murdering revenge on the bastard who had killed her brother.

She refocused, picking out more details. Beyond the trucks on the far side of the house, a makeshift corral had been erected out of silvered barbed wire. The corral was empty, but the gate stood open like a mouth expecting a meal. Harper shuddered again. She didn't want to know what Samir had planned for that. Just looking at it made her sick inside.

The whir of a truck engine broke the quiet. Two more wolves loped up the road ahead of a large truck pulling an enclosed trailer. Three more men came out of the house, pulling on coats as they tramped down the drive to meet it. Harper slowly turned her head and watched as the wolf that had been on sentry behind her made a beeline for the house, his attention on the incoming vehicle and not the woods.

He passed a dozen feet from where she lurked. The coast behind her looked clear. Time to go.

Except. The truck.

What was in the truck? What if it was one of her friends, or all of them? She'd been in and out of consciousness for at least a day, probably more. Enough time for Samir to spring his trap, maybe.

Harper turned back to the action at the front of the house. Curiosity was apparently going to kill the fox, too. It was probably just Samir coming back, and that would make everything more dangerous. But she had to know.

The big man got up from his spot on the porch, leaving his cigar burning in a tin ashtray on the railing. Behind the truck, the trailer shook as though something inside were putting up a fight. The truck came to a stop near the house, and Samir climbed out of the passenger side.

"Careful," Samir warned his men as they converged on the trailer. "You all can look your fill later. Get the package secure in the paddock first."

"Where's Dal?" the big man asked, looking from Samir to the man coming around the truck from the driver's seat.

"He did not make it," Samir said with a casual lift of his shoulders. "He was slow."

"Unicorns got him, but he kept them off us, did his job," the driver added. He was a younger man with brown hair and wind-chapped skin, with a flat, cautious voice. He gave the big man a tense nod.

Unicorn. Unicorn. Oh, no.

Harper watched with growing horror as two men muscled a small white body free of the trailer, half dragging him with chains hooked to a thick, silvery wire halter. The unicorn was a colt and, she was guessing, born recently, though the lifespan and growth rate of unicorns weren't something she'd ever put skill points into. But she knew horses, and he looked maybe two months old at most. Past the initial super-awkward stage but still small and weak. He had a nub instead of a horn, and he was trying to put his teeth into anyone he could reach, snorting and neighing when they jerked his head to the side.

"Careful! I need him alive for Balor," Samir said. "Get him to the paddock."

The paddock was on the opposite side of the house from her. Everyone was watching the struggle with the baby unicorn. Harper doubted they'd notice if she danced across the open ground to the woods naked with theme music playing.

Harper looked behind her with longing and then sighed. Whatever Samir was up to, this seemed important to him. He'd mentioned Balor, too, which rang a lot of alarms in Harper's mind. They'd had a hell of a time shutting down the Fomorian before—what if Samir planned to open his Eye again? Or something worse. With Samir, she was willing to bet on *worse*. The unicorns helped safeguard the wilds. If Samir wanted one alive and trapped, there was probably nefarious, awful reasoning behind it.

Besides, in the end, it came down to WWMD. *What would Max do?* He'd save the damn unicorn. She knew it in her bones.

So, that's what she was going to do. Be a big damn crazy hero.

Harper looked around, taking in her resources, and came up with a really stupid plan. *Time to kick ass and take screenshots.*

CHAPTER FOUR

I was awake long before Noah tapped on the door and led me to the sitting room with the couch and two chairs. He left me at the door with a nod.

Walking in, I saw Yosemite standing by the couch. The huge druid's hair was tangled, and his multicolored eyes, one green, one blue, had bags under them that spoke volumes about how much rest he was getting. I hadn't realized until I saw him how close to the precipice of losing my shit I was. Seeing him there, alive and more or less well, dragged back the memory of his death, the images of all of my friends dying.

I failed my willpower save and practically threw myself into his arms, clinging tight to his barrel chest, breathing in his scent of snow and pine.

"Jade," he said softly, patting my back with a gentle hand. "What happened? The spell had you—why aren't you with us? Why are you here?"

It felt like pulling two strong magnets apart to step away from him, but I managed.

"Sit," I said. I had to decide how much to tell him. But first, I had to know the things I'd been dreading.

Yosemite sat on the couch and raised a red-gold eyebrow at me.

"Is everyone—I mean . . ." I said, but couldn't get the full question out.

I already knew everyone wasn't okay. But I wanted to keep hoping, just for a moment.

"Alek, Ezekiel, Levi, Rosie, and Junebug are safe in a grove of mine. Freyda and her surviving wolves are around as well." The druid took a deep breath as though he would say more, but instead he held it, staring at me. With him sitting down, we almost were eye to eye.

Junebug was safe. "Junebug is okay?" I said, avoiding the nine-hundred-pound gorilla in the room. Or, really, the fox. "I saw her get shot."

"Freyda's wolves found her, brought her to me in time for me to heal her. She's still injured but should recover. Shifters are strong." His smile was faint and faded quickly, like a flash of sunlight peeking out from a storm cloud.

"And Harper?" I asked, forcing myself to say the words.

Yosemite shook his head, shadows filling his eyes. "We don't know," he said, letting out another long, sighing breath.

I thunked down into the chair and closed my eyes. Harper's face was waiting for me there in the darkness behind my lids. Her green eyes wide with pain and betrayal as we left her behind. *I'm so sorry, furball*, I whispered to her in my head. Then what Yosemite had said sank in and my eyes popped open.

"Wait, what do you mean, you don't know?" I looked at him, trying to squash my thin hopes. He hadn't said *she's dead*, after all. "I saw her get shot," I added. "I saw her being left behind, out of range of your magic."

"I know," he said. Yosemite stared down at his big, tattooed hands and gave a small shake of his head. "In the forest we found pieces of Harper's shirt, covered in blood. Freyda scouted back to the grove where the fight was. Harper's body isn't there."

"Samir could have her," I whispered. I didn't know if this was worse or better.

"He could," Yosemite said. "Or he could have her body, though the shifters swear the blood was fresh, not days old."

I stood up and paced the length of the small room, clenching and unclenching my fists until my fingers cramped. Harper could be alive. Alive and held hostage by my psychotic ex. Noah knew where Samir was; he'd said as much. Which meant, if Harper was alive, we could go get her.

"It's a trap, Jade," Yosemite said. His voice held a weariness in it that made me wonder if he'd been arguing the same thing with Alek and my friends. They wouldn't want to leave Harper in Samir's hands any more than I did.

"You think I don't fucking know that?" I said, spinning around. I made a face at my own tone. "Sorry," I muttered.

"We're all under a lot of stress." Yosemite managed a smile, his teeth flashing through his beard.

"I'm guessing they want to go get her?" I asked.

"Ezee and Levi, yes. Alek and I, no. Rosie, well . . ." He shrugged, splaying his hands. "If she wasn't hurt and if Junebug didn't need her, I think she'd go herself."

Rosie would want to go get her daughter, but she was also one of the most pragmatic people I'd ever known. She wouldn't want anyone else risking themselves.

"They can't fight Samir," I said. "It isn't a matter of *should* or *shouldn't*. They cannot."

"I believe we learned that lesson quite well," Yosemite said, putting a tiny bit of bite into his tone. "What are you doing here, Jade?" Leaving unspoken, of course, the whole "why the hell did you abandon everyone after making me take us away from a fight before we even found out if we could win" part of the sentence.

It was okay. I caught the subtext.

"It's complicated," I said by way of non-answer to buy myself a few precious seconds to think. I had no idea how much to tell him. Anything I said would probably get back to my friends, to Alek. I needed them safe.

How safe will they be, going after Harper without you with them?

"Jade?" Yosemite tipped his head to one side and his eyes narrowed. "Your magic? Your aura is changed somewhat."

I took a deep breath. "I am going to tell you what I'm doing, at least what I can. But you have to promise me, Iollan," I said, using his given name instead of the nickname we all called him by. "You cannot tell this to the others. Not even Alek."

"Not even that you are alive?" He shook his head.

"You can tell them that, if you must. But not where I am or what I'm doing. No specifics. Only that they must wait for me. They cannot go after Samir. Cannot. Samir is trying to draw me with Harper as bait, if she's alive. That means he'll keep her alive for now. They cannot go after her, or they'll just become more bait. Or die. I doubt that bastard thinks he needs more than a couple pieces to hook me."

Harper is enough. Alek would be more than enough. It wasn't a pretty thought to consider how expendable or not your friends were. I glared at the druid, trying to beam how serious I was into his brain.

He pressed his lips together and gave another head-shake. "Fine."

I didn't know if I believed his promise, but in the end, it didn't matter.

"The fight with Samir didn't go quite how you think. The short version is that I used the power of the nodes to turn back time, because we all died. Everybody. That's when I yelled at you to get us out. Doing that, though, it burned me out." I held up a hand to stall his questions. "That's why I'm here. I had a vision, of a sort, and Noah is going to help me get my magic back, as well as maybe find a way to defeat Samir so that we all don't just die again."

"You turned back time?" Yosemite put his head in his hands.

"It's okay if you don't believe me," I said. It was a big pill to swallow, even with our magical experience.

"Oh, I believe you," he said. "But you've changed the world, Jade. No possibility you haven't. Not with magic like that."

"I don't know about the world," I said, rubbing my thumb over the mystery divot in my talisman. "Just the future. I hope. Now isn't exactly the time for a debate about the long-term effects. I'm more worried about everyone being alive next week."

"I will keep them safe," Yosemite said, rising to his impressive seven-foot height. "But your friends are not helpless."

"I know," I said, mentally adding that they weren't except against Samir. It wasn't Yosemite's job to protect them from my ex. It was mine. So, I shut up.

"Good luck, Jade Crow." Yosemite opened his arms.

I hugged him again. "Iollan," I said softly as he pulled away. "If you do have to tell them you saw me . . ." I hesitated.

"Yes?"

"Tell Alek I love him. Tell him to trust me." I bit my lip. "Please," I added.

"I will. Come back safe, and soon." Yosemite walked toward the door, which opened immediately as he reached it.

Noah stood in the hall. "Our other guest is here," he said. "And breakfast is served."

"Iollan," I said to the retreating druid's back.

He stopped and turned, looking at me expectantly.

"Just . . . stay safe," I muttered. There was so much more I wanted to say, but the words clogged in my throat. For a moment, I almost begged him to take me back with him, but I had work to do there. My best chance seemed to lie in being away from my friends. I had to cling to the plan, such as it was.

Yosemite nodded, a sad, understanding smile crinkling the corners of his eyes. Then he walked down the hall and I followed Noah instead, heading to breakfast and an unknown future.

HARPER

Harper slunk across the frozen ground back to the edge of the house, waiting for shouts of discovery or bullets or fireballs or worse. Though she doubted Samir would throw a fireball at the house. She had yet to see him pull any of the really obvious magic that Jade liked so much. He was more of the brutally-hurting-people-and-being-evil kind of sorcerer.

With those comforting thoughts, she crept up to the porch and peeked up over the deck. Everyone was still busy with the unicorn. So far, so good. She popped up on her hind legs and snatched the still-burning cigar from the ashtray. Tobacco acid burned her sensitive tongue, reaffirming a lifelong commitment to never smoke the shit. She tucked tail and ran along the edge of the house until she felt it was safe to dart back under the cars.

No shouts or fireballs or bullets yet.

Stealth check, total success.

Harper dropped the cigar as carefully as she could onto the frozen mud. It kept smoldering. She shifted back to human, red dots swimming in her vision as her battered human body brought back all its pain, and picked up the cigar again. This part would need opposable thumbs.

On her belly, she crawled to the car with the gas leak and rolled over, suppressing a groan. There. She guessed that salt on the roads had rusted out a little of the undercarriage. The leak was tiny, but Harper intended to fix that if her nipples didn't freeze off first. Without fur or even a shirt, she felt the full brunt of the Idaho winter.

Once again throwing a nervous glance toward the crowd around the paddock, she laid down the cigar, propping it on a tire edge to keep it burning, tapping the ash off as she did so. The cherry was fading, so she took a quick, acrid drag of it, spitting the smoke out quickly and suppressing a cough.

Keeping her eyes on Samir and the mercenaries, she felt around for a rock and dug it out of the half-frozen mud with her less-injured left hand. Then she went to work on the gas leak, rubbing the rock as quietly as possible against the rust. It felt like it took forever, but the damp smear of gas became a drip even as the unicorn was wrestled into the paddock and Samir ordered everyone out. It looked like he was doing something at the gate, which worried Harper when she risked another glance, but she shoved all worries away. Part two was her focus now. No thinking ahead. Too much danger she'd remember what a dumb idea this was.

She let the gas drip into the mud, digging a little channel for it. The fumes were the most flammable, she remembered vaguely from chemistry. Harper started to wish she'd spent less time programming games into her TI-86 and more time actually studying. Her rough plan was that the cigar would ignite the fuel and travel up the fumes to the gas tank. She had no idea what would happen then but didn't care as long as it created a distraction.

Go time. Harper laid the cigar next to the pool of gas and backed out from under the SUV, moving quickly under the next vehicle over. She shifted back to fox form and headed along the back edge of the house, tense and ready to go. People were leaving the paddock, Samir and the big bear man moving for the porch, sentries heading out into the snow again, back in wolf form.

For a long moment, nothing happened. She almost went back to check on her distraction, afraid there weren't enough vapors or the cigar had burned out. Way her luck had been going, it probably had.

Come on, real life, she thought desperately; *for once, just be like the movies*. She just wanted one fucking break.

Shouts rang out like gospel music to her ears.

"Car's on fire," someone yelled.

"Grab a hose."

"Boss, sir!"

Harper saw no one around the paddock anymore. She didn't know how long she had, especially since she realized even as she bolted for the fence that she hadn't thought about how a mage could probably squash a fire real quick. Hopefully, he was worn out from capturing the unicorn. Even he had to have limits.

Not looking back, she darted under the fence, half waiting for her skin to fry off with a magic trap or something. The unicorn colt turned and snorted, shaking his haltered head. Betting that he wouldn't kick her, Harper went right up to him and then dared to look back at the house.

Black smoke billowed up, from burning tires Harper guessed, and metal screeched and whined as the SUV went up in flames almost good enough for a Vin Diesel movie. Burning debris smashed into the cars next to it. Nobody was near Harper or even looking in that direction.

Harper shifted to human and murmured softly at the unicorn to hold still. To her surprise, he pressed his soft nose into her palm, trusting. She doubted he'd been born when they'd saved the unicorns a few months before, but maybe his parents had passed on word that Harper and her folk were good. Or maybe he was smart enough to recognize any port in a storm.

The colt was pure white, but this close, Harper saw that his hair was blackened as though singed under the silver wire of the halter. *New step one: removing that.* It was constructed like a rope halter, a single thick strand that was looped around his nose and over the ears, all held with a knot under the chin. She took a deep breath and started pulling on the knot.

Her fingers burned as though she'd grabbed a handful of hot coals, but Harper mentally added it to the list of physical suckitude and kept working the knot. It came free all at once and the halter fell away to the ground.

The colt snorted and turned, making for the fence. Harper looked at the gate, saw the thick, intricately woven silver chain on it, and past it the mass of people slowly containing the fire as Samir played director from the porch. Seeing all that, she quickly went over to the unicorn. The fence hadn't stopped her from going under, and the unicorn was pretty small, so she had a vague hope she could lift the wires or lift him over.

The barbed wire was looped to fence posts and looked standard feed-store issue but had a small modification as she examined it more closely. More of the silver wire was braided through it. Her burning hands didn't want to grab it again, but she was this fucking close to freedom and wasn't about to let acidic pain stop her now. Harper reached for the bottom strand.

The unicorn jumped the fence, popping into the air as though he had wings and landing on the other side in a tiny puff of snow. He looked back at her with another snort as though to ask what she was doing still in there.

"You're welcome," she muttered. Then she was fox again, slipping her body under the fence.

"No! Stop them!" A terrible shout rang across the open field as Harper charged through the snow after the colt. Her luck had run out.

The colt ran across the top of the snow like an elf straight out of *Lord of the Rings*. Harper floundered along behind him in the deepening snow, struggling to get to the trees. *We make it out of this, I'm naming you Legolas*, she silently told the baby unicorn.

A wolf charged her from the right, barreling through the snow. She barked warning at the unicorn, mentally willing him to keep going, to get to the trees. He was a lot faster than she. If she saved him plus stuck it to Samir in doing so, it was all worth it.

The first bullet zipped over her head close enough, she felt as much as heard it miss her. The second hit her in the ass, tumbling her forward.

Then the wolf was on her. Harper snapped at him, catching his foreleg, but got only a mouthful of fur. His jaws closed on her back, tearing white-hot gashes across her barely healed flank. She was big for a fox, but he was huge for a wolf. His powerful jaws lifted her right out of the snow and he shook her like a rat.

Her last thought as snow and sunlight turned to pain and darkness was that she should have been born a tiger.

CHAPTER FIVE

Breakfast was in the same room where we'd had dinner. Apples, bananas, bacon, hard-boiled eggs, and Old Fashioned donuts were piled on the table this time. From the depleted platter of bacon, it looked like everyone else had gotten a head start on me.

I was relieved to see Kira and her crew. If they were still there, hopefully it meant they would help.

The other person at the table surprised me. He was a Hispanic male in his mid-thirties, with short brown hair and deceptively sleepy brown eyes. His suit was different from the last one I'd seen Agent Salazar wearing, but it had the same kind of understated tailored cut. I'd last seen him in Wylde, after walking naked out of a fire that had destroyed my game store.

"Salazar," I said, taking a seat across from him. "We meet again."

He was seated where I had been the night before, next to the twins. Kira had the head of the table again. I glanced at Jaq as I sat, nodding a greeting.

"The Archivist told you I was coming?" he said. "You don't seem surprised."

"He didn't," I said, grabbing a donut and an egg. "But you being a special agent of some unspecified secret agency, combined with us needing information about a secret government prison, I just can't find it in me to feel shock right now." Which was true. I'd been surprised for about half a second seeing him there, but logic had quickly drawn the lines for me.

"I hear you want to break into Custer," he said. "Because you haven't done enough crazy shit."

"I need to talk to one of the inmates," I said, unsure how much Noah had filled him in. "It could be the key to defeating Samir." I knew I was overstating things. I had no idea what would happen when I met my father for real. *I don't always make life-or-death decisions that impact everyone I love, but when I do, I go off vague ancestral vision memory thingies.*

"Don't hurt yourself with the convincing," Alma said. She and her twin giggled.

I glared at them, glad my twins didn't giggle at least, though their smartass qualities seemed similar enough to put on a real cage match against each other.

"Jade doesn't need to convince me," Salazar said. "Things are changing, have been for a while. My time with the NOS is nearly over."

"NOS?" I asked around a mouthful of donut.

"My agency. Not Otherwise Specified. Our government does love their acronyms," Salazar said. He blew on his cup of coffee.

"So, you'll help us break in?" I said. Ideas were already whirling around in my head. "You have codes or clearance or whatever?"

"Ooh, maybe he could take you in as a prisoner!" Alma said.

"Or pretend you are some kind of government inspector," Cora chimed in.

"I do have clearance, but stop whatever you are thinking," he said. "You all have seen too many spy movies. Spy movies always forget one thing."

"Paperwork," Jaq said with a chagrined smile.

"Paperwork," Salazar confirmed. "It would take weeks to process a new prisoner in. There are holding facilities all over the States where people and such are evaluated before transfer. Almost no one is sent directly to Custer. And before you ask, no, I can't fake the paperwork."

"Before you ask me, neither can I," Noah said from the other end of the table. He'd been so still, I had forgotten he was there for a moment. Pesky vampires and their lack of breathing and noise-making.

"So, we can't walk in the front door," Kira said. "Obviously, or we wouldn't be needed."

The twins made faces at her. I felt a pang of longing. These people were friends; Kira had her crew with her. I was alone in a room of near-strangers. No history, no camaraderie.

Whose fault is that, exactly? the traitorous voice of reason whispered in my head. I mentally slapped tape over her mouth.

"I can get in myself," Salazar said. "Though it will likely come back on me and I'll have to burn this identity."

"You mean your name isn't Salazar?" I asked. I cracked an egg against the table and started peeling it onto my plate. I was hungrier than I had felt in days. Maybe because I knew that my friends were safe, for the moment, and that if I could get my magic back, I might even have a chance at saving Harper, too. Hope can really work up an appetite.

"It is, but I was placed in the NOS by the Council of Nine. The government doesn't like to hire shifters and supernaturals directly. Only on a contract basis. The Council pulled some powerful strings so I could keep track of Custer and the NOS. I reported to them." His shrug was careful, belying the tension in his body.

"To them, and to the Archivist," Kira said. She had her ice-blue laser beam gaze focused on him.

"The Council knows, I'm sure," Salazar said, returning her look with bland acceptance. "As long as I reported to them too, they didn't care."

"Why do you keep using the past tense?" Alma asked.

"After I help you, I'm out. It's complicated."

"Need-to-know-basis?" I asked, though I had a pretty good guess why he wasn't going to report to the Nine anymore. Alek's words about the Council being dissolved ghosted through my brain.

"That's right," he said, throwing me a small smile that told me he'd guessed that I knew.

It was like a word puzzle. He knew that I knew and now I knew that he knew that I knew . . . Fuck it. I preferred puzzles that gave me levels.

"Why do you need us, then?" Kira asked, directing her question down the table to Noah. "Can't secret agent man here walk in, open the cell that has the guy we want, and then walk him out again?"

"He could, though getting out with a prisoner would be complicated, I imagine. But we are not breaking Ash out. We must get Jade inside," Noah said. "Her father is in there voluntarily."

"Well, he's locked up," Salazar said in a mildly defensive tone. "But he doesn't wake up much. Just eats and sleeps, and occasionally binge-watches television before passing out for another few months. Nobody knows what he is. He just walked in about forty years ago, or so the stories go, anyway. Asked for a room. Killed a guard when they told him it was a prison and he couldn't have one. So, they locked him right up. He's never been a problem since, not in all the years I've been in NOS."

"What does he look like?" I asked. It wasn't relevant really, but this was my father, my biological one, at least. Curiosity nudged out sense.

"Who cares?" Kira said. "Fine, he won't walk out, and I assume you can't carry him out. How do we get in?"

I really wanted to tell her to go fuck herself, but I needed her, rudeness and all.

"I can open a secret hatch, a side door. It's an emergency exit. Here." Salazar shoved his plate to the side. "Let me show you the layout."

We all started moving dishes down the table toward Noah, clearing a spot in front of Salazar so he could unfold a piece of paper he pulled from an inner pocket in his suit coat. On the paper was a rough sketch of something shaped like an infinity sign.

"This is Custer," he said, tapping a finger on the figure eight. "Whole thing is underground. It's almost like a Möbius strip, which I'm going to assume I don't have to explain." He waited for us to nod or glare at him, depending, before continuing, "The front is here, at the crossing of the sides. It is actually two levels, this loop being on top, the other the lower level. Lower level is the more dangerous one."

"Let me guess," I muttered. "That's where we have to be?" It would be with my luck, lately.

"No, that's the good news," Salazar said. He wasn't smiling, which worried me. "Upper level, here on the bend where it starts to straighten? That's where you want to get to. And here . . ." He indicated the middle of the upper bend. "This is where the hatch I can open for you is."

"So, we creep up to the side, you open the door, we go get the guy, easy peasy?" Alma asked. I shared her skepticism.

"What are all those little dots?" Cora leaned forward to examine the paper more closely.

"Those are why we need you," Noah said from directly behind me.

I barely flinched. Really. Except my knee hit the table hard enough to leave a bruise and jump the cutlery around. Damn quiet vampires.

"Those are magical landmines, more or less. They trigger nasty things, most of which I don't know about, not specifically. It is hard to sort what is Agency legend and what's reality, and I can't ask too many questions. Rumors are the traps trigger magical creatures that attack whatever steps on them. Or they just might be like regular mines and explode." Salazar spread his hands and gave us an apologetic smile.

"Why would they build an escape hatch into a deathtrap?" Kira said.

"The hatch leads to the helipad. No one is supposed to just walk across the field."

"It's open ground?" Jaq asked.

"Yes. About twenty acres are kept clear. I haven't even gotten to the best part." Salazar picked up his coffee, took a big drink, and set it down, looking from Kira to me. "There's an invisible magic fence around the whole place except the road in. Maybe more than one fence—the water-cooler stories vary from one to three fences."

"If it is magic," I said, thinking things over, "it is most likely three. Three is a common and powerful number."

"There are one or three invisible fences. There are invisible magical landmines, or possibly just straight-up normal landmines. The whole facility is underground and, this time of year, under snow. We'll have to cross open ground in full view to deliver the package, over dangers we can't even see," Kira summed up, ticking off the problems on her fingers.

"Hey," I said. "I'm not a package." The way she'd kept ignoring me, and her rudeness, was starting to grate.

"Did your magic come back while you got your beauty sleep?" she asked, her voice as icy as her eyes.

"No, but . . ." I said. I stopped talking, because I had nothing to add after the *but*.

"Can you shoot?"

"Not if you want me to hit what I aim at," I muttered. Now I knew how a deflating balloon felt.

"Fight hand to hand?"

I shook my head. Alek had been teaching me some stuff, but I had no illusions about my skills versus anything deadly.

"Detect landmines? See invisible fences? Fly a helicopter?"

"Kira," Alma and Jaq said at the same time.

"Kira, come on," Cora echoed.

"She has no practical skills; that's why we are here. I won't have a normal fucking up my team. Tell me what you can contribute, or get out and let the grown-ups plan." Kira glared at me.

I opened my mouth to say a lot of words that began with the letters *F* and *C*, but Salazar cut me off.

"None of you can fly a helicopter in. They'd see you coming and shoot it down without questions." He gave me a sympathetic look.

"Fine, genius," I said, standing up. I'd had enough. "You figure out a plan, since that's what you're being paid to do." I stormed out of the room, brushing past Noah.

I didn't know where the hallway led, but I tried to return to my room. I needed to think. I needed to breathe. I really, really needed *not* to cry in front of that bitch. Or start trying to punch her. As she'd just pointed out, I wasn't a match for most humans, much less a giant tiger shifter. Punching would just end in tears. Mine, probably.

The door I opened wasn't to my room. Instead, I found myself in the library I'd first been in months and lifetimes before with Yosemite, when we had traded Samir's dagger for the druidic book. Tall shelves lined the room, stretching up into the shadows. Lamplight bathed the room in a cozy golden glow, adding to the mysterious atmosphere. It gleamed off leather spines and gold-leaf titles. This was as good a room as any for a sulk, I decided, and shut the door.

Kira's words had hurt because I had to acknowledge, much as my smarting pride didn't wish me to, that she was right. Not that I couldn't think strategically, of course. I was a gamer; I'd planned more imagined assaults and break-ins of facilities and castles and dungeons and whatever than most people. But those were all imaginary.

I didn't know Kira. I didn't know her team. I had no clue what the resources available looked like. I couldn't fight. I couldn't protect us with magic. It was worse than that, however.

Samir was still in Wylde. He potentially had Harper captive, doing Universe knew what to her. My friends, Alek . . . they were all out there in the wilderness, licking wounds, hiding from a mess I'd made, from an evil I was responsible for bringing into their lives. I couldn't go to them either, because what could I offer? My best hope for saving them was to find my father, get my magic back, and *then* go kick some ass.

Kira had more or less said I was useless. Sitting there alone in the library, I could grudgingly admit that maybe I was. I half-expected Noah to come after me, but he left me alone to wallow. It felt totally shitty to be sidelined like this, no matter how much truth was in it or how dangerous it might be for me to try to get too involved. There was probably a life lesson in there somewhere, but I was speeding along the Sulk Highway to Pityville so fast, I didn't want to detour down Introspection Lane.

There was only so much sulking I could handle. I was in a library, after all. I walked slowly around the room, gently touching titles, thrilled that I could still read the spines. I hadn't lost my wicked cool ability to read any language. I had seen a red book last time I was there, with a dragon on it. I went hunting for that, but another title caught my eye almost immediately. It was new leather, black with gold stitching, standing out among the other books for its thickness and its shiny newness.

Jonathan Strange & Mr Norrell by Susanna Clarke. I'd never read it, opting to watch the miniseries instead. I'd been impressed with the magic system and meant to read the book, but I'd had so little time the last year for reading. Gaming was my first love anyway, right after trying not to get killed by my ex.

I thumbed it open. It was a special edition, signed by the author. Made sense, I supposed, though I wondered how Noah had it in there among thousands of far more archaic books. Maybe it had been mis-shelved and there was a fantasy section around somewhere.

If only I had a couple magicians to imbue me with all of English magic right about now.

I should have been born a wizard, I guess. But I was a sorcerer to my core. I'd even learned to control my magic through D&D spells the way a sorcerer would, not learning them by the book but taking the essence of the listed spell and practicing with my will, bending my magic to do my bidding without ingredients and incantations, or study. Prestidigitation had been my favorite. It was fun to say, too, a good word to work into random sentences. It was a wonder I hadn't been more popular at parties. Using something like Ray of Frost would have made me way cooler but probably raised too many questions.

I took the novel back to one of the padded benches and sat down. I figured someone could come find me if or when they got a solid plan. Meanwhile, I could read and cool off, and hopefully, Kira and I would stop wanting to kill each other. Who knew? Maybe I'd learn a thing or three from Jonathan Strange.

I started to smile at the thought and my cheeks froze in mid-pull. My heart started to thud into my ribs. I almost face-palmed for realsies.

I didn't *have* magic. That didn't mean I couldn't *do* magic.

People, normal humans and witches and whatever, they did magic all the time. Well, not all the time—it took rituals and knowledge, and discipline and a non-fake spell to go on, but . . . Magic wasn't the province of sorcerers. We were just better at it.

I dropped the book onto the bench and started for the door. Then stopped. I had a lot of suspicions about this warehouse and its owner. Time to test one of them.

"Noah Grey," I said, trying not to yell. I didn't think I needed to speak too loudly.

Suspicions were confirmed when he walked through the door not thirty seconds later.

"Yes?" he said. His angular face carried a half-amused, half-curious expression.

"Do you have spell books?" I said. "Real ones, not like fake New Age bullshit."

The vampire tilted his head to one side and raised both eyebrows.

"Okay," I said. I started thinking as quickly as my excitement would allow. "Stupid question, I guess. I need spells. Ones that deal with seeing invisibility, also some simple stuff, too, so I can test and see if this will even work."

He studied me for a moment and I wondered if he'd start demanding another drop of blood or something. I was willing to give it. Anything to be of use, anything to do magic again, even if it wasn't exactly the same.

"Wait here," he said. He left as silently as he'd entered.

Fuck, yeah. Allowing a small fist pump, I grinned. I was about to gain my first level of wizard. *We'll see who is useless now, bitch.*

HARPER

Harper wasn't unconscious long, unfortunately. She came to, still a fox, with Samir looming over her. The moment her eyes opened, he kicked her.

"Stupid fucking animal," he spat, lifting his boot again.

She didn't hesitate, despite her ribs letting her know they were going on strike and her hip screaming its death scene.

Harper sprang as soon as she had a leg under her, shifting to human in mid-leap and slamming into the surprised Samir. She went for his throat with her hands and teeth, uncaring this was her weaker human body. Human teeth could still rip and tear, and she was still shifter, still strong.

Samir slammed his elbow into her ribs, knocking the wind from her laboring lungs. His hand snapped up and closed on her throat, barely keeping her teeth from his neck. Her hands closed on his jacket, and for a moment, they struggled before he threw her backward into the snow, her strength waning.

She curled on the snow around her aching ribs, spitting blood and wheezing. Samir made a fist, and crackling energy, barely visible in the fading daylight, formed around his hand.

"That's right, motherfucker," Harper snarled. "Kill me. Kill me, pickle-dick. Fry me. Do it."

Dying had been, like, plan Z, but she hurt so much, she found she didn't care. The unicorn was free. If she was dead, the pain would stop. Samir wouldn't be able to hurt her anymore or use her to hurt anyone she loved.

"No," he said. "Stupid bitch. You are going to live and watch your friends come and die here, one by one." He kicked her again, but she twisted and took the worst of it on her thigh muscle. "Get the cage," he told one of the men.

Harper allowed herself the tiniest feeling of relief. Not dead. Not yet. She clutched her hands to her chest as one of the mercenaries grabbed her legs and started dragging her back to the house. She started reciting Pi in her head to keep herself conscious. It was back to plan C.

Plan C was in her hands. Literally. Harper closed her fist tighter around the ruby vial she'd taken off Samir's neck in their struggle. She mentally thanked Uncle Darragh and his lessons with the bells.

Still alive. Almost kicking.

Samir didn't take chances this time. No more chains. He had two of his men bring a heavy cage up to the room she'd been in before, and they stuffed her into it. It locked with a thick chain through bars and a welded loop on the top, nowhere near the slits at the front. No way for someone inside to reach and pick the lock.

Harper let herself pass out once inside the cage, after tucking her tiny prize into her jeans pocket. She heard Samir giving instructions that some-one was to remain in the room with her at all times before exhaustion and injury pulled her back into the dark.

She didn't know how long she was out, but the pains had faded somewhat and the room was full dark when she awoke. A guard, the young-looking, flat-expressioned brown-haired man who had come back with Samir and the unicorn, leaned against the wall near the door, flipping a coin. Could have put his picture next to the dictionary definition of *boredom*. A different guard from before. Time was definitely slipping away from her.

Her friends would come for her. Hopefully, they wouldn't be totally stupid and walk right into an obvious trap, but Harper didn't feel much like waiting around to be rescued. She was no kitten and she'd get her own damn self out of this tree. Somehow.

"My mouth tastes like ass," she said, opening conversation. "Water?" She didn't see any around him, not even a cup or a bottle, but maybe she could get him to leave and get her some.

"No," he said.

"No? Just no?" she asked, licking her chapped lips. She really did want water.

He shrugged and slipped the coin into his pocket.

Harper tried a different plan.

"You're stuck in here with me," she said. She awkwardly tried to pull down her filthy bra strap, exposing an equally filthy, and bruised, breast. "We could pass the time more pleasantly."

It was a Hail Mary to end all Hail Marys, she recognized, but figured at worst he would say no again.

"Not into rape," he said with another shrug, his voice still calm and flat.

"Not rape if I'm willing," Harper said, pressing her cheek to the bars. This always worked way better in the movies. She needed a makeup crew. And a nap. And a hidden gun.

I watch way too many movies, she thought, still trying to look even marginally appealing. She mostly felt utterly pathetic.

"Technically," he said, moving away from the wall and walking toward her, "it's still rape. I have total power over you in an illegal situation. You can't consent."

"Great," Harper muttered, dragging her bra strap back up into a position that didn't push too hard on her bruises. "What are you, a fucking lawyer?"

"No," he said, his mouth twitching in the barest hint of a smile. "I'm not a rapist."

Harper leaned back against the side of the cage and drew her legs up. She couldn't reach the lock. This guy wasn't going to fall for stupid movie tricks. She'd have to wait for another opening. Maybe his replacement wouldn't have qualms and would only see a helpless female.

"Besides," her guard said after a long moment. He bent down in front the cage, out of reach. "You're just trying to get me to unlock this thing for you so you can try to escape again."

"Now you're fucking Sherlock Holmes." She closed her eyes. "Aren't you people worried about the Council of Nine sending a Justice after you?" she asked finally, trying one last line.

"No," he said, his tone so sure, she opened her eyes and looked at him again. "Lots of us have been operating for years without trouble. Long as you don't do certain things, nobody cares. The Nine aren't quite the all-powerful gods some think."

"You going to explain that?" Harper glared at him. She was learning the hard way that he was right. The shit that had gone down with the rogue wolf Justice and the alpha of alphas mess had shown that. Plus whatever weird stuff was going on with Alek.

"No," he said.

Harper sighed. She was bone tired, hurting, and out of ideas. Maybe the next guard would be a lot more stupid. A nap sounded like the only real plan left to her.

"You could ask nicely," the guard said after a long moment, his smile sly and big enough to flash a hint of teeth.

"What?" Harper eyed him, feeling like she'd lost some key context. Maybe she'd passed out again without knowing it and missed a whole chunk of conversation? More likely he was messing with her.

"You want out of the cage?" he asked.

"Is that a trick question?" she asked back.

"No, but I suppose it is an obvious one. I could let you go. I don't think you'd get very far, though." His eyes were a shade lighter brown than his hair; his smell was clean and woodsy, tinged with the scent of wolf. A hint of weariness in his gaze made Harper guess that he was a lot older than he looked.

"You could let me worry about that," Harper said. Her heart sped up. He was fucking with her. She tried to remember that.

"Of course, if I let you go, I'll be held responsible. The boss isn't a very forgiving man, nor, I think, is our employer." He sat back on his heels, his tone still conversational, but that sly look was getting more obvious by the second.

"Escape with me?" Harper suggested. This bastard was a real sadist, she decided. He was hurting her with the only thing she really wanted, damaging her with hope.

"No. I like my job, and I like living. You fuck up in this business, you get retired with flowers and an unmarked grave." He shook his head. "But maybe I can get someone else to let you out. After that, whatever happens isn't my problem. We catch you, we kill you, understand?"

It's a trap, it's a fucking trap, stop even thinking about this, her brain screamed at her. She shoved away the voice of reason. None of her choices were good, so she was going to choose the one that dangled freedom.

Harper licked her lips again. "Why would you help me?"

"I know who you are," he said. "You're XHarperX, right? I watched you win the StormMasters Cup. When you transfused a Baneling?"

StarCraft. He was talking about a live stage tournament she'd won at the big Master Gamers' League convention what felt like an entire lifetime ago. Before she'd known her friend Jade was running for her life. Before Samir.

"You're a gamer?" she whispered, starting to believe, starting to really hope.

"We are legion," he said with a solemn nod. "I'd hate to see you die here without at least a fighting chance."

He glanced at the door and added, "And maybe being killed escaping is better. A better death than what that sorcerer plans for you."

"What do I have to do?" Harper said.

"Play along," he said. He rose and went to the door.

She heard him call out for someone, and another man, this one slightly shorter, only an inch or two taller than Harper herself, entered. The new man was packing a big, obvious gun on his hip and had a big knife sticking out of his combat boots. He looked like he wished he were Rambo. Harper sniffed the air, trying to determine his animal, but his scent was human through and through.

A fighting chance, that was what the gamer guard had promised. Human was better than shifter. Injured as she was, she'd have a hard time overpowering a flea, but damned if she wouldn't rather tackle a human than a wolf or bear any day.

"Girl has to shit," Gamer Guy said with a disinterested shrug. "I want coffee. She's your problem for the moment."

"What you want me to do? Get her a bucket?" Human Guy whined, glaring over at Harper.

Gamer Guy handed him a key. "Take her to the bathroom, let her shit, lock her back up."

"Why me?"

"Because I said so," Gamer Guy said. He put a little growl into his voice, standing up taller, and Harper sensed the wolf in him.

Human Guy apparently did also. "What if she tries something? We're not supposed to let her out."

"You scared of an injured little girl?"

"I really gotta go, please," Harper chimed in.

"I ain't scared. Just let her shit in her cage. Who cares?" Human Guy took the key and made a face.

"You'll care when it stinks up everything and you have to spend the next twelve hours locked in here with her." Gamer Guy went to the door.

Human Guy had already thought of that, apparently, because he was moving to the cage. "At least stand at the stairs in case she does something stupid?"

"No problem," Gamer Guy said. He gave a slight nod to Harper behind Human Guy's back. His message was clear. Up to her now.

She faked being weak and hurt, which wasn't that difficult or faked, as she unfolded herself from the cage and staggered to her feet. She clutched her gut and groaned, hoping she wasn't hamming it up too hard.

Human Guy grabbed her upper arm, making her hiss in pain as his fingers dug into bruised flesh. He dragged her out the door and toward the bathroom she'd escaped from who knew how many hours before. She staggered some more, leaning heavily, and managed to spit up a little blood, letting it run down her chin.

"Jesus," Human Guy muttered. He shoved her into the bathroom.

"Door?" she asked.

"Fat chance," he said, and waved an arm at the toilet. "Go."

"At least turn around?" She made big eyes at him, trying to look as weak and waifish as possible.

He looked around the sparsely decorated bathroom as though checking to see if she had a giant sword hidden in the wallpaper or something, and then turned around with a sigh, his body blocking the doorway.

Harper put the toilet seat down and took quick stock of her options. The toilet was as old as the cabin, heavy porcelain stained with time and use. It had chipped in some parts, showing what looked like iron underneath.

One chance. That was all she'd have.

Time's up; let's do this, she told herself.

She pulled the top of the toilet tank off and sprang at Human Guy, swinging the heavy porcelain and iron lid into the back of his head. He went down with a sickening thud.

The hallway beyond him was clear. No sign of Gamer Guy. She figured he was downstairs getting his alibi cup of coffee.

Ignoring the intense protest of her body, Harper dragged the human into the bathroom and closed the door. She took a risk and ran a little water in the sink, ignoring her reflection as she shoveled a handful into her mouth. The water was the best she'd ever tasted.

She bent and felt a thready pulse in Human Guy's throat. Harper hesitated for a moment. She thought about using his knife but realized all that blood would tip off the shifters in the house, giving things away too soon. She picked up the heavy lid again instead and this time pushed it down onto his neck. He never woke up and barely even twitched. In the back of her mind, she knew Max would be frowning, but he was dead and not there. Things would never be the same and she couldn't afford to be weak. Not ever again.

Besides, as she'd once told Jade, some people needed killing. This meant one less asshole coming after her and her friends.

Harper hit the light and went back to the window. It wasn't quite dark outside; the horizon had the greyish tinge of false dawn about it. Dark enough that she might get away, she thought. She shoved the window open and had seriously painful déjà vu as she pushed herself out and landed on her old friend, the snowy bush.

With another prayer to whatever benevolent forces might be listening, Harper shifted. Agony tore through her ass and hip. Bullet wounds took longer than a few hours to heal, apparently. She compartmentalized the shit out of this pain, too. Her human form would be too damned slow and too damned cold.

No wolves moved in the trees that she could see. Time to go.

Harper bolted through the faint path she saw toward where the sentries had been patrolling earlier, taking the faster route instead of the stealthier one. She wasn't sure her hip was up to wading in untouched snow. She was almost to the trees, their dark branches reaching out like old friends, when she heard yelling behind her and then the howl of a wolf.

No looking back. Harper went for the trees. She left the snow with a leap, darting into bare brush at the edge of the woods. She had no idea where she was going, and once in the darkness of the forest, she could see almost nothing more than a few feet from her face. She ran on instinct, desperation, and adrenaline.

The first wolf caught her in the side with a leap she saw just in time to roll away from. Blinding agony ripped through her hip and back as her wounds reopened. She spun and snarled at the circling wolf. A second joined it, its form a darker shadow, circling away from the first, surrounding her.

Harper resolved to go down fighting. Gamer Guy was right, she figured. Better to die this way than be used as bait. She also had the fleeting but satisfying thought that if she died in fox form, Samir's stupid ruby vial, whatever it was, would be lost to the Veil inside her human jeans pocket forever.

I'd like to live, she thought, even as she resigned herself to being ripped apart. *I wanted to see him die. I'm sorry, Max. I'll explain when I see you. Soon.*

She crouched, eyes watering from the pain, and snarled a final time.

The dark wolf sprang at her but never made it. Soft white light filled the woods around them and a blur of silver hit the wolf, throwing it into a tree, where it collapsed and didn't rise. The blur resolved itself into a unicorn.

Lir. Harper recognized this one. Jade had saved its life after the evil sorcerer Clyde tried to kill off the unicorns with Fomorian hounds. She knew as sure as gravity it was the same one.

The first wolf snarled and tried to go for a hamstring. He took a horn in his ribs as the unicorn spun, again a blur of speed and deadly power. The wolf limped back, side gushing blood, and howled. Answering howls filled the woods, echoing.

Lir turned to Harper and bent his foreleg, dropping into a kind of strange bow. Harper took the hint and shifted to human, stumbling toward him. His mane was strong under her bruised and acid-burned fingers, his fur thicker and softer than a chinchilla's. She climbed onto his back with the grace of a sack of onions, and he sprang away through the woods as the howling grew nearer.

Harper clung on as they ran. Branches that should have slapped her silly seemed to pull away from her at the last second, and she swore the trees were shifting out of the way. Glancing back, the woods were thick and dark behind them, looking impassable for something as large as a unicorn.

"I love magic," Harper murmured. Her grip was failing her, her mind trying to run away to a nice dark place where there wasn't so much pain. The unicorn had the smoothest gait of anything she'd ever ridden, but there was still enough up-and-down movement to make her want to vomit as she felt every bruise, every bullet hole, and every cut she'd ever gotten in her life, in either body.

Lir seemed to know where he was going, so Harper turned her entire waning attention to staying on his back. She was riding a unicorn. Max would have shit himself with jealousy. They crossed a stream as daylight turned the woods from black to grey and white. They reached a clearing where a massive oak stretched welcoming branches toward the weak winter sun, and the unicorn stopped abruptly. Harper lost her grip and slid from his back. She lay where she'd fallen, unsure she'd ever be able to rise again. The snow felt soothing on her skin.

A huge white tiger emerged from the woods and turned into a tall blond Viking-looking dude as he ran toward her.

Alek. Harper was sure she'd never been so excited to see anyone in her life. He was alive. Then the druid, Yosemite, his flame-red hair curling around his face and his eyes bright with green flame, emerged from the woods behind Alek and bowed to the unicorn.

"Wolves. Samir," she said, trying to get her brain and her mouth to coordinate into a proper warning. "Chasing us."

"Harper, shh," Alek said, pulling her into his arms as carefully as he could. "You are safe now. I have you."

She looked up at him, his eyes pale as the winter sky, his cheeks lined with worry and white-blond stubble. He was absolutely the most beautiful thing she'd ever seen in her life.

"Now I know how Jade always feels," she murmured as she passed the fuck out.

CHAPTER SIX

Noah brought me three books and a bona fide scroll. He also gave me a notepad and a box of pens and pencils.

"These are reproductions, so don't worry about touching the pages, no matter how old they seem," Noah said.

"Thank you," I said, taking the books and putting them onto the desk.

"Good luck," he said. Then he left with a half-smile playing around his lips.

I tried not to think about what that meant. Either he approved of what I was trying to do, or he thought I was crazy and was just handing over things to keep me from picking more fights with Kira. Like giving the rowdy kid a coloring book and some crayons to distract her.

Only, my crayons could maybe do magic. I shrugged off worrying about the vampire's motivations and got to work at the small desk.

One of the books was a thick tome bound with red leather and closed with three brass clasps. It looked like a proper spell book, so I started with it first. It was written in Latin, with some of the spells in older languages, variants of Coptic and Greek. I turned the pages carefully, almost wishing I had gloves, despite what the Archivist had said. The spells in this book were complex, rituals for harvest or dealing with spirits, though I found two that might help us see the invisible. Both required a full moon and specially prepared garments. I set that book aside.

My wizarding was off to a grand start. Sorcery was so much easier. This material-components-and-casting-time stuff was bullshit.

The next book I picked up was a slender volume with the title *Triewe Lacnunga*. A grammatically suspect Anglo-Saxon title that meant roughly *True Remedies*. I was guessing the title had come after the book itself, though the text was mostly in Anglo-Saxon, with a few of the spells in Latin. I paged through the book quickly. These spells were far simpler, mostly based in herbs with basic invocations. Tearing up a piece of note paper, I made bookmarks and marked off a couple promising spells. One was very simple, dealing with making light, and I figured I could use it as a practice spell. I had no clue if I could make magic work even with real spells, after all. Going from zero to seeing invisibility was probably a mistake.

Not that I had time to give myself a true crash course in working this kind of magic. Even with spells and ingredients and everything else right, I was pretty sure it took witches and other human magic-users years or more to be able to master gathering power and executing these spells. It had taken a full coven just to flood my shop with bugs, for example. My only hope was that since I was used to bending power to my will and totally comfortable with the idea of magic itself, that I could skip the whole "years of study" thing.

I didn't have years. My friends didn't have years. We might not even have days.

The third book had a stitched binding and carved wood panels for its case, painted with blue and red knot work. It was in this book I found a seeing-invisible-things spell that wasn't too complex. I started writing down a wish list of ingredients and components. The spell wouldn't last long; it would go for the length of time a candle burned or be broken at full sunset, whichever came first. The candle part was super unspecific. What candle? There wasn't one involved in the spell. Fan-fucking-tastic.

I opened the ivory scroll case just because. I was pretty sure I was going to use the Celtic invisibility-seeing spell, but come on. Scroll case. Had to be opened just to satisfy my curiosity.

The scroll inside was made of white leather, scraped thin but still soft and flexible. It was beautifully illuminated with bright patterns in red, purple, and gold around the edges. The incantation was simple enough and in more or less modern English. I murmured the words aloud, not quite saying all of them. There was a rhythm in the phrases, a cadence that I could feel forming an arcane pattern. Definitely real magic there.

I wrote down the ingredients listed on the scroll in the short paragraph of instruction before the spell proper. This one also would be broken at sunset and had to be cast in daylight under an open sky, and would apparently only work under said sky. I was pretty sure *open sky* meant just not indoors, but the scroll wasn't exactly super specific.

"Noah," I said aloud. "I have a shopping list for you."

He opened the door less than a minute later.

"What time is it?" I asked him.

"Just past ten," he said, taking the list I handed him.

"Can you get this stuff for me? And I need somewhere to try out the practice spell." I put on my best *don't kill me* smile.

Noah's silver eyes narrowed as he glanced over my list and he sighed, the hush of air leaving his mouth totally incongruous with the whole not-breathing thing.

"Come with me," he said.

I ended up in the large loading dock and garage area, with an audience. Noah brought me the things I needed to try the simple light spell. He was followed by Kira, the twins, Jaq, and Salazar.

The ingredients, I wanted. The others, I could have lived without. I was too stubborn to order them to leave, so I took my things and the spell book and set up away from the RV.

"What is she doing?" Cora asked as I drew a rough circle with a piece of natural chalk.

"Casting a spell?" Alma answered, her voice pitching up at the end into a question.

"She's figuring out if she can do magic so that she can maybe find a way for us to see invisible shit," I said. I was proud of myself. I'd only sounded annoyed, not homicidal.

"Could be useful," Kira said grudgingly. She ruined it by adding, "If you can actually do it."

"Stand back," I said, glaring at the peanut gallery. Odds were the worst that could happen was nothing at all, but if I had to deal with an audience, they could at least not be crowding me.

I finished the circle and got the four red candles, placing them at compass points. The spell didn't specify if the points had to be actual compass points, so I just tried to make them equidistant. I lit the candles with a strike-anywhere match after stepping into the circle. In the middle of the circle were a gourd and three bowls of herbs and spices. Cinnamon, clove, and dried basil.

"She casting a spell or making pie?" Kira muttered.

I continued ignoring her and picked up the wooden athame, a ceremonial kind of knife that had a thin maple blade and ebony handle. Then I sat cross-legged in the center and started murmuring the incantation. Going clockwise, or sunward as the spell called it, I sprinkled the dull blade with cinnamon, then clove, then basil. Uttering the words of the spell, focusing all my will and not just a little desperate hope into it, I plunged the knife into the gourd. I lifted the blade out in a smooth motion and gripped it in my left hand, saying the final word of the spell.

For a moment, nothing happened. Then the candles extinguished

217

themselves and my fingers uncurled of their own volition. I dropped the knife, holding my left hand aloft. In my palm, floating over my skin, was a small ball of white light.

The difference between this magic and what I was used to was impossible to explain. Like the difference between holding an ice cube and *being* cold. There was no rush of power in me, no euphoria like I felt when working my own magic. Just a weightless ball of light and a grim satisfaction that I'd made something work.

"Cantrip achieved," I said, risking a look at my audience. I was afraid to move. The light wouldn't last outside of the circle anyway, if my interpretation of the spell was correct.

Alma and Cora clapped. Jaq and Salazar were smiling. Noah stood in shadow near the door, his face unreadable from this distance. Kira gave me a slight nod, like a fencing opponent acknowledging a touch.

Not so useless after all. Feeling better than I had in days, I got slowly to my feet and closed my hand, extinguishing the ball of light.

"Can I come back to the big table now?" I asked.

"Hey," I said to Jaq, since we were bringing up the rear of the group heading back to the war room.

He turned and looked at me, his bland face expectant.

"Uh, so, do you have a preferred pronoun?" I asked. Yeah, that had sounded more polite and way less awkward in my head.

He chuckled. "*He* and *him* is fine. I find it easier to be male in this world, most of the time," Jaq said. "But thank you for asking. Most people just assign whichever they are more comfortable with."

"Thanks," I mumbled. At least that was out of the way. He'd smoothed it over and made me feel less like an ass. I appreciated that.

Breakfast dishes had been cleared away, but there was fresh coffee at one end of the table. I grabbed a mug, adding milk and sugar to make it palatable.

"Want a little coffee with your sugar?" Cora asked. She and her twin giggled.

"All right," Kira said, calling the meeting to a semblance of order before I could respond. "So, Jade, you can make us see the invisible fence? What about the mines or traps or whatever?"

"I probably can," I said as I took my seat by Jaq. While I wanted to be useful and look competent, overselling my new wizard powers could get us all killed. Pride goeth before the fall and all that jazz.

"If I can see the fence," Jaq said, "I can nullify the magic."

I gave him an appraising look, wondering not for the first time what exactly this mild guy was. I'd asked enough awkward questions for one day, however, and in the end, it was probably none of my business.

"Can you do that to the mines, if this spell lets us see them?" Alma asked.

"I assume touching them would set them off?" Jaq looked at Salazar, who nodded. "Then no. We could try, but likely they would trigger before I was able to destroy the magic."

"If we can see them, we can walk around them," Kira said.

"What about guards and cameras and stuff?" I asked.

Kira sighed and the twins giggled. From their looks, I guessed this stuff had been covered. Too freaking bad. I hadn't been there.

"No cameras," Salazar said. He smiled at me and gave a slight nod, as if to reinforce that he didn't mind going over it again and was on my side. "The government would have to pay someone to watch them. With the magic and the nature of this place, nobody is that worried about people coming in. Which works to our advantage, fortunately. There are external guards, but they are stationed at the main entrance tunnel and garage, which is here." He tapped his drawing a short distance away from the twist in the building. "If you're careful, no one will be looking this way, and the building creates a hill, so there isn't line of sight from the main entrance."

"Speaking of magic," I said, trying to order my thoughts. "Who put these protections in place? Is there a coven or resident magic-user we need to worry about?" For all I knew, they had a sorcerer on staff. That would make things even more dangerous.

"No, nobody in the building," Salazar said. He shifted his weight in his seat and met my gaze with an uncomfortable grimace. "It was done by a sorcerer, on contract."

"Samir," I said. I recalled what Salazar had said at the scene of Peggy's murder a few days before. Had it only been days? A week, maybe. It felt like a lifetime. I started to wonder if the order to cover up the supernatural nature of the crime and get out of town had been because of whom Samir was friends with. "He's got friends in high places, I suppose," I added.

"I wouldn't call them friends, but he's greased a lot of palms over the years." Salazar picked up his coffee mug and swirled it around, his lips pressed into a tight line.

"At least he's otherwise occupied," I said. *With trying to kill me and my friends.* I left that part unsaid.

"Best to go in near dusk, though," Salazar said after a moment of silence.

"The spell won't last past dark," I said.

"It's not that far from where we can set up to the hatch," Cora said. "If we can see where to go, even at a very slow walk, we should be able to get inside within twenty to thirty minutes at most."

"If she can see the mines and the fence, Jade could walk herself in, maybe?" Alma said.

"No." Kira looked at me, then at Jaq. "She needs Jaq to nullify the fence or fences. There might be more than one, remember? And since neither of them can fight, at the least, I'm going with them as contingency."

"No plan survives engagement with the enemy," Alma said. "We're going too."

"You are?" I pictured them wheeling across a minefield before remembering they were shifters. I had the grace to blush. "Sorry," I muttered.

"Hey, it's okay," Cora said, smiling.

"We might look like two wheelchair-bound, joined-at-the-literal-hip cripples, but with our powers combined, we kick serious ass." Alma grinned and high-fived her twin.

"You two kick virtual ass also," Kira said. Her whole expression softened when she looked at them, making her appear almost human. It was hard to dislike someone who clearly cared so much about her people, but I kept right on trying.

"By day, we're white-hat hacking mavens," Alma said.

"But by night, we become a Mayan jaguar goddess!" Cora laughed.

"You're Mayan?" Salazar asked, eyebrows raised.

"Well, a couple generations back. We were raised in Las Vegas," Alma said.

"Mayan sounds cooler than kids from Nevada," Cora said.

"So, we have a rough plan, then," Kira said. "How long will the spell take to cast?"

I took a sip of my coffee and thought about which spell to use. The scroll one was elegant and fairly simple, though the ingredient list was longer. The one in the book was more complex verbally, but with a shorter list of things. I wasn't sure which I wanted to try yet, so I gave it my best guess.

"Not long, I don't think. Ten minutes at most?"

"Can you cast it here first?" she asked.

"No," I said. I'd thought about this already. "There are two spells that might work, but both have time limits on them that aren't clear. Sunset is pretty clear, but there's stuff about the length of time it takes a candle to burn down, and one spell only works outside, I think. To be safe, I should do the magic as close to the time we'll need it as possible."

"All right." She sat back, wheels clearly spinning in her mind behind her icy eyes. "Here's the plan. We'll drive up behind the prison. Salazar said there is an old logging access road that can get us within a mile. We'll hike closer, do the spell there, and then head in. Salazar will meet us at the hatch. Once there, the alarms go off, yes?" She looked at Salazar.

"Yes, alarms, guards, the works. The place is guarded by a few NOS agents but mostly contracted shifters." Salazar added that last part looking at me, so I assumed he'd been over that and was saying it for my benefit.

"Jade heads to her father, we head toward the entrance, hopefully drawing attention with us. After that, we leave, and Jade, you're on your own." Kira gave me a look that spoke volumes about her opinion on my chances of success.

"How do I get into the cell?" I asked Salazar, ignoring Kira.

"I'll get you a passkey. It's a room, technically, not a barred cell. I would tell you the number right now, but I have to look up the exact one in the system. Doing so will flag me, but fortunately, bureaucracy being what it is, I won't be questioned until long after we've escaped."

"We could try to hack in now and find out," Cora said. She cracked her knuckles.

"Internal system. No way to hack from the outside," Salazar said.

"Damn," Alma said.

"How are you guys going to get out?" I asked.

"In a blaze of teeth and glory!" Cora said. They both started giggling again.

"We'll worry about that," Kira said with a quelling look at the twins. "You just do whatever you have to do. The Archivist says your father will get you out."

"He will, if Jade can convince him to help her," Noah said from his post against the wall near the door.

"Okay, final question," I said after I'd drained the last of my coffee. "How do we get there? Isn't South Dakota, like, a day of driving away? Also, covered in winter?"

"Leave that to me," Jaq said.

"We can drive there in less than four hours," Kira said. She smiled at me, all teeth.

"How, exactly?" I set my coffee mug down and raised an eyebrow at her.

"Magic," she said.

CHAPTER SEVEN

I took another shower and gathered my few things. This was it. All the worry-
ing and planning were more or less over. In a few hours, I'd have answers.
At least, I hoped.

Someone knocked on the door as I was getting dressed. I finished
tugging on a clean-ish long-sleeved shirt and called out for whoever it
was to come in. It was the Archivist, which surprised me. He hadn't been
the knocking type up until now. Maybe he'd known I hadn't been fully
clothed yet, which sort of defeated the politeness of his knock, since I
couldn't think of an explanation for how he'd know I was half-naked
that wasn't more awkward than walking in on me.

"They ready?" I asked Noah as he entered.

"Yes," he said. He closed the door behind him and stood with his
hands behind his back, almost like I imagined a formal butler would stand.
"There is a box of the things you asked for in the vehicle, along with the
book and the scroll. I'd like those back, by the way."

"I don't plan on taking them with me. I'll leave them in the RV and tell
Kira to return them. Good enough?"

"That will do," he said. He brought his hands out from behind his
back, revealing a sheathed dagger in them. "This is yours."

"I meant like a pocketknife or something," I said, not understanding. My ingredient and spell component list hadn't had a dagger on it.

Then I looked more closely at the knife, taking it in my hand. I nearly dropped it when I realized what it was. Samir's dagger, only somewhat changed.

"I traded this to you," I said. "Why are you giving it back?" He didn't seem like the charity type.

"I have a feeling you might need it," he said cryptically. "These are blades of prophecy, which you might find useful."

"Blades of prophecy? That sounds not at all ominous," I muttered. I pulled the dagger from its sheath. It was changed from when I'd had it. The blade *was* silver on one side now, black on the other. Marks ran down the blade, runes and symbols in a myriad of languages, the least ancient of which was Greek. Alpha and Omega. Each symbol pretty much meant the same thing. Beginning and end.

"The blade is joined together again. It will not leave you like before. Be careful with it. It is a knife of ending. It can kill almost anything." Noah's gaze was so intense, it made me uncomfortable.

"Almost anything?" I peered at it. Looked like a knife to me. It had acted pretty strangely when I'd had it, though. I had no problem believing it was magical. "What would happen if I were to stab Samir with it?"

"I have no idea," Noah said. "I do not like guessing, but I imagine it would destroy his flesh, at the least."

"Leaving his heart?" I guessed. Guessing was like my middle name lately. "So, again, why are you giving this to me?"

"Prophecies," Noah said with a smile. "We'll call it a hunch."

"I thought you didn't like guesses."

"Instinct is not the same as supposition," he said with one of his deliberate, creepy shrugs.

"Fine," I said, resheathing the blade. "But can you hand it to me again, and this time say, 'It's dangerous to go alone! Take this'?"

"No," the vampire said, his smile disappearing. "Follow me."

"Everyone's a critic," I muttered as I shoved the dagger into my backpack and followed him out.

"There are a few rules of van club," Jaq said. He stood in the doorway between the driver's section of the RV and the living room section.

"Rule one: you don't talk about van club?" I guessed.

It got me a giggle from the twins, at least. They were seated on a narrow couch to one side, canes leaning between their legs. Apparently, they could walk, but Cora had told me they preferred the chair due to their twisted hips. Kira, Salazar, and I were crammed on another bench behind a narrow table.

"Sure," Jaq said. "Actual rules. Don't come up here or bother me while I'm driving, for any reason. You are spurting blood out your neck, there's a first-aid kit in the bathroom. Any reason. I mean it. Next rule: do not open the windows or pull back the curtains until I tell you it is safe to do so. Do not try to exit the vehicle. If you hear something weird outside, ignore the shit out of it. Clear?"

"Crystal," I said. "What is going to happen, exactly?"

"I'm going to drive," Jaq said. "The roads I'm taking aren't really meant for mortals, so we go fast and hope nothing notices."

"What if something notices?" I had an image of Cthulhu in my head, the way he was talking. Waking old ones or whatever. There was definitely a vast amount about this world I had no knowledge of. It made me feel very small.

"We die," he said. "But don't worry; I've never had that happen. I'm good at what I do."

"Let's go," Kira said. "We are on a clock, after all."

All the curtains were closed and Jaq went into the front, shutting a sliding door behind him.

"I'm going to grab a nap, if that's all right?" Salazar said to Kira.

"We'll show you to a bunk," Cora said. The twins heaved themselves up, leaning heavily on their canes. "Then we're gonna sleep too, I think. It's easier to make this kind of trip if you aren't awake."

That left Kira and me sitting in silence at the table. The engine started and we rolled out of the garage. Kira pulled out a gun and started taking it apart, her message that she wasn't interested in small talk loud and clear.

I moved to the couch and tried to close my eyes. All my worries were waiting there for me. Could I work the spell? Was Harper still alive? Would Alek ever forgive me for abandoning them? Sleep was so not a thing I was going to be able to do. I opened my eyes again as the RV went over what felt like a speed bump. The road noise died, leaving behind only engine sounds as though the tires were no longer on a hard surface. It was eerie.

Kira was bent over her gun, wiping down parts carefully with a soft cloth before fitting them back together again. She looked so much like Alek in that moment. I swallowed around the lump in my throat. She looked up at me and raised an eyebrow.

"So," I said. I couldn't talk about Alek—that seemed like a hot button from hell for her—so I went with the only other topic we had in common. "What kind of games do you play?"

"What makes you think I play games?" she said.

"Your tee shirt? Things you've said? It's pretty obvious." I fought not to glare at her. She made it damn hard to crack her icy exterior.

Kira looked down at herself. She was wearing black cargo pants and a grey tee shirt that said FRAG THE WEAK on it.

"*Counterstrike*," she said. "Though I play other things, especially any kind of horror game. You?" she added in a tone that made me think she might actually want an answer. Maybe the ice was cracking.

"RPGs, mostly. You're good with guns, I bet, like . . ." I stopped.

Shit. It was too damn tough not to mention Alek. I missed him like hell.

"Like my brother?" she said. She slammed the clip home in the gun.

"Sorry," I said. "The twins said he executed a friend of yours? As Justice?" Fuck it. If we were going to talk about him, I figured we could talk about all of it.

"He didn't tell you?" Kira put the gun into a holster and set it aside, which made me feel marginally less nervous.

"No. He doesn't talk about family much." I shook my head.

"My friend's daughter was slain by a group of human scum. We shifters don't have children often or easily."

I nodded, not daring to interrupt.

"We were hunting them down, but my friend got to them first. He went a little mad—understandably, mind you," she went on. "He killed the three men who had taken his child, but he went further than that. He killed their families." She looked down at her hands on the table and took a deep breath. "It was bad, I know. But he was so lost in hurt and grief. Human law enforcement was up in arms about the killings, and it was going to be tough to keep it quiet. I think that's why the Council sent a Justice."

"Alek," I said. *Damn.*

"He passed judgment, as he does. It didn't matter that the humans had wronged Daniel first. The only sentence he knows how to deliver is death. He executed Daniel right in front of me. I wasn't strong enough to stop him. We haven't spoken since." Her mouth pressed into a tight pink line and her eyes were cold enough to slow global warming.

I tried to think of anything to say, but my brain came up with dust kittens and platitudes.

"So," Kira said after an awkward, tense moment. She unclenched her fists. "He still have a stick up his ass?"

"Guess how we met?" I said. "He walked into my game shop and accused me of murder." My laugh was more nerves than humor.

Her face cracked in a smile and she shook her head. In a blink, the ice seemed to melt, and I saw care and longing in her eyes, emotions I recognized easily. She might be angry with Alek for what he had done, but it was crystal clear in that moment that Kira also still loved him and missed her brother.

"Sounds like Aleksei," she said. "And now you are mated."

"We worked it out," I said. I tried for a safer topic. "Why don't you have an accent? He does."

"Because I don't want one, so I worked hard to lose it," Kira said. "I'm a six-foot-three muscular woman with a short temper. Getting work is already a bitch. Being a giant Russian as well? Not really something that would put my very American clients at ease."

"'Murica," I said.

"Fuck, yeah," she finished.

"I know that the Archivist is paying you, but I really do appreciate you all risking your lives to help me," I said. We were on more solid ground now, and I felt like the tension was fading. A truce had at least been called.

"It's what we do," she said. Then she tilted her head to one side in a very feline gesture. "Why isn't Aleksei heres with you? He's almost as good a shot as I am, and his tiger is stronger. My brother has his faults, but leaving his mate to face danger doesn't seem his style."

Did I say *solid ground*? I meant *hot lava*. Awesomesauce.

"I left him. Without magic, I can't protect him, and I've got a giant target on my back. It's me that Samir wants to kill, in the end." I folded my arms across my chest.

"So, you don't trust my brother?" she said.

"I trust him. I just don't want him hurt." I pulled my legs up, wrapping my arms around them. It was a super-defensive posture, but I didn't care.

"Not enough to let him make his own decision about risks?"

We were definitely back in I-want-to-punch-Kira land.

"I watched him die," I said. It felt weird to say it aloud. I'd told Yosemite the bare details but nothing specific. There hadn't been time even if I'd wanted to. "I was barely able to bring him back. I can't go through that again. I'll do anything to keep him safe."

"So, your feelings matter more than his?" Kira said with an infuriatingly smug look on her face.

"You don't care about your friends? Want to keep them safe? Would you deliberately put them in danger if you knew it might kill them?" I said instead of answering directly. I could fight fire with fire.

"Yes," she said. "I am right now."

Oh. There was that. She was really good at deflating me. "You don't worry?"

"Of course I worry. I'm not a sociopath. But I trust them. Jaq, Cora, Alma . . . all of them are capable and intelligent people. They understand the risks of what we do and they can take care of themselves, and of each other. We watch each other's backs; use our strengths to make the group better as a whole. That's what a team is about, no? If I don't trust them, let them do what they can, it'll distract me. As worrying about me would distract them. It would make us all weaker."

She had a point. I let it sink in, growing more uncomfortable as I thought it over. Had I been stifling my team, minimizing what they could do? I'd been trying to protect everyone.

"I let them help," I said, as much to myself as to her. "And they all died."

"They aren't dead now," she said.

"Because I brought them back," I said.

Kira raised an eyebrow at that and looked almost impressed. "So, you protected them." She leaned forward and laid her palms flat on the table. "I am a tiger, Jade. We're as lone-hunter as it gets in many ways. But I've learned the hard way over the years that everyone needs friends. We all have weaknesses. True friends are never a weakness."

I sighed. "Thanks," I said after a moment. "You've given me a lot to think about, I guess." I didn't want to think about it. I wanted to keep doing whatever I felt was right, but I wasn't so pigheaded that I couldn't feel the truth in her words. They stung because they were hitting their marks.

"Don't mention it," she said, and pulled out another gun to resume her cleaning-weapons-and-ignoring-me routine.

I dragged the box with the spell books and supplies out from under the bench and set a bamboo calligraphy brush and a folder of rice paper on the table.

"Can I borrow a knife?" I asked Kira as I sat down next to her. The RV was moving, but there was no road shake. We might as well have been floating, for all I could tell. I tried not to think about it too hard.

"What do you want it for?" she asked, squinting at my supplies.

Oh, you know. To cut myself so I can use the blood to write ancient Japanese spells I sort of remember that I learned from an assassin whose heart I snacked on. Probably not something I should say in my out-loud voice. Nope.

"Magic stuff," I said.

The look on her face when I sliced open my arm and let my blood drip into the ink stone was worth it. I had no idea if the exploding papers I was trying to make would work. Haruki, the assassin whose power and memories I'd absorbed, had studied his whole life, using discipline and techniques drilled into him through intense practice to master this kind of magic. I was going to use incomplete memories and desperate prayers to reproduce it. It probably wouldn't work, but it kept my mind off the trip and what lay ahead. That was good enough for me.

ALEK

Alek stared up at the darkening winter sky. The trees were wrong, the air a little too warm at only just below freezing, but for a moment, the scent of snow and wet pine brought him back to his childhood roaming the Siberian forests. A slight breeze ruffled his thick fur. Night came on quickly in winter; the setting sun had left a gash of color in the sky, turning the outline of the trees to jagged wounds.

His ears flicked around, his nose keeping watch as well. He had no desire to fight Samir right now, not without Jade, but part of him wanted a wolf or three to find them. He needed to sink his teeth into something and feel like he was doing anything at all to help.

Even Harper had rescued herself, the crazy fox. She'd fallen off the unicorn half-dead, covered in filth and blood from an unknown number of injuries. Yosemite said she needed rest but that he was sure she'd live. It was a morale boost they all needed, and hopefully she'd have information. Alek had worried that Samir had Jade, at least until they found Harper's bloody shirt laid out as obvious bait leading back toward Wylde. There'd been a big argument about following the trail despite them all being sure it was a trap. Rosie had said the trail led in the direction of a couple of old farms.

Then Yosemite had been called away, disappearing the day before while they scouted out and tried to figure out if Harper was alive or not. Another argument ensued. Alek was damn tired of arguing. Rosie was distraught, Junebug still healing from being shot. They were all scared and exhausted.

They were all looking to him. And he couldn't find it in himself to admit he had no idea what to do. His whole life, he'd relied on the guidance of the Nine. On visions and purpose given to him. Before, he had felt this was the One True Path, hadn't questioned anything.

The world, his world, had changed. Or perhaps, he thought ruefully, he'd finally just started to see it for what it really was.

Yosemite was back, though refusing to answer questions. It didn't matter. Alek knew he'd gone to see Jade. He'd smelled her on the druid's jacket. For a moment, he'd wanted to punch information out of the bigger man, but sense won out. If the druid wasn't saying something, he likely had a reason.

Besides, it was a comfort just to know Jade was alive and, for the moment, he guessed, safe enough. If she was staying away from them, she had her reasons. Stupid, overprotective, Jade Crow brand-of-special-logic reasons.

He huffled out a breath and watched steam rise in the chill air. Trust. It was all he had.

He heard Yosemite before the druid reached him, though the big man made little noise even walking through snow.

"Harper's awake," Yosemite said.

Finally. Alek turned and followed the druid back into the camp. Druidic magic had woven a thick-branched dome around everyone, which kept the worst of the cold out and the snow off. They had no fire, but Freyda and the few survivors in her pack had brought them sleeping bags, food, and a small gas camp stove, so there were coffee and warm food, at least. She'd left then, going deep into the wilderness to search for Softpaw. Reinforcements.

Not that they'd do much good without Jade. Nobody could kill a sorcerer except a sorcerer. Alek wouldn't allow himself to think about how badly they'd lost the last fight. They would regroup, plan, and find a way. The only alternatives were terrible. Run. Or die.

He preferred fight. Always fight.

Everyone was huddled around Harper. Her face was still bruised, but at least it was clean now, and someone had found her a sweater. Her green eyes were brighter and less sunken than before. She even managed a smile as he entered the camp and shifted back to human.

Ezee made room and Alek seated himself on a sleeping bag in the circle of friends.

"Tell us everything," he said, since someone had to say things like that and everyone was looking at him.

She did, piecing together parts they had already guessed, like the trap with her bloody shirt, and explaining about saving the unicorn foal.

"You escaped twice? That's badass," Levi said, giving Harper a mock fist bump.

"I know, right?" she said with a weak grin. "Think they'll get ScarJo to play me in the movie?"

"Tell me again the part about Balor," Yosemite said, cutting the banter short.

Alek glanced at the druid and didn't like what he saw. The man's eyebrows were pulled into a single worried line, his ruddy cheeks pale, and fear scent wafted off him, putting Alek's teeth on edge.

"There wasn't much, sorry. He said they needed Legolas, the colt, for Balor. That was, I think, the only time I heard the name, but I remembered it because of what happened before," Harper said.

"What is that look, Yosemite?" Ezee asked softly. All the shifters could smell the druid's fear, see his tension. "That's the 'oh shit, I just remembered something really bad' look, isn't it?"

"Is he going to open the Eye again?" Alek asked, trying to piece it all together. They'd dealt with Balor's Eye before. They could do it again. The unicorns were safe this time, at least. *For the moment.* Alek shoved the dark thoughts away.

Yosemite stood and paced the short length of the camp. He stared into the twisted branches, breathing slowly and deeply. Then he turned back. His face looked haunted now, cast in shadow since he'd walked away from the single electric lamp.

"There's a legend. It's truly legend, mind you, but it is written in the book and was told to me by my master when I was young. Balor is not truly dead; that's why his Eye is still dangerous. He could be raised back to life. It takes three impossible things, however."

Alek couldn't suppress his growing sense of dread as Ezee asked softly, "What three things?"

Yosemite closed his eyes and recited, with a cadence that suggested tales around campfires in the long ago and far away, "The first feather of the Phoenix. The last drop of blood from a dragon's heart. The final breath of a unicorn." He opened his eyes. "If he took the unicorn for that, we should assume he knows a way to collect or already possesses the other ingredients."

"Shit," Ezee said, echoing what they were all thinking. "He said he was going to become a god, right? So, he raises Balor, eats his heart, and presto, godhood?"

"This is seriously the suck," Levi said.

"Wait," Harper said. "That's awesome." She slid a hand into her sleeping bag and pulled out a small red vial. "Think this is dragon blood?"

Yosemite crossed quickly to her and took it. "Perhaps. Where did you get this?"

"I stole it off Samir's neck. It seemed like he was attached to it, kept touching it all the time like a creeper. I figured if he liked it, I wanted to take it away."

"Is it like the One Ring? Or can we burn it or something?" Levi asked.

"It can be destroyed," Yosemite said, still holding the ruby-colored vial as though it might bite him.

"Destroy it," Alek said. He rose to his feet. "We cannot let him raise Balor." If Samir ate the heart, he'd be well beyond Jade's power to destroy. Alek refused to consider that he already might be.

They risked a small fire just outside camp and burned the vial. The flames turned purple and roared upward for a breath before smoldering down. Only cracked, smoky glass remained. They buried the coals and covered it over with snow and rocks.

"What do we do now?" Rosie asked once everyone had gathered. She had been very quiet the last few days, but her color was better now that her daughter was back. Alek felt for her. She'd buried one child already this winter, and nearly collapsed in fear and relief when he'd brought the other back to her. But she was strong, holding together, making sure everyone was warm and fed, keeping busy and refusing to whine or openly worry. The woman was a rock. He prayed she wouldn't crack. They needed her.

"We can't kill Samir," Junebug said softly. Levi reached over and squeezed her hand.

"Jade can," Ezee said.

"Jade's not here," Harper pointed out, her mouth going into a tight, angry line. "Where even is she?"

"She's safe," Yosemite said. Every head turned to him. "I saw her yesterday."

"Thanks for sharing with the group?" Ezee said with a glare.

"She asked me not to; I'm sorry. She's . . ." He hesitated and sighed. "She told me she knows what she needs to do to beat Samir. It requires doing something else, getting a secret weapon or maybe someone who can help? She wouldn't give me details, said it would just put us all in danger."

Alek bit his lip, repressing the urge to demand more answers. *Trust her.* It was becoming his new mantra. He wanted to go to Jade, find his mate, kiss or shake some sense into her beautiful, stubborn head. He looked around the group, seeing their hopeful, exhausted faces. They needed him more than Jade did, as much as it hurt his heart to admit. So, he stayed silent.

"That's Jade," Harper muttered. "I wish she'd let us help. We're going to anyway."

"We are?" Rosie asked. "How, exactly? We have you back, sweetheart. We should get out of these woods. Find somewhere to hide."

"What if Samir raises Balor?" Alek said, shaking his head. Rosie's plan was likely the safer one, the sane one, but Alek already knew the druid wouldn't leave the woods, not with Samir hunting the unicorns. "We can hide well enough in the woods. We're shifters and there are tens of thousands of acres here."

"I won't leave the unicorns, and they won't leave the Frank. If Balor is involved, the unicorns will try to fight and stop the pollution of their woods. They can't help themselves; it is what they are here to do," Yosemite said, confirming Alek's thoughts.

"We can't kill Samir," Harper said. She held up a hand as Levi started to interrupt her. "But we can fuck up his plans. Look what I did all on my own." She managed a grin that had a lot of teeth in it. "Plus, if we do somehow get him pinned, we can seriously damage him. String him up and serve his heart to Jade on a platter."

"I agree," Alek said. He almost chuckled at how surprised everyone looked. "He found this dragon-heart blood once. He might be able to get more. We have to prevent him from completing his plan."

"And buy time for Jade," Ezee added, nodding slowly.

"I'm in," Junebug said, glaring at Levi as he turned to her and tried to protest. "This is about more than just us. Jade is trying to protect us. If that bastard eats Balor's heart, he'll gain too much power, and who will protect her then?"

Rosie looked at her daughter's angry, determined face. "I am in as well."

"Levi?" Ezee said, meeting his twin's eyes.

"So, to clarify this plan," Levi said. "We're going to run around the woods, playing keep-away with unicorns from a bunch of shifter mercenaries and a super-powerful sorcerer. Who, by the way, we can't kill, and who totally kicked all our asses, like, seven ways from Sunday. We're going to do this while buying time for our own sorceress, wherever she is and whatever she's doing there, to come back with a person or weapon or cookies of death or whatever, in the hope she saves the day?"

There was silence for a moment. Alek swallowed a chuckle and took a deep breath.

"Yes," he said.

"That about sums it up," Ezee said.

"Fuck it; I'm in," Levi said. "You all realize this makes Jade into Goku, right?"

"Goku?" Alek asked. He was certain this was a videogame reference or something he wasn't getting. That feeling was familiar and strangely comforting. Things might be dire, but at least he was among friends.

"It's a show. Where people spend a lot of time holding off bad guys waiting for the hero to power up and defeat them." Harper did laugh now, wincing as though it hurt to do so.

"Next time on *Running Around the Woods, Beating Up Samir*!" Ezee was grinning now as well.

"We have a plan, then," Alek said, suppressing his annoyance. He hoped they would all live long enough that he could get in on the joke. Someday.

"Yep. We keep the unicorns safe and wait for Jade," Levi said.

"And hope she brings all seven Dragon Balls with her," Harper added softly.

Alek rose and left the camp, shifting to tiger and moving silently into the dark woods. The druid followed him.

"I'm sorry," he told Alek as they stood, giant and tiger, side by side. "I wasn't sure how you'd react."

Alek shifted to human so he could speak. "I knew," he said. "I smelled her on you."

"You still said nothing?"

"If you did not tell me, I assumed you had reason, and I guessed that reason was Jade being stubborn."

"She is that." Yosemite chuckled, the sound like dry leaves rustling in an autumn wind. "She told me that you would find out and to give you a message."

Alek stayed silent, watching the druid's face in the starlight.

"She said to tell you she loves you, and to trust her."

Shifting back to tiger, Alek padded away, deeper into the woods.

Be safe, love, he silently told the stars. *Come back to us, and we will fight, side by side.*

CHAPTER EIGHT ▶

The journey through whatever crazy magic shortcut we were taking went by without event. I felt us hit the logging road, the tires making noise again and the RV shaking as it jounced along.

The air was freezing cold as we emerged into a quiet, snow-covered copse of trees. After checking to make sure the magic dagger was securely tied by its sheath to my waist, I zipped up my hoodie over it. I wished I had thought to ask Noah for a proper winter coat. At least I couldn't actually freeze to death.

Alma and Cora jumped out of the RV in their jaguar form, answering my earlier speculation about how they would shift. Single jaguar. I wondered how that worked mentally. Did they share a brain when shifted? Questions for another time, if we made it through this alive and I ever saw them again. Sobering thought. I was so good at those. I'd never seen a jaguar outside of a zoo. The twin's form was spotted, not the black kind, and their shoulder came up to my waist. They bounded off into the snow, looking back at us like an expectant puppy.

"We call them Ladies in this form," Jaq said, walking up beside me. He looked exhausted, sweat matting his hair to his forehead, and his olive skin had a pale cast to it.

"Good to know," I said. "You okay?"

"It was a long drive," he said. "I'll be fine."

"Let's cast the spell here so we don't have to drag this box up to the prison," Kira said. She'd pulled on her leather jacket but was standing with it open as she finished strapping on her arsenal. I counted three handguns and at least five knives.

"I'll go on ahead," Salazar said. "Make sure I'm in position when you get there."

"How will you get in?" I asked.

"I called in a favor," he said. "There's a car waiting for me down the road. I have clearance to enter Custer. It won't be a problem. Good luck. See you soon."

Salazar walked out from under the trees and shifted into a huge golden eagle. With powerful flaps of his wings, he took off into the clear, cold air and flew away. Remembering how awesome flying had been, I envied the hell out of him. Life had been so much easier with real magic involved. It was like that song. *You don't know what you have until it's gone.*

"Spell?" Kira said, looking at me.

I turned and went to get my box.

"I'm going to do this on myself first," I explained as I got out the ingredients and spread them on a tarp that Jaq had found for me from the RV. "I don't know exactly how it is going to work."

"How will we know if it has worked?" Kira asked.

I held up a small velvet bag. "I'll be able to see this."

"It's a bag." She looked skeptical.

"With an invisible ring in it," I said, grinning. Thank you, Archivist. He really was the guy who had everything. "I got us covered."

Cora and Alma, or, I guess, Ladies, bounded back over to us and sat in the snow, watching me closely with green-gold eyes.

I unrolled the scroll and set it where I could read it. Then I took a quart bowl and carefully measured out pinches of poppy seed, dried sword fern, a ball of spider silk, and three woolen fibers from a black ram. Finally, I added a drop of camphor oil. Murmuring the words of the spell, I picked up a pestle made of amber and started grinding the ingredients together.

"My friends of the shadows," I invoked. "Of mist and of moonlight, you who are seldom seen. Be with me now." Keeping up the litany, I divided the paste into two portions and carefully painted over my closed eyelids. I finished the last words of the spell and opened my eyes.

"Houston," I said. "I think we have a problem."

Where there should have been trees and snow and an RV, there was nothing. Just pale, almost greyish light.

"What do you see?" Kira said from somewhere beside me.

"Nothing," I said. "Like, actually nothing."

"What about this?" she asked, her voice very close now.

I turned my head toward it and saw a glowing ring floating in the air.

"Okay, I see the ring. I just can't see anything else. At all." Magic. It is not for beginners.

I heard Jaq laugh and then it cut off. I could imagine Kira glaring at him. The ring disappeared and I assumed she'd put it back in the bag.

"So, we'll be able to see the fence at least. And maybe these magical mines." I could almost hear her thoughts grinding away, her tactical brain looking for ways to make this an advantage.

"Who is this *we*, white woman?" I muttered, my own thoughts spinning around. "I can't cast the spell on anyone else. I didn't exactly memorize it, and these things aren't kind to imprecise casting. At best nothing would happen."

"Klaatu barada necktie?" Kira said with a snort. I was glad she was amused at least.

"Yeah, kind of like that." *Fuck my life.* I stared around at the nothingness. "I might be able to get into the RV and dispel it. It says it only works under the open sky."

"No," Kira said. "This is fine. I can make this work. We don't want us blind anyway, or we won't be able to see the entrance or any threats coming at us. You'll just have to guide us in, tell us where the fence is."

She was right beside me. I felt the warmth coming off her body. It was amazing how much I noticed now that my sight was missing. I just had to channel my inner Daredevil. No problem.

"Okay," I said, carefully rising to my feet. There wasn't much choice. We had to go with what we had. "Um, how do I walk through the woods to the minefield? I can't see the trees. Or the ground."

A fuzzy head bumped against my palm and the tarp crackled as Ladies stepped up beside me.

"No worries," Kira said, taking my hand in her own. Her skin was calloused and warm, her hand dwarfing mine. "We've got you."

I don't know how long we walked through the woods. I could smell the snow, hear it crunching under my hiking boots. Felt the wet and cold soaking into my socks. Visually, though? My world was a grey-tinged white screen. I walked with one hand clutching Kira's arm and the other resting on the jaguar-twins' head. It was like one of those trust exercises you have to do in school, only a lot scarier.

Three parallel, silvery lines appeared ahead of me. I was so excited to see something that it took a second for my brain to catch up.

"Stop," I said, tugging on Kira's arm. "I see the fence."

"We're not out of the woods yet, though I think I see the field ahead. How far is it?" Kira halted beside me, her voice coming from above my right shoulder.

"I'm not sure. I can't see the ground. This is really disorienting," I said.

I squinted, as though somehow that would help. The fence was three silver wire-looking lines. There were faint shadowed posts at intervals of about six feet, if my eyes weren't lying to me.

242

"There are three wire-like lines," I continued. "One at my knees, one at just above my waist, one probably about eye level with Kira."

"Everyone get in a line just behind Jade," Kira said. "I'll walk slightly behind you as well, keep you from hitting a tree. It's clear directly in front of you, so try to walk straight. Stop before you hit the fence, obviously."

"Obviously," I muttered.

Kira moved behind me, her hand gripping my elbow, her body a warm comfort at my back. I remembered what she'd said in the RV about having each other's backs, but also trusting each other that we could do what we needed to do. They were strangers to me and I to them, but there we were. Risking. Trusting.

I guess I had taken that detour into Life-lesson-ville.

Agonizingly slowly, we made our way toward the invisible fence. Up close, the wires were thick ropes of energy hanging in the air that hummed audibly and glowed bright enough to put dots in my vision. I wished for my magic, wondering what kind of spell this was and how it had been done. Even without being able to touch it magically, I could see Samir's handiwork in this. He loved crafting shit. I shuddered and came to a stop with the fence about a foot away.

"It's about a foot away from me," I said. "I could touch it, but I really don't want to."

"We're at the edge of the trees," Kira said for my benefit. "There's a big open field that rises up to a hill in the middle. Can't really see from here, but I think the helipad is on that. Do you see anything else?"

"No, the fence is glowing pretty brightly. If there are mines, they might be under snow or ground. I can't see the ring when it is in the bag, for example." I realized I probably should have thought of this before. "I can hear it, though; can you? The fence is humming. Like bees."

"No," Kira said.

"I can't hear it either," Jaq said. He had come up beside me. "Jade, I want you to crouch down so you are eye level with the bottom strand. Put your hand out so that it is within in an inch or so. Hold there and I'll see what I can do. Don't touch it."

"Don't have to tell me twice," I said. I did as he instructed, crouching down and holding out my hand.

I heard Jaq crunching forward in the snow, and then the hum intensified for a moment before the strand snapped and disappeared.

"I think that worked," I said.

"It did. We can see it now. It's just broken wire on the ground," Kira said.

"Stand up and do the same with the middle," Jaq said.

We repeated this for the middle and top strands. The grey world I was in grew darker again as the fence died. I peered into what I thought was ahead of me and picked up very faint traces of light in a direction that might have been down. As I said. Disorienting as fuck.

"Nothing is coming to kill us and I don't hear any alarms, so we're probably good," Kira said.

"I think I see the mines or traps or whatever they are. And I think I'll hear them as we get near. We're going to have to do this really slowly." I took a deep breath.

"We can't be too slow," Kira said. "Not to rush you or anything, but the sun is setting. It's going to get dark and your spell will break, yes?"

"FML," I muttered.

"Do you see another fence?" Jaq asked.

"No," I said. "I think if there was one, given how far off I saw this one from, I'd see it. How far is the crest of the hill from us now?"

"Three hundred feet? Like a football pitch."

"We call it *soccer* and *fields* in 'Murica," I said.

"You call it wrong," Kira said. "If there are no more fences, Jaq, you should go to the RV. We'll need you more there than here."

"All right," he said, reluctance obvious in his voice. "Good luck, Jade."

"You too," I said. "And thank you."

I listened to him crunch away through the snow. After a moment, Kira spoke again.

"Okay, like before. We line up. Ladies, step only where Jade steps. Fortunately, with this snow, we'll be able to see that pretty clearly."

"Time's up," I said as much to myself as to them. "Let's do this."

"At least we had chicken," Kira murmured behind me, making me smile.

I might blow us all up or even worse by missing a mine, but at least I'd die among nerds. It was something. I took the first step forward through where the fence had been.

"Am I facing toward the top of the hill?" I asked.

"You are good to go," Kira said. I felt cold air on my ears as my hood was pulled down, and then a tug on my braid. I realized it was her hand. "Is this okay? You don't have a belt I can grab."

"Yeah, just don't yank." I could deal with cold ears. My hair was loosely braided, so it covered the tips at least. I wondered what Alek would think of the situation. Me, walking blindly through a minefield with his sister holding my hair like a leash, and a giant jaguar following in our footsteps. I hoped he was safe, but I couldn't think about him now. No distractions.

Whatever magic was in the mines was strong enough that I could see it with my spelled eyes. It glowed and hummed like the fence.

"Okay, there's sort of a grid pattern, but it's hard to make out since I can only see the ones near me," I said. "The circles are about six to eight inches across, and some of these are only a few feet apart, so I'll try to step right between. Don't weave behind me. This could get really hairy."

At least I could see my own feet. That would have made shit really exciting. I had no idea why I could see myself when I wasn't invisible, but that's the thing with magic. It makes its own rules.

Step by step, heel to toe, I walked across the field. The mines hummed in warning as we moved around them, their silvery glow muffled, like LEDs stuffed in a pillowcase. Sweat beaded on my forehead and ran

245

down my spine from the tension only to freeze in the winter air. The mines seemed to stretch into forever, new ones appearing ahead no matter how many I walked past.

"Adjust left if you can," Kira said. Her own tension radiated enough to feel, tangible heat prickling the back of my neck.

"There's a big cluster that way, but I think I can get through them."

I shifted to the left. Another few steps and it felt like we were definitely traveling uphill. My thighs burned and the snow had gotten deeper, making the lights dimmer and soaking my jeans to the knees.

"Not too much further," Kira said soothingly. "Relax. We're doing great."

She really shouldn't have said that.

My foot caught something beneath the snow and I stumbled forward. Kira jerked on my braid, pulling me back, but it was too late. I overbalanced and did a full sideways sprawl into deep, icy snow.

Right onto a humming, glowing mine.

It didn't explode. The light extinguished with a hiss.

"I just fell on one," I said, trying not to panic as I climbed to my feet. "What's happening?" Obviously, I hadn't exploded.

"Nothing," Kira said, her voice tight with worry.

The jaguar snarled.

"Strike that," Kira said. I heard a scraping noise and then the crack of a gun going off.

"What do I do?" I said. My voice came out in a shriek and I made myself take a deep breath. I couldn't see shit except for the other mines around us.

"Come back toward my voice," Kira said.

I walked the couple steps back until she put a hand on my shoulder.

"What is it? What did you shoot?" There. My voice was way less panicked. Kinda.

Ladies snarled again, very close to me now.

"Zombies, I think." Kira's gun went off again, two shots this time in quick succession. My ears started ringing. "Climbing out of the ground. We need to go. Fast."

"Which way?" I said. All I saw was mines, but from the glow, I thought I could tell which way was uphill. Not well enough to trust it.

Kira grabbed my arm and turned me in what I guessed was the right direction. "Fast zombies, seriously. Go."

I went far more quickly than I was comfortable with, but fighting undead wasn't an option for me. I tried to navigate the remaining mines without stepping into any lighted circles, praying to the Universe that my friends could keep up and follow my path. Gunfire rang out just behind me, shot after shot. An animal screamed, though more in anger than pain.

Gasping for air, my thighs burning, I passed through the last ring of lights and felt the ground flatten out.

"Clear ahead of me," I called back.

Something slammed into my side, knocking me over. I curled instinctively and kicked out, my boots connecting with something hard that shrieked on impact. Gunfire, this time sounding like it came from ahead of me, cut through the air.

Hands grabbed my shoulders, and before I could react, I was being dragged across the snow and then pulled upright. Icy crystals caught in my hoodie and slid down the back of my neck. I tried to punch upward.

"Jade." Salazar's voice came from above me. "It's me; come on."

"I can't see," I said. "Get me inside." I hoped that would break the spell.

Salazar picked me up as though I weighed nothing and carried me for a few terrifying strides. Then he set me down, pushing me to my knees.

"Just in front of you is the opening. There's a ladder on the left."

I flailed out with my hands as I heard him clear a gun and start shooting again. My fingers met a metal rim and I scrabbled around until I felt the first rung. Closing my eyes, I crawled into the hole and started climbing down.

When I opened my eyes, I could see.

CHAPTER NINE

The hatch opened into a small room with copper walls. There was a single closed door at one end that looked like something I'd seen in submarine movies, with a big lever handle. I moved quickly out of the way of the ladder as Kira came sliding down like a total badass, her feet on the sides instead of the rungs.

"Jump," she called up to someone.

The jaguar came next, the twins diving in headfirst and landing with a heavy thud as they shoved off the ladder with their back feet.

"Sal," Kira yelled up.

More gunfire and then he was there, sliding down the ladder much the same way Kira had.

"Button," he said, gasping. "Close the hatch."

I looked around wildly and saw a panel near the door with the lever. It had two buttons on it that both looked exactly alike. I dashed toward it and hit the top one.

The hatch started to slide shut with a grinding protest. Something ugly and misshapen, its form backlit by the grey sky, stuck its head in. Kira shot it right between the glowing red eyes and it reared back. The hatch stopped grinding and slid shut with a clang.

"Holy fucking shit," Kira said.

"Nice shooting," Salazar said. He leaned against the ladder, still panting, his gun dangling in his hand.

"I've spent lot of hours playing *Left 4 Dead*." Kira grinned. "Never thought it would translate to real-life zombie killing, though."

"Alarms are going; we have to move," Salazar said. He pulled a white keycard from his suit pocket and held it out to me. "This is yours. The room you want is in the blue section, number forty-two. Can you remember that?"

"Life, the universe, and everything, blue. Got it," I said, taking the card. My hands were shaking, my fingers numb with cold and buzzing with adrenaline. I was soaked from my spill into the snow and starting to feel the cold.

"God, that's a horrible sound," Kira muttered. She checked the clip in her gun and nodded to Salazar.

"I don't hear anything," I said.

"Alarms are pitched for the shifters that patrol the corridors. Come on." Salazar moved past me and opened the door.

The door opened into a wide hallway that stretched to the left and right, curving away. The wall had a green stripe painted on it. From Salazar's diagram, I had pictured a single hall running in an infinity sign. This corridor was wide but had other openings in it, hallways that led off to wherever. It was more like a strand of DNA, I guessed, than a real figure eight.

"Jade, this will lead you to the blue corridor. Go right, then hang left when it turns. Find the hallway opening with the blue stripe. Good luck."

"Thank you," I said. I hesitated, looking at the three of them.

A shout rang down the hallway and I heard boots slamming down on metal.

"Take care of my brother," Kira said, giving me a somber nod. "Time to go make some noise."

They took off running to the left. I turned my back on them and started up the hallway to the right. I unzipped my wet hoodie and pulled out my dagger. I had no idea how to use it, but it seemed like a better option than the possibly-not-exploding spell notes I had folded in my jeans pocket. I was quite sure the blood ink had been damaged by me face-planting into the hill. My clothing was soaked. Small consolation that the spell probably would have failed. *No sour grapes here, nope.*

The blade was warm and pulsed in my fingers. Its weight was comforting, though I knew that must be magic or psychosomatic illusion. I had no idea how to use a knife, not really. A few lessons with Alek did not a master make. Being able to see again was also comforting. I hadn't quite realized until it was over how nerve-destroyingly awful being blind like that had been.

I turned the corner. The hallway I was in bent in a wide turn, continuing left. The roof and walls were the same copper-looking metal the room had been, but the floor was made of metal grating, like the kind you see on a footbridge. Faint blue light glowed up from under the grates. I tried not to wonder too much about it. No time. Three halls opened off it to the left. I sprinted down the corridor, looking at each side passage as I went by. First one was red. No go. The second was painted a dark purple.

Boots on metal rang out ahead of me. Putting on the last bit of speed I had, I bolted for the third hall. The paint was blue, the color of sky and hope and everything good. At least at that moment.

I hung a hard left and started looked at the doors. Salazar was right: they weren't cells but rooms like in a hotel, complete with a keycard reader on them. Only with a bulletproof glass window in each door. A Stephen King type of super-creepy hotel.

This hall stretched on forever, it seemed, though the light was dim there, making it difficult to read the numbers. Thirty-two. Thirty-three. On and on. I heard a shout somewhere behind me but didn't dare to glance back.

Forty-two. I reached the door and shoved the card into its slot, swiping it so quickly I got an error and a red light for my trouble. I did glance down the hall and saw a large wolflike creature glide past the opening to the green corridor. It didn't seem to see me. I swiped again, more carefully.

The light flicked to green and the door slid open like a barn door on a track inside the thick wall. I dived into the room and pulled it shut behind me, dropping down below the level of the window as it closed.

My heart in my throat and my lungs threatening to go on strike, I leaned against the cool metal and looked around. The room was about ten feet by ten feet, with a toilet and sink in one corner opposite me. On the right was a television bolted into the metal wall. A bed stretched along the left wall with a small side table bolted to the floor next to it.

The only light in the room was from a soft yellow bulb above my head. There was enough of it to illuminate the figure asleep in the bed. I crawled to the side and stood up, still pressed against the wall, hoping I was out of sight if anyone looked in. I doubted they'd be searching the rooms, but I had used a card. They might notice this door had been opened.

No idea how much time I had. I took a deep breath and went to wake up my father.

He was half-covered in a grey blanket, one arm thrown over his greying head, the other propped on an ample belly. He looked old, tired, and dead to the world. His hair was iron-grey, cut short like it had been in the diner. His face was brown and lined. He looked seventy, at least, and fat, very fat. I guessed his weight at three hundred pounds or more. So very different from my vision. A small bubble of spit grew and popped from his half-open lips as I approached the foot of the bed. He smelled like musty old grass. It reminded me of the smell in a hayloft that hasn't been swept enough.

I took a deep breath and sheathed my dagger. No point waking him up with a knife out. Might give entirely the wrong idea. Then I reached down and shook his leg.

"Must be new," he mumbled, not even opening his eyes. "Leave the tray on the table."

"I'm not here to feed you," I said. "You have to wake up."

"I'm tired, girl. Go away." He rolled over, pulling the blanket up to his chin.

In all my mental imaginings and rehearsals of this scene, I'd never pictured it going anything like this.

"I'm not a girl, I'm your damn daughter. I need your help." I reached down and shook his leg again.

"Don't have a daughter," he mumbled.

"Oh, for fuck's sake," I said, trying to keep my voice down but totally failing. We didn't have time for this shit. For all I knew, Salazar and Kira and the twins were out there getting shot or ripped to pieces, and I was in here arguing with a half-asleep idiot.

"Ash," I tried again. "Get up. I am your daughter. My name is Jade Crow. I am the daughter of Pearl Crow, who you fucked like almost fifty years ago." I gave his leg a very hard shake and dug my fingers in.

"Pearl?" He opened his eyes and finally looked at me. His eyes were dark brown with none of the red flecks I'd seen in the diner. "I remember her. Beautiful woman. Oh, how she could sing."

My mom can sing? I tried to remember if she ever had. I shoved the thought away. Not the time for reminiscing.

"Yes. You slept with her. She got pregnant with me. I'm your kid."

He squinted at me and heaved himself into a sitting position. "No. Unlikely I'd even have a child. Anyway, my kid would be a sorcerer. I don't sense any magic on you."

That stung. I had hoped that whatever had happened, it was just a matter of time until my power came back on its own. Hopefully this guy was wrong.

"I time-traveled," I said, going with the truth, as crazy as it sounded. "It burned out my power. That's why I need you. You showed up in a diner a few days ago and told me to come find you."

Okay. That definitely sounded insane. Great.

"Come here," he said. Intelligence glinted in his eyes and he looked far more awake.

I walked around the bed and crouched down. "I don't want to be seen from the door," I explained. "I kind of broke in here and they are looking for me."

He chuckled. "I broke in here too, I think. A long time ago."

Ash held out his hand and I took the hint, placing mine in it.

"If you are really a sorcerer," he said, "this will probably hurt."

His hand closed tightly on mine before I could respond and pain sliced into my head at my temples. The world went black and I squeezed my eyes shut. I wanted to pull away or start punching him or something, but I made myself hold still. Whatever he was doing, I had to hope it would confirm who I was. He was my ticket out of here, after all. He was the golden ticket to everything, in the end.

So, I breathed through the intense pain and silently recited the litany against fear from *Dune*.

Then, as quickly as it had come, the pain was gone, leaving me gasping. I opened my eyes to see Ash staring at me and smiling.

"Shit on a stick," he said, his voice taking on a slight drawl. "You really are my kid. Kind of fucked yourself up good, didn't you?"

Maybe I'd inherited my potty mouth. That thought almost got me to smile. No time for smiling. Right.

"Yeah, I did. Can we get out of here and discuss it somewhere else?" I glanced back at the door as I heard boots and someone yelling something down the hallway. Whatever was happening out there, they still seemed to be looking for me.

"How are we going to get out?" Ash asked.

"What? You are supposed to get us out. You can do that," I said. I stood up and glared down at him, willing him to start being more useful.

"Who told you that, exactly?" He pushed the blanket off his legs. He was wearing a vast tee shirt that said BEER IS GOOD! on it and a pair of red sweatpants. His feet were bare.

"A vampire," I said. "He helped me break in here. It's complicated."

"You listened to a vampire?" Ash shook his head and chuckled again. "Guess I better get you out. I'd like more sleep, but I suppose time is of the essence, et cetera, et cetera, and so on?"

"Very," I said, glancing at the door again.

"Help me up," he said.

He swung his tree-trunk legs over and I grabbed his hands, pulling him to his feet. He closed his eyes as he reached his arms overhead in a long stretch. I struggled not to growl with impatience as his joints popped and crackled.

"Up it is," he said after a moment, opening his eyes and looking at me again. "I'll just have to carry you, I reckon. Get on my back and hold on tight."

I did as he said, using the bed to boost myself up. He was just about six feet tall but with shoulders like an ox, broader than Alek's or Yosemite's. I wrapped my legs around his middle as best I could and clung to his thick neck. The wet-hay smell was a lot stronger now.

He took a big breath, his ribs expanding enough that I feared my legs would unclamp. Then he threw his arms upward again. A wide circular portal opened directly above us, revealing a clear and star-filled night sky. With a wild yell, my father leapt into the air, flying upward like a super-hero, taking me up, up, and away.

CHAPTER TEN ▶

The sky we flew up into wasn't a South Dakota sky. Looking below, I saw lights as though we were passing over a town, not the dark forest and receding prison I had expected. The air was freezing and we flew so quickly, I couldn't keep my eyes open. I felt my tears turning to ice on my cheeks and put my entire remaining energy into staying on Ash's back.

We flew long enough that after a while, I figured falling off and dying might not be so awful. I'd be warm again or at least not care about the hypothermia and frostbite that were surely setting in. As though sensing my suicidal thoughts, Ash dropped out of the sky at the same terrifying speed at which he'd flown up into it.

He landed in a field that was blissfully clear of snow. I had no idea how far we had come or where we were. I guessed still Northern Hemisphere, because the air, while not the biting cold from before, was still winter. I spied the Big Dipper in the sky as I lay on my back and tried to learn how to breathe again.

"I think my limbs fell off," I muttered. I felt the tingling pain in my feet as blood started to circulate again. I risked wiggling a toe.

"Bullshit," Ash said. He stood beside me. He held up his hand and white light coalesced around his fingers, illuminating the area. "No kid of mine is going to die of a little cold air."

"That was freezing," I said. I pulled my hoodie sleeves down over my icy hands and started rubbing them together vigorously. "Where are we?"

"Oregon. About ten miles from the ocean. Now, where did I put it?" He started walking in a spiral out from where we'd landed.

Oregon. Not so far then, at least, from Wylde and my friends. I sat up, wondering what part of the Oregon coast. It stretched for over three hundred miles, if I remembered correctly.

"Ah, here it is. I'll leave you the light," he said. Ash fixed the glowing sphere in the air.

I remembered keenly when magic had been so simple for me, and sighed.

"Wait," I said, as his words sank into my frozen and exhausted brain. "Leave me?"

"Back in a jiffy." He laughed and sank into the ground, disappearing from view before I could get another word out.

Yep. This had gone exactly how I imagined. Not.

I stood up and walked to where he'd left the glowing sphere. I jogged in place to warm up, re-zipping my hoodie after checking that my dagger was still in place. Noah had been right about it, apparently. Now that it was joined with its other half, it had abandoned its former habit of falling out of wherever I put it and trying to get left behind.

The ground shook. Then it shook again, harder, tumbling me off my feet. I crawled to my knees and reached under my hoodie for the dagger hilt.

A huge snake uncoiled from the ground. Its eyes glowed with infernal red light and its scales were gold and silver, patterned like a diamondback rattler.

"Ash?" I said, not knowing what to make of this thing. Had he somehow transformed?

The snake reared back, and flaps like a cobra's opened on its neck as it hissed at me, a tongue flickering out. Its fangs were as long as my body. It was like a dire cobra crossed with a late night Syfy movie creature.

I drew the dagger, keeping my eye on the hissing snake as I got to my feet. It was pitifully short and small in my hand. Why couldn't Noah have given me a spear of prophecy instead?

Even as I thought this, the dagger glowed blue and elongated, transforming into a sword. Not a polearm, but slightly better.

"Thanks, totally-not-creepy knife," I muttered.

The snake coiled and struck. I threw myself to the side and slashed with the sword, my tired body remembering Alek's combat lessons.

I wished I had my magic so badly, it hurt almost as much as coming down on my ankle wrong. Which I did, like a total boss. I felt something pop and my leg gave out.

I rolled and dragged myself up to my good leg, putting as little weight on the other as I could manage. The snake hissed and circled. I turned in place, waving the glowing sword in front of me.

"Back, shoo, go away," I yelled at it. "Bad snake."

At least I was about to get eaten without any witnesses to my terrible one-sided I'm-about-to-die banter.

The snake struck again, its scales grazing me as I leapt to the side. I lashed out with the sword, but the serpent was too quick and dodged my wild swing. It slithered away beyond the circle of light.

Staying on my feet sucked, but I managed. I turned slowly, my eyes searching the shadows beyond for any sign of movement, any flash of gold or silver or glowing red eyes. The night was deadly still.

"Ash," I yelled. "Ash, damnit, help me."

Of course, I was still working on the desperate assumption that Ash wasn't the snake. My father was clearly a powerful sorcerer, so who knew what he could turn into? This was not my night. This hadn't really been my week. Or my year.

Eyes flickered like ruby stars in the night, warning me. The snake rushed me again, rearing back and striking down. I was already moving, limping sideways as I tried again to slice the fucker with my sword. No dice. The snake recoiled quickly. At least it seemed afraid of my glowing blade. That was something.

Not afraid enough to stop trying to eat me. No luck there.

I kept staggering out of the way, my movements getting more painful and sluggish. My arm felt like I'd been swinging a lead bar, though the sword probably weighed only a couple pounds. I wasn't going to win this fight. There was no sign of my father. I was alone and I was going to die there, on this random fucking hill somewhere only miles from the Oregon coast.

Die. I reeled from another dodge and fixated on that word. I wasn't able to use magic, but I'd been healing just fine. I'd been able to read the books in Noah's library, too.

I was still a motherfucking sorceress.

I couldn't die. The only way to kill me was to be a sorcerer and eat my heart. As long as this thing wasn't my father in some kind of mega-evil-snake form, I was probably safe from the whole death thing.

New tactic time. I clenched my jaw, gritting my teeth. This was going to hurt.

"Hope you are right about this blade," I muttered as I stood and waited for the snake to strike again.

It did, predictably. This time, I didn't dodge. I let its jaws close around me, one giant fang jabbing and slicing right through my abdomen. It lifted me into the air and shook me as though to knock me loose from its fang.

I clung to my sword like the lifeline it was and stabbed that hell serpent right in its stupid face.

The snake convulsed, throwing me free of its mouth. I landed hard on the grass and stayed there, in far too much pain to want to move. From my sideways position, I watched the serpent writhe and twist.

Then, with a last terrible convulsion, it dropped into a gold and silver heap, unmoving.

I closed my eyes and let the sword fall from my hand. I knew I should do something about the gaping hole in my guts that was currently gushing blood, but I couldn't bring myself to care. It would heal or it wouldn't. At least my blood was warm.

"Lucy!" A man's voice lifted me out of the dark fog of pain. "Shucks, I forgot about her."

"Lucy can't come to the phone right now," I babbled. "She's dead."

"I see that," Ash said. His face swam into my red-flecked vision. He looked different, but my pain-addled mind wouldn't tell me what had changed. "You really should stop getting hurt like this."

"Go fuck yourself," I said. His face started to double, his eyes crossing, and the stars over his head grew brighter.

Ash laughed. He picked up my sword and looked it over. "Behave," he said as it started to glow more brightly. The sword dimmed and turned back into a dagger. He slid it into the sheath at my waist.

"Let's get you somewhere and take a look at this cut, hmm?" He lifted me up.

Darkness swirled over my eyes. I reached for unconsciousness like I would greet the embrace of a long-lost friend. Here I was again, being carried away from a fight by a man. Same Bat-time. Same Bat-station. Nothing changes.

CHAPTER ELEVEN

"Alek," I whispered. His hands were on my cheek, warm and familiar. I tried to reach for him, but the dream faded away before I could even grasp its memory. Instead, memory of my fight with the snake flooded back into my head. There was a bed under me and while my belly still felt like it was on fire, the flames were at least dying down. Wherever I was, I was warm and not dead. It's the little things in life, I was learning.

"Normally, I'd be insulted to be called another man's name," Ash said from somewhere beside me. "But I have a feeling this is somebody special."

I opened my eyes and blinked against the yellow light. When they adjusted and focused, I saw I was in a one-room log cabin. A fire crackled cheerfully in a huge stone hearth, lending the air a cozy woodsmoke scent. Ash sat on a hewn wood chair next to my bed. My dagger was in its sheath on a table just beyond him, resting next to an iron teakettle. I looked down at myself. The wound was under a flannel shirt. A Navaho-style blanket covered my legs.

"Hi," I said, looking back at Ash.

He looked like he had in my vision, only now his hair was long and pulled into two braids. His face was only slightly lined, looking forties instead of seventies, and his skin had lost is dull brown tone, looking more reddish and healthy. Red flecks burned in his eyes.

"How are you feeling?" he asked.

"Like I got bit by a giant fucking snake," I said. "What was that? Where did you go?"

"That was Lucy. I forgot I left her to guard my heart."

"Your heart?" I blinked at him.

"I had to go get it so I could remember. So I could be whole. Can't help my kid if I can barely remember I have one, am I right?" He grinned at me.

"You *didn't* know you had one," I pointed out.

"Of course I did. I knew about you the moment your cells started splitting inside your mom."

"That's creepy," I muttered. More loudly, I asked, "If you knew about me, why didn't you ever come see me? I didn't know about you."

"I was bending the rules just being here. You were safe enough where you were. I knew you'd need me later, though. So, I buried my heart to keep inside the Oath and went somewhere safe to take a nap. The part of me that knew about you wasn't able to travel with me. But see? It all worked out." He shrugged and patted my shoulder gently.

"I think I hate you a little," I said, too tired and hurt to keep from saying stupid things aloud.

"Fair enough," he said. He rose and went to the table. He flipped over a small ceramic cup and poured an amber liquid into it.

"What are these rules? What oath? What are you?" I asked. I tried to sit up as he came back over and handed me the cup. My abs, which still had a hole in them from what I could tell, protested with a sharp stab of white-hot pain. Lying down was good. I decided to do that some more.

"We'll get to that," he said. "You need to heal. When you wake up, come outside."

"I don't have time to heal," I said. I sniffed the tea. It seemed safe enough, some kind of chamomile and mint medley. Taking a sip, I looked at my father. "I have to regain my magic," I said. "People I love are depending on it. They don't have time for me to rest."

"They have time," Ash said. His face grew fuzzy. He took the cup from me as my eyes closed of their own volition.

"Drug me?" I slurred.

"Good night, Jade," he said. It was the last thing I heard before my dreams reclaimed me.

I awoke feeling more rested than I had in weeks. I was alone in the cabin. Sunlight shone in through two windows set high in the far wall. I unbuttoned the flannel shirt. My belly had a nasty puckered scar on it, but the flesh was fading from pink to brown. When I moved, I felt no pain. My ankle took my weight without protest.

My shoes were by the single door. I tugged them on, lacing them quickly. Ash had said to come outside and find him when I awoke. I had no idea how long I'd slept, but I feared it had been more than a single night, judging by how much my wounds had healed. Who knew what danger Alek and my friends were in or how close Samir was to finding and hurting them?

Who knew if Harper's time had run out?

I thought about Kira's words as I finished tying my shoes and stood up. *Trust.* Yeah, that. My friends weren't helpless. They were shifters, strong and powerful. And they were gamers. Intelligent, used to thinking on their feet. They'd come through the latest Samir shit with me, at my side nearly every step. They had home-territory advantage and a freaking druid protecting them.

Alek was one of the smartest people I'd ever met. Great with a gun, a brilliant fighter, and the most powerful shifter I'd ever seen. He'd protected me as many times as I had saved his ass.

Trust. I could do that. For a little while. They needed me, yes. But Ash had been right. They needed me whole and strong. They needed the sorceress. And they needed me to trust that they could handle shit, trust that they could help.

Amazing how much clearer things looked when I'd had a good night of sleep, eh?

I took a deep breath and opened the door.

Beyond the cabin was a meadow. Golden grass, as though it was high summer, stretched as far as my eye could see. A white sun burned high above in a painfully blue sky. I walked out into the meadow, turning in a circle, looking for Ash.

Then, in the distance, some of the golden grass detached itself. A huge serpent-like creature rose up. No, not a serpent. A dragon. I held my ground as it approached, undulating through the grass.

"Morning," its voice boomed, its tone reminiscent of Ash's.

"Ash?" I said.

"In the flesh," he said. The dragon chuckled, the sound rippling over me like a physical force. His breath smelled like fresh-baked bread.

I stared up at him. He was more of an Asian-style dragon than a European one. His body was long and almost serpent-like, but with a thick mane that rippled in the breeze and ran the whole extent of his thirty- or forty-foot spine. He had spindly arms with three clawed fingers and a clawed thumb. I saw no legs because of the length of the grass, but he had haunches, so I guessed he had some down his length, hidden from my view.

His head was wide, with a long jaw somewhat like a wolf's. Long tendrils trailed off his chin like a segmented beard. His forward-facing eyes glinted, dark as a night sky but with flecks of ruby fire in them instead of stars.

"You're a freaking dragon," I said.

"Indeed." He grinned at me, which was unnerving, given the amount of teeth he had. "I figured I'd just show you. Most people don't believe in dragons anymore."

I just nodded, still staring up at him. Then it hit me.

The bomb that the rogue Justice Eva had set. Alek saying he'd seen a dragon in the flames. The feeling of total strength and ingrained knowledge that fire wouldn't hurt me when I'd fought the elemental destroying my game store.

"I'm a half-dragon?" I said softly. I was going to have to add a new template to my character sheet.

"No, don't be ridiculous," Ash said. He snorted, intensifying the fresh bread smell in the air.

"Oh," I said. I looked at my feet, embarrassed that I'd assumed.

"There's no half about it," he added. "You are completely dragon."

"Um." I looked back up at him. "I can't turn into a dragon. I think I could have noticed."

"Your powers have been locked away. I had to do it when you were a baby. It is technically breaking the Oath for me to have a child."

"What oath? You keep mentioning this." I dug my foot into the grass. "Can we sit? Staring up at you is kind of painful. The sun is really bright."

"Oh, sorry," Ash said. In a blink, he was human again. He dropped down into the grass and sat cross-legged.

I joined him, resting my hands on my knees.

"Story time," Ash said. "I'll make this as brief as I can. Many thousands of years ago, magic was at its peak. Gods and creatures that are now legend, like dragons, roamed the Earth. It was pretty much a sucky time for humanity, however. Deities meddling in their lives all the time. Things with teeth and claws and magic roaming around, murdering them for food or sport. Not a good era to be born mortal."

I thought about the myths I'd studied in school. I could see his point. The gods had been real dicks in most of those stories.

"Okay," I said.

"So, many of us banded together. A group of gods and other immortals. We created the Oath and sealed away the demons and those gods and their ilk who stood against us. Humanity's time was rising, magic shrinking. We knew it was time to follow our ancestors and go into the lands beyond the stars."

"So, you just left?" I said. "But not all of you. What about shifters and the Fey, things like that?" I also thought about Brie, who was really like three goddesses sharing a single body.

"Not all the gods left. Some stayed to diminish, to guard the world from what magic was left to it. Many of the Fey Folk retreated to their own kingdoms, though some also stayed. They were not bound by the Oath, being lesser creatures. Same with the shifter folk. They were even rarer before than they are now."

"You stayed," I said. It was half a question, half a statement.

"No," Ash said. "I left, choosing to guard a seal, and made a life in the Veil. But two thousand or so years ago now, the Seal that I watched over in the Otherworld cracked open, and I came through, curious what had done it."

"And?" I said. I leaned forward, wrapped up in story time.

He shook his head with a sigh. "I don't know. But magic has been creeping back into the world drip by drip."

"So, you had a kid?" I prompted. "On purpose?"

"There are prophecies older than I am," he said, smiling at me. His smile was sad somehow and did not touch his dark, red-flecked eyes. "Some speak of a child born outside the Oath to a dragon and a crow."

Prophecies? About me? Um, yeah. Do not want.

"Let me guess: I'll bring balance to the Force?" I said, making a face at him.

"Not exactly, Jade Skywalker." He rolled his eyes, making a face right back at me. "It's unclear what this child will do, since clarity and prophecy are antithetical to each other, but I couldn't resist the opportunity."

"Wait, you've seen *Star Wars*? I thought you were asleep in prison for like forty years?"

He raised his hands in a what-can-you-do gesture and said, "They had Netflix."

Maybe nerd was genetic. I couldn't resist a smile.

"So," he said after a moment. Story time was apparently over, though I had a lot of questions. Questions that would have to wait. "What's your story?"

I took a deep breath. I'd come so far for his help. He deserved the truth, all of it, if he wanted.

"Where should I start?" I asked.

"At the beginning. Childhood should be early enough, I think."

I thought about that for a minute and gathered my memories along with my courage. Then I told him everything, spilling my guts and leaving out pretty much nothing. I had a suspicion that he knew at least some of it already.

The sun was dropping to the other side of the sky by the time I finished.

"That's where things stand. My friends are hiding out in the wilderness. My best friend is probably being tortured or has been killed by my evil ex, and I'm totally without magic." I flexed my fingers, letting blood flow back into them. Apparently, I'd been making tight fists through the last part of my tale. My hands hurt almost as much as my heart.

"Then I had better start training you," Ash said. "I will show you how to unlock your dragon side. When you do that, your magic should return stronger than it has ever been."

"How long will that take?" I looked up at the sky, wondering how long I'd been away from my friends already.

"If you are a quick study, maybe two months? Just unlocking your power won't be enough if you can't control it properly. It would be far too dangerous to unleash an immature dragon on the world."

"Two months?" I jumped to my feet. "Fuck, no. I can't take two months. I don't have that kind of time. Two days might make the difference between my friends living and dying. It could already be too damn late."

"Where do you think you are?" Ash rose gracefully to his feet.

"Not in Kansas anymore?" I said, still upset. I looked around, suspecting a trick question. "Or Oregon? It doesn't feel like winter here."

"You aren't anywhere, not really. We're in a pocket of the Veil. This isn't Earth, kiddo. Time won't pass outside at the same pace as in here. Minutes out there will feel like hours or even days here."

I looked around again. Golden grass stretching toward a deep blue horizon, the breeze sending a shivering and unending wave through it.

"Seriously? What you are saying is that I'm in Narnia, basically," I said. My heart stopped trying to punch its way through my chest and I unclenched my fists.

Ash threw back his head and laughed.

"More like the magical equivalent of the Matrix," he said, his face split by a huge grin.

"You're going to teach me to dodge bullets?" I said.

"When I'm done, you won't have to," he answered, not quite nailing the quote.

I let it pass, figuring he'd seen it a while ago and probably while half-asleep. I'd been shot enough to realize never getting shot again was a pretty sweet plan.

"All right," I said. I spun in a slow circle, taking in this place. Grass, sun, sky, cabin. Dragon.

I turned back to Ash and nodded. "I'm your grasshopper. Show me your dragony ways."

Samir, you have no idea the pain and destruction coming your way, I promised silently. *I will crush your face with my scaly might. Just wait, you bastard. Just you fucking wait.*

But my final, much happier thought as I followed my father through the door and into his cabin was that my friends were never going to believe this. I smiled.

MAGIC TO THE BONE

THE TWENTY-SIDED SORCERESS: BOOK VII

CHAPTER ONE ▶

I decided somewhere around day two that if I ever wrote an autobiography, I'd title that fucker *Leveling Up Is Hard to Do.*

Throughout my whole life, my answer to pretty much any problem had been to either run away or throw a lot of fireballs at it and *then* run away. I was done running. So, that left fireballs. When all you have is a hammer, so the saying goes, every problem looks like a nail.

Not having magic was proving to be the Gojira of nails, and I was all out of hammer.

My father Ash's solution so far had been rest, food, and enough meditation and "focus practice" to turn me into a monk. Finally, after a week of curbing my urge to start smashing furniture with my bare, utterly nonmagical hands in frustration, he conceded that his current method was not getting results.

"You are blocked," he said. "Not burned out as I thought."

"Okay, great. How do we unblock me?" I asked. "And if you say meditating more, I swear I'm gonna start punching logs," I added through gritted teeth.

We were seated on the knotted rag carpet in front of the huge stone hearth, the fire popping and crackling behind an iron screen. Ash smiled at me, the expression putting deeper lines into his mid-forties-looking face, the red flecks in his black eyes dancing. He tipped his head back, contemplated the log cabin's ceiling, and tugged on one of his braids in a gesture I was growing far too familiar with.

He didn't speak for a long moment, but I'd learned to let him be. There was no rushing Ash into working through his thoughts out loud and using his words.

"No," he said eventually. His gaze dropped back to mine. "Is there something you've forgotten?"

I knew he was musing from his tone, not really asking the question, but my frustration wouldn't let me shut my mouth.

"That's like the TSA asking if anyone has put something into your luggage without your knowledge," I muttered. There was likely a ton I had forgotten in my life, but the important bits all seemed to be there. Samir trying to kill me. Samir destroying my life over and over. The people I'd lost because of him. Their names and faces were a litany in my mind, a list that had started with my first real family and ended with Harper. A list I would never let grow. Not a chance.

There was only one name left to add to the list of the dead, and it started with "Sa" and ended with "that fucking asswipe bastard who will die horribly-mir." I rubbed my thumb over the divot in my twenty-sided die talisman. I'd picked up that habit since the mark was a reminder of my failure.

"Indeed," Ash said softly, dragging me out of my murderous thoughts. I wondered what he had read in my face, for his eyes were sad though his expression was still contemplative. He unfolded his long legs and rose. "I have to go get something," he said.

"I'm guessing not something in the cabin?"

"No, and while I'm gone, you must not leave the cabin. Under any circumstances." Ash fixed me with a deadly serious gaze, tension in his shoulders. Like he knew that saying those words was putting candy in front of a starving toddler.

"Great," I said. "Why don't you also say 'I'll be right back,' too?" I guessed he didn't watch a lot of horror movies while he was locked up in the secret government prison for magical critters.

"I mean it, Jade," he said.

"I know. I won't. I've read enough fairy tales, thanks." I smiled. I wasn't lying, either about the reading fairytales or the no intention of going outside. I figured when a dragon tells you not to do something, the wise response is to under no circumstances do that thing.

"Wait for me," he said. Then he opened the door without even putting on shoes or a coat, and disappeared into the darkness as the door slammed shut behind him, the latch turning itself.

I flopped back onto the carpet. He'd been gone ten seconds and the silence was already starting to wreck me. I made myself get up and go to the table. There was a box there with a deck of cards in it. They were old, no numbers on them. Ash had said he picked them up in Prussia, and while he might have been fucking with me, something about how he said it and the look of the cards made me believe him. I wondered if he knew there was no Prussia anymore, but he'd only been incarcerated for about forty years, so I hadn't said anything.

I didn't know how long my father would be gone. Left alone with only my thoughts, sorrow and anger threatened to wage war in my heart, and despair prodded at my mental defenses like a bored velociraptor. My choices were to brood, meditate some more, or play solitaire.

I played solitaire. I didn't even cheat. Much.

Ash didn't come back for a very long time. I slept twice, but without windows, I had no idea of the passage of time. I drank water from the sink when I was thirsty and made short work of the bread and cheese he'd left in a basket on the table. The weirdest part about being in the Veil pocket, whatever that was, was that while I got tired and thirsty and hungry, I didn't ever have to pee. I wondered if I was going to explode when I finally got back to Earth.

These were the deep thoughts I was pondering by the second "day" of Ash's disappearance. It was so damn tempting to go outside, but I resisted. Barely. I started to contemplate what I'd do if he didn't come back, but the truth was, I had no idea.

Living in a limbo land without magic, locked in a log cabin, and wholly dependent on someone else for everything was stupidly terrifying. Maybe one of the most nerve-racking things I've endured in my life. Which is saying a lot, considering I was a homeless non-white teenage girl living on the streets of New York in the eighties. But even then, I'd had magic as a fallback, knowing I could and would fry the shit out of anyone who fucked with me.

Here, I had nothing but time to dwell and brood.

Ash returned before I did anything truly stupid, like open the door. I didn't know if I'd ever been happier to see anyone in my life.

He came through the door with a grocery bag in one hand and a soccer-ball-sized leather pouch in the other. He set both bags down on the table.

"Took you long enough," I said. There was too much relief in my voice for the words to be as reproving as I meant them.

"You listened to me," Ash said. "Good."

"You said not to leave. I stayed." I gathered up the cards from the carpet in front of me and put them back into their box as a crazy thought dawned on me. "This wasn't some kind of stupid test, was it?" Was I supposed to go outside?

"No," Ash said. "I had to leave the Veil. It wasn't safe without me here keeping this pocket isolated and stable."

"Why didn't you just explain that before you left?" I made a face at him.

He lifted one shoulder in a half-shrug. "I did."

I started to argue, then shut my mouth. There wasn't a point.

"So," I said instead, eager for something that wasn't solitaire and brooding, "what's in the bag?"

The grocery bag had food, shockingly enough. Despite my raging curiosity about the mysteriously plain leather pouch, I managed to sit quietly enough and eat the sandwich Ash had brought for me. He even knew I liked root beer. It was endearing, if a little creepy.

We finished, putting the wrappers back into the bag. I wondered what trash service in the Veil was like but resisted saying that out loud also. I might've not had my magic back, but I was gaining uber levels in shutting up and patience. Life skills. Really. I watched silently as Ash opened the leather bag. I didn't know what I'd hoped for, but a small silver cup, a vial of green liquid, and a bunch of assorted roots wasn't exactly exciting.

"Wazzat?" I asked. "Looks like spell ingredients, I suppose?"

"I'm a dragon, not a witch," Ash said with a half-smile. "But you aren't far off, *I suppose*. I'm going to make tea. Then you will drink it."

"Tea? Your solution is tea?" I crossed my arms and swallowed a nervous chuckle.

"It's more like poison. If you were human or even shifter, it would kill you." Ash pulled out a small folding knife, unfolded it, and started shaving slivers off the various roots and into the silver cup.

"You are going to poison me?" There was no holding back my incredulous laugh now. "That's . . ." I trailed off. Maybe it was brilliant. If my body had to fight off the poison, maybe it would unblock my magic while it did so. For a moment, I was totally on board with this crazy plan, but then reality crashed in.

"Wait," I said. "That's not going to work. Remember Lucy? She damn near bit me in half. If that didn't wake up my magic to help me heal, I don't think poison will do it." His snake-shaped Guardian had nearly killed me and I was still magicless.

Ash's dark brows knitted together and then he chuckled. "No, not poisoning you so that you'll heal, though I can see why you thought that. This tea pulls the inside to the outside."

That sounded really disgusting. I pictured my skin turning inside out and my guts prolapsing. He laughed outright at my look of horror.

"Inside, in a metaphysical sense," he added as he went back to his work. "It should, if it works, show you what has been lost and give a path to get it back."

I pushed aside thoughts of being turned inside out and focused on what he was saying. Finding my lost magic was good. But . . . *wait a minute.*

"Seriously?" I said. "Like, seriously?"

"What?" Ash asked, looking up from his concoction.

"My dragon-mentor secret father is mixing up a poison drug to send his Native American sorceress daughter on a fucking vision quest." I leaned back in my chair and pressed my lips together.

"Perhaps you'll meet your spirit animal," Ash said.

I made a face at him, but something about those specific words bothered me. *Spirit animal.* For a moment, I almost remembered something, but it flitted away from my active thoughts before I could catch it, leaving a weirdly aching emptiness behind. Perhaps Ash was right. Perhaps I had somehow forgotten or lost something essential to myself, to my magic. I decided to shut up and let him work.

When it was done steeping, the poison tea looked like sunshine in a cup. It also smelled like overripe bananas and sadness. I really, really, *really* didn't want to put that in my mouth.

Too bad I didn't have a choice. It was time to suck it up and be an adult. And sometimes that meant doing things because they had to get done. Like taxes and standing in line at the DMV.

So, I adulted the fuck up and lifted the cup of poison. "Sláinte mhaith," I said with a grimace. Then I drank it down.

Worst. Shot. Ever.

"Do I get a chaser?" I gasped, my eyes watering as my throat burned enough that I wondered how flames didn't accompany the words out of my mouth.

"Best not to drink anything else with it, sorry." Ash gripped my elbow as I stumbled sideways.

The room was tipping, though I knew in some corner of my brain that it was me falling. The rug looked nice, a swirl of sky blue and grass green knotted into the cheerful yellows. It looked nice, but it was sure coming at my face really fast.

My father caught me before I bruised the rug. I lay in his arms in agony. Inside my head, weird images formed. It seemed as if a flaming Zerg army was spawning inside me and swarming through my limbs. Just when I was ready to cede the whole planet formerly known as Jade to the Queen of Blades, the swarm leapt into a Nydus Worm and my mind cleared.

My belly was still on fire, but it was at "shouldn't have left the seeds in that jalapeño" levels instead of "I just inhaled a field of ghost pepper" levels. I struggled to sit up, and Ash let me.

"I saw a vision of a computer game," I said. "I don't think this is working."

"Hold on to whatever you saw, no matter how strange," Ash said. "Come with me."

He helped me up. My legs were rubber but not on fire, so I managed to stand without leaning too heavily on him. I followed him to the cabin door.

It was broad daylight outside. The white sun hung at zenith and the sky was perfectly azure. Golden grass waved in the never-ending breeze. More of my head-fog cleared in the fresh air and I sucked down a breath full of summer warmth and the scent of ripe hay.

"Ah, well," Ash said. "I thought I felt a change. Perhaps not."

"Um," I said. "What about that?" I pointed to the left of the cabin.

For the last week, the landscape had always been unbroken rolling hills of grass, as far as my eye could see. Now there was a big bare patch with a mounded lump of earth in the middle only steps away from the cabin. I walked toward it. The mound had an opening, like a burial barrow or a giant ant nest. Not quite a Nydus, and I was nothing but glad about that.

"What about what?" Ash said. Curiosity gleamed in his eyes.

I described what I saw and he nodded, back in contemplative dragon mentor mode.

"Let me guess," I said. "I'm supposed to go in there?"

Ash shrugged, but I was already moving. The poison had brought me to this place. The key to unblocking my magic and defeating Samir could be down there. If I wanted to save my friends, if I wanted to ever be with Alek again, to be safe and happy again...

No choice. Not really.

I walked forward and let the earth swallow me.

CHAPTER TWO ▶

Two steps in, I fell down the rabbit hole. Well, maybe less a rabbit hole than dropping into freefall in a moist, nearly airless tunnel. I stretched my fingertips out but couldn't find walls. This was going to be the worst quest ever if I ended up a pancake at the bottom. Worst in many ways, not least of which was that I wouldn't die.

Anyone who says flying is just like falling but without the sudden stop at the end has never fallen very far or flown much; that's all I'm saying.

There was no sudden stop. One moment I was falling and trying to distract my fear-soaked brain with remembering what the terminal velocity for a human was. The next, I was on my hands and knees in a roughhewn tunnel. The ground was rocky with a thick layer of coarse dust over it. Dust and musty air tickled my nose. A soft blue glow emanated from around me like an aura. I looked down and realized I wasn't on my hands and knees after all.

I had no hands. Just paws. Huge black paws that were glowing pale blue. They were almost like a wolf's paws, but as I raised one to examine it, sitting back on my haunches for balance, I realized I had retractable claws. Some kind of panther, then? I wasn't sure. Twisting my head revealed a long, furry body that ended in a very long tail that was definitely catlike.

If my fur hadn't been black, I would have guessed snow leopard based on that tail. Weird.

Guess I'd found my spirit animal after all. Un-fucking-believable.

The tunnel stretched out ahead and behind me, so I arbitrarily chose the direction I'd been facing as the one to go in. I was on a quest, after all. No lollygagging.

The tunnel split into three, all descending. It reminded me of a mine shaft, though there were no tracks, just thick dust and rock beneath my paws. The dream version of a mine shaft, perhaps. I froze as I heard footsteps coming from the middle corridor. There was nowhere to hide, so I moved into the opening of one of the side tunnels. Not that anyone coming could fail to miss the huge glowing panther cat thing.

Two teenage boys in dirty jeans and flannel shirts picked their way to the intersection, both holding flashlights. The yellow light glinted off their black ponytails and their wide, nervous eyes. I recognized them as they stopped at the crossroads and turned. John and Connor. My cousins.

I hadn't thought about them since I was dealing with Not Afraid. I had no idea why they would be there now. They had nothing to do with my magic or the loss of it. What the frak had been in that cup?

They scented the air and John pointed to the way I'd come. "That way," he said.

"We're supposed to collapse the tunnel," Connor said. He rubbed his free hand on his jeans and looked back the way they had come.

"She's got no light," John said. "She's got no nose for this. No way she gets out. This place is rotten, but it could take us forever to collapse it. We'll just close up the front, okay? I mean, what if we brought it down on ourselves?" He peered up at the wooden supports.

"Sky Heart said—" Connor started to say.

"He ain't here. He won't know. We did what he said. She won't make it out of here. Come on, before we lose the light."

Sky Heart. At the sound of my grandfather's name, I growled. I couldn't help it. Neither one of them seemed to be able to see me, but at the growl, they both whipped their heads around, eyes searching the corridors. They still couldn't see me, I realized, as their eyes passed over me, unfocused and terrified.

"Okay, let's go." Connor led the way, and they disappeared into the damp darkness.

Sky Heart had killed a lot of people, most of them children. I wondered whom he had told them to abandon here, and why. His preferred method had been to throw them off a cliff if they didn't become crow shifters. Was this the past? My cousins had looked early teens, which meant I was still living at Three Feathers among the People. I'd be just a little kid at this point.

That thought poked at the weird, empty space I'd sensed earlier while Ash was brewing his magic potion. Again I couldn't grasp it. But this was what I was shown, so it must be important.

I went down the path my cousins had taken. I wanted to see whom they had left, though I was beginning to suspect I knew. But I couldn't *remember*. I reached for other memories of my childhood. My mother singing. The smell of the kitchen on baking day. How the quilt on my bed had a bright purple satin patch that I loved to stroke over and over, until I'd worn a hole in it. I'd cried until Mom had patched it with another piece, and Jasper, the man I'd thought was my father, had told her she spoiled me.

So, at least there was that. I remembered childhood, including the worse parts that came later. Including never fitting in, never being quite like everyone else.

The shaft grew tighter and closer, the air so stale that my lungs labored to draw enough in to support my huge body. It branched again, going down and down, and I followed pure instinct now. This was very like a bad dream, and I trusted that every road would lead wherever it wanted me to go. There was no way out but through.

Eventually, I heard a child sobbing. I followed that noise through the all-encompassing dark and found a little girl. Blood ran from a cut on her head, matting her dark, filthy hair. She sat curled against the wall, her arms wrapped around skinny knees. Her brown eyes were puffy from tears. One shoe was untied. She couldn't have been older than four or five.

But I knew that she was four. I knew because some of that empty space filled in.

I was in the mine near Three Feathers. That little girl was me, Jade Crow, age four. I remembered now my cousins leading me down, teasing me that I was afraid of the dark, that I was too little to come on such a grand adventure. I remembered those hours stuck in the darkness, all alone and sure I was going to stay there forever.

I couldn't remember how I got out; that piece of memory eluded me, as impossible to grab as a handful of cloud.

Baby Jade stopped sobbing and stared at me in shock. She could see me; that was very clear. She hiccupped and curled tighter as though her knobby knees would shield her from the giant cat beast. I crouched down, putting my belly on the cold floor, and tried to look as unthreatening as possible. Carefully I slunk toward her on my belly, stretching out my head. A soft whine escaped my throat.

She held still, watching me with eyes that seemed to glow as they reflected the blue light radiating from my body. Just before I reached her, the ground between us split open, a seam of pure silver running like a river, dividing us. My paw touched it and the universe opened to me.

It was only a moment, a terrifying, awesome, overwhelming glimmer of vast understanding. The world turned from solid and known to an undulating tapestry. Threads were woven into pictures too vast to grasp from my all-too-limited perspective. I saw what my time-reversing spell had done; the damage it had caused radiated out from a single knot. Threads broken, threads rewoven, threads knotted and tangled. I couldn't even begin to comprehend how to undo what I had done.

But there was one silver-and-purple thread that hung broken and caught my eye as it sparked like live wires. It was broken away from the knot of my time spell, and some deep gut feeling told me this wasn't my doing. The ends were frayed and stretched toward each other like fingers. Two lost halves searching for their mate in the darkness.

I held my head still mere inches from her legs and stared up into baby Jade's tear-stained face. I held my breath. I couldn't touch her. She had to choose.

Baby Jade slowly unwound her arms from her legs. Then she stretched out her hand, closing the gap as she dug her fingers into my fur.

"Hello, nice wolf," she said.

The ends of the threads found each other. Strands joined to strands and we were made whole.

I stepped out into the bright sunlight and faced Ash with a shit-eating grin. I'd never felt better. I must not have been gone very long, despite what it had felt like inside the mine shafts, because the sun was still at zenith.

"You found what you needed," he said, his tone certain.

"I found my spirit animal after all," I said.

Wolf was back with me, inside me now, a part of me as she'd never been before. I felt her in my mind, waiting patiently inside a silver circle, guarding Tess and all the hearts I'd consumed, keeping my ghosts at bay, protecting me as she'd been doing all along. Magic coursed through my veins, infusing every cell of my being. I felt whole, remade, stronger, better, faster, all that jazz.

I felt so powerful it scared me a little.

"You have a Guardian," Ash said. "Interesting."

The plains were back to where they had been, the barrow gone as soon as I left its entrance. We retreated to the cabin's shade and I tried to explain what I'd seen. I stumbled over the tapestry images.

"Somehow I forgot Wolf," I said. "I mean, Samir destroyed her when he killed Max, and she was just gone, but I could still remember she was missing. Then, I'm not sure when, I couldn't anymore. It was like she was *gone* gone."

"He broke her connection to you; he didn't destroy her. The Undying can't die, or they'd be very poorly named," Ash said with a forced chuckle. "You pushed the connection further away when you turned back the universe."

"So, why did finding her give me my power back?"

"It made you whole, though I think seeing the Patterns had as much to do with that as finding your Guardian again."

Patterns? I filed that away for about five minutes from now. First questions come first.

"What is she? Why do I have her?" I poked at Wolf in my mind, but she was as unforthcoming as ever, merely lifting her big head and staring me down with unblinking, star-filled eyes. Still, I wanted to weep with joy that she was back.

Ash shrugged. "Not even a dragon can explain the Gods, or their Undying, I'm afraid. You'd have to ask them."

"I wish this all made more sense," I muttered.

"It's magic," Ash said. "If it made sense, we'd call it science."

"Touché."

"The good news is that now I can show you how to use your power more effectively." Ash smiled at me. "After we have tea."

"Can I turn into a dragon now?" I already knew how to use magic, damnit. I wanted to get to the fun stuff. I still didn't feel particularly dragon-y. I just felt like me, except all leveled up in strength.

"You have to walk before you fly," Ash said. He shook his head. "First I must teach you more control. Then we'll see how you handle the dragon."

"I just want to kill Samir."

"Jade." Ash's tone turned serious. "Trust me a little longer."

I made a big show of sighing loudly and rolling my eyes at him like the super-mature kid I am, but I nodded. He'd helped me get my magic back, just as he'd promised. I was impatient and worried about my friends, but hopefully, in their world I'd been gone only a couple days. The druid had said they were hiding out and safe enough.

Trust. Right. That thing I was working on. Well, practice makes perfect.

"After enlightenment, chop wood, carry water," I said.

ALEK

Days turned into weeks. Over three of them now. It snowed and snowed some more, making it easier to avoid Samir's mercenaries in some ways, but rougher on Alek's ragtag band. He was used to the cold, used to living in woods and snow and surviving on what he could hunt. The rest of them besides the druid? Not so much.

He scouted Samir's home base as dawn tinged the grey sky the color of raw meat. Alek was at home there in the silence and the patterned shadows of black and white. His coat blended into the landscape, his stripes breaking up the visual field. His big paws trod lightly and easily through the snow. Alek could almost imagine he were home, wandering the Siberian forests of his youth, about to be ambushed by his siblings at any moment.

Unfortunately, the only ambush he could expect here would be by shifters, wolves, or bears, mercenaries hired by Samir to guard him while he prepared to raise Balor from the dead. Once Samir did that, it was unlikely anyone could stop him. All the evil sorcerer had to do was eat Balor's heart, and all the dead Celtic sorcerer's power would go to Samir, effectively rendering him a god.

Samir needed a unicorn to accomplish the spell, according to the druid and what Harper had told them from her time in captivity. Yosemite was keeping the unicorns as safe as he could, and Alek, with the help of Harper, Ezee, and Levi, was trying to keep close tabs on Samir's comings and goings.

It wasn't easy, despite his comfort in these woods. Samir didn't have wards up that they could tell, so there was some advantage there. Yosemite theorized that Samir needed to conserve power for the spell. Just having ingredients wasn't enough; one had to have the raw ability and strength to make it happen.

The mercenaries were the real problem. Most were shifters. The ones that weren't were still well armed and stayed in vehicles or around the house. Nobody moved out alone. Alek had narrowly avoided hunting parties multiple times. Sentry wolves prowled the perimeter as well, and while Alek had been tempted a time or two with killing them off, his less frustrated and more rational side had prevailed. If they started killing off Samir's forces, he'd bring more and might start actively hunting them in force, instead of the small parties he'd been sending.

So many risks. So little action. It was taking its toll. Alek swallowed a growl and pushed forward through the snow.

He got near where a patrolling wolf would likely pass and settled himself low to watch, blending into the background as though he were a statue carved of snow and shadow. In the dark coniferous branches above him, birds flitted and made their morning greetings. Within minutes, the tenor of the woodsong changed and he felt the approach of the wolf. Alek was upwind, the nearly imperceptible breeze blowing the wolf's scent into his face.

Again he withheld his instinct and desire to spring, and allowed the wolf to pass. It was one of the younger, smaller ones, a rangy beast with a red-brown coat. Alek waited until the wolf was long gone, then moved inside the perimeter to take up a spot on the very edge of the woods where he could see the farmhouse and clearing.

There was little movement at this time of morning. He counted the cars and saw there were six, plus the burned-out one that was Harper's handiwork. The air held the scents of human and shifter; traces of coffee and cigar smoke lingered as well. No strange activity. Samir appeared to be in a holding pattern, though he was definitely up to things.

Junebug was keeping watch on Wylde as best she could, volunteering because an owl could get around and go unnoticed more than any of them. Alek had argued they all had to assume that Samir had given descriptions of each of them to his men, so it wasn't safe to venture into town in human form, and their animal halves would stand out more than a little.

Wylde was quiet, from Junebug's reports. Too quiet, in many ways. After the murder of the witches—Samir had gotten to five of the thirteen, as far as they could tell—and the burning of Jade's building, everyone was either taking a winter vacation or hiding inside in fear, human and shifter alike. Dark SUVs came and went from some houses at odd hours; strange men openly carrying guns and dressed in paramilitary attire abounded. Junebug hadn't seen Sheriff Lee in two weeks, either, and the last report from Freyda had been over a week before, as she had to keep her head down also, her pack decimated in Samir's first attack. Human law enforcement was suspiciously thin on the ground as well, given the recent crimes. Somehow, Samir had Wylde isolated, even from a human response. He had thrown out the rulebook on keeping the supernatural quiet from humanity, it appeared, and that boded very ill indeed for everyone.

It was small consolation to Alek that Samir clearly didn't have what he wanted yet.

No Jade.

Alek could admit to himself that was what he truly looked for on these scouting missions. If Samir had her, Alek liked to believe he would have been able to tell. The way Samir had acted before meant he would flaunt her, try to use her as bait. That was Alek's guess and his grim hope. Samir wanted to destroy Jade, to kill everything she loved before taking her down. For all the evil sorcerer had told Harper that he had bigger plans, Jade was still enough of a priority that Samir had risked his plan to try to draw them in. Samir had kept Harper alive, and it had cost him two of the three ingredients he needed to raise Balor.

Jade was Samir's weakness. Alek was sure of it.

She was Alek's weakness as well. And his strength. Without her, they had no hope of truly defeating Samir. Without her, he had no hope, period. He protected her friends, he tried to present a strong front and lead them, but inside, he roared in his empty, lonely heart.

Alek settled his head on his paws and controlled his breathing so the mist of warm air wouldn't give him away. He would wait for Jade. They must wait.

He loved her. She loved him. She would return. These were facts of the universe, and he used them like claws to tear down the tide of frustration and despair threatening to swamp his weary heart.

Sunlight broke through the cloud cover and glinted off the silver paddock fencing. Movement there drew Alek's eyes. There was something inside the paddock. He lifted his head and drew a deep breath, sorting the scents again.

He couldn't scent it, but he saw the white shape move again. Unicorn. Light gleamed off its coat as it came to the side of the paddock nearest his hiding place. His eyesight was sharp, but it was still far away. He didn't recognize it as one of the unicorns supposedly safe with Yosemite, but that didn't mean much at this distance. A big white horse with a horn was pretty unmistakable.

There was no denying what he saw.

Alek slunk back into the woods, picking up speed as he moved away from Samir's base. He had to find the druid and the others. Samir had a unicorn.

I'm sorry, kitten, he whispered to Jade in his mind. *Our time is nearly up. Come home.*

Worried about the unicorn, Alek wasn't as careful as he usually was. He sprinted away from the clearing and nearly ran right into the patrolling wolf.

The wolf sprang back before Alek could react, and growled, hackles raised. It shouldn't have been there, as this was not its normal path, but Alek had no time to worry about that. The time for hiding was over if Samir had what he needed for that spell. This wolf had to die.

Alek leapt for the wolf, intending to snap its neck before it could raise a cry and bring any others. He was lucky the wolf was as surprised to see him as he was to run into it, for it was only snarling and not running. Stupid wolf. Dead wolf.

A red shape streaked out from the dark underbrush and threw itself between Alek and his prey. A fox, one that turned into a girl even as he twisted to avoid crushing Harper.

"Alek, don't," she said, panting. Her green eyes were wide, her skin sweaty, and her hair matted to her head.

Alek growled. What was she thinking? She was supposed to be farther behind him, watching his retreat to make sure he wasn't followed. Not nearly on top of him like this. And definitely not stopping him from preventing this wolf from bringing all its buddies to the fray.

Harper turned to the wolf, giving her back to Alek. He growled and moved sideways, ready to strike.

"Shift," Harper said to the wolf.

To Alek's shock, the wolf obeyed. A thin young man wearing cargo pants and a black tee shirt crouched warily in the snow, his brown eyes darting from Harper to Alek and back again.

"This is the guy who saved me," Harper said quietly, her gaze still fixed on the wolf shifter. "I owe him."

"You should both get far away from here," the wolf shifter whispered, glancing behind him and then again at Alek. Fear thinned his voice and turned his scent sour. He was terrified, but not of Alek or Harper.

Alek crouched, unable to decide if he should shift. He had questions for this man, but they were still in patrol range of the clearing, and if this wolf had doubled back, who knew what the others might be up to now that they had a unicorn to guard? They were close enough that shifter hearing might pick up sounds of a fight or even of normal voices.

"Go," Harper hissed. "Go, and we're even. You understand?"

"Got it," the wolf said.

Alek made his decision. He shifted, shivering in the blast of cold as his fur left him and was replaced with a wholly inadequate wool sweater.

"Wait," he said, as softly as he could. "The unicorn?"

The wolf licked his lips and shook his head. "You don't want to get involved. Get out. This ain't a fight anybody can win, believe me."

"Unicorn?" Harper said, more loudly than she should have.

Alek winced and brought a finger to his lips. She mouthed *sorry* at him.

"Go," the wolf said, as though he had any say in the matter and it were *their* life *he* was sparing.

Which, Alek thought, was fair enough at this point. The wolf shifter could have raised the alarm but was choosing not to. The less-charitable voice inside whispered that it was because the moment the wolf called for help, he must know that Alek would kill him.

Alek nodded and reached for his tiger again. Warm fur enveloped him. He knew what he needed to know now. The wolf's response had confirmed what Alek thought he'd seen. Samir had a unicorn. The wolf's fear made it very likely the ritual was at hand. He jerked his head at Harper and she shifted, following him away from the clearing. They took a winding path back to their own camp, careful to leave as little trail as they could.

Alek looked up at the steel-and-smoke sky, and sent another silent call for his mate. Time was up. Soon, all too soon, it would be too late for Jade to save them.

CHAPTER THREE ▶

I thought that I'd been training to take on Samir before, working with Alek and my friends to get stronger, gain more control of my magic. I'd thought wrong. What I'd been doing before was more like a toddler waving a piece of grass around, pretending it was a sword, compared to Ash's training.

Ash made me *use* my magic. Dawn till dark and often into the night. But it wasn't just the use of magic; it was the thinking he made me do behind it. We spent as much time talking as we did with him trying to think up new ways to throw magic at me.

"You have patterns you are comfortable with," Ash said. "Things you fall back on, things that come more easily to you."

"Is that bad?" I asked. I was too predictable, apparently. I leaned back in the grass and looked up at the moonless sky. There was a seductive peace to this place that I fought in my mind. I couldn't stay there. I couldn't tarry. I had to learn what I must and get back to my friends.

"It is, and it isn't. Think of it like riding a horse. The more you do it, the less you have to think about the parts, about how to stay on the horse, how to communicate where to go."

"Muscle memory," I said. "That's good, right?"

Ash chuckled. "It is, and it isn't."

"Gee, thanks." I sat up and glared at him.

"It makes some things your go-to plan and lets you do them quickly. It also means you are predictable. I know that no matter what I do, you will likely use a shield to ward off an attack and then try an offensive that is built on raw power, lightning or fire."

"That's not fair," I said. "I've been trying different things. I nearly knocked you out of the sky with that cyclone I made."

"Except you were too focused on it, so it made you slow. Practice it a hundred more times, and perhaps you can do it when the pressure is on."

That spell had taken a lot out of me, especially multitasking to keep my defenses up and manipulate time around me in small ways to speed my body and reactions. I was glad that I could still do that, that I still had Tess's memories to guide me. No more full-on time travel, though. She'd been right about that. I felt way more powerful than I ever had, but I wasn't stupid enough to try that shit again.

Though I would do it again in a heartbeat if it meant stopping Samir from killing everyone. Again.

Hopefully, it would never come to that.

"I don't have time. Besides, when do I get to turn into a dragon? Then I can just eat him." I grinned.

"You can't," Ash said.

"I can't be a dragon?" I hoped I was misunderstanding him. He'd said I was a dragon. He'd said I could transform when I was ready. I felt pretty fucking ready.

"You can choose a dragon form here in the Veil," Ash said, holding up a hand to stop my further protest. "But out there, in the mortal world, you will not be able to transform."

"You were planning to tell me that when?" Okay. No dragon form. Damn. There went my brilliant plan of eating Samir, heart and all.

Ash sighed. His dark eyes glinted in the light shining out from the open cabin door. He was quiet for a long moment, something I was growing used to. My father liked to think things through. I'd learned not to interrupt. There was no point in being impatient with Ash. It was about as useful as wishing the tide would come in more quickly.

"I tell you things as you need them," Ash said. "Focus. You have what you are good at. You are not unique in this."

I started to ask what that meant and then closed my mouth. I had things I fell back on, things I did because they came more naturally. Shielding, throwing more elemental magic around, pulling ideas from the D&D spellbook and morphing them into my own thing. I was not a creature of finesse or subtlety, not like . . .

"D'oh!" I said. "Right. Samir has his habits too." I knew this, of course; I just hadn't really thought it through. It was how I'd almost beaten him the first time. Using his weaknesses, his predictable desire to personally destroy me to get close to him.

I could have killed him then, even as my heart beat in his hand. It just would have cost everyone I loved. Too heavy a coin.

Saving them had still cost me too much. Steve. Max. Harper.

"Fight Samir," Ash said gently. "Not yourself. What is he good at? What will he fall back to when the pressure is on him?"

I closed my eyes and made myself face my memories and all the sneaky emotional demons lurking there.

"He likes to make things," I said. "He's very good at objects, putting power into things. He uses people and his vast wealth, too. He doesn't like to fight head-on unless he's utterly sure of victory."

"And when he is left no choice? When he fights face-to-face?"

I bit my lip as I wrapped my arms around my knees. In my mind, Wolf roused and growled, pacing the silver circle around my deepest memories.

"Exploding stones, weapons. That dagger, the Alpha and Omega, was originally his, though he only had one half, thank the Universe. He'll always fight with backup and weapons. He doesn't believe in the concept of a fair fight." I opened my eyes and looked at my father.

"We'll practice your defense against objects, then." Ash nodded to himself. "You'll have to try to anticipate what he'll do, where to get to him, perhaps remove his allies."

I couldn't decide if the tightness in my throat was from wanting to laugh or to cry.

"Fat chance," I muttered. "He's always one step ahead, at the least. Why can't you come with me? He wouldn't be able to predict you."

I'd asked that question already, and I knew that Ash's response wouldn't change. But damn, it would be so much easier with his help.

"Kiddo, you know I can't. I've interfered enough. I shouldn't even be in the mortal world. Every moment I spend there with my full power weakens the Seal."

"I know, I know. Magic apocalypse bad. It still sucks. I don't know if I can play his game, if I can beat him when he's the one always calling all the shots."

"Don't like the game? Change the rules," Ash said with a loose-shouldered shrug. "Be predictable, until you aren't."

"Know what would be unpredictable?" I said with a sly smile. "Turning into a fucking dragon."

Ash laughed. "Irrepressible kid. Ain't going to happen, not with the Seals in place, which is a damn good thing. But perhaps you are ready to pick a form here, and perhaps we can figure out a way for you to incorporate some of its strengths into your abilities outside the Veil."

"Squee!" I said, jumping to my feet.

"Squee? Who says that?" Ash shook his head.

"Me, so focus. How do I turn into a dragon?" I was so ready, I couldn't even come up with a simile in my head for how ready I was.

"You have to pick a form first. Solidify it in your mind. Once you turn, you'll only ever have the shape you pick, and your human one, of course."

"Can it be any dragon?" Images flashed through my head, from Disney-style Maleficent to Ash's own more Asian take, and everything in between.

I knew dragons. Like any proper nerd, I was obsessed with dragons.

"Doesn't even have to be a dragon, if you really want something else. The more complex, the more difficult the transformation, however."

"Wait, I could be like a wolf or a tiger or something?" I tipped my head sideways and made a face at him. "Where's the point in that?"

"Dragon is a concept. A word given to our kind by mortals. It has no more meaning than why we call apples apples or think the sky is blue," Ash said.

I held up a hand to forestall another long conversation on the nature of magic and what Ash called the Pattern. Apparently, that was what I'd glimpsed in my poison-vision, or at least, from how Ash explained it, what my mind had interpreted the data to mean, because what I'd seen were the very foundation of the entire universe and the magic coursing through it.

That magic-theory stuff made my head hurt. I couldn't do anything with it, in the end, except the magic-using part. But thinking about it as a tapestry wasn't useful. I preferred to stick with my feeling of magic, the sensation that it was more like water or electricity pulsing through my veins. I was no weaver. I couldn't even knit.

"So, you chose your dragon form?" I asked.

"No," Ash said. "I was born that way. I took the form of my mother, as you took the form of your mother."

Oh. That actually made some kind of sense. It was weird to think of him as having a mother. Weird to think I had a grandmother who was a dragon. I wanted to ask about her but pushed the questions aside. Knowing about extended family wouldn't help me defeat Samir.

"So this," I said, waving my hand up and down to indicate his current human shape, "that's the form you chose, the way I have to choose my alternate shape?"

"Yes. I look much like the first human I met who didn't run from me in fear. He told great jokes and was very wise. Human form seemed useful in many ways, and I liked humans more than most of our kind. So, when I chose a form, I modeled myself after him."

"Good thing you didn't get fascinated by a sheep, eh?"

"Funny," he said. "It's late. You should rest."

"Take the bed for once," I said. "I'm gonna grab a blanket and come back out here." I had to think, and I wanted the dark and the quiet.

Ash, being Ash, seemed to understand this without needing clarification. I grabbed a blanket and went a little distance from the cabin. It wasn't cold in this place, but the warmth of the blanket was still comforting, and it kept the grass from poking me in the butt.

So, I wouldn't be able to transform outside the Veil. That was pretty disappointing. I'd gone my whole life so far without being anything but me, so I guessed I could get over it.

Still. I wanted to pick a form. To come fully into whatever I really was. I lay back in the grass and thought about my favorite dragon-y things.

Prismatic dragons were pretty boss. I mean, I could be epic level at this point, right? When adding a template, why go half-ass about it? But I didn't really want to be a European-type dragon. They seemed clunky, plus I was kind of not European. By that logic, though, I wasn't Asian, either. But I had precedent for that, since my father had a more snakelike form. With that cool wolf-type head.

I definitely wanted something like that. Or . . . I laughed.

I could be a dragon cat. Wolves, tigers . . . I loved those creatures. But with scales. I tried to imagine the look on Alek's face if I turned into a winged, scaly tiger in front of him. Longing twisted in my heart. I missed his face, the scruff of his beard, the winter sky reflected in his pale eyes. He'd never see my dragon self.

Except he kind of had. I remembered what he said after I'd stopped the bomb and saved the alphas. He'd seen a dragon in that fire. We hadn't talked about it after, about what kind of dragon it had been or what it had looked like. Did his perception matter? I wasn't sure. It probably didn't. Ash would likely tell me that Alek had seen what his brain could interpret, just as I had in the poison-vision.

My dragon body would be mine. Mine to decide. So, why not a scaled, winged cat thing? I loved big cats; I loved purple and silver; I loved flying. Retractable claws seemed useful. I didn't need to gesture or anything to cast spells, so paws wouldn't be an issue, and I would totally make sure I could breathe fire or something. That was important.

Not a tiger. Tigers were overdone. Also not exactly American. I wanted a dragon form that was part of me, part of where I was born, who I was. Lynx, maybe? But with a long tail. A tail seemed useful.

I realized that I could pretty much have just visualized Wolf, put a more cat-like head on her, and stuck wings on, and been at nearly the place I was already. Maybe my subconscious was telling me something. Except definitely more scales. Definitely black, silver, and purple.

I was up most of the night visualizing my dragon self, putting details into the image in my mind. I hoped I hadn't complicated it so much that I'd end up looking like a Dr. Seuss character instead of a badass.

Ash brought me bread slathered in honey and a cup of tea. We watched the sun rise together in silence.

"Ready?" he asked finally.

"I'm scared I'll fuck this up and look crazy," I admitted.

Ash laughed and stood up. He unbuttoned his shirt, revealing abs that rivaled Alek's. The fact that he was my father made it super awkward.

"You think I visualized this human body exactly? I didn't care about muscles or even symmetry or being attractive to the humans. You build the picture as the base, your magic will take care of the rest. That's why it is best to keep things simple. Let the power flow. Let the pattern fit where it wants to go."

"Got it," I said. "You can put your shirt back on."

He did, hiding a smile as he looked down at the buttons.

"Take the image of what you want. Fix it in your mind until there is nothing else, until it feels as real as the grass under your feet, as the air coming in and going out of your lungs. Then let the magic flow and don't fight it."

Sounded simple enough. Which scared me. Simple and magic meant disaster sometimes, in my experience.

I walked some distance away from Ash and closed my eyes. I pushed away everything, every worry, every aching muscle. In my head I pictured my lynx-dragon. Head like a cat's but with scales. Ears tufted with soft black fur. Whiskers, because they seemed useful. Big black wings with deep purple scales, and a long, scaly tail that ended in its own tuft of fur. A compact, strong body with purple- and silver-tipped scales shimmering along its length. Perfect scales, armor against anything that might try to hurt me. I built my dragon to be fast and strong, and to keep me safe.

Air in, air out. Just me and the dragon. I pulled on my magic, letting it spill through me unchecked. I was caught up in the onslaught, filled until I felt I would burst. I waited to burst, to transform, but the magic swelled and then ebbed.

Nothing. I opened my eyes and turned to look back at Ash. I had failed.

Except my gaze met a scaled back and a large pair of folded black wings. And Ash seemed much smaller than he had before. I twisted fully around and reared back, looking down at myself. Paws! Retractable claws and purple paws. I unfurled my wings with barely a thought and beat them. Magic swelled through me again and I soared into the air. I didn't need the wings to fly, but after a couple scary dives, I found a way to use them to help stabilize and change direction with greater agility. My tail helped with that also, just like I'd envisioned. I turned huge circles above Ash, my keen eyes making out his shit-eating grin as he watched me soar and spin.

I raised my head to the heavens and opened my jaw, roaring purple flames out into the sky. Screw that weak human body, I thought. I wanted to stay this way and never turn back. Nothing could touch me, not up here, not with my armor. I would be safe forever.

Safe, but alone.

Reality reasserted itself and pulled me back toward the field and Ash. I couldn't soar forever. Not if I wanted to save my friends. I saw my choices laid out before me like the Pattern that Ash spoke of. I could stay in the Veil, stay a dragon-cat, be safe from the Samirs of the world.

Or I could go back to the imperfect Jade, the me I was born with instead of the me I'd chosen.

I dropped heavily to the ground and let instinct put me back into my body. Tears stung my eyes as I became human again. It was hard to let go, but I had shit to do and an evil ex to kill. I couldn't fight him as a dragon, so I had to resume my training as a human.

Some things are simple after all.

"I thought I'd have to go up and drag you back down in a few days," Ash said. "You could spend more time in your other form if you want." He was still half-smiling, but his eyes looked sad.

"I can't," I said. "It's glorious, but I can't fight Samir like that. Besides, pretty sure that form would suck at videogames," I added, trying to smile.

"True," Ash said. "You chose a beautiful dragon-cat thing, though. It's very you. I'm so proud." He reached out like he was going to ruffle my hair, and I stepped out of range.

"Ack, no. Don't get all weepy parental on me now. We gotta get back to you trying to kill me the way Samir will."

"As you wish," Ash said.

I followed him back to the cabin, wondering if the prison he'd been in had *The Princess Bride* on Netflix, too.

Days and nights blended into each other. Ash made exploding stones explode at me. He even made a rope that cut. On one of his shopping trips, he brought back a duffle bag full of guns. I resisted asking where those had come from. Probably safer not to know.

He shot at me. He attacked me with magic. He turned invisible and made me practice sensing spells and my otherworldly awareness techniques, or whatever the hell I was supposed to be developing. He drilled me in the use of the magic dagger, as well, which was kind of awesome. The Alpha and Omega would turn into a sword at my command, light and responsive in my hand. We never fought directly with it, though. Too much risk, since it was supposed to be able to kill anything.

Not a sorcerer, however. Ash was fairly sure of that. "I'd have a hell of a time regenerating from whatever it did, I imagine," he said when I asked. "It would most likely destroy everything but my heart's essence."

"So, if I stab Samir with it, I'll still have to eat his heart?" I looked at the dagger resting in its sheath. I had to admit that as much as I wanted to kill him deader than dead, I wasn't looking forward to giving his memories a permanent home in my brain. At least now that I was whole, I didn't have ghosts like mind-Tess lurking anymore. I didn't even want to think about what a horror show it would be to have Samir living on as a strong presence in my thoughts. Ick.

I trained. I slept. I ate. I fought. Sometimes, just for a little while, I turned into my dragon-cat form and flew, letting it all fall away for a precious, stolen moment.

"It's time," I said one night. I had been putting off saying so, but I could tell that Ash knew. I'd never be totally prepared. "I have to get back to my friends. Time is passing. Even days could be the difference between them surviving or not."

"Sit down, Jade," Ash said. He motioned to the rug in front of the fire.

His tone was deadly serious, and it scared me enough that I sat without making any smartass comment about not being a dog. He sat as well, crossing his legs and resting his hands on his knees. His mostly unlined face looked harsher, older somehow.

"There's one final thing I have to explain to you," he said, meeting my gaze with troubled eyes.

"You are freaking me out," I said. "Just say it." My stomach churned like it was full of acid and bees.

"You cannot, under any circumstances, kill Samir."

"The fuck you say?" I fisted my hands on my knees and glared at Ash. "I'm killing him. What the fuck has all this been for if not that?"

"You must defeat him, I agree. But you cannot swallow his heart. Destroy him with the Alpha and Omega, trap his heart in a container— anything but eat it." Ash leaned forward, emphasizing his words with a curt gesture.

"Why?" I asked. Killing Samir was the entire focus of my existence at the moment. This made zero sense.

"Two thousand years ago, a Seal cracked, leaking magic back into the world in greater and greater quantity. I believe that crack was caused by Samir. His pattern is tied to the Seal. If he is destroyed, it could break the Seal, which could be enough to nullify the Oath entirely. Magic would overflow the world, the time of humans would be over, and the gods and demons and all the creatures of magic could return."

That sounded pretty bad, sure. Yet . . . there was a lot of uncertainty in what Ash was saying, despite his deadly serious tone.

"You are saying *could* a lot," I pointed out. "So, you aren't sure?"

Ash took a deep breath and let it out in a sigh. "I am not sure. I am sure enough, however, that I will not let you go without your promise, Jade. Destroy him, but do not kill him."

"What, you want some magical oath from me?" I got to my feet and paced away from him. I wanted to punch something. Samir had to die. I didn't want to end the world, though. It seemed too stupid and yet so fucking fitting of the RNG of my life that something I wanted would have consequences like this. Never lucky.

"No," Ash said. "Your word will suffice."

"I'll think about it," I said. I folded my arms across my chest and shook my head as he started to speak again. "That's the best you are going to get."

Ash stared up into my face and nodded slowly. "Don't think too long," he said.

I knew what he'd seen in my expression. I trusted him. I trusted the vision I'd seen on my hunt for my magic. I knew all too well the long-reaching and terrible consequences of fucking with super-powerful magic. I'd made the mistake once, though for a damn good cause. If a magic apocalypse could be avoided, I would do what I must.

I walked out into the night and drew a deep breath of fresh air. I would leave in the morning, though it was probably silly to delay. I wanted one more night to marshal my thoughts and get ready to return to the real world.

Not killing Samir? Would destruction of his corporeal form and keeping his heart locked up in a box like the one he'd made for Clyde, his apprentice, to stuff me into be enough?

Not for Harper. I could hear her angry words in my memory, her white-hot determination on getting revenge for Max. And I almost felt relief along with the pang of deep loss. She was dead, and I'd never forgive myself for leaving her behind like that.

But if she were alive, she'd never forgive me if I didn't kill Samir.

"Sorry, furball," I whispered into the darkness. "I hope you will understand, if you are watching from some afterlife. I'm so sorry." I scrubbed the tears from my cheeks and went back inside to make my father a promise I wasn't sure I could keep.

HARPER

Harper crouched under the dubious cover of a stunted fir tree and watched the muddy, frozen dirt road that led away from Samir's base of operations. She'd argued for a position closer to the house, but with Junebug's return, she'd lost that position to the far-stealthier owl. Watch their movements, wait for an opportunity to perhaps sneak in. That was the brilliant plan—or really, compromise—they'd arrived at.

At least they were doing something. Yosemite had argued with Harper that they had to free the unicorn, though the druid had confirmed it wasn't one of the unicorns in the Frank's usual group. Ezee, Levi, and even Harper's mom thought it was a terrible plan to go back to the farmhouse. Harper could grudgingly admit they had a point. Nothing good had happened to her in that place, and it was crawling with mercenaries they didn't have the firepower or numbers to fight head-on.

Not to mention that bastard Samir. He alone was enough to make anyone think twice about attacking.

"He doesn't have the dragon blood, right? So, the unicorn is captured but safe," Ezee had argued.

"We don't know what he has or doesn't. He found another unicorn. What? You scared of a little fight?" Harper wanted to fight something, someone. Do something. Weeks of lurking in the woods, watching and waiting, wasn't getting her any closer to avenging Max. They were a mere annoyance, and barely that, in Samir's side. Not even a thorn. More like a tiny splinter.

"There might be alternate things he could use to raise Balor," Yosemite had interjected, stepping physically between Ezee and Harper. "I am not good with the language yet, but my book has some passages that might say more."

"Which we could read if Jade were here," Levi had said softly.

"Our knight in magic armor isn't here, and I don't see her riding up anytime soon," Harper shot back. "There's just us."

"She is right," Alek had said, surprising Harper most of all. "We cannot wait while Samir becomes a god. We will watch them more closely, but we have to be more careful. Junebug said they are more active in town, no? So we wait. If Samir leaves, perhaps with cover of darkness we can get the unicorn out."

There had been more arguing, but it was clear nobody had their heart in refusing. As scared and tired as they all were, Harper realized, they were all feeling the same frustration of inaction. Wylde was under siege in a quiet, deadly way, and nobody was stepping up to save their home. It was up to them.

Engine noise rumbled in the distance. Harper pressed herself as flat as her fox body would go. One of Samir's SUVs appeared after an agonizing minute, followed by two more, and both of the trucks with the huge cages in their beds. Harper tried to remember how many vehicles the mercenaries had in total. Five? Six? This was most of his forces moving out. No horse trailer, so it was likely the unicorn was still in the paddock.

She stayed hidden until the vehicles had rounded the bend and turned onto the road heading into Wylde. Then she counted to one hundred, lifting her nose and tasting the air. No smell of wolf or man, only mud, pine needles, and the lingering traces of exhaust fumes. All was quiet.

"He's definitely gone," Junebug said. "He was in the second vehicle. He's not hard to pick out; all the others seem to kowtow to him. Even though I can't see faces from that distance, I can read the body language."

"See? He's gone. Only one car remains. Most of them are gone. This is go time." Harper paced through the snow, kicking up chunks with her boots. By Junebug's count, there couldn't be more than a half dozen of the mercenaries left to guard the unicorn. They'd never have a better chance.

"I don't like it," Ezee said.

"Me either," Levi echoed. "Harper, think about it," he added as she glared at the twins. "He has his prize, something that you took from him, and he just goes off to do whatever in town, leaving barely anyone there to guard? This has 'trap' written all over it in letters fifty feet high."

"Perhaps," Junebug said. She laid a hand on Levi's arm. "But he did something first to the paddock with the unicorn. It's not just fencing now but a dome. The silver wire almost looks like chain link. Even if we got the halter off, the unicorn wouldn't be able to jump out."

"And why make it so much harder and more protected, with magic, no less, if it is a trap?" Harper added. She folded her arms across her chest. Levi had a point, but some risks had to be taken. Thwarting Samir's plans was the next best thing to killing his ass. She could do one, even if she lacked the power to do the other. Harper refused to be helpless.

"We do not know how soon they will return," Ezee said.

"Which is why we go now," Harper said. "We have to do something. Alek?"

She looked at the big tiger shifter. The former Justice had his head bowed, his pale blue eyes fixed on some unseen point in the middle distance.

"I will go," Alek said. "Harper is right. If there is a chance to stop him, we must take it."

"There's more trouble with this plan," Yosemite said. "If you go now, I cannot come with you."

Harper glared at the druid. "Why?"

"The confluence," Ezee said, comprehension dawning on his face.

"Oh, shit," Harper said. Yosemite had mentioned that he might have a chance of reaching into Faerie and contacting Brie and Ciaran, but he had to wait for a special day and time. Magic was too stupidly complicated. Harper wished spellcaster types could button-mash in real life. It would solve so many problems.

"At dusk. It may be my only chance for a while. If I could let them know what is going on, perhaps they can come home more quickly."

"There will be, what, one or two on patrol? Maybe four in the house?" Levi asked. His expression gave Harper hope. He was thinking, planning. He'd come with them.

Of course he would. Alek had spoken. They still followed what he said; even she herself did for the most part. He was the alpha, in the end, Justice or not. Harper figured now would be a poor time to start resenting that. She was exhausted, that was all. Tired and full of hate for the one man she had zero chance of killing. *Feels bad, man.*

No time for riding the pity train to sad town. Harper gave herself a mental shake as Alek started outlining the plan.

Junebug would watch the road in and be prepared to try and signal if the cars were returning. Harper and Alek would go in from the west, killing the sentry there and using the fact that there were few windows on the rear of the farmhouse as cover for getting across the open ground. Ezee and Levi would hunt down the sentry on the other side and be prepared to run in as a distraction if Harper and Alek needed it. Rose was going to stay behind with Yosemite in his grove and keep guard. Harper was happy about that last, though she knew her mother wasn't.

"This isn't the time for heroics," her mom told her, pulling Harper into a hug.

"I have to go. I know how to get that wire off," Harper said, squeezing her mother back until she felt like her arms would pop.

Not that there was much trick to it. Grab hold, ignore the horrible burn, pull. Harper wasn't about to share that detail yet. She wanted to be in the thick of things. Alek was huge and tough and shit, but he couldn't be allowed to have all the fun. Or take on all the danger. Harper prayed that Samir hadn't put any serious whammy on the fencing.

Torch that bridge when you are over it, she told herself.

Harper pulled away from her mom and smiled in what she hoped was a brave way. Then she reached for her fox and shifted, following the giant white tiger into the woods.

Round two, motherfucker, she thought. She was going to be a damn thorn, not a splinter, if she had any say at all.

▲ ▲ ▲

The sentry wolf was walking his normal route. It wasn't Gamer Guy, as Harper had nicknamed her reluctant benefactor. She felt thin relief at that as she looked at his corpse. This wolf hadn't stood a chance against Alek, not when Alek was hunting and ready. The tiger had snapped the wolf's neck to where it hung at a sickening angle. There was barely any blood, just a tinge of its scent on the air. That was good. It wouldn't give them away.

Harper was used to activity in the clearing around the farmhouse. Dusk was falling, the tired winter sun sinking behind black spears of pine and fir. Her breath puffed out from her nose as the air chilled to below freezing. The snow had started to form a thin crust and crunched beneath her paws. The sound was faint, something unlikely to be heard from the house, but it still made Harper jumpy. Nothing moved in the clearing except the dimly seen white form inside the wire dome.

Junebug had reported correctly. What had been a paddock made of silvered barbed wire was now a cage of the stuff, the silver wiring glowing faintly where it curved upward and formed a lattice-like dome. There were still gaps in the fencing, especially between the bottom wire and the snow-covered ground. Harper could get in the same way she had before, just going underneath it. Tiger-Alek wouldn't fit.

To get the halter off, she would have to shift. After that, she had no plan.

Didn't matter. *No plan survives contact with the enemy*, she told herself. Harper would do what a gamer did best: improvise and try not to die. *Life, on Hardcore mode*, she thought with a twinge of bleak humor. No do-overs. No save files.

Harper hung back at the edge of the woods, waiting with Alek while he took in the silent scene. Just one SUV left. A few lights in the windows, though the bathroom window she had escaped out of twice was dark. She met Alek's gaze and he gave a soft huffling grunt.

They moved in a line, small red fox and giant white tiger, crossing the open ground between the woods and the house with low, quick strides.

Alek held himself back for her, Harper knew, letting her stay on his tail, using his bulk to clear the snow. They were going to leave a hell of a trail, but it didn't matter. There was no hiding they had been there now, not with a dead wolf behind them.

She wondered if Ezee and Levi were all right, but immediately pushed that worry from her mind. They had their job to do and they would do it. The brothers would look out for each other, and Levi's wolverine was more than a match for a wolf, even a shifter wolf.

Harper reached the edge of the house behind Alek. Still no noise, no movement. She smelled nothing out of the ordinary, but not many ordinary smells, either. Snow, mud, Alek's tiger scent. Fainter smell of wolf and human. And horse. Which was odd, because unicorns didn't smell like horses exactly. Without waiting for Alek, Harper slid around the side of the house. No one was on the porch. No sounds of movement from inside.

Alek slunk out into the open ground by the paddock, his huge white form obscenely visible against the muddy, churned up ground. Harper watched as he circled the house. He seemed like he was just asking to be shot at, but nobody tried.

The house appeared abandoned. Alek snarled, moving back to Harper where she crouched beside the porch.

Okay, she admitted to herself. *It's maybe a trap.* But there was still a unicorn. She could see the white body moving inside the paddock. She couldn't see if it had a horn from here. She had to get closer.

Ignoring Alek's warning snarl, Harper ran for the paddock. She was almost to the fence, ready to duck beneath it, when she heard a woman yell out, "It's a trap; stop!"

Harper froze. It was a voice she recognized, a voice that she had started to despair of ever hearing again. Jade had returned.

CHAPTER FOUR ▶

"So I just have to click my heels together and think of home?" I looked at Ash with as much skepticism as I could muster, given that I was a dragon, in a pocket of unreality, talking to another dragon. Still, teleportation seemed kind of dangerous to me.

But . . . I wanted to be back with Alek and my friends. I wanted to know they were all right. I wasn't sure I was ready to face Samir again. I wasn't sure I'd ever feel ready. I guess part of being a big damn hero is that you do things anyway, no matter how scared you feel.

"Visualize a place you know well. It will be the quickest way back," Ash said.

We were standing in the open field by the cabin. I looked around and sighed. It would be so simple to stay, to put things off another week or two. Time wasn't passing much outside there, or so Ash said. Would another week mean the difference between winning and losing? I had no way to know.

"Everywhere I knew is gone," I said. My shop was burned. The Henhouse B&B was burned. I had no idea if Alek had his trailer with him or where it would be. Had he left Wylde? If my friends were smart, they would have gotten the hell out of there. But no, the druid had said they were hiding out in the River of No Return wilderness. "If they are in the woods, how will I find them?" I vocalized my worries.

"You could try going to a person and not a place, but it is less accurate." Ash folded his arms across his chest, his red-flecked eyes fixed on my face.

"Why can't you just drop me off in Wylde?" I asked. He'd explained why he couldn't come with me, that he had to stay in the Veil and become guardian to the cracked Seal again. Him being fully in the real world would be one dragon too many, apparently.

"Holding this pocket has been tiring enough," Ash said. He shook his head. "The Seal weakens. I cannot leave the Veil again. I've played chicken enough with the Oath for one lifetime, I think."

It was interesting to have my very existence referred to as playing chicken, but I let it go. Things were tense now that I was leaving. He'd accepted my promise not to kill Samir, but I had a suspicion that Ash was perfectly aware how thin that promise was, and that if push came to dying horribly, I'd break it in a heartbeat.

A person. Not a place.

"I can do this," I muttered. "Goodbye, Ash. Thank you," I added. He didn't offer a hug and I didn't ask. Ash nodded at me and smiled. I decided to pretend his smile was less sad than it looked.

There was only one person I wanted to be with, if I got right to the core of it all. I closed my eyes and let all awareness of the field and my father slip away. Instead, I pictured Alek. Tall, strong, ice-blue eyes, soft, pale skin, lips curving in a smirk that said he could see through all my bullshit. My tiger, my rock, my mate. I let my magic flow through me and focused all my will on being with Alek, on feeling his arms curling around me again, on the wild, musky scent of him.

Then I clicked my heels, because why not.

"There's no place like home," I whispered.

Turned out there was no place like home. There was fucking cold air, shitloads of snow, and my damn friends about to get themselves killed.

▲ ▲ ▲

I popped out of the Veil and ended up standing on the roof of an SUV in the middle of a big clearing. There was snow everywhere and my thin flannel shirt felt like nothing against the below-freezing air. I gasped for breath and squinted to look around in the dimming light. I barely had a moment to register that Harper was here and alive. The damn fox was about to get herself killed. Samir's magic coated this place like sugar on Frosted Flakes. It was writhing all around a paddock formed of silvered barbed wire, and radiated out in a spiral from there. I couldn't tell what the spell would do once triggered, but I couldn't imagine it was anything good.

There was a two-story farmhouse to my right with a huge white tiger crouched by the porch. Alek. Alive, for the moment. His blue eyes met mine and I held up my hands in a stay-put gesture.

"It's a trap; stop!" I called out to both of them. How the hell Harper hadn't triggered it yet I didn't know, but I could puzzle that out later. Provided later wasn't too late, of course.

The fox turned and looked at me. Her mouth opened and then shut. It was almost comical except for the dire circumstances. I gave her a thumbs-up. Fox-Harper didn't move, staying frozen in place. Tiger-Alek shifted to human, but also stayed where he was.

"Jade," he called out. "What is it?"

I rubbed my thumb over my talisman, using my newfound skills to examine Samir's spell. His power smelled honey-sweet and sickened me. I forced myself to remain calm. Destructive magic. Coming into the area hadn't triggered it. The spiral looked like a whirlpool of power, pulling in toward the center. It encompassed the house, the paddock, even the area I was in.

"Jade?"

I turned my head as Ezee shouted from across the field, his voice another balm on my worried soul. He and Levi stood at the edge of the clearing, just outside the spell's range.

"Stay back," I yelled to them. "Stay at the tree line." The last thing I needed was for two more of us to be caught in this.

"What about the unicorn?" Levi yelled. "We're here for it."

I looked back at the dome of glowing wires over the paddock. For a moment, I saw the white horse, but something about it seemed off. Samir's magic colored it as well. I summoned more of my power into myself and really stared. The unicorn seemed to melt away, leaving a grotesque construction of silver wires, a white horse hide, and chunks of carved wood behind. The spiral of magic was anchored at the center, buried inside the construct.

"It's an illusion," I said. I had a feeling that touching that thing would have caused the spell to trigger, but I doubted that was the only way to set this off. It was too elaborate, thrown too wide across the clearing.

Alek cursed in Russian. Fox-Harper started to move away from the paddock back toward Alek, being careful to stay in her old tracks, and the spell shivered in response, the honey-thick magic rising. The magic clung to her fur, outlining her in a glow apparently only I could see.

"Harper, no," I called out. "Don't move."

Her movement had confirmed my second assumption. The spell was a trap with multiple triggers. It was open right now, waiting for one of those trapped within to try and leave it.

I looked down at my own legs and feet. The car wasn't covered in magic. The spell was focused along the ground. I followed the spiral and began to pick out small points of concentrated power. As Ash had said, Samir was going with his comfort zone. He'd anchored the spell along the arms of the spiral with ensorcelled stones. I hadn't touched the ground, so I wasn't caught in the spell yet. The spell was designed for people who had to be in contact with the earth.

I didn't think I could dispel it without triggering it. That left getting

Alek and Harper out quickly. Samir was predictable in that he would probably have rigged the effect to be some kind of explosion. He liked explosions. The messier and showier, the better. Plus, if this trap was designed to catch my friends, he would have made sure it would do lots of damage. No guarantee of killing a shifter otherwise.

I shoved away that thoroughly unpleasant thought.

"Okay," I called out. "I have an idea. Ezee, Levi, back out of here. Like way, way back."

They must have picked up on how deadly serious I was, because they disappeared into the trees with little more than a worried look in our direction.

"What do you need?" Alek asked me.

"For you and Harper to hold really still. This might feel weird. Harper, I think it is safe for you to shift." It would be easier to do what I wanted if everyone was human since we might need to hold on to each other.

Harper shifted to human but stayed in place.

"Holding still, got it," she said.

"I'm going to yank you guys to me and then fly us out of here. When you get within reach, grab ahold of each other. This might be kind of explosive. Ready?" I pulled on my magic, letting it sing in my veins. I'd been training for weeks. This was just two little spells at once, with the lives of the two people I loved most in the world on the line. No biggie.

"Ready," Alek said.

"Let's do this," Harper said.

Throwing my arms wide, I snapped out two long coils of power and wrapped them around Alek and Harper. In my mind I drew the shield, summoning it around me as I yanked them into the air and across the field. I was already rising, towing them along like action heroes being dragged into a rescue helicopter. Only, instead of a helicopter, they just had a giant glowing sphere of shield magic. I hoped it was up to the task.

Alek's hand closed on my forearm first, warm and solid. Then Harper slammed into us as Samir's magic reacted and his spiral unwound in a spectacular burst. I slammed my shields closed and let the wave of Samir's magic throw us into the air like a punted soccer ball. Wind streamed past my face, whipping my hair free from its braid. I leaned into Alek and held on to my spell, pouring everything into the shield.

Then we were free from the explosion, sailing high above the trees. I opened my eyes and looked down with tear-blurred vision. Below us, the clearing was blackened and cratered. The house was gone. It looked like a meteor had hit, the trees around all bent and broken in a circle leaning away from the point of impact. There was no fire, just destruction. I hoped the twins had gotten far enough away from the edge.

I let go of the shield and wrapped us in magic so we wouldn't plummet to our deaths. I'd never flown with someone else clinging to me, much less two someones, but I managed a more or less graceful descent toward what looked like another clearing. Open ground seemed better than trying for a forest landing.

We crashed less than gracefully into the snow, Alek twisting at the last moment and catching me so I landed more on him than anything else. We just lay like that, Harper next to me, her hand still gripping my arm, my body sprawled half over Alek, and caught our breaths.

Alek's arms came up around me and squeezed me hard enough that I had to squeak in protest. Then his mouth was on mine, and for a moment, I forgot everything. This was what I had fought for. This was what I had missed, had craved.

"You two want to get a room?" Harper's voice pulled me back to reality.

I let go of Alek and turned to look at her. She was sitting up in the snow. Whole. Healthy. She looked tired and her eyes had dark circles below them, but she wasn't looking at me with that haunting glare of utter betrayal. I ignored a twinge of guilt. I didn't have to tell her about not being able to kill Samir yet.

"I thought you were dead," I said as I crawled off Alek and wrapped my arms around her.

She hugged me back, burying her head in my neck. "I ain't so easy to kill," she said. Her words were flippant though her tone was anything but.

"I'm sorry, furball," I whispered into her snow-caked hair.

"Jade!"

I let go of Harper reluctantly and looked up to see Ezee and Levi stumbling through the snow toward us.

"When you said way, way back, you meant it," Levi said with a grimace. His coat was torn across his chest, and fresh blood stained the ripped material.

"Are you all right?" I got to my feet. The snow coating my shirt was starting to melt and I was getting colder and colder by the second.

"Just a scratch from some branches I didn't dodge," Levi said.

Ezee stopped a couple feet from me. He, too, looked tired. They all did. Tired and more careworn than I'd ever seen them. I had a sudden and uncomfortable suspicion that more time had passed than I realized or than Ash had said would. I hoped Ash had merely been wrong and not lying to me.

"So, what did I miss? What happened to you guys?" I said with an only half-forced smile.

"Mercenaries," Ezee said, returning my smile, his white teeth flashing brightly in the dimming light. "What happened to you?"

"Training montage," I said. "Is everyone else safe?"

"Mom is back at camp guarding Yosemite while he tries to contact Brie and Ciaran. Junebug is keeping an eye on the road. We should probably find her. I can't imagine she missed the giant explosion."

Junebug was alive? The last thing I remembered was her being shot. Relief was truly a tangible thing when it was this strong. I hadn't realized how deeply I'd buried all my worries about my friends until just now. I felt like someone had removed a thousand pounds of iron from off my shoulders.

"Good, gang's all here," I said.

"Except Max," Harper said behind me.

I had no response to that.

"Let's get back to camp before Jade freezes, yes?" Alek said. He pulled off his jacket and draped it over my shoulders.

"Don't you need this?" I asked, trying to be polite even as I shoved my wet arms into the warm sleeves.

"I have fur," Alek said.

Good point. I pulled his oversized coat around me and felt marginally better.

My friends shifted to their animal forms and led the way. I followed Alek's tiger, my brain already working out how to tell my story. I owed them all a lot of explanations. They deserved the truth from me, about everything.

I watched Harper's red fox shape disappear into the gloom, and despaired. I was so damn glad she was alive, and so damn dreading having to tell her that I couldn't kill the man responsible for murdering her brother.

All I could hope for was that somehow she would understand.

I had a feeling asking Harper to understand we had to let Samir live would be a lot like asking the sun to rise in the west.

CHAPTER FIVE ▶

Levi peeled off to go collect Junebug. I followed Alek to their camp. It was cold, slow going through the woods, and the sight of the camp was a welcome thing indeed.

Iollan, the druid, must have made the camp. It was a tangle of branches and vines that didn't look native to the area grown into a domed structure that was covered in snow. The snow proved insulating, for the inside of the dome was far warmer than the outside. There were sleeping bags on rough pallets made of branches, and a small camp stove, along with some electric lanterns. It was rough but cozy.

The best part of arriving at camp was seeing Rose. Harper's mother came out of the dome and wrapped her wiry arms around me. I let myself indulge in her hug, wrapping my arms around her and holding on for a long time. It was nice to feel missed, to feel a little mothered as well.

"It's good to see you," Rose said. Her face had more lines in it than I remembered. Her eyes were shadowed with grief and determination. She was alive and vibrant and strong, and I was glad to see that.

Turning back time had been worth it, I knew then, in a deeper way than I had realized. Having Harper alive, sinking down onto a sleeping bag next to Alek as everyone gathered around, I looked at my friends and felt a strange satisfaction, a warm sense of belonging. If only I'd been able to save Max and Steve.

I shoved that thought away. I was there. Everyone was whole and alive. I looked around.

"Wait, where's Iollan?" I asked, not seeing the huge druid.

"He was in here, contacting Ciaran and Brie," Rosie said. "Then he came out to where I was keeping watch, said he had to check on something, and walked into a tree before I could get a word out."

"Typical," Ezee muttered.

I glanced at my friend, wondering if there was trouble in paradise. I knew his relationship with the druid was complicated. As Ezee had told me, they came from different worlds. A cosmopolitan-ish coyote shifter who loved his fine wines, modern-day comforts, and being professorial, versus the big druid who loved the wilds and looked like he hadn't seen a tailor or a razor in three hundred years.

"He can handle himself," I said. I dreaded my next question, but it had to be asked. "How long have I been gone?"

"You don't know?" Harper asked.

I shook my head.

"Little over three weeks." Levi was crouched in front of the camp stove's dubious warmth, heating a pot of water for what I hoped would be tea.

Three weeks? Shit. That was longer than I thought.

"So, what's been happening?" I asked.

"Where were you?" Harper said at the same time.

There was an awkward silence as we stared at each other.

"You first?" I said lamely. I needed a little more time to figure out what to say and how to say it. There was so much. For them, it had been three weeks. For me, it had been months. I felt so much had changed. I *was* changed.

"Samir captured me after you left," Harper said with a shrug that looked far too casual. "I escaped, but I figured out his plan first. Oh, and I rescued a unicorn."

Of course she did. I smiled and shook my head. "What's his plan? Besides apparently killing us all?"

Harper looked at Alek, who slid his arm around me.

"We think Samir is going to resurrect Balor, then eat his heart," Alek said.

"He wants to become a god," Ezee said.

"Fucktoast on a stick," I muttered. "Will that work?"

"Yosemite thinks it is possible, yeah," Harper said. "Samir seemed very convinced too."

I wanted to ask her more about her captivity, but I was afraid. It was partially my fault she had ended up like that. I kind of didn't want to know what had happened. I had enough guilt clogging my brain. I vowed to ask later, maybe after that bastard was dead as fuck. Or at least destroyed. Thinking about him hurting Harper, I was on the fence again about killing him. If the dagger didn't work, I wouldn't have a choice. He had to be destroyed.

Before he turned into a god. Because why would life take it easy on me? Ha.

"He needs a unicorn?" I asked, thinking of the illusion at the farmhouse.

"Last tear from a unicorn, last feather of a phoenix, last drop of blood from a dragon, I guess," Ezee said. "Harper also stole what we think was dragon blood, and we destroyed it."

"Phoenix feather? Like in Final Fantasy?" I asked. Last drop of blood from a dragon sounded pretty bad, considering I'd just brought him myself. I had no intention of giving him my last drop of blood. Or any drops.

I was glad it was the last drop, because Noah the vampire had taken some of my blood. I hated the idea of him helping Samir at all, but I didn't trust the Archivist and wouldn't put it past him. However, the blood he had was hardly my last. It wasn't even the last blood I'd shed.

"Yeah, I guess. Magic is weird," Harper said.

Levi dipped out a cup of boiling water and dropped a tea bag into it. He repeated this until the water was low, then dumped the final amount into the final cup. There weren't enough to go around, so he and Junebug shared. I watched him hand the cups around and accepted mine gratefully. It helped thaw my hands. This was how they'd been living for weeks.

I had amazing friends. I was going to get maudlin if I wasn't careful.

Tea handed out, everyone sat around in the circle of sleeping bags and looked at me. They were waiting for an explanation.

I leaned into Alek's warmth. I'd taken off his coat when we sat down, but now I wished I still had its bulk so I could hide in it. No. No more hiding. Time for the truth. Or at least most of it.

"This is going to sound kind of crazy," I warned them.

"Jade, seriously? We're a bunch of shapeshifters and a sorceress camped out in the wilderness in a shelter grown by a druid, all because your evil ex-boyfriend is trying to raise an ancient god so he can eat its heart and attain phenomenal cosmic power." Harper folded her arms across her chest and made a face at me as she finished speaking.

"Okay, good point," I said. Right. Out with it all. "I set up the contingency with Iollan before the fight with Samir in case we were in over our heads. I didn't tell you guys because I knew you'd probably be pissed about the idea of running away."

"Damn right," Harper muttered. "So, you ran before things even got going. Who wouldn't be pissed about that?"

"Let Jade speak," Rose said, touching Harper's arm gently. She and Harper were seated directly across from me.

I toyed with my mug for a moment, not wanting to meet Harper's eye. There was nothing for it but to keep going, as Rose said, and hope they understood. Hope they even believed me.

"That's what you remember," I said as I looked up and met Harper's angry green gaze. "But that isn't how it went down. We did fight." I held her gaze while I recounted the events, trying to maintain clinical distance from my memories. "Junebug got shot out of the air. Then Samir hit Iollan with a spell and ripped out his throat. Alek took a spell meant for me. It ripped his chest open. A giant bear killed Ezee and Levi. Everyone was dead or dying. Even me."

I stopped and took a deep breath, looking upward at the tangle of branches.

"Samir ripped out my heart," I said. I had told Ash all this, but it still wasn't easy to say aloud. "He had it in his hand. I still had the ley line magic. So, I did the only thing I could think to do. I turned back time."

I looked around at their faces. Ezee had his head tipped to the side, considering. Levi and Junebug were holding hands, both of them looking at me with raised eyebrows. Rose nodded, seeming to accept this. Harper shook her head, but the gesture was more contemplative than negating. I turned my head and looked at Alek. His ice-blue eyes looked down into mine and he nodded slowly.

"That makes sense," he said, his voice soft.

"It does?" Ezee asked.

"The Council of Nine told me once that if I stayed with Jade, I would die. I saw myself with a mortal wound in my chest. So, yes, this thing makes sense."

"That's why you told Iollan to get us out?" Harper said, half-question, half-statement. She looked like she was working something out in her head. "That's why you couldn't do anything. You had used too much magic already."

I didn't tell her that I'd had Iollan getting them all out before I turned back the clock. Better she didn't know that little detail.

"It was worse than that," I said. She'd given me the perfect opening to explain why I'd been gone so long. "I only turned back time a couple minutes, but it totally wrecked me. It burned out my magic. I couldn't use any magic at all. I couldn't even feel it."

"That is why you left?" Alek said. I loved him for the lack of reproach in his words. I had hurt him, I knew, but he was able to comprehend why.

Alek would never judge me too harshly for having to make tough calls and tougher decisions.

"I needed to get my magic back," I said. I filled them in on the rough details, though I savored the look on their faces when I mentioned I'd met Alek's sister.

"Kira?" Alek said. His eyes narrowed to slits. "She is still angry?"

"Yeah," I said. I figured I'd ask him about what he'd done, why he had killed her friend, and hear his side of the story, but not until later. Much later, at this rate. We had way bigger problems. "She helped me, though. We broke my biological father out of prison. Then I followed him to a magical pocket of time and space and he helped me get my magic back." I handwaved mentioning the Veil. There just wasn't time to explain it, and I wasn't even sure I knew exactly where we had been or what was happening.

"So, you are stronger, faster, better?" Levi said with a grin.

"Oh, it's better than that." I took a deep breath and smiled slowly. Then I told them the rest.

Being back with my friends, sitting next to my lover, and knowing everyone was safe? Worth everything.

Getting to tell my friends that I was a freaking dragon? Priceless.

In the excitement and explanations that followed, I conveniently forgot to mention the whole "can't kill Samir or else magic apocalypse" thing. Whoops.

Yosemite still hadn't returned by the time we were all figuring out sleeping arrangements. It worried all of us, but as I'd told Ezee, the druid knew these woods and could take care of himself.

I was worried, too, that Samir had set a trap at the farmhouse he'd been using as a base. Junebug offered to fly into Wylde and scout around, but while her owl-self didn't mind the darkness, with the druid missing it felt unsafe. I was bothered that Freyda and her wolves were missing as well. They had gone to find Softpaw, apparently, but even so, that was over a week past now. Between that and whatever Samir was up to with all the mercenaries in town, things looked not-great for the good guys.

But I was back. I was here and ready to fight. It wouldn't go the same as before. I wouldn't let it. Nor would I shut out my friends or refuse to let them help. They had done more these last few weeks to delay and threaten Samir's plans than I had, after all. I had learned the value of trust and I wasn't going to fuck up again.

At least, I wasn't going to fuck up in the same way. No plan survives contact with the enemy, after all.

I pulled on Alek's coat and went outside with him to take first watch. We wanted to be alone, and while it was cold, it was better than nothing.

"Moon is full," I said as he wrapped his arms around me. I leaned back into his warmth and looked up past his face at the sky. The moon sailed through a sea of stars, not a cloud in sight. It made the snow-covered trees around us into a softer world of glitter and shadow.

"Not quite," Alek said, dropping into Russian. His voice rumbled in his chest and into my back. "Tomorrow night."

"You going werewolf on me now?" I said with a laugh.

"At home, in the forests, sometimes the moon is all I would have for light. I know it well."

"I'm sorry I left you," I said softly. "I had to."

"I know," he said. "You fight your way. I am just glad you came back to me, Jade Crow." He tucked his head down beside mine, pressing his cheek against my cheek. I breathed in the warm musk of him, summer sunlight and vanilla spice. He was everything good in the world packaged up just for me.

"If I hadn't come back right when I did, you would have died. Harper would have died. Maybe the twins, too," I murmured. I hated to even think about it.

"But you did come back," Alek said. "What worries me is that Samir left, as though he knew we would come. That trap was for us, I think."

I felt as disturbed and confused as Alek sounded. It wasn't quite a Samir thing to do. My ex seemed overly attached to the idea of wrecking my life and killing my friends as a way of tearing me apart before he killed me himself. For him to leave a trap he didn't even know would get sprung meant things were in motion, meant he likely had to move on with his other plans.

It meant we were running out of time. *Time's up; let's do this* went through my mind. Only Samir would damn well be Leeroy.

"Whatever he is doing, it is soon," Alek added, echoing my thoughts.

"I won't run again," I said. "It ends. Tomorrow, I'm going to track him down."

"Alone?" Alek said, his voice a murmur of damp fog over my skin.

"No," I said. "Not alone."

I twisted around and hugged myself into his warmth, pressing my face to his chest. I had turned back time for this moment, for all the moments I would have after this. I could kill Samir to keep them safe. To help remove the shadows and pain from Harper's eyes. To alleviate my own guilt. For Max and Tess and Steve and Todd and Sophie and Kayla and Ji-Hoon.

The people I loved who had died because of Samir was a list that was burned into my heart. I wouldn't add to it. Not ever again.

Even if that meant breaking the Seal and letting magic back into the world. If it came down to a choice between that and letting those I loved die?

I would choose Samir's death. Every. Damn. Time.

CHAPTER SIX ▶

"It's like living in your own freezer," Levi said brightly as he dragged a side of bacon out of the snow piled up behind the druid's grove.

"Complete with lack of showers," Harper said as she brushed off a round of wood to sit on.

The day was clear, if cold, so we were gathered around outside. Rose had brought the camp stove out and was making coffee. I wasn't normally a coffee person, but I'd been outvoted and drinking battery acid was small payment to see my friends smiling, alive, and well enough. Junebug and Ezee had gone to look around. The druid wasn't back yet, which had us all worried. I'd made them promise to stay away from Samir's former camp and from town.

Once I was fed, I was going to Wylde myself. No more hiding. It was time to be the hunter. I rubbed at my talisman, feeling the divot in the silver. It was a constant reminder of what I had almost lost.

"You smell like sunshine and flowers," Levi told Harper. "Like . . . azaleas!"

"You smell like old bacon," she said.

"That's why Junebug loves me."

"She's a vegetarian."

"Both of you stop or we won't have any bacon. Bring that here," Rose said, cutting them off before it could end in fists and someone being tossed in the snow.

Bacon was soon sizzling, making my stomach growl almost as loud as Alek's. I held my metal plate in anticipation, breathing in the hot scent of cooking fat.

The screech of an owl broke the relative peace of the clearing. Junebug's huge white owl form swept down into the grove. She shifted even as she landed, dropping into a superhero landing pose in the snow at the edge of the cleared space around the dome.

"Jade, come, please," she cried out. Her hands had blood on them.

I dropped my plate and ran toward her. "What is it? Ezee?"

"No, Yosemite," she said. "I think he's dying."

We ran. Junebug flew ahead of us, dodging trees. I used my magic to push myself up and stay light on the snow, running like freaking Legolas to keep up with the shadow of wings ahead of me. Alek had shifted to tiger and stayed even with us. Levi and Harper were dark streaks of speed among the underbrush and evergreen boughs.

Not too far from the camp, we came to a huge spreading oak. A druid's tree if ever there was one. It reminded me of the one in the first camp, in Iollan's first grove where the fight had gone so poorly. This wasn't the same place—however, it was deeper into the wilderness and the ground beneath the oak was piled with rocks that, strangely, had no snow on them.

Iollan lay prone under the oak, half propped on its giant roots. Blood spilled out of his mouth with every agonizing breath, turning his red beard almost black. Ezee knelt beside his lover, pressing what had been his own shirt onto a wound I couldn't see on Iollan's chest. Ezee looked up at me with wild black eyes as I ran toward them.

"Save him," he commanded.

It was Max all over again. Time blurred for me and I saw Harper's face instead of Ezee's, her green eyes screaming at me to save her brother. I had failed Max.

I'm a sorceress, not a doctor, I wanted to say. But no. It didn't matter. I would not fail again.

I knelt next to the druid. He was cold to the touch but still breathing. His eyes were closed but his pupils were responsive to light when I pried one open. That was good, right?

"Move the shirt," I said. "I have to see the wound."

Ezee complied, spawning a fresh gush of blood as he removed the pressure. Blood pulsed from three neat holes in Iollan's broad chest. They looked like such tiny openings, but clearly they went deep. His swirling blue tattoos glowed faintly.

"Do the wounds go through?" I asked.

"No," Ezee said. "I checked beneath him when I got here. The bullets must be still inside. But he's not healing."

"He's unconscious," I pointed out. "Can he heal like that?"

Ezee gave me a helpless look and shook his head. He didn't know.

With the amount of blood he was losing, I was surprised Iollan was still alive. But he was cold, which I recalled might be a good thing. Didn't paramedics have a saying that someone isn't dead until they are warm and dead? I summoned magic and used it the way I had with Alek when he was poisoned. I tried to look inside. Maybe I could see the bullets and somehow coax them out. Magical surgery. First time for everything.

I found three small, round metal objects. They looked like dark obstructions to my magic. Iollan's magic was fighting them. I felt his power as a foreign thing, twisting in his body like vines pushing through bricks in a time-lapse video. His magic wasn't around the bullets; they existed in a strange void inside him, sending out a pulse of rusty-feeling magic themselves. No, not magic, more like anti-magic. The druidic magic was unfamiliar to my powers and it tried to fight me, too. His magic shoved on mine, driving the tendrils I'd extended into the wounds out.

"There's bullets in him. They are like musket balls or something," I said. "His magic doesn't want me poking around. I think the bullets are magic, or impeding his magic?"

"Cold iron," Ezee said instantly, nodding. "Get them out?" He laid a hand on Iollan's forehead. "His breathing is getting worse. Now, Jade."

I closed my eyes. The druidic power didn't want me there, but fuck it. I was stronger than it. I sent tendrils of power back into his body, using his wounds as my openings both physically and metaphysically. The vines writhed and twisted, growing thorns and attacking my magic, but I sheared through them.

"Careful," Ezee said as Iollan moaned in pain.

I gritted my teeth. There was no choice but to cause more pain. Two of the balls had taken fairly straight courses into his body and lodged next to bone. The third, however, had bounced around and was buried far off course in muscles that were likely his diaphragm or something. I wished I'd paid more attention to those crazy anatomy charts in health class back in high school. That was a long-ass time before, so it probably wouldn't have mattered anyway.

Grabbing the first iron ball, I yanked on it, visualizing my magic as though it were surgeon's tools instead of raw power. It popped clear of the wound with a gross sucking sound. I let it drop and reached for the second. That one came out more easily as the druidic magic inside him changed its course and began flooding the now iron-free wound.

The third one had no clear channel to pull it through. I wrapped my power around it but wasn't sure how to draw it out. Iollan's insides were a mess of blood, and even using magical x-ray vision, I wasn't sure how to do this without more damage. The ball wasn't that far away from the surface. Just a layer of fat and muscle stood in its way. No organs or bone blocking it.

"The way out is through," I muttered. Praying to whatever powers might protect a druid, I yanked hard on the ball and ripped it straight out of him in a gush of warm blood that spilled over my hands where they rested on his chest.

"Goddamnit, Jade," Ezee said.

I opened my eyes. "The iron is out," I said. "Sorry."

Ezee pressed his shirt back to the wound as I moved my fingers. "It's still bleeding."

"I'm not a healer," I said. "His magic is working on him now. Anything I try to do to stop the bleeding might make it worse. His power and mine don't play very nicely."

"Move your hands, Ezekiel," Alek said from behind me.

I rocked back on my heels and looked up. Alek had a giant snowball in his arms.

Ezee moved and Alek started packing snow around the druid's chest.

"Is making him cold a good idea?" Harper asked.

"It'll slow the bleeding." Levi came up behind his twin and laid a hand on Ezee's shoulder.

Alek packed the druid around with a pile of fresh snow. The snow turned pink but not red. I wiped my bloody hands off in more snow as best I could.

"It's working," Ezee said softly.

I came back under the tree and saw that his magic had kicked in fully. Thick green vines sprouted from the frozen earth, shoving aside rock and dirt as they unfurled and wrapped Iollan in their grip. Within a minute, he was covered from chin to ankle in thick greenery. His rough breathing slowed and no more blood sprayed from his mouth. His features relaxed into sleep.

There was nothing to do but wait. So, we found seats on the rocks and waited to see if the druid would live.

CHAPTER SEVEN

Iollan opened his eyes after an interminable couple of hours. The vines slid away from him, leaving bloody but unbroken skin behind. His tattoos were just faded blue ink again, the animal patterns and dots and knotwork no longer glowing. His ruined shirt hung off his shoulders as he sat upright.

"I thought you were dying," Ezee said. He took the druid's hand and pressed the back of it to his lips.

"Not so easy to kill," Iollan said as he laid a huge hand along Ezee's cheek. "How did you get the iron out?"

"Jade did it with her magic," Ezee said.

"Hi," I said with an awkward wave as I came to stand by his feet. "I'm back."

"Who shot you?" Ezee asked, not taking his eyes off Iollan's tired face.

"Mercenaries. I'll explain but I'm freezing." He shivered—for effect, most likely, but he did look chilled.

"Can you walk?" I asked.

"Only one way to know," he said.

Iollan got to his feet with Ezee's help. It turned out he could walk, but it was slow going. I used my magic to wrap us in warmth. Maybe I'd call this spell Mordenkainen's Space Heater? I was burning power like it was going out of style. Fighting Samir might have to wait a day or three for me to sleep and freshen up, but it was worth it to keep my friends alive.

Junebug had flown back to camp to warn Rose what was happening, then flown back to us to wait. She went ahead again, and there was a sleeping bag for Iollan to fall into. Coffee, camp toast, and reheated bacon waited for the rest of us.

"I need to talk to Jade alone," Iollan said.

Ezee made a face at that and Harper started to protest. Alek shut them all down with a soft growl. I was going to have to learn that trick.

"They will hear whatever we say anyway," I said to the druid. Shifters had fantastic senses, after all.

"Not inside my hut." He waved his hand at the dome of vines and branches above us.

Everyone filed out, Alek leaving last, as though to make sure they actually left us alone.

"Wait," I said. "Alek should stay." I didn't know what the druid had to say, but I didn't want to hear it alone. I had a feeling it wasn't good news.

There was a protest from Harper outside that fortunately my weaker sorceress senses couldn't hear clearly. Alek looked to Iollan, and the big druid nodded.

Alek dropped the thick piece of canvas covering the opening and then touched his hand to the vines. Silvery light flickered out over the whole of the structure.

"Secondary measure," he said with a shrug.

I sank down beside Iollan and sipped at the brown acidic water everyone else called coffee.

"Samir?" I said.

"I talked to Brie and Ciaran," Iollan began, not confirming but not denying my assumption. "They cannot return yet. The Fey are waiting. Did everyone tell you what Samir is up to?"

"Raising Balor? Yeah," I said. "So far as we know, right?"

"It's confirmed. Samir bought information from some of the Fey. He made his plans known in exchange, at least the gist of them. They want him to succeed, so they are keeping Brie and Ciaran away. They tried to get their oath they wouldn't interfere, but of course neither would give it." Iollan lay back against the shelter wall, pulling the sleeping bag up over his chest and wrapping his arms around himself. He was giant and broad, taller than Alek by half a foot, but he seemed reduced now, crumpled and a little broken.

"Fuck me sideways with a chainsaw," I muttered.

"That would be uncomfortable," Alek said.

I started to say that was the point but caught the gleam in his eye. I loved that he could even begin to joke at a time like this. We'd be perfect for each other right up to the end.

"It gets worse," Iollan said. "But first, Brie made me promise to make you promise not to kill Samir."

"Et tu, Brute?" I said.

"She cannot kill Samir?" Alek said. His gaze traveled from me to Iollan and back. "You knew?"

"Ash said the same thing. If I eat Samir's heart, it could apparently bring about some kind of magical apocalypse." I made a *cheers* gesture with my coffee mug and swallowed the bitter brew down. "But it's cool. I have a crazy plan to stab him with my magic knife and destroy him that way without killing him."

The plan sounded just as silly aloud here as it had talking to my father about it. Awesomesauce.

"Good," Iollan said. "If he raises Balor, however, it will not matter. He eats the heart, he could potentially break the Seal anyway."

"And the Fey want this?" I asked. I set down my mug and rubbed at the hilt of the Alpha and Omega where it hung, securely strapped to my ankle.

"They believe it will revive their lords, allow them to return and rule as they should. That magic flooding the world will bring the return of the Tuatha Dé."

"Right. So, we don't have Ciaran or Brie's help." I took a deep breath. They had been missing in action for a while. I hadn't been counting on them, but it sure would have been nice to have a little goddess and leprechaun backup when facing down my nemesis.

"It's worse," Iollan said with a grimace.

"How worse?" Alek asked. He slid his hand over my forearm and squeezed. That small gesture reminded me of his strength. I was not alone.

"Balor's head was taken by Samir last night," the druid said. "That's what I went to check on after I spoke with Brie. We took away the unicorn and destroyed the dragon blood. But there are apparently other ways to raise Balor. Like a sacrifice."

"If he's taken the head, he could be anywhere." I put my hand over Alek's and burrowed my fingers between his. We were fucked. I couldn't track him magically. There had to be some way to find him. He couldn't have gotten too far in a single night.

Except, you know, *magic*. It made a lot of things possible.

"He'll be near Wylde," Iollan said with a firm nod that set his matted curls bouncing. "Why was Balor's head here of all places in the world? Think about why you came to this place, as well."

"Ley lines," I said. "This place is crazy with magic."

"Not just the lines," Alek said softly.

No, not just the lines. I had come here to hide a leaf in a forest. Wylde, Idaho was the shifter capital of North America. Not just shifters, either. Witches, a few Fey, probably other supernatural people that I didn't even know about who had kept their heads down.

"How big a sacrifice?" I asked, not wanting to know the answer.

"Bigger the better. The more powerful the beings sacrificed, the better the chance of the spell working and bringing Balor fully back to life."

"The witches?" I asked.

They seemed a likely source, being easier to grab than shifters. Witches couldn't defend themselves with tooth and claw. After Samir ate Peggy the librarian's heart, they were supposed to have gotten out of town, but I didn't know if they had.

"We forgot to tell you," Alek said with a deep sigh. "The witches might be dead. Samir got to at least half of them."

I let out a long and varied string of every swear word I knew in Arabic, Russian, French, and Japanese. I probably made some up, but those were the most satisfying languages I could think to curse in. I ran out of breath before I could move on to Dutch.

"It gets even worse," Iollan said as I paused for air.

"Worse than Samir having all the knowledge and memory of women who were embedded in the very fabric of life in Wylde?" I said. Those women had been school principals, daycare workers, science teachers, bar owners, librarians—basically tapped into everything in Wylde. They would likely know who was human and who wasn't. They'd thought I was a hedge witch, a solo practitioner, and left me alone until it became clear I wasn't.

That they had spied on me for Samir didn't matter. Peggy had been a bitch to me, but I understood her motivations, her fears. Samir was not a man anyone with an ounce of self-preservation said no to.

"Balor can only be resurrected under the full moon of Mac Tíre." Iollan closed his eyes.

"Mock . . ." Alek tried to repeat the Irish word and looked at me questioningly.

"It's a word for wolf," I said. "When is this wolf moon supposed to happen?" I hardly had to ask. My stomach felt like someone had transportered a hive of bees into it, and the bees were angry. Tonight was a full moon. Never lucky.

"Tonight," Iollan said, confirming my suspicion.

I let go of Alek's hand and wrapped my arms around myself as I rocked back on my heels. We were super fucked, but worrying about that wasn't solving the problem.

"Okay. Samir is going to raise Balor tonight?"

Iollan nodded at my words.

"He's going to need a huge sacrifice. So, he'll need supernaturals. He has to get those from Wylde, probably. I imagine they won't come quietly." I chewed the inside of my lip. I tasted coffee and anger.

"He has cages," Alek said. He looked frustrated, as though he were only now seeing something that should have been obvious to him before. "In his trucks. Big cages. Harper was worried when she first saw them, because she thought they might have been used to capture us, as well."

"He's going to capture shifters," I said. "How many does he need?" I asked Iollan, looking back at the druid's exhausted face.

"I don't know. There was little time to ask Brie questions, and I am not sure even she knows. The Fey are not happy with her right now. They believe she should be on the side of bringing magic back fully into the world. It would free her." Iollan added that last part in Irish as he glanced at Alek. Alek didn't know that Brie was actually three Irish goddesses crammed into one feisty package.

Secrets upon secrets. I was sick of it all. And yet . . .

"We can't tell Harper or the others that I am not going to kill Samir," I said. I wasn't sure that I could not kill him. If it came down to him or me, I was going to eat his heart and deal with the consequences.

"All right," Alek said. His ice-blue eyes searched mine and he nodded slowly. He would keep my secrets. He was good like that. I imagined he also understood how pissed off Harper would be if she knew. We needed her focused.

She might find out later, but I'd deal with that then. Hopefully much later.

Right. Back to the "what we know" game.

"We should bring in the others," I said. "We'll just leave out a few details, yeah?"

Alek fetched everyone and I sketched out what we knew.

"So, we have until moonrise to find Samir and stop him?" Levi asked.

"Why move Balor's head?" Ezee asked.

"Yes to the first," Iollan said. "I think because he needs to be close to the sacrifice. The spell is not simple. It will take a ritual and lots of power. Druidic magic is as much about timing and ritual as it is about raw power. He is trying to do things our way, so he is somewhat bound by our rules."

That was the small bit of luck we had. What Samir was attempting wasn't something that could be strong-armed with raw power. He wouldn't have gone through all these preparations and risked so much if it were. Sorcery alone couldn't raise Balor.

But sorcery could stop Samir.

"We'll go to Wylde," I said. I stood up and looked around the group. Their mouths were hanging open, with the exception of Alek's. "What?"

"You said 'we,'" Harper said. "You aren't going to argue it is too dangerous and we should stay here?"

"Nope," I said, enjoying her baffled look. "I'm probably going to need help. More hands make light work and all that jazz."

"Are you a pod person? What have you done with Jade?" Harper squinted at me and held up her fingers in a crude cross.

"Okay, you give me shit, I will leave you behind," I said, smiling to take the bite from my words.

"No chance of that. I'm going. I'm going to watch that motherfucker die." Harper's smile slid into a snarl.

"I am too," Levi said, standing up.

Ezee looked at Iollan and then at his twin, clearly torn between staying with his injured lover and going with his brother.

"Go, Ezekiel. I will be safe enough here." Iollan smiled at Ezee. "I need to sleep in the earth again soon. I am sorry I cannot help more," he added, looking at me.

"Rest," I said. "We got this." I sounded pretty confident. Go me. The druid had risked his life to confirm that Balor had been moved, and he had gotten us the information we needed about the ritual. More backup and more information would have been nice, but he had already done so much.

"I will stay and guard him," Rose said.

"You don't want to see justice done for Max?" Harper said. She folded her arms over her chest and glared down at her mother.

"Revenge is not justice," Rose murmured, shaking her head sadly. "And I am no fighter. Go, sweetheart. You are not a child anymore and I cannot make you stay here and safe with me. We must make our own peace now, in our own way."

Harper looked like she might cry for a moment, her green eyes suspiciously bright, but she gave a curt nod and turned back to me.

"I will stay also," Junebug said. "I can keep watch better here. An owl is not much use in a straight-up fight. Getting shot once was enough for me in a lifetime."

Levi wrapped his arms around his wife. They made a pair, her with her hippy braids and hair longer than mine, him with his mohawk and myriad piercings, her skin pale against Levi's, dark and light twined together. I wondered if Alek and I looked that complete when we embraced.

"All right," I said, fighting my own urge to shed a tear or three. "Let's go storm the castle."

Nobody followed up the quote. Serious eyes focused on me, and one by one, everyone nodded.

I had my posse, such as we were. A coyote, a tiger, a wolverine, and a fox. There was a bar joke in this somewhere.

Now we just had to find out where exactly this castle was. And do it by moonrise. Just another day in the life.

Let's go end this, I thought, as I followed my furred friends outside. It was the last midnight and we were going into the woods.

CHAPTER EIGHT

Deep winter in Wylde was never a crazy busy time. The students at Juniper College were gone, and most people were at the ski places or staying in more hunting-friendly counties for the holidays. By the time we escaped the woods, slowed down by me being on foot, and went to where Levi had hidden his Jeep, it was later than I liked. Moonrise would come just near sunset, and this deep in winter, sunset came damned early. We drove into town, ready for anything.

Quiet greeted us. Eerie emptiness. I wasn't sure what day it was, but everything looked nearly deserted. The courthouse had no cars in front of it, not even one of the deputy or sheriff's vehicles. The road had been plowed since the last snowfall, but no one was driving. The lights were on at the gas station and I thought I saw someone moving inside the small convenience store attached, but nobody was filling up.

"Where to?" Levi asked me, his dark eyes flicking to mine in the rear-view mirror.

"Vivian's," I said. Nobody was trying to stop us from driving through town, so I figured we might as well start with the vet. She would know what was happening, if anything was.

I failed my will save and ended up staring as we drove past my burned-out comic store. Pwned looked even more dead and forlorn after a few weeks of snowfall. The snow couldn't entirely cover the blackened beams and caved-in walls. The building looked like a monster that had been slain, robbed for parts, and left to rot. Alek's arm tightened around my shoulders as we drove by. Someone had put up caution tape and a plastic fence, but the snow had nearly covered those, rendering them useless. No repairs had been started on the partially burned buildings to either side, and their windows were dark, CLOSED signs prominent.

Wylde, Idaho had become a ghost town in the short time I'd been gone.

"Where are the cops? Why isn't anyone repairing things? Why isn't anyone even out on the road?" I wondered aloud.

"Everyone is terrified because of the murders. We were getting press, there were talks of the FBI getting involved, and then it just stopped. Nobody is covering it anymore. It's like Area 51 or something." Harper peered out the window, her breath fogging the glass as she spoke.

Remembering what Detective Wise and Agent Salazar had said about not wanting to be involved in sorcerer stuff, plus knowing that our own government had hired Samir to build them a magical prison, I had a feeling it was more like the government had shut down all word getting out and decided to let Wylde and her supernatural beings handle their own mess. Easier to let a bunch of nonhumans disappear or die than to explain to the world that hey, by the way, magic is real and there's a lot of people who can turn into giant scary animals.

Nothing sent the message that we were truly on our own with Samir louder and clearer than the dead silence of the empty town.

"At least there's none of those heavily armed men in black that Junebug reported," Ezee said.

"Don't jinx us," Levi muttered.

We pulled up at Vivian Lake's big Victorian office-slash-house without seeing a soul. There were lights on in the houses around her office, but her own home was dark except for one window on the bottom floor that I thought must be her office, if my memory of the layout was any good. She lived above her workplace, the way I had before mine got destroyed.

We exited the car cautiously. I sensed no magic around, but I let Alek go ahead up to the door. It was dark in the office and the closed sign was turned to face outward, but the door was unlocked.

Inside, the office was a wreck. Someone had tried to tidy up slightly, but the cracked front counter, the jumble of paperwork that had been hastily restacked, and a broken lamp shoved into a wastebasket were all signs that this place had been the scene of a fight. My heart felt like it was going to break my ribs and nervous snakes twisted in my belly as I pulled up magic, ready for anything. Nothing good had happened there.

"I smell blood," Alek murmured, his voice barely audible. "It's not fresh," he added. He had his gun out as he moved expertly through the office, waving at us to stay back behind him.

"I'll watch the front," Levi whispered.

I watched Alek's back as he went down the hall, past the exam rooms, and toward the office, where the light shone under the door.

The door opened and a stocky Asian woman holding a gun appeared around the side. For a moment, she and Alek stared at each other, then both lowered their weapons.

"Rachel," I said. Wylde's sheriff, Rachel Lee, was still alive and still there. Relief crawled over me.

"Jade, Alek, thank God," Rachel said. She holstered her gun and waved us back.

Levi stayed watching the front, nodding to me when I looked a question at him.

"I'll be able to hear whatever you say from here if you leave the door open," he said.

Vivian's office was in better shape than her front reception area. Whatever fight had happened hadn't reached here. Harper, Ezee, Alek, and

I crowded in. Vivian was nowhere to be seen, and the sinking feeling started again in my belly.

"Where's Dr. Lake?" Harper asked before I could.

"They took her," Rachel said. She folded her arms across her chest, and I realized she wasn't in uniform. No badge, just a gun strapped on over a thick sweater and jeans. I remembered vaguely there had been talk about suspending her, but it felt like a lifetime ago.

"Who took her? How?" Ezee said.

"Samir," I answered, guessing. He wanted sacrifices, and Vivian was well known as a shifter to the other supernaturals. I clenched my hands into fists.

"Yeah, him and those humans he has working for him. They've hit quite a few of the shifter families. They even captured the alpha. Used her unconscious body as bait right in the middle of the damn road to grab a few others. Then they took the kids, even the ones not yet gone through the change, right out of school yesterday. Fucking coordinated." Rachel spat the words out. Her face was lined, her eyes angry and hard.

"How?" I repeated Ezee's question. Shifters, even kids, weren't easy prey. Taking Freyda, the alpha of alphas, would have been damn near impossible. At least, taking her alive would. "And why isn't anyone out there?" I added, waving a hand at the window. "Kids got kidnapped and nobody is doing anything?"

"The humans are hiding or have fled. Shifters that tried to flee got grabbed, like they were watching for that. They have tranq darts fit to maim an elephant that have to have some kind of magic going on. Get hit with one, and a shifter falls over like they're dead, except they aren't. I barely got away when they came for me at the station."

"Why aren't people leaving Wylde?" Alek cut in.

"There was a roadblock up on both sides going into and out of town until last night. Guess they got what they wanted. State cops are pretending Wylde doesn't exist, my damn deputy disappeared, and I'm suspended.

We've been abandoned. Fucking humans." Rachel's eyes glittered, and I was glad she wasn't still holding her gun.

I understood her rage. The human world not knowing about the supernatural world usually worked in our favor, but it had downsides. It was painfully clear that as far as the human Powers That Be were concerned, our mess was ours. I wondered if they would feel the same way if Samir achieved godhood.

Of course, if the Seal was broken and magic flooded the world again, and all the gods walked the Earth, every human on the planet was in for the rudest awakening ever. Sheer numbers wouldn't matter a whit against actual immortals.

"Fine," Harper said. "So, we're abandoned. It doesn't matter. We're going to go fuck that bastard's shit up. Where did they take the kids and Dr. Lake?"

"I don't know," Rachel said. "We're meeting up at Mikhail's trailer park, those few of us left. I came to grab some first-aid supplies here, but then we're going to track them down. They left town in trucks heading toward Juniper."

"Could they be there?" I asked, looking at Ezee.

"No students are allowed to stay over winter break, but there's some security and janitorial staff on, plus a few professors usually around catching up on work," he said. He shook his head. "So, maybe?"

I stepped forward and leaned a hip on Vivian's desk. Something was teasing at my brain, something Rachel had said. I was missing an important detail and needed to work it out quickly. My instincts were screaming at me. I rubbed my fingers over the bridge of my nose and squeezed my eyes shut, thinking.

Samir knew about the shifters; he knew about the college; he knew about Wylde. Because of the witches.

"You dealt with Peggy and her coven a lot?" I asked Rachel, opening my eyes.

She tipped her head to the side at my apparent non sequitur but nodded. "Sure. She helped me keep some things quiet from time to time, deal with non-shifter supes on occasion."

"Meeting up at Mikhail's, was that a normal plan? Or something you made up just now on the fly?" I said. Things were falling into place in my head, pieces fitting together to form a horrible picture.

"That's the plan in general. We'd often meet up there if we needed to talk about things on neutral ground. When the kids were taken, that's how the remaining shifters knew to come here. Not that there are many of us left. The Pearsons, Kameron, couple others, plus Mikhail and his younger son."

"So, Peggy knew about meeting up there," I said.

From the corner of my eye I saw horrified looks pass across Ezee and Harper's faces as they figured out what I was getting at.

"Yes," Rachel said, a line forming between her eyebrows.

"So, Samir knows," Alek said softly. "How long since you left there?"

"A few hours. I wanted to check on people now that the roadblock is down, see who might be around. Oh, shit." Rachel grabbed up a duffle bag that had been hidden behind Vivian's desk. "Shit," she repeated.

"Come on," I said. "We've got to get to Mikhail and Sons right fucking now."

Maybe Samir had all the shifters he needed. Maybe he wouldn't bother going after them.

Maybe *Firefly* would be revived with a full second season.

Yeah. I wasn't going to bet on any of those things, either.

CHAPTER NINE

Alek and I piled into Rachel's SUV. Levi, Ezee, and Harper took Levi's Jeep and followed us. No traffic meant no one to slow us down, just the slick roads, but Rachel and Levi had both grown up driving in these kinds of conditions and handled their vehicles like they were racing on a dry track in perfect weather.

"Guess we won't get a speeding ticket," I joked as I clung to Alek's arm with one hand and braced myself against the dash with the other.

"I'll cite myself later," Rachel said with a teeth-baring grin.

"Just make sure to let Levi off with a warning. I don't think his license can handle more tickets." I returned her smile.

Mikhail's RV park was on the very edge of town directly off the main road leading into Wylde from the southeast. In non-winter months, it was a scenic, lovely spot for a park. Bear Creek flowed past it in a jumbled rush of boulder-filled rapids, and the park had permanent structures for grilling and picnics, also including a laundry room, a huge river rock–lined hot tub, and showers. Mikhail lived in a two-story log cabin with his younger son, Vasili. The older son drove trucks most of the year. I couldn't remember his name. In winter, the park was mostly shut down, the stalls empty, the campsites snowed under.

It wasn't empty now. The snow on the drive was churned up and ridged from many vehicles using it recently. We headed straight down the long driveway. Two big trucks with cages in their beds were pulled up in a haphazard wedge formation in the big RV turn-around area in front of the main cabin. Men in black-and-white patterned fatigues scrambled around a big flatbed trailer hooked up to one of the trucks. A huge, unconscious—or dead—brown bear was strapped down to the bed, and another lay in a heap of ropes and cables at the foot of the trailer.

I feared we were too late. Except they were still there. These bastards were going to regret that.

We didn't go for subtlety or stealth. Rachel yanked hard on the steering wheel and brought her SUV sideways to partially block off the driveway. She was out of the car with her gun drawn before we'd even stopped skidding.

Levi took her cue and pulled his Jeep to a quick stop behind us, keeping the SUV as cover. That was all I had time to see as I lurched sideways out of the truck behind Alek.

The mercenaries started shouting and bringing guns up. Alek and I had come out on the wrong side of the truck if we wanted cover, but I had shields up instantly, blocking fire for us both. The snow under my feet was dirty, and spattered with red. We weren't the first to fight there.

"Body armor," Rachel yelled from behind the truck where she had smartly grabbed cover.

"Drop it," Alek told me. I let the shield go for a bare second, and Alek took the nearest man down with two rapid shots to the head. My ears rang and I gritted my teeth. Guns were freaking loud when fired this close to my damn head. A dart bounced off my shield as I summoned it back into existence just in time. Rachel had said they were tranqing the shifters. These guys were in for a rude awakening now.

Another went down as Rachel shot his legs out from under him. That still left about six men, who were all wising up and going for cover.

A bullet slammed into my shield, the force rocking me back on my heels. I skidded in the snow and nearly fell backward as my foot hit a chunk of ice. They were wising up in other ways. Damn. Bullets, not darts. Alek put a steadying hand on my shoulder, keeping himself behind me and the shield.

The mercenaries scrambled back, getting behind the truck and trailer. Shooting at them now meant risking the bears. I heard Rachel cursing behind the SUV as another spatter of gunfire bounded off my shield and clipped her vehicle. I hoped she wasn't hit. The mercenaries were shooting over the truck beds, spraying and praying. They had the advantage of more guns and better cover.

An advantage I was going to take away from them.

"I'll keep my shield up," I said to Alek, hoping my voice was quiet, since my ears were still hating me from the shots he'd fired. "We're gonna go take their cover away."

"Ready," Alek said. He squeezed my shoulder and stepped up just behind me.

I poured more magic into my shield. I had to fight Samir today, but conserving too much magic now might get us all killed. I couldn't afford to take a bullet or ten. My magic was much stronger than it had ever been, but I knew the limit was still out there. I compromised, using the shield but not trying to do a second spell. I still wasn't the world's strongest at multi-casting.

We walked forward step by step. I braced against the shocks of bullets slamming into the wall of my shields. Purple sparks blossomed and fell away on impact, my magic slipping in to fill any cracks. The mercenaries were the ones swearing now. I heard the crackle of a radio. Were they calling for help? Not good.

One tried to make a break for the cabin, and Rachel took him out. He sprawled, blood spattering the snow. Two others jumped up behind the giant bear, crouching to fire at us again, still using the poor creature, which I assumed was Mikhail himself, as cover. The bear's sides rose and fell, and from this close, his heavy breathing was audible even to my injured eardrums.

"Go now," I said in Russian, hoping only Alek would understand me.

We were almost to the trailer; my knees would touch it in another step. I dropped the shield and Alek sprang to the bed, his speed and height allowing him to fire down directly over the bear and into the men.

Ignoring the protest of my leg muscles, I jumped also, using magic to push myself much farther into the air. From this vantage I saw two more men scrabbling back in the snow, bringing assault rifles to bear on Alek.

"No, you don't," I yelled. Lightning crackled from my fingers as I zotted them.

Body armor was apparently shit against magical attack. They fell back screaming in the snow.

The remaining man went for the cab of the truck and made it before Alek could get over the bear and try to stop him. I dropped to the ground and ran to the side, reaching out with magic for the door of the truck.

The engine kicked in and he floored it, running the truck straight at Rachel's SUV.

Not today, motherfucker. I didn't even think, just threw magic in a force wave from my hands, all my mind focused on bricking that engine beyond usefulness or recognition.

The truck slammed forward and to the right. Metal screamed as the trailer bed went with it, chains snapping. From the corner of my eye I saw Alek running backward in the snow to avoid the flipping trailer. The truck crumpled like a soda can and smashed through a tree and into a bigger tree.

I grabbed at the trailer with my magic, pulling it back toward me. My muscles screamed in protest and spikes of pain slashed into my head. I hadn't practiced moving large objects that often. The trailer rolled up on its side and then bounced back down, rolling to a jerking stop. The bear was still strapped to it, unconscious but safe.

Silence reigned for a long moment as I hunched over, breathing in deep, painful breaths of cold air.

"Jade? You okay?" Harper called out.

"I'm okay," I said, looking up.

Alek was checking on the downed men, moving guns away from their hands, checking for signs of life. They looked pretty dead to me; even the ones I'd electrocuted were still and silent now. Blood spattered the snow and ice chunks, not all of it fresh. The snow lumped over the picnic tables made them look like white coffins as I scanned the area for any other threats or signs of life.

"Lee is hit," Ezee said, loping up to us.

"Shit." I followed him around the SUV.

Rachel was on the ground but still conscious. She smiled grimly up at me.

"Leg gave out, sorry," she said, waving a hand at her blood-soaked pant leg.

"Let's get you inside," I said, nodding at Levi and Ezee. They could carry her, no problem. Go go shifter super strength.

"Where are the others?" she asked with a wince as Levi lifted her himself, careful of her leg.

Harper had pulled the duffle bag of medical supplies out and held up a baggie of gauze pads.

"Inside," I said to Harper. To Rachel I said, "I don't know. Just two bears; I think Mikhail and Vasili. Maybe the others are hiding?"

All that blood and the churned-up ice and snow around the drive said they were long taken, but I figured that speculation could wait until Rachel was inside and safe.

"They are breathing but will not wake," Alek said to me as we passed him.

"Any of the bad guys alive enough to talk?" I asked.

Alek shook his head. "I will check the truck," he said, starting toward the truck I'd smashed.

I seriously doubted that guy was even in one piece, but it couldn't hurt to confirm. Damnit. Having someone alive to question would have been good. The guy Rachel leg-shot had ended up in the path of the truck and trailer. He was pedestrian pancake now. Everyone else had taken magic to the heart or bullets to the brain. We were a little too efficient.

Searching my heart, I tried to feel something other than relief that these guys were down. We'd just killed a bunch of humans. Nope. Nothing. Maybe tomorrow, I'd feel remorse. Somehow, I doubted it. They were capturing my friends, citizens of my damn town, for my evil ex-boyfriend to use in a sacrifice. Choices had consequences. They had made their choice. I was their consequence.

A part of me hated Samir even more for making this my reality.

I walked to the edge of the turnaround. From there, the burble of the creek sang up through the snowy trees. Snow dusted the rocks down the slope like powdered sugar. Looking in this direction, it was like the carnage behind me had never happened. Out there in the woods, life went on. Despite men with guns. Despite sorcerers and shifters and vendettas and ambitions.

It was a world I barely remembered and wasn't sure I'd ever return to.

Harper's footsteps pulled me back to my world.

"Nobody inside. Levi's putting pressure on the wound and the bleeding is already slowing. Normal bullets, I guess," she said. "What should we do about the bears?"

"Unstrap Mikhail. I don't know that we can or should move them, but I hate having them in the open like this." I remembered the man swearing at the radio, the crackle of a reply I hadn't quite caught. "There are more of them somewhere, and I think one got a call out."

"Shitballs." Harper summed up the situation eloquently.

I looked up at the flat blue sky. The sun was sinking already.

"We're running out of time," I murmured.

Alek made his way around the trailer toward us. Then he froze, his gaze on the woods to our left. He had his gun back out before I could blink, but didn't fire.

Turning, I saw a rangy red-brown wolf lope out of the trees. It dropped its head and then flopped down, baring its belly. In a blink, it became a man. He was thin and plain in appearance, wearing a grey sweater and tan cargo pants. He was unarmed, his hands up in the air as he lay there in submissive position like a roach that had been flipped over. I called up my magic and searched for signs of a spell or Samir on him. I sensed nothing, no trace of Samir's sickly sweet power.

"Goddamnit," Harper muttered beside me. "Not him again."

"Him again?" I asked, giving Harper a sideways glance.

"I just came to talk," the wolf shifter said. "I think we can help each other."

"I would rather shoot you," Alek said, though he didn't. Yet.

"He works for Samir," Harper explained. "But he did help me escape."

"You trust him?" I didn't take my eyes off the prone man again, but I caught her nod and half-shrug in my peripheral vision.

The wolf shifter looked from him to Harper and me, resting his gaze on me. He licked his lips in a quick, nervous flick of his tongue.

"That would be the biggest mistake you'll ever make," he said.

He sounded utterly confident for an unarmed guy lying in the snow.

"Let's hear him out," I said. At the least, he was someone alive to question. Best case? He was going to be the key to unlocking Samir's doom.

CHAPTER TEN ▶

The office had a front desk area that was just a standing case full of candy and other snacks. Beyond that was a good-size room with a rustic carved-wood coffee table and a random assortment of chairs and cushioned benches that looked as though they'd been collected from the side of the road at various times in history, which they probably had. Rachel was sprawled on the floor, propped against one of the benches, holding a thick gauze pad to her leg. Ezee was standing over her, and Levi came down a set of steps at the back of the waiting room as we entered.

"Nobody here," Levi said. He sent a curious look at our guest. "Who's he?"

"You got a name?" I asked the wolf shifter as we arrayed ourselves in an uncomfortable semicircle among the chairs. Alek kept his gun in his hand and stayed between the wolf and the door. Nobody sat.

"Cal," the wolf shifter said. "Those guys took the other shifters who were here. You missed them by half an hour. These were staying to try to load the bears up."

"Who are you?" Rachel said through gritted teeth. "Why weren't you helping?"

"'Cause he's one of Samir's," Harper said. She folded her arms over her chest and pressed her lips together.

"I helped you escape the sorcerer," Cal said.

"He did?" Ezee and I said at the same time.

"Nominally. We're even for that now. I got a feeling you were using me to clean up someone you didn't like anyway." Harper glared at him.

"Clean up?" I looked between them. Clearly, I had missed something in her explanation of how she escaped Samir.

"She killed one of the other mercs. Crushed his throat with a toilet lid." Cal raised an eyebrow at her as if to say "Good luck explaining that."

"Badass," Levi said, drawing out the vowels in the words to form a half-whistle.

Harper shifted her weight from foot to foot, betraying her nervousness. Her eyes flicked to mine and I made sure to smile. None of us were clear of blood on our hands. I wasn't going to judge.

"You were part of the group capturing shifters?" Rachel said. Her lip curled in disgust.

I felt the same disgust. Shifters capturing shifters for sacrifice was shitty as hell. Doing it for a sorcerer must have been the worst kind of sacrilege in Rachel's, and probably everyone else's, minds.

"No," Cal said. "Our group is guarding the sorc. We're not dealing with the shifter stuff or town. I overheard them on the radios doing a last-minute grab at Samir's request, so I came to see what was up. I couldn't stick around where I was. I got a horrible feeling we're not going make it through this one."

"You are not," Alek said. His voice was winter ice and bitter winds. It was the voice a rabbit hears in its mind just before the eagle drops from the sky.

I glanced at him, but his beautiful face was unreadable.

"Radios? I saw some on the guys out there. Can we use them to track what they are doing?" Levi started toward the door.

"No good," Cal said with a swift shake of his head. "One of these guys squawked for help. They'll have changed the channel to an alt now they haven't heard back. They might monitor this channel for communications, but they won't use it."

"It doesn't matter," I said. "You know where Samir is and where the shifters are being kept. So, spill it and I'll keep the tiger from killing you."

Cal gave me a bitter, tight smile. "No," he said. "I need to know things first."

"Like hell you do," Harper said, starting toward him with her murder-face on.

"We should try the diplomatic chat option before hitting the kill button." I put out my arm, stopping her. "What do you want, Cal?"

He looked me over with an obvious up-and-down sweep of his eyes, assessing. He was a predator through and through. In some ways, he reminded me of a shorter, brown-haired, less dramatic-looking Alek.

"You're a gamer too," he said after he finished his assessment.

"Talk," Alek said with a soft growl.

"I want you to save my boss," Cal said. "I think he's under some kind of spell."

"The big white bear?" I guessed, thinking back to the fight that happened in the alternate timeline.

"Vollan," Cal said with a nod. "Been running with him a long time. He's a damn good boss. Keeps us safe, gets us paid. This job, well, it ain't usual. We've taken people before, held 'em for ransom, that kind of thing. Taking other shifters? We don't usually do that."

"You took my brother," Harper said, her voice barely above a whisper.

"The kid? Yeah. Nobody was supposed to die. After that, couple of us tried to talk to the boss. Tried to say how the job wasn't what we'd expected. Arenson had point on that; he'd always been good with the boss, had his ear. Vollan shut him down. Then he left him on patrol after we all pulled out. When we asked where he was, boss just said he wasn't coming back."

"The two wolves?" Levi asked. "That whole camp was rigged to blow with magic, you know."

Cal seemed to sag in place, his shoulders dipping. "So, he is gone. Szabo too?"

"Both," Alek said, his voice still ice.

"Fuck," Cal said. His brown eyes met mine. "That isn't how Vollan is. He doesn't do this. We don't work with humans, either, or other merc groups. Capturing girls, bringing in kids to get killed, all this, it's shit. Total shit."

"Okay, so your boss took a shitty job. Walk away." I still didn't see how this was my problem. I wanted his information, but I didn't know what he wanted yet. If his own people hadn't been able to change this Vollan's mind, I didn't see how I could.

"No, I'm not explaining it right," Cal said. He threw his hands up and then squeezed his fingers into fists as though he'd crush the air around him. "I think my boss is under a spell," he said. "I think he's being mind-controlled."

"Is that possible?" Ezee asked me.

I searched my memories as quickly as I could. Tess seemed to have no idea if Samir could do that or not. I had no idea. But Samir had been around a long time.

"It's not impossible," I said finally. "I need more information. What makes you think it is a spell?"

"How he acts, what he does. Like he's angry but he can't take it out in the right way. After Harper got away, Vollan called me out and we walked the perimeter. I thought he knew I'd helped her, but he didn't say shit. Finally, he just looked at me and nodded with this strange look in his eye. I don't even know how to explain it. Like desperation. Like he wanted to speak but just flat couldn't." Cal took a half-step toward me, desperation in his own eyes. Alek growled again and he stopped moving.

"If this was a D&D game, I'd think it was a geas," Ezee said.

I glanced at Ezee and he shrugged. He was right. It did sound like some kind of control thing. Maybe. If Cal wasn't just crazy. But this guy had helped Harper escape; she didn't deny that. He was here now and he knew where Samir was and what he was planning.

"Geese?" Cal said, his eyes flicking between us.

"Ge-as," I repeated. It was magic so outside my own experience and utility that I had to take a moment to wrap my head around how I'd even do something like that. But Samir . . . he would. I could see it. A spell like that would take a lot of power to maintain, since magic often weakened with distance. Unless . . .

"Does Vollan have something he wears all the time? Something he never takes off, ever?" Samir loved objects, I knew. He was good at making them.

Cal's eyes lit up. "His dog tags. He fought in the Second World War. Talks about it all the time. How he was out there killing Nazis. He never takes those things off."

"Samir could have anchored a spell to those, maybe. It's not guaranteed, just a guess," I added.

"It makes sense," Cal said, clearly latching on to whatever hope he could.

I almost felt sorry for him. He was a killer who had helped Samir wreck my life and kill my friends, but in some ways, he was also a victim of Samir's evil machinations. And he really did seem to want to help his boss. He was there, risking his life to try to do that. Loyalty like that, I understood and kind of admired.

"Great, that's solved—where is Samir and where are the shifters?" Harper said.

"Can you break the spell?" Cal asked me, ignoring Harper.

"Maybe," I said. I'd seen that question coming from a mile away. "Killing Samir, which I'm going to do anyway, will break it. So, you are going to get what you want no matter what."

Cal shook his head. "Not good enough. You have to break the spell first. You help me, save Vollan, I will help you."

"No," Alek said. "There is no time for this." He pointedly glanced out the window. The sun was dropping behind the trees. He was right.

"Do you know what Samir is going to do?" I asked Cal. "He's going to raise an Irish god from the dead, then eat the heart and become a god himself. So sorry, but our quest is, like, a million times more important. We only have until moonrise. So, quit fucking around and tell us what we need to know. Once Samir is gone, your boss will be free anyway."

"No," Cal said again. "I know he's doing some ritual. He knows that you will try to stop him. He's got my whole pack arranged around him with high-powered rifles. You think you all can fight through that?"

"I'm a sorceress," I said, trying to imitate Alek's cold confidence. "You think a few guns are going to stop me?"

"What if those guns were on your side? Or at least gone?" Cal said. He dropped his chin and folded his arms. He was stubborn and brave; I'd give him that. "You free my boss, I know he'll get us out. Or even help you. He won't be too well disposed to Samir. Boss doesn't like anyone calling his shots. And you are going to need help." He cast his gaze over our admittedly ragtag group.

"One of those guys outside called for help," Levi reminded us. "Are they going to come here?"

Cal shrugged. "I doubt it. They might send a few guys, but as you said, shit is going down soon. They'll assume their guys are gone. I haven't seen much loyalty in that crowd." He looked like he wanted to spit, his lip curling at the thought of the human mercenaries.

Everyone was looking at me. Ezee and Levi had mirrored looks of speculation and interest. Harper looked torn between believing Cal and killing him. Alek looked very much on the side of killing him. I turned my head to fully meet Rachel's gaze, and she gave a little shrug and nodded down at her leg. She wasn't going with us, regardless.

"He telling the truth?" I asked Alek baldly.

"He is," Alek said. "To his knowledge."

"He's not bespelled," I said. "I checked him when he first showed up."

"Please, this will work for us both," Cal said.

"Fine," I said. He had a point. I didn't really need Alek's Justice senses to tell me he was genuinely concerned about his boss. "To break the spell, I have to be with your boss. I can't do it from here."

"Okay," Cal said. He reached slowly down and drew a small flip phone out of his cargo pants pocket. "I'll call him. I think I can get him to meet us. I don't know if he'll come alone, but he might if I word it right. I think he wants help and I think he knows I suspect something. He still trusts me."

"Where is Samir?" I asked. "You've got my promise we'll help. Time to hold up your end."

"Juniper College," he said, confirming our speculations. "They got the shifters and some others locked up in a church-looking building. Samir is down on some kind of sports field; it's all surrounded by trees, which is why he has us watching his back. Human mercs are in charge of the shifters."

"Student Commons," Ezee said. "It's a converted chapel. Stone building, only two ways in or out. Narrow, high windows with steel wire to keep birds off the stained glass. It's practically a fortress. We always joked if zombies attacked, we'd hole up there."

"Well, shit," Harper said, echoing my thoughts.

"One problem at a time," I said. "Call your boss. Let's get ourselves over to Juniper, or as close as we can get, and then figure out a plan."

"I'm staying here to guard Mikhail and Vasili," Rachel said. "Not much use anyway until this heals. I should shift."

"You gonna be okay here alone?" Levi asked.

"You will need all the help you can get at the college," Rachel said. "I'll be fine. Bears will wake up, then we'll try to get to you if we can. There's a couple rifles, a shotgun, and a spare Glock in my car, if you want them."

I bent over and shook her hand. "Thank you, Sheriff," I said. "Good luck."

"You too, Jade, you too," Rachel said. Then she shifted, turning from stocky human to a black-furred wolf.

We walked outside, Rachel limping behind us. She flopped on the welcome mat outside the door. Ezee left the cabin open so she'd have easy cover if shit went down. The bears were still enjoying their forced beauty sleep in the snow and on the trailer. The sun was setting. Moonrise would follow soon after. I stared at Cal's back as he opened his phone and dialed a number, hoping I wasn't making a horrible mistake.

CHAPTER ELEVEN ▶

Harper sat on Ezee's lap in the front seat. Alek and I wedged Cal between us in the back. There was no way to be comfortable or to not come into contact with each other, so we sucked it up and squished in.

Alek tried to interrogate Cal more while we drove toward Juniper, but the merc was silent, just shaking his head every time Alek growled a question. After a few minutes, Alek gave up.

I sat there gripping the arm on the door for balance and to keep minimal contact with Cal. I tried not to panic about how quickly things were happening now. Vollan would meet Cal at the bottom of the college drive, where there was a turn-around and a small gatehouse. Cal couldn't be sure the other mercenaries, the human ones, wouldn't be there, but he said Vollan had confirmed that everyone was busy at the moment.

I had a short car ride to figure out my new problem. How to break a geas or a control spell or whatever it was. If this were a game of D&D, it would have been simple enough: cast Wish or Miracle or Remove Curse. Though that last one wouldn't work. I was pretty sure Samir was still levels higher than I was, even with my new dragon subclass. I smiled to myself, almost wishing I could share these thoughts with Harper and the twins. They were silent, focusing on their own inner demons and desires, I imagined. So, I stayed quiet too.

This was no game. There was no simple answer. Or was there? Remove the tags. Nullify the magic. Samir would have some kind of protection on the dog tags. A compulsion not to remove them, perhaps, or a spell that would trigger or cause horrible pain if anyone tried. He'd put necklaces on both myself and Tess that had things like that involved. Samir wasn't likely to change his MO for no good reason. Why fuck with what had worked for who knew how many centuries?

Tess. I almost face-palmed. I'd brute-forced my own necklace off. But Tess had removed hers with a much more elegant bit of magic. I had her memories, her powers. There was a chance I could use the same magic to remove Vollan's tags. The danger was that Samir might feel his spell falling apart, but there was nothing I could think of to negate that. It didn't matter if he knew I was coming for him or not, in the end. I was going to come for him anyway.

Plan in place, I closed my eyes and sifted through Tess's memory, matching it up with my own. I'd witnessed the magic; now I just had to study how to recreate it.

We arrived too soon. I climbed out of the Jeep, not at all confident. I was just going to have to fake it until I made it. Levi pulled the Jeep off to the side. Vollan was nowhere in sight. The drive was plowed, the turn-around clear with snow piled on the sides like walls. The road turned and was forested with ancient oaks and some transplanted, stumpy-looking juniper that gave the college its name.

"He's going to see us and bolt," I said. "I really think we should hide, put the Jeep up the road or something." It was an objection I'd raised back at the RV park.

"No, he won't," Cal said.

"He is already here," Alek said softly as he moved up beside me.

A huge white bear emerged from the woods, moving with speed and silence I would not have thought possible. He paused after he leapt the snow wall, head down, looking at Cal and then at us.

Then he shifted, became a big man with a shock of silver-threaded black hair. He was wearing a green parka. A gun appeared in his hand like magic. I hadn't even seen him move.

"Cal," he said. "You all right?" His eyes flicked to Alek, who had a gun out now also.

Shifter speed. I was never going to get used to it.

Magic coursed through me with a thought. They weren't the only ones who could be quick. I wrapped my power around Vollan in ropes, not pulling tight until I had him mummified. Then I squeezed with my mind, jerking him off his feet and down. His arms flattened to his sides and he hit the icy pavement hard, trying to kick free of my magic.

"Don't fight her," Cal said. "Please, trust me."

Vollan started cursing and promising to do terrible things to Cal's mother.

I had no idea if there was anyone close enough to hear him. We had to get the second part of the plan rolling, and now. Levi and Ezee grabbed rifles out of the back of the Jeep and spread out, keeping an eye on the road leading up to the college. Alek and Cal moved quickly to Vollan, pinning him with their bodies. I was going to need to let my Hold Person spell go in order to get that necklace off without killing him. I wasn't dumb enough to multitask magic I hadn't practiced or performed before.

Vollan quit swearing and glared at me as I dug his dog tags out of his parka. Samir's magic dripped from them like the sickly honey it smelled of. It mingled with the cigar-smoke stench clinging to the bear shifter and turned my stomach. My guess had been right.

"It's the tags," I said to Cal and Alek. "Hold him." I released the spell.

Vollan didn't do more than a token struggle. He also didn't shift. I had a feeling maybe Cal was right. Looking into Vollan's pale eyes, I saw a man who was trapped and couldn't help himself. He had to fight us, because I bet the spell was making him fight, but he could skirt around really fighting it.

I gripped the tags, swallowing bile at the feel of Samir's magic. Consolation prize was that this would hopefully be the last day of my life I'd ever have to deal with it.

If it wasn't just the last day of my life, period.

With that happy thought, I closed my eyes. I gathered my magic and thought of Tess, of her magic, clear and cold and precise. The air around us grew thick, the world holding its breath as I messed, only a little, with time itself. Then I hummed a soft note as I opened my eyes and yanked on the dog tags.

The chain and tags slid clear of Vollan's neck, the chain moving straight through his flesh as though it weren't there at all. For a moment, Tess was there in my mind, a ghost of a smile on her ruby-red lips. She nodded to me, pleased, before she faded away into the silver circle that Wolf had constructed inside my head to hold my ghosts at bay.

I threw the tags into the snow beyond us as I stood up. They sank away into the white wet, the feel of Samir's power fading as the snow engulfed them.

"I am free," Vollan said with awe in his voice. "I can't hear him anymore." He looked at Cal, and a wild grin broke out on his face.

Alek looked at me and I nodded. He released Vollan and backed up, his hand casually resting on the gun at his waist.

"Good to have you back, Boss," Cal said, offering Vollan a hand up.

"How did you know?" Vollan asked.

"Talk later," Alek said. "We upheld bargain. Your turn."

"Bargain?" Vollan looked at Alek and then to Cal.

"We free you, you help us stop Samir," I said. "What's his plan? Where is he now?"

"That the deal you made, son?" Vollan said to Cal as he bent and retrieved his gun. Alek growled, but the big bear shifter just made a sour face at him. "I ain't gonna shoot you," he said. "Just not leaving my weapon on the ground."

"Yeah," Cal said. "That's the deal I made. We shouldn't be here, Boss. This isn't our thing."

"All right." Vollan ran a hand through his hair, making it stand up in the growing chill. "Sorcerer is up that way, in that field tucked down at the bottom of campus. Not that far if you go through the woods. The humans are up doing something around that church. I think they are going to blow the place up. Lot of shifters been taken up there in cages. We ain't been a part of that."

"Blow the place up?" Harper said, moving toward us. Behind her I saw Ezee and Levi exchange a worried look.

"I smelled some things, like Semtex, maybe. I never did much with demolitions, but you don't really forget the smells," Vollan answered her.

That made sense in a sick way. Samir liked explosions. He had blown up things before. Like my adoptive family. At a school, no less. Maybe time really was a flat circle.

"Could you bring down the building with that? Enough to kill shifters? He needs a sacrifice," Harper said.

"He could if he augments it with magic, I suppose," I said. Not a happy thought. He'd used a regular old dynamite-type bomb before but also had exploding stones placed at intervals to magnify the blast. The school had burned for days. My nails dug into my palms hard enough to hurt. Freyda, her pack, Vivian—all of them were locked up in that chapel. *Not again. Not fucking again.*

"Worse than that," Ezee said, exchanging another worried look with Levi. "There's an old boiler room and some steam tunnels that run right under the Commons. I ran a Spycraft game set here once, before Jade's time. We used blueprints and figured out you could drop half the school in on itself if you put enough explosives in those tunnels. Put them right under the chapel? Boom. No more chapel."

I'd been in those tunnels with Ezee before. An evil warlock had been using them for his lair. It was true; nothing good happened to gamers in steam tunnels.

"We stop Samir, the bomb won't go off, right?" Harper said.

"Humans are in charge of the bomb," Vollan said. "I don't know what their orders are, but given where they put their trailers? I'd say they are expecting the center to go. Samir seems the type to build in contingencies, too."

"He is," I said. I rubbed the bridge of my nose. We were fucked.

"I know a way into those tunnels," Ezee said. "What if we got to the bomb—could we disarm it?"

"This isn't a spy movie," Levi said.

"Yes, I could," Cal said. "It's what I did for the army."

"You waited until now to say that? Seriously?" Harper glared at him.

"Dramatic reveal," he said with a half-smile.

I couldn't decide if I wanted to shake his hand or punch him. He was almost likeable, for a stone-cold killer.

"I kind of hate you," Harper muttered.

Cal just shrugged.

I looked up at the sky. It wasn't dark yet, but we could count the daylight left in terms of minutes, not hours.

"Can you get your men away from Samir? Or at least get me through the line?" I asked Vollan.

"Maybe," he said. "I can get you through to the sorcerer. We've got orders not to shoot you until he gives the signal, anyway. That's why I came out of the trees when I saw Cal wasn't alone. I remembered you. The little part of my head that was still mine hoped you could help."

"Glad you were right," I said. "Can you stop them from shooting?" Last thing I wanted to worry about was dodging bullets and shielding myself from gunfire while trying to fight Samir also. It warmed my heart that my ex was scared enough to give orders to shoot me if he needed it, though. He wasn't as confident as he appeared. That or he was just a deck-stacking asshole. Probably a little from column A and a little from column B.

"If you give me enough time to get around to their positions," he said.

"I can stall Samir," I said, hoping I wasn't full of shit. I could certainly distract him, at least.

"What about the bomb?" Harper asked.

"You guys are going to have to handle that," I said, turning to her. "Think you can get Cal into those tunnels? Show him where the room is?"

"Zomg, you are letting us help?" Harper leaned forward and squinted at me. "Pod person, I'm sure of it."

"Maybe I learned that friendship is magic," I said. "Don't push it. Don't do anything stupid and do not get yourself killed. I'll raise you from the dead and kill you again if you do. Promise."

"I go with Jade," Alek said in a tone that shut up any argument I had.

"I face Samir alone," I said. "Nonnegotiable, Alek."

"Ah, there's our girl," Harper said.

We hashed out a quick plan that was likely suicide. But we were gamers. Rushing into certain death, hoping we could win, was pretty much par for the course for us. I was putting my friends' lives in the hands of a mercenary who had helped kidnap Max and Rosie. Who had also helped free Harper. I was putting my and Alek's safety in the hands of a bear who had, in another timeline, killed two of my friends.

Desperation breeds strange bedfellows. With quick hugs all around, I followed Alek and Vollan into the woods. It was endgame. The boss fight loomed, and no matter how unready I felt, there was no turning back. Not this time. Not ever again.

HARPER

In fox form, Harper ran along behind Cal, Levi, and Ezee. Cal and Levi stayed in human form, carrying the guns. Ezee was in his coyote shape, running slightly ahead, scouting for them. As they got to the edge of the first set of dorms, they had to slow down.

Three big RVs were parked in the lower lot, barely visible as the team ran through the trees toward the center. A dozen men were clustered around the Campus Security building, but they were definitely human. None of them even glanced their way, though a shifter probably could have heard or smelled them coming. The wind was not in Harper and her friends' favor.

Ezee skirted the brick dorm building. The Student Commons lay in the center of everything, like the circle at the heart of a wheel. Ezee had explained there were two ways to get to the old boiler room below it. One was through the Commons itself, but that had been sealed off when the renovations were done to convert the chapel into what it was today. The other entrance was in the math and science building to the right of the Commons, dead ahead of them now.

The campus was dead quiet once they sneaked past the men around the security office. When she glanced that way, she saw the Commons' main doors were locked with a web of silver wire. Harper shivered as she ran, and it had nothing to do with the snow. Samir's magic was sealing the door; she was sure of it. Not a good sign.

Three men sporting automatic weapons and wearing body armor emerged from the math and science building. She'd been so focused on what was beside and behind that Harper didn't see them until they were shouting and raising their guns.

Cal dropped one of them with a headshot worthy of any zombie killer. The shot rang out like a clarion call in the silence. Harper dove into the deeper snow off the path. Ezee charged ahead as Levi dropped the rifles he'd been holding and drew a pistol. A bullet whizzed by Harper's ear.

More shouting. More gunfire. All three of the men ahead of them were down. Harper charged past them and into the building, shifting to human as soon as her feet hit the tiled floor.

Cal took up the rear and yanked the door shut behind them.

"We've got seconds. Let's go," he said. He wasn't even breathing hard, the bastard.

Harper reminded herself that he was on their side, and shoved away her annoyance and anger. She followed Ezee, who had also shifted to human, down the hall and then down a narrow set of stairs.

Harper stayed on his heels as they crashed through a fire door and into an even narrower hallway. Ezee stopped abruptly and threw her to the side as a bullet clipped his arm, spraying her face with warm blood. The gunshot sound was booming and disorienting in the narrow space. More shots from behind them rang out and Harper twisted, shifting back to fox to lower her profile.

The fire door banged shut, cutting her off from Levi as he and Cal turned to fire up the stairs. Ezee went down beside her, shifting as he fell. No shots came at them. Down the hallway, Harper saw the silhouetted figure of a man. He was messing with something in his hands. His gun? She didn't care.

Harper threw aside her fear and charged down the hall at the gunman. His gun had jammed. He threw it at her and tried to pull something from his belt, but she was too fast. Harper remembered body armor, so she went for his throat, letting her animal instincts guide her. Her teeth sank home, blood filling her mouth, flesh squelching and crunching in her jaws. It was disgusting but she ripped and tore, thinking only of survival.

Ezee barreled past them, leaping over them both as Harper took her prey down to the ground. He grabbed her by her scruff and dragged her forward with him, still running. Harper didn't fight but got her legs underneath her and scrambled beside him. Ezee was shouting. Shouting a word over and over.

Blood rushed in her ears, and they still rang from the gunfire, but Harper made out what he was saying.

Grenade.

The gunman hadn't thrown his jammed gun at her. He'd thrown a grenade.

The explosion rocked the world, or so it felt like. Chunks of concrete rained down and the ceiling groaned. A wave of force threw Harper and Ezee down, knocking the air from Harper's lungs. There was a secondary crash and then all she heard was ringing, like an alarm someone had forgotten to shut off.

She reached into the mist and found her human form, shifting away from the injured, unhappy fox.

"Harper, you okay?" Ezee whispered. Or shouted. She couldn't tell. His face was caked with cement dust.

"Biblethump," she said.

"Thank God," he said. He helped her to her feet.

Feet. She still had them. Small mercies. Her human body had been safe from the mess of the blast, so she bet that she looked ridiculously clean compared to Ezee. Harper turned to look behind them and saw only a pile of rubble. Complete cave-in. The blast had shoved the body of the gunman down the hallway with them. He lay in a dusty, crumpled heap. She could still taste his blood.

Harper swallowed the bile that rose at that thought. *Nope. Big fat cup of nope.* She wasn't going to barf. They had to figure shit out.

Her ears were healing, the ringing retreating. She looked at Ezee.

"How do we get out of here?" she asked.

"That's the bad news," he said, brushing ineffectually at his coat. "That was the only way in or out."

"Where's the boiler room?"

"That way," Ezee said.

Harper started walking. Her heart was still beating. She could mostly breathe. She felt strangely numb and wondered if that was shock. They found the boiler room right where Ezee thought it was, about thirty feet farther down. There were no other gunmen in their way. They seemed to be completely alone down there.

"Least there are no more bad guys," Ezee said from behind her. "We can't get out, but nobody can come down here, either. Hope Levi is okay," he added, almost too softly for her to hear.

Pushing through the metal door into the boiler room, Harper groaned.

"Never lucky," she muttered. "Great. We're locked in with a freaking bomb."

CHAPTER TWELVE

The old lower field wasn't used much except by the Ultimate Frisbee team. It was tucked down into the woods surrounding Juniper and a bit of a walk down a hill from the main part of campus. The woods around it were kept clear of invasive species and brush but otherwise left to grow wild. Vollan was in his bear form, but he pointed with his muzzle in the direction of the field, his silent intent clear.

I was to go that way. He and Alek would go along the perimeter and alert his men to the change in plan.

I leaned into Alek's chest and he curled his arms around me. We didn't risk words, just stood for an all-too-brief moment.

I love you, I mouthed to him as we pulled apart finally.

Alek smiled and mouthed *Good* back to me.

There was nothing more to say. He shifted to tiger, and then he and the huge white bear disappeared into the trees, moving quickly and quietly, Alek's black-and-white tiger blending into the shadows.

I turned and made my way to the edge of the field. Magic and adrenaline flowed through me, washing away my fear and my fatigue. This was it. The last midnight. The boss fight.

First would come the talking in the hopes I could distract him so he didn't blow up my friends.

Yeah. Some things never change.

I felt his power in the form of a ward on the field before I stepped out of the trees. The field was pristine with snow except for a huge charred circle burned into it. Samir stood at the center of the circle, his honey-sweet power rippling around him. A stone box carved with ornate patterns I couldn't quite make out at this distance lay to one side of him. Balor's head, I assumed. Samir was prepared for the ritual, waiting for moonrise.

Moon wasn't up yet. I walked out of the trees, ready to shield myself and hoping nobody shot me in the back. I'd been shot enough for one lifetime.

Samir didn't seem surprised to see me. He stood silently, watching me approach. When I reached the edge of the circle, he held up one hand. I stopped, mostly of my own volition. I wasn't ready to provoke him yet, so there was little harm in doing what he wanted. For the moment.

He was dressed more like a man attending a nice dinner than someone preparing a winter ritual. He had on dark grey pinstriped slacks and a maroon sweater. Samir's only concession to the snow and cold was a very functional-looking pair of black boots. Not a hair was out of place and his face still looked thirty, handsome and unlined.

His golden eyes were wary, tiny creases giving away a hint of strain. I might have been imagining that part. Wishful thinking is a powerful thing.

One thing was painfully clear to me. I was not ready for this. I didn't know if I'd ever be ready. My heartbeat slowed. My fingers tingled with more than the chill of the air. I tried to think up something clever or snarky to open with, but my mind wouldn't obey.

"Jade," Samir said. "I had a feeling you would come."

"What? Miss you trying to do something this stupid? Never," I said.

"Stupid?" His golden eyes narrowed slightly.

"Raising Balor? A god of blight and other bad shit? You think he's going to stand here while you eat his heart?" *Keep him talking*, I thought. *Let's go.*

"No, I don't intend to let him stand at all. This circle isn't just for resurrection." Samir motioned to the black circle, and I saw there were other patterns cut into it, burned down into the bare and blackened earth. Looking at them made my brain hurt.

"The Fey are letting you do this because they think the gods will return. You won't be the baddest thing out there anymore," I said, playing one of my trump cards. I doubted that Samir cared, but I was willing to say just about anything to keep him talking.

"You always were too clever," he said. "I underestimated you, Jade. I don't do that often."

I snorted. "Really? You might want to reexamine your track record."

His eyes were slits now, his mouth tight. Samir definitely didn't like me laughing at him.

"Raising Balor will not break the Seal," he said. "But it will weaken it. More magic in the world is a good thing. The humans and other animals have ruled too long. We used to be revered, not hunted and hiding in the shadows." So, he knew about the Seal. And didn't care. Not a surprise there.

"What if I smudge this line?" I asked, poking a toe forward at the black line.

"It's representational. The magic is in place. The lines were just there as a guide. Mess with it all you want." Samir shrugged, too casually. His eyes flicked over my head.

I worried he had noticed some kind of movement in the woods, and then I realized that the moon would be rising in the direction he looked. He was keeping track of the time. Which meant I was running out of it. Samir would want to end me before he had to do his ritual.

"Moon up yet?" I asked, not wanting to turn and look. I knew it wasn't. Not quite. The sky was still too light. The sunset made the woods behind Samir look like they were on fire.

"You will know when it is," Samir said. "We'll be celebrating with a bang."

"The bomb you have under the Student Commons?" I said. His eyebrows went up. He hadn't realized I knew. "I don't think so." It felt so damn good to be able to surprise him.

His sickly sweet magic rippled out from him in the direction of the college center. To my dragon-enhanced mage-vision, it looked like a thick cord running up the hill. Until he awakened it, I hadn't noticed it among all the other magic stacked up around us. His line to the sacrifice. I was going to have to snip that somehow.

But not yet. No telling what effect that would have. I decided to wait on that as a last resort. Seeing magic was apparently a dragon thing, not a sorcerer thing. It was a big advantage that I had. Samir could probably detect magic. He'd dodged my spells easily enough in the past, but I bet he had to use concentration to do it. I had for the most part, until my dragon-self had fully integrated. Now I just saw magic if I looked for it.

"I'm surprised you are here, then," Samir said. "Not up there, trying to save them. Going to let them all die just like before?"

"Not exactly," I said. "I'm going to stop you." *Keep him talking, and nobody explodes.* Time was running out like sand through my fingers. I hoped that Vollan and Alek were ready. I hoped that Cal had made it to the bomb.

Samir laughed, the sound chilling me far worse than the icy air. His magic coalesced around him, and I knew time wasn't just running out . . . it was gone.

HARPER

The grenade had collapsed a section of the tunnel just inside the doorway. It must have found some kind of old structural weakness to cause this much damage, Harper thought. She scrabbled at the debris, pulling bits of stone and twisted rebar away. There was no telling how thick the cave-in was or if the stairs behind the door were safe. If Levi was safe.

She pushed that thought away. No point worrying about him when she had no way to know. At least nobody was shooting at them anymore.

"This is like that scene at the end of *Cabin in the Woods*," Ezee said. He had stripped off his coat and was working beside her.

"What? Waiting around for the world to explode?" Harper made a face at him in the dim light. She'd been relatively clean before, but digging in rock debris had fixed that.

"I guess I'm the fool and you are the virgin," Ezee said, pulling free another chunk of concrete. More dust and rock slid into place in the dent he'd just created.

"Hey, now," Harper protested. "How do you know it isn't the other way around? I'm pretty funny. I have antics."

"Honey," Ezee said, his dark eyes glinting in the light filtering out from the boiler room, "I am no virgin."

"Neither am I," Harper said.

"When's the last time you had sex?"

"Whoa, now. Just because the Sahara is a desert doesn't mean it never rains there." Harper gave up on her section and walked a few steps down the hall. The dead mercenary was still heaped there. It was a testament to how much rock dust must have been in the corridor that she couldn't really smell the blood anymore.

She nudged his body with her foot. They were going to die here because of this asshole. It was totally unfair.

"It's all fun and games until someone throws a grenade," she said, punctuating her words with a hard kick to the corpse's stomach.

A rectangular piece of plastic shot free of the body and spun into the corridor.

Harper looked at Ezee. "Radio," they said at the same time. She kicked herself for not remembering one of the first rules of adventuring: *Always loot the corpse.*

Harper snatched it up. Ezee followed her down the hall to the boiler room as she brought it into the light for examination.

The radio seemed intact. A red light blinked on it.

"How do we call for help?" Harper asked. "This thing has numbers on it. Must be the channels?"

"It's the bad-guy radio," Ezee said. "They'll be monitoring the signal. Is it even working? We haven't heard it."

"Volume was all the way down," Harper said, twisting the knob. "What are the odds that Levi or Cal are near a corpse?"

"And not buried under that rubble?" Ezee said, his face grim.

He'd clearly been trying not to dwell on his own fears for Levi. Harper empathized with that.

"Worth a try," Harper said. She clicked the side button to talk. "Leviticus," she yelled into it. "This is Fox paging Leviticus, over."

Levi hated his full name as much as she hated hers. Hopefully, if he were alive and could hear the bad guys' radios, he'd find a way to answer.

The radio crackled almost immediately, making Harper flinch, as she still had it near her face with the volume all the way up.

"Azalea," a voice said. It wasn't Levi's but Cal's. "Channel not clear."

"He didn't say 'over' yet," Harper said as Ezee tried to grab for the radio.

"I don't think anyone actually talks like that," Ezee said.

"I'm a condemned woman," Harper said, motioning toward the bomb she was trying not to look at. "Don't ruin my paramilitary dreams."

"Ask him if Levi is okay," Ezee said.

"He called me Azalea. I'm sure Levi is fine. But he said 'Channel not clear.'"

"We're on the bad guys' channel. See those numbers? We have to change somehow, but if you say a number to switch to, they can just switch to listen in or jam it or something."

"Not if we use code," Harper said, her mind racing. She studied the numbers and then clicked the button. "Zerg cheese, I repeat, go to Zerg cheese," she said into the radio.

"Zerg cheese?" Ezee raised an eyebrow.

"Cal is a gamer. He plays Zerg. He'll know." Harper clicked the dial over to the channel, praying she was right and that this worked.

"Six pool," the radio said. "Funny."

"Is Levi okay?" Harper asked, relief flooding through her. He'd understood the channel change.

"I'm okay," Levi's voice came through the radio. "You guys?"

Ezee fist-pumped and muttered a prayer of thanks to the ceiling.

"Ezee is here with me. We're good. Except this bomb."

"Um, Harper?" Ezee said, looking at the bomb.

There was what looked like a circuit board on top of a pile of orange putty bricks. The board had a line of lights. Lights that had been dark except for a single red one earlier. Now they were green and blinking on and off in a line.

"The bomb just started blinking," Harper told Cal.

"Describe it," Cal said. "And describe where you are, what tools you might have."

Harper took a deep breath and looked around the room, then back at the bomb.

"Red bricks, maybe twenty of them all wrapped in gold wire? It's just a block in the center of the room, on the floor. There are wires from a circuit board thing going into the bricks. Two sets of wires with metal at the brick parts. Not much else here. A sink. Some folding chairs. No tools."

"I'll check the corpse," Ezee said, heading out the door.

"You ever played that game where you disarm a bomb while the other person has the manual?"

"I suck at that game," Harper said.

"You're one of the best pro gamers I've ever seen," Cal said. "You got this. Tell me about the bomb."

"The bricks look like C-4, but they are orange. Oh, there's a weird crystal taped to the side, too. Looks like smoky quartz or something?"

"Do the bricks have numbers on them?"

"No, writing. Not English."

"Cyrillic," Ezee said, coming back into the room. He had a flak jacket and the gunman's belt with him. "Leatherman," he added, holding up the belt. "So, we got tools."

"Cyrillic," Harper repeated to Cal.

"How many red wires?" Cal asked.

Harper moved closer to the bomb. She bent and examined the wires. They were all white.

"No red wires. They're all white," she said, hoping that wasn't bad.

"No red wires," Cal repeated. Then there was silence over the radio for what felt like eternity.

Sweat trickled down the back of Harper's neck, itching in the cement dust and hair stuck there. She was no bomb expert and this was no game. *Deep breath*, she told herself. *Don't panic.*

"There are two spots the wires go into the C-4?" Cal said, the radio crackling.

"Yes."

"Hand the radio to Ezee," Cal said. "You are going to need both hands."

Harper looked at Ezee. He put down his loot and took the radio, giving her a quick thumbs-up.

"You kill us, at least we don't die alone," he said with a forced grin.

Harper bared her teeth at him.

Ezee clicked the radio on. "Go ahead; she's ready," he said.

"Okay. Harper. Put both hands on the wires where they join the metal pins."

Harper did so and nodded to Ezee.

"Done," Ezee said.

"Now, on the count of three, I want you to pull. Smooth and fast, got it?"

"Got it."

Harper felt the wires under her fingertips, felt the cool metal pins and their slightly rough edges. Time seemed to slow. Just her breath easing out and the sound of Cal counting down from three over the radio.

Three. Two. One.

She pulled. The long metal bits slid out of the C-4, leaving Harper crouched in front of the bomb with two probe-like things attached to wires in her hands. She looked at Ezee and raised her eyebrows. The circuit board was still blinking green.

"She did it," Ezee said. "Circuit board is still blinking."

"Good," Cal said. "She said there's a sink? Take it to the sink."

"Okay," Harper said. She kept hold of the pins as Ezee helped cut the tape off the sides of the board. They walked it together to the sink and put it carefully down. Harper set the pins down carefully, too.

"It's in the sink," she said, taking the radio back from Ezee.

"Turn on the water," Cal said.

Ezee and Harper shared a look. They had no idea if the water worked.

"Here goes nothing," Ezee muttered. He twisted the tap.

Water choked and spat and then flowed out in a brownish rush. It smelled heavily of metal and rust, but it splashed down onto the electronics. The lights blinked off and then something popped and sizzled. Water plus electronics when powered was bad. Harper could put that together.

"It's wet. Lights aren't on anymore." She left the water running.

"Congrats, you just disarmed your first bomb." Cal's voice was full of laughter.

"Wait, what? That was it?" Harper glared at the radio. "What about the explosives?"

"This isn't the movies," Cal said. "C-4 is very stable. Without the blasting caps and electric trigger, you could light it on fire and cook dinner with it and it wouldn't blow up."

"What about the crystal?" Ezee asked.

Harper repeated that question.

"Probably magic," Cal said, sounding more serious. "Secondary trigger? Amplifier? That isn't my area."

"Let's remove it," Ezee said. "We can wrap it in the flak jacket and put it at the end of the hall."

"Better than leaving it," Harper agreed. She relayed the plan to Cal and Levi.

At the far end of the hall was a set of doors that were long sealed, the tunnel beyond bricked up and closed off. It was weird to think that only feet above her head was a room full of shifters awaiting their fate. In the end, she and Ezee dragged the body down there, too, piling it on top of the flak-jacket-wrapped crystal.

Nothing exploded.

"Can you guys come help dig us out? What's going on up there?" Harper asked Cal as she slumped to the floor, leaning against the cool wall in relief.

"We're on an upper floor, pinned down. They have retreated a bit, though. We're going to try getting out and finding some more guns. Levi is a crack shot," Cal added.

"Of course he's a crack shot," Ezee muttered. "Raised on a rez in Idaho. Geez."

Harper grinned at him and shook her head.

"We'll be here," she told Cal.

Ezee and Harper stared at each other for a moment, and then both sighed.

"So, you wanna go keep digging? Or sit here and stare at a bomb while we talk about my sex life some more?" Harper asked.

"Digging sounds great."

CHAPTER THIRTEEN

Gunfire crackled through the rising gloom, coming from up the hill. My friends must have gotten to the mercenaries. Time was definitely short.

Samir stopped laughing and looked toward the noise. He gave a small shake of his head.

"So, you chose to come here, to stop me," he said. "Stupid girl."

Calm slid over me. This was it. It was time.

"See," I said, gathering my magic into an invisible shield. I took a deliberate step into the circle, smudging the black line as I went. "You are older than I am, more powerful, way more tricky, but there's something you just super suck at."

"What is that?" Samir tipped his head to the side, watching my slow advance with narrowed eyes.

"Making friends," I said. We were less than twenty feet apart now. It would have to be close enough. I threw up my shield, making it purple and sparkly and visible as hell.

Bullets zinged by me. Three bounced off Samir's own protections, but the fourth found an angle he hadn't shielded quickly enough. It cut a deep furrow into his arm, blood spraying in a mist in its path.

"Traitors," Samir hissed. He wasn't bleeding as much as I'd hoped, but he was definitely hurt. Score one for the good guys.

"Traitors?" I said. I threw an exploratory bolt of lightning at him. He bounced it away with a gesture. "Forced loyalty isn't loyalty. Not hard to betray someone coercing you. Maybe you should have tried not being an evil motherfucker."

A golden lash of power whipped toward me. I sprang back, barely keeping my feet on the uneven ground. His magic fizzled on my shield.

"Live long enough, Jade, you'll learn that everyone betrays everyone eventually," he snarled.

"I almost pity the lonely, sucking black hole inside you," I said with a grunt as he whipped more power at me.

Samir changed his attack, throwing magic into the ground at my feet. Stones rose around me, burning with honey-sick power. I poured magic into my shield and charged at him. The stones burst, forming a thick, burning mist. I couldn't see him anymore. One moment there was field and snow and Samir's angry face, the next just burning fog.

I thrust my left hand out, my right gripping my talisman, and sent a wave of force to part the fog, calling up wind to disperse it.

Samir had moved. I barely dodged the golden whip of power snaking in from my left.

For a second, my concentration wavered and my shield weakened. The burning fog coated my left hand, my skin blackening and blistering instantly.

Choking back a scream, I grabbed my shield around me again, running to my right, bringing the whirlwind to bear on the fog. It dissipated in time for me to dodge another whip.

"Running out of time," I gasped at Samir, hoping to distract him. I was defending myself, more or less. But I wasn't able to attack. Without offense, I couldn't end this fight. I'd expended too much magic in the last two days, or maybe never had enough in the first place. I needed an edge, or I was going to lose and fast.

The moon was rising. I saw a sliver of it over the trees beyond Samir.

He turned his head, and I threw the power in my shield at him in a slam attack.

Tricks. Samir was so good at them. My shield rammed through his illusion as the real Samir jumped me from the right, materializing out of thin air. Only my dragon sense of his magic warned me.

I twisted and threw myself sideways, rolling on the hard ground. Burning golden power, reinforced with actual physical chains he'd thrown, wrapped around my legs instead of my body as he'd intended. I slashed at it with my own magic, forming purple blades as extensions of my hands, cutting through his power. He yanked, dragging me along the ground toward him. The chain attached to my left leg wasn't fully cut. I felt my femur bend, then snap.

Pain shot through me and I caught the wave with my magic, forcing myself not to feel it, cocooning the injury in power. I tried to stand, but my leg wouldn't hold me.

I was losing. All the magic in the world wasn't going to save me. He was too powerful.

Powerful. But predictable. I heard Ash's voice in my head again. Samir was on his A game, working with the things in his comfort zone. Why wouldn't he? They had never failed him.

He'd approach me, just as he was now, moving slowly toward me, gathering his power to him. He would want to gloat, to savor the moment he took my heart. I let my shoulders slump and pulled my own magic in close. It wasn't that tough to look like I was defeated. I almost was.

Come a little closer, bastard. I let my right hand slip to the hilt of the Alpha and Omega but didn't draw it. I didn't want the motion to catch his attention. Not yet. I wasn't the using-weapons type, which Samir knew. This surprise was best saved for the last moment.

"You could have been amazing," Samir said. "You should have stayed with me."

"Until you ate me," I said through gritted teeth.

"Perhaps I would have kept you," Samir said with a half-shrug. His eyes darted to the sky. "Ready to feel your friends die?" he asked. He released power, and the line up the hill became visible again.

"Not today," I said. I released the knife hilt and slammed my good hand into the ground. I pictured my magic like a huge scythe and threw it toward the glowing umbilical cord of power. My magic met his and cut clean through it, burning away Samir's gold with purple vengeance.

I slumped for real as the power faded. It had taken more than I had thought to cut the cord.

Samir swore and advanced the last feet to me, caution gone.

"Stupid, meddling bitch," he said. He grabbed me too fast for me to react.

My muscles were lead, my magic a whisper in my veins, my left leg screaming in pain. It was like my nightmare unfolding all over again. Another snowy field. Another dusk. Another moon.

Samir's hand formed claws as he lifted me up. I tried to push him off with my bad hand and get to my knife with the good one. My ankle was too far away, my body bent unnaturally upward by Samir's strength.

His sweater had pushed back, and the angry scar, a wound that wouldn't quite heal, showed on his forearm.

Wolf had done that.

Wolf, whom he had been afraid of.

Wolf, whom I had found and rejoined with.

I brought my good leg up hard, going for his balls or his abs or whatever I could connect with. Samir plunged his clawed hand into my chest even as the knife hilt touched my fingertips.

Now.

Wolf flowed out of her silver circle in my mind and manifested. She slammed into Samir from the side, hard enough that he lost his grip and his fingers slid out of me with a sucking sound that was worse than the pain.

ANNIE BELLET

"No," he said, his face a death mask of hatred and horror as he stared at her.

I drew the Alpha and Omega and threw myself forward, my legs refusing to hold me. Samir and I ended up in an embrace as he caught me instinctually. The dagger slid into his chest, up through the soft tissue beneath his ribs.

We were eye to eye, close enough to kiss, his arms around me, half kneeling in the snow.

"Did I ever tell you the story of the scorpion and the frog?" he murmured.

I had no idea what he was trying to say. It didn't matter.

I was all out of fucks to give.

I twisted the Alpha and Omega and shoved it up, straight into his evil heart.

CHAPTER FOURTEEN ▶

Samir didn't die so much as explode in a puff of glittering golden dust. Without him to hold me up, I fell forward into the snow. My bad hand caught my fall and I cried out, my own voice rough in my ears.

My hair had come out of its braid and fell around me in a curtain. Something red and glowing caught my eye on the ground in the shade of my hair. It was a tiny gem, no bigger than maybe half a carat, ruby or garnet in color.

Samir's last drop of heart's blood. It glinted in my palm as I lifted it with my blackened fingers. A trace of his power lingered on in it, the red depth shining gold for a second as I studied it. I touched the blade of the Alpha and Omega to it and the glow died.

All I had to do to end him for good was to swallow this little thing. Such a small drop of blood. It would be good-bye, Samir.

And hello, all Samir's power. His memories. Also . . . hello, magic apocalypse.

I licked my lips and shook my head. Nope. I wanted him dead, but the consequences were too great. At least, like this he couldn't hurt anyone. If I could keep the heart stone safe. I wasn't leaving it here.

Wolf bonked my good shoulder with her bony head and I looked up into her starry night eyes. A thought formed in my mind as though it were mine, but I knew it was hers.

I dropped the dagger and lifted my talisman, turning the twenty-sided die until the one showed. Or where the one should be. Now it was just a pockmark. A divot about the right size to slot in a tiny gem. I rested the die on my bad hand and picked up the heart stone.

"Here goes nothing," I said to Wolf. I dropped the gem into the divot.

Silver light flashed, bright enough that I closed my eyes and still saw stars. When my lids were dark again, I opened my eyes. The gem was sealed into the metal as though it had been forged that way. I picked at it with a broken nail and found it glued tight. Samir's heart wasn't going anywhere. I resolved to make sure I touched it with the dagger at least once a day, but this was a solution I could live with for the moment.

Wolf bonked me again and then faded away, resuming her place inside my mind.

"Jade," Alek called to me.

He was making his way across the field. He had not a scratch on him, from what I could see. I didn't want to think about how tough it must have been for him to stand and watch me almost lose. I didn't want to think about what he would have done if I had fallen.

From up the hill I heard more gunfire and hoped that was a good thing.

"My leg is broken," I said to Alek as he got near. "Help?"

"He is destroyed?" Alek said, kneeling down beside me and feeling me over gently for other injuries.

"He's gone, but I didn't eat him," I said. "No apocalypse."

The wounds on my chest were already closing. My blistered arm looked worse than it felt now. It was mostly the leg. As Alek lifted me, I could almost hear the sections of bone grinding against each other. I pushed what magic I had left at it, trying to dull the pain. It took it down to a six on a scale of one to kill me now.

"Vollan?" I asked.

"Heading up to take care of the mercenaries."

"Well. We won," I said, leaning my cheek on his chest. "Let's go find the others."

"I should take you away from here," Alek said.

"No. They might need a mage up top." I glared up at him.

"I said 'should,' not 'would,'" Alek murmured.

My glare turned in to a grin. "Giddyup," I said.

It was a sign of how relieved he was for me to be alive that he didn't even growl.

Vollan's crew made swift work of the remaining human mercenaries. Levi and Cal had apparently already decimated them, forming a two-man army of doom. Harper and Ezee had disarmed the bomb but were trapped below the Commons.

Samir's magic still clung to the doors, so I ended up being needed after all. Wolf and I managed to cut through the silver wires. I was going to need to sleep for a week after this.

Freyda emerged first, her face thin and tired. Vivian followed and started immediately coordinating the full rescue after giving me a quick once-over and assuring Alek I'd live. The shifters were in bad shape—some of them had been locked up for days without food or water; some were still injured from their capture—but nobody had died. I sat propped in a chair Levi had dragged out of a building, and watched them file out to freedom. There were more shifters in Wylde than even I'd realized. Children, too.

Many of them thanked Alek and me; some were crying. I sat awkwardly and tried to smile.

I had saved them. It was enough.

▲ ▲ ▲

It took hours to dig Harper and Ezee out, but they were in decent shape and made it to Levi's house with the rest of us while Alek took off into the woods to tell Yosemite, Rose, and Junebug that we'd won.

Mikhail offered Alek and me the use of an RV on his property until my place was rebuilt. I told him we'd think about it. Rachel was up at the state offices, giving the higher-ups some serious hell. She was confident she'd be reinstated. Vollan and his people had taken care of disappearing the bodies at the RV park and up at Juniper. I figured the less questions asked, the better. The Dean at Juniper was an owl shifter and had been one of the people locked up. She was handling the explanations to the returning faculty and students.

Brie and Ciaran were free from the Fey. They called from the Dublin airport. I realized I hadn't told them that they had no home to come back to, but I figured another day wouldn't hurt until I faced that reality.

Rose left the day after the fight with Samir. She was going to go see family, she said. She'd been up late talking to Harper, but I hadn't heard the conversation. Her eyes were still full of grief as she hugged me.

"I'll be back in the spring," she said. "Rebuild the Henhouse. I just need some time."

"Take all the time you need," I said, hugging her back as best I could. I was still not great at standing, so she was bent over me. Seated hugs are always awkward.

Alek and I shared Levi's guest bed, Alek's feet hanging over the end. My leg ached and I couldn't sleep. The clock said five. It was still dark out.

I pushed Alek's heavy arm off me and slid out of bed, wincing as I put my left foot down. I limped from the room, closing the door behind me as quietly as I could. Making my way to the kitchen, I saw a duffle bag sitting by the back door.

The door opened, light shining in from the rear porch, and Harper stood there, her green eyes wide like a deer in headlights.

"You leaving?" I whispered, aware of Ezee sleeping on the couch in the living room behind us.

"Come on," Harper said. She picked up her bag and I followed her out into the freezing predawn morning.

She had an old Honda pulled up there, trunk open. Harper tossed the bag in and came back up to the porch.

"I'm taking off for a while," she said.

I wrapped my arms around myself, shivering.

"How long?"

"I don't know." Harper didn't look at me, staring off into the middle distance, seeing things I could only guess at. "I've been meaning to do some more tournaments, go to more cons. I can't stay here, Jade. I just can't."

"Everywhere you look, you see Max," I guessed. I knew that feeling. That grief.

"Everywhere," she whispered. She stepped up beside me on my good side and slid a warm arm around my waist. "Does it go away?"

I wrapped my arm over her shoulder and pulled her in closer. "Kind of. It gets easier to bear. With time."

"I see him. I keep expecting him to come through the door or phone me asking for a ride someplace. I hear his voice in my head. Everywhere I look, I remember Max. There's no part of Wylde that isn't also part of him."

"Oh, furball," I murmured, turning to pull her into a full hug. My arm twinged and my leg complained, but I ignored them. Fuck pain. This was more important.

"Thank you," she said, pulling back a little so she could look into my face. "For killing that bastard. I'm just sorry I missed it."

Guilt clogged my throat. I resisted the urge to rub my talisman, to feel the heart gem still embedded there. I hadn't told her the truth, only that Samir was destroyed. I had let her assume he was dead.

A dark voice inside my head whispered that maybe Samir was right. Maybe in the end, we did always betray the ones we loved.

"You'll always have a place at the table," I told her instead.

"Say goodbye to the twins for me? I don't meant to sneak away, but I can't stand the thought of long goodbyes. I'll email and Skype and stuff." She sniffled, her eyes bright with tears.

"Of course," I said, squeezing her into another hug. "Good luck; have fun."

I stood in the freezing morning air and watched my best friend drive away. I watched until long after her brake lights had disappeared. Then I went back into the house and tucked my freezing feet against Alek's legs. He pulled me in closer and didn't even complain.

CHAPTER FIFTEEN ▶

My leg healed within a couple days. My heart took a little longer. I was bone tired after the fight and all the aftermath of seeing everyone home safe and sound and a million rounds of explanations. It was hard to accept that after all these years of running, it was over. No more Samir. No more hiding. The weather turned wet and then warm. I finally got the city to approve my permits and began the fight with the insurance company over my building.

The day was sunny and warm enough that I only had a hoodie on as I sat on a folding chair across the street from where my store had stood. I wasn't great with power tools, so I was leaving the demo and cleanup to Levi and Junebug. They were directing the construction crew I'd hired like pros. Ezee was trying to drive a tractor and scoop up debris.

Trying being the operative word there. Levi hung off the side of the Caterpillar, yelling instructions as Ezee jerked the tractor around in fits and starts. I had been laughing all morning so hard, my face hurt. Alek went to get us some lunch with a shake of his head.

"There's my favorite sorceress," a lilting Irish voice said.

I was out of my chair and wrapped up in a hug before I could even register Ciaran's presence. The leprechaun was wearing his usual red jacket with gold buttons. After he let me go, Brie stepped in and gave me a quick hug as well. She had her red hair in two braids pinned around her head, but looked odd without her apron. No bakery, though, so no apron. Which was all my fault.

"You came. Thank you," I said. They'd taken the news of Brie's bakery and Ciaran's curios shop with a shrug and the Irish equivalent of "shit happens." Still, I hadn't been sure they would come today and talk to me about the new plans.

"As I said, I totally understand if you guys want to scoop up another location. This is going to take months. But I'm hoping you'll want to stay. I'm going to make the building way better." I smiled at them, sweeping my arm in a grand gesture at the pile of burned wood and rubble across the street. It was going to take every penny I had saved over the years, plus whatever insurance would get me, but it would be worth it.

"Rent somewhere else? No," Brie said. "Don't be silly."

"We've got a proposition for you," Ciaran said, grinning at my obvious relief.

"Oh?" I motioned toward the stack of folding chairs we'd borrowed from the sewing shop behind us. "You guys want to sit?"

Ciaran and Brie shook their heads, but they were still smiling like they'd eaten canaries or something.

"We want to be partners. Help you out with the building. Go in for thirds."

"That's not going to be cheap," I said. In my surprise, I forgot little details like manners and politeness.

Ciaran laughed. "I'm a leprechaun," he said with a wink.

"You got a pot of gold hiding in a rainbow?" I made a face at him, not exactly enjoying being the butt of a joke they weren't letting me in on.

Ciaran leaned in toward me and flicked his fingers by my ear. He pulled his hand back and a gold coin appeared there. When he held it out to me, I took it. It was heavy, solid. One side was stamped with a shamrock, the other with a triskelion similar to the mark that he, Brie, and Iollan all had tattooed.

"There's more of that, whatever you need," Ciaran said.

"Thanks," I said. "Is Iollan still out in the Frank?"

Brie nodded. "He's finishing up the new safeguards on Balor's head."

"Good," I said. I had no idea where the three of them had relocated the head to, and I was glad of that. The druid had argued that nobody should know except him, but he had needed Brie and Ciaran's help. That stone box wasn't light even for a giant to carry.

"I've got a meeting set up with Perkins tomorrow at two, to hammer out some paperwork and details. Will that work for you?" Brie asked me.

"Yeah, sure, of course," I stammered. "I'll be there."

"Great, see you tomorrow," she said. She and Ciaran walked away, waving to Levi as he leapt free of the Caterpillar.

I stood and watched them go, the coin still in my hand.

"Sandwich for your thoughts?" Alek said. I hadn't heard him approach, but I rarely did.

I turned to him and accepted the meatball sub, but I dropped it into the chair beside me and instead held up the gold coin.

"Ciaran and Brie want to go in on the building," I said.

Alek put his own sandwich down.

"Good," he said, looking not the least surprised.

"They tell you?"

"No, but it makes sense."

Alek stepped up to me and pulled me into an embrace. He'd barely let me out of his sight, much less his arms, since the fight with Samir. It was the most obvious sign I had that he had been terrified for me. I twisted in his arms to face the street and leaned back into his strength.

"Think Harper will ever come back?" I said softly as I watched Ezee chasing Levi around the tractor, trying to whack his twin with a baseball cap.

"Yes," Alek said. His voice was a deep rumble that vibrated in his chest, almost like a purr.

"You sound so confident," I muttered. "How do you know?"

"This is her home," he said. "You are her family. This is where she belongs. Her heart will draw her back when she is ready."

I watched my friends laughing in the rubble of my shop and took a deep breath of air that held the promise of spring. Then I lifted my chin, tilting my head back until I could see the golden stubble on Alek's own chin. He tipped his head down and pressed his lips to my forehead.

And thinking about it, I understood his confidence. He was right. Alek usually was.

He was my family. This was my home.

I closed my eyes and let him hold me. For the first time in a very, very long time, I was at peace.

ABOUT THE AUTHOR ▶

ANNIE BELLET lives and writes in the Pacific Northwest. She is the *USA Today* bestselling author of the *Gryphonpike Chronicles* and the *Twenty-Sided Sorceress* series.

Follow her at her website, www.anniebellet.com.

STOP!

HAVE YOU READ *LEVEL GRIND* AND BOOKS 1–4?
IF NOT, TAKE A LOOK AT WHAT YOU MISSED HERE. . . .

Life-changing moments are sneaky little bastards. Often, we don't even know that nothing will ever be the same until long after, and only in hindsight can we look and say, "There! That was it! That changed everything."

Well, at least we could, if we're alive to do it.

For me, it was just another Thursday evening on a blustery spring day. I was finishing up a Japanese-to-English translation job and only somewhat pretending to mind the register in my comic and game shop. That's the benefit of being the owner, I suppose. No one was going to tell me to be cheerful and pay attention to customers.

There weren't any, anyway. Thursday nights are game night and we close early. I hadn't flipped the sign yet as I was waiting on Harper, my best friend of the last four years, to stop swearing at her game of *StarCraft*.

"No amount of Banelings in the world are going to save you here," I said, glancing over at her screen.

"Marines are overpowered," she growled.

"Sure," I said, trying not to laugh. It was an old gripe. Whatever race her opponent played in the game was always OP, according to the logic of Harper. "Maybe you should play with a mouse instead of just your trackpad?"

"I'm practicing my hotkeying," she said. "Shut up; you're distracting me."

The string of bells on the door tinkled and I turned away from my laptop to face the front of the store, figuring it was either a college student or a harried mother looking for *Pokémon* or *Magic: The Gathering* cards. Those types, beyond my regulars, are about all that trickle into my store on weekdays.

The man who came in was no college student, and he definitely wasn't a soccer mom. He walked through the door and paused, his head turning and his eyes wide from the change between daylight and the strategically placed lamps I keep in my shop. He took in the front display of the latest adventure releases and the wall rack of new-release comics, then stepped farther in, head turning as though searching for something or someone.

His uncertainty gave me a moment to look him over. He looked roughly thirty years old and somewhat like a Hollywood version of a Norse god. About six foot six with shaggy white-blond hair, features that a romance novel would call chiseled, and more lean muscle than a CrossFit junkie. He was also packing a handgun, mostly hidden beneath his custom-fitted leather jacket.

So, you know, not your average comic book or tabletop gaming enthusiast.

There was also the part where my wards hummed for moment, a sound only I could hear. Which meant he wasn't human, either.

Not that this was weird for the town of Wylde, Idaho. Most of the non-college-student population isn't wholly human. We're the shape-shifter capital of the West. Harper herself is a fox shifter; two of the other three in my game group are a wolverine and a coyote. Guy who owns the pawnshop next to me is a bona fide leprechaun, and the woman who runs the bakery on the other side is some kind of witch or maybe a druid.

The thick ley lines that run through the River of No Return Wilderness at the edge of town draw all kinds of supernaturals to the area.

It was what had drawn me here. I'd always heard the best place to hide a leaf is in a forest.

I was immediately on my guard. Wards aren't really my strong suit, so I didn't know what flavor of preternatural this giant was, but the gun didn't bode well. Nor did the way he looked at me like he recognized me, or the way he came over to the counter, moving with preternatural grace around the comic book displays. I gathered my power inside myself, preparing to send a bolt of pure energy into his chest if needed. I hadn't cast a real spell like that in years, but I figured I could get a single one off without knocking myself unconscious with the effort. Probably.

"Can I help you?" I asked, glad the counter was between us, even if the glass case full of dice and card boxes would be little more than a stutter step to clear for a shifter.

"Who are you?" he said. His voice was deep, with a slight accent. Russian, maybe. His eyes were the blue of glacier ice and his expression about as welcoming.

"Jade Crow," I said, teeth grinding with the effort of speaking and keeping control of my magic. "Who are you?"

"Hi, handsome," Harper said, climbing out of the overstuffed chair next to me that she'd been gaming in. She snapped her laptop shut and gave the newcomer a dazzling smile. She was angular and punky, with spiky brown hair and a way of making men forget what they were going to say when she smiled.

Then she stopped smiling and her eyes got huge, focusing in on the silver feather strung around his neck. "Oh, shit. Justice. Forgive me." And she bowed her head like she was addressing some kind of royalty.

"Justice? Like one of the shifter peacekeepers, right?" I said, my voice shaking a little with the effort of holding on to my powers for this long without letting loose. "The fuck is going on?" I glanced at Harper and then back at the intruder, keeping my eyes on the feather talisman. Yeah, it was better to look at his neck. Or his chin. His lips were way too kissable.

I shoved that thought away for later. Much, much later.

"I am Aleksei Kirov, a Justice of the Council of Nine. And you," he said, gesturing at me, "are a murderer."